also by
Laura Thalassa

THE BARGAINER SERIES

Rhapsodic

A Strange Hymn

The Emperor of Evening Stars

Dark Harmony

Rhapsodic

LAURA THALASSA

Bloom *books*

Published by Bloom Books, an imprint of Sourcebooks
P.O. Box 4410, Naperville, Illinois 60567-4410
(630) 961-3900
sourcebooks.com

Originally self-published in 2016 by Laura Thalassa.

Cataloging-in-Publication Data is on file with the Library of Congress.

Printed and bound in the United States of America.
KP 10 9 8 7 6

To my family
Because life takes a village

PROLOGUE

May, eight years ago

There's blood on my hands, blood between my toes, blood speckled in my hair. It's splashed across my chest, and to my horror, I can taste a few droplets on my lips.

There's far too much of it staining the kitchen's polished floors. No one can survive that much blood loss, not even the monster at my feet.

My entire body shakes, adrenaline still pumping through my veins. I drop the broken bottle, the glass shattering as it hits the ground, and fall to my knees.

Blood soaking into my jeans.

I stare at my tormentor. His glassy eyes have lost their focus and his skin its color. If I were a braver person, I would've placed my ear to his chest just to make sure that his cold, blackened heart had stilled. I can't bear to touch him, even now. Even if he can no longer hurt me.

He's gone. He's finally gone.

A shuddering sob pushes its way out of me. For the first time in what seems like an eternity, I can breathe. I sob again. God, it feels good. This time, tears follow.

I'm not supposed to feel relief. I know that. I know people are supposed to mourn the loss of life. But I can't. Not him anyway. Maybe that makes me evil. All I know is that tonight, I actually faced my fear and I survived it.

He's dead. He can't hurt me anymore. He's dead.

It takes only a few more seconds for that realization to hit me.

Oh God. He's *dead*.

My hands begin to shake. There's a body and blood, so much blood. I'm drenched in it. It speckles my homework, and one fat droplet obscures Lincoln's face on my history textbook.

A harsh shiver courses through my body.

I stare down at my hands, feeling like Lady Macbeth. *Out, damned spot!* I dash to the kitchen sink, leaving a trail of bloody footprints in my wake. Oh God, I need to get his blood off me now.

I rinse my hands furiously. It stains my cuticles and embeds itself beneath my fingernails. I can't get it out, but it doesn't matter, because I notice the red liquid coats my arms. So I scrub those. But then it's on my shirt, and I can see it congealing in my hair.

I whimper as I do so. It doesn't matter. It's not coming out.

Fuck.

I lean over the granite countertop and assess the pink mixture of blood and water that stains it, the floor, and the sink.

Can't hide from this.

Reluctantly, my eyes slide to the body. An illogical part

of me expects my stepfather to sit back up and attack me. When he doesn't do just that, I begin to think again.

What do I do now? Call the police? The justice system protects kids, so I'll be okay. They'll just call me in for questioning.

But will they protect me? It's not like I killed just anyone. I killed one of the wealthiest, most untouchable men alive. It doesn't matter that it was self-defense. Even in death, men like him get away with the unthinkable all the time.

And I'd have to talk about it—all of it.

Nausea rolls through me.

But I have no choice. I have to turn myself in. Unless...

The monster bleeding out in our kitchen knew a man who knew a man. Someone who could clean up a messy situation. I only had to sell a bit of my soul to speak to him.

No cops, no questions, no foster care or jail.

You know what? He can have whatever's left of my soul. All I want is out.

I dash to the junk drawer, my trembling hands struggling to open it. Once I do, it's short work grabbing the business card and reading over the peculiar contact information. There's a single sentence written on it; all I have to do is recite it out loud.

Fear washes through me. If I do this, there's no going back.

My gaze sweeps over the kitchen. *It's already too late to go back.*

I squeeze the card in my hand. Taking a deep breath, I do as the business card instructs.

"Bargainer, I would like to make a deal."

CHAPTER 1

Present

A file folder drops to the desk in front of me. "You've got mail, Callie."

I lower my mug of steaming coffee from my mouth, my eyes flicking up from my laptop.

Temperance "Temper" Darling—swear to God, that's her name—my business partner and best friend, stands on the other side of my desk, a coy smile on her face. She drops into the seat across from me.

I kick my ankles off my desk, reaching across it to drag the file closer to me.

She nods to the folder. "This one's easy money."

They're all easy money, and she knows that.

Her eyes drift around my cupboard-sized office, the twin of hers.

"How much is the client offering?" I ask, propping my feet up once more on the edge of my desk.

"Twenty grand for a single meeting with the target, and she already knows when and where you're to intercept him."

I whistle. Easy money indeed.

"Rendezvous time with the target?" I ask.

"Eight p.m. tonight at Flamencos. FYI, it's a fancy restaurant, so—" Her gaze drops to my scuffed-up boots. "You can't wear *that*."

I roll my eyes.

"Oh, and he'll be there with friends."

And here I was looking forward to getting home relatively early.

"Do you know what the client wants?" I ask.

"The client believes her uncle, our target, is abusing his guardianship of his mother, her grandmother. The two are going to court over the issue. She wants to save some legal bills and get a confession straight from the horse's mouth."

Already, a familiar exhilaration has my skin beginning to glow. This is the chance to potentially help an old lady out and punish the worst kind of criminal—one who preys on his own family.

Temper notices my glowing skin, her gaze transfixed. She reaches out before she remembers herself. Not even she is immune to my glamour.

She shakes her head. "You are one twisted chick."

That is God's honest truth.

"Takes one to know one."

She snorts. "You can call me the Wicked Witch of the West."

But Temper's not a witch. She's something far more powerful.

She checks her phone. "Crap," she says. "I'd love to stay and chat, but my perp's going to be at Luca's Deli in less than an hour, and with LA lunch hour traffic, I really don't want to be forced to part the 405 like the Red Sea. That sort of thing looks suspicious." She stands, shoving her phone to her pocket. "When's Eli getting back?"

Eli, the bounty hunter who sometimes works for us and sometimes works for the Politia, the supernatural police force. Eli, who's also my boyfriend.

"Sorry, Temper, but he'll be gone for another week." I relax a little as I say the words.

That's wrong, right? To enjoy the fact that your boyfriend's gone and you get time alone?

It's probably also wrong to find his affection stifling. I'm afraid of what it means, especially because we shouldn't be dating in the first place.

First rule in the book is not to get involved with colleagues. One evening of after-work drinks six months ago, and I broke that rule like it'd never been there in the first place. And I broke it again and again and again until I found myself in a relationship I wasn't sure I even wanted.

"Ugh," Temper says, her hair bouncing a little as she leans her head back, her eyes moving heavenward. "The bad guys always love to stir things up when Eli's gone." She heads for my door, and with a parting look, she leaves my office.

I stare at the file a moment, then I pick it up.

The case isn't anything special. There isn't anything particularly cruel or difficult about it. Nothing to make me reach for the Johnnie Walker I keep in one of my desk drawers. I find I want to anyway, that my hand itches to pull the bottle out.

Too many bad people in this world.

My eyes flick to the onyx beads that coil around my left

arm as I drum my fingers against the table. The beads seem to swallow the light rather than refract it.

Too many bad people, and too many memories worth forgetting.

The swanky restaurant I walk into at eight p.m. sharp is low lit, candles flickering dimly from each two-seater table. Flamencos is clearly a place rich people come to romance each other.

I follow the waiter, my heels clicking softly against the hardwood floor as he leads me to a private room.

Twenty grand. It's a crap ton of money. But I'm not doing this for the payout. The truth is that I'm a connoisseur of addictions, and this is one of my favorites.

The waiter opens the door to the private room, and I enter.

Inside, a group of people chat amicably around a large table. Their voices quiet a little as soon as the door clicks shut behind me. I make no move toward the table.

My eyes land on Micky Fugue, a balding man in his late forties. My target.

My skin begins to glow as I let the siren in me surface. "Everybody out." My voice is melodious, unearthly. Compelling.

Almost as one, the guests stand, their eyes glazed.

This is my beautiful, dreadful power. A siren's power. To compel the willing—and unwilling—to do and believe whatever it is I wish.

Glamour. It's illegal. Not that I really give a damn.

"The evening went great," I tell them as they pass. "You'd all love to do this sometime in the future. Oh, and I was never here."

When Micky walks by me, I grab his upper arm. "Not you."

He stops, caught in the web of my voice, while the rest of the guests file out. His glazed eyes flicker for one moment, and in that instant, I see his confusion as his awareness fights my strange magic. Then it's gone.

"Let's sit down." I direct him back to his seat, then slide into the one next to him. "You can leave once we're finished."

I'm still glowing, my power mounting with every passing second. My hands tremble just the slightest as I fight my other urges—sex and violence. Consider me a modern-day Jekyll and Hyde. Most of the time, I'm simply Callie the PI. But when I need to use my power, another side of me surfaces. The siren is the monster inside me; she wants to take and take and take. To wreak havoc and feast on her victims' fear and lust.

I'd be hard-pressed to admit it out loud, but controlling her is hard.

I grab a piece of bread from one of the baskets at the center of the table, and I slide over a small plate one of the guests hasn't touched. After I pour olive oil, then balsamic vinegar onto the plate, I dip the bread into it and take a bite.

I eye the man next to me. That tailored suit he wears hides the paunch of his belly. On his wrist, he wears a Rolex. The file said he was an accountant. I know they make decent money, especially here in LA, but they don't make money this good.

"Why don't we get right to the point?" I say. As I talk, I set up the video on my phone so the camera can capture our conversation. "I'm going to record this exchange. Please say yes out loud and give your consent to this interview."

Micky's brows stitch together as he fights the glamour in

my voice. It's no use. "Yes," he finally says between clenched teeth. This guy is no fool; he might not understand what's happening to him, but he knows he's about to get played. He knows he's *already* getting played.

As soon as he agrees, I begin.

"Have you been embezzling money from your mother?" His senile, terminally ill mother. I really shouldn't have read the file. I'm not supposed to get emotionally involved in cases, and yet when it comes to children and the elderly, I always seem to find myself getting angry.

Tonight's no exception.

I take a bite of the bread, watching him.

He opens his mouth—

"From this moment until the end of our interview, you will tell the *truth*," I command, the words lilting off my tongue.

He stops, and whatever he was about to say dies on his lips. I wait for him to continue, but he doesn't. Now that he can't lie, it's only a matter of time before he's forced to admit the truth.

Micky fights my glamour, though it's useless. He's starting to sweat, despite his placid features.

I continue eating as though nothing is amiss.

Color stains his cheeks. Finally, he chokes out, "Yes. How the fuck did you—"

"Silence."

Immediately, he stops speaking.

This sicko. Stealing money from his dying mother. A sweet old lady whose biggest failure was birthing this loser.

"How long have you been doing this?"

His eyes flicker with anger. "Two years," he grits out against his will. He glares at me.

I take my time eating the last of the bread.

"Why did you do it?" I finally ask.

"She wasn't using it and I needed it. I'm going to give it back," he says.

"Oh, are you?" I raise my eyebrows. "And how much have you...*borrowed*?" I ask.

Several silent seconds tick by. Micky's ruddy cheeks are turning a deeper and deeper shade of pink. Finally, he says, "I don't know."

I lean in close. "Give me your best guess."

"Maybe two hundred and twenty thousand."

Just hearing that number sends a slice of anger through me. "And when were you going to pay your mother back?" I ask.

"N-now," he stammers.

And I'm the queen of Sheba.

"How much money do you have available in your accounts at the moment?" I ask.

He reaches for his glass of water and takes a deep swallow before answering. "I–I like to invest."

"How much money?"

"A little over twelve thousand."

Twelve thousand dollars. He's emptied his mother's coffers, and here he is living like a king. But behind this façade, the man only has twelve thousand dollars at hand. And I bet that money will get liquidated soon as well. These types of men have butterfingers; money slips right through them.

I give him a disappointed look. "That's not the right answer. Now," I say, the siren urging me to be cruel, "where is the money?"

His sweaty upper lip twitches before he answers. "Gone."

I reach over and turn off the camera and the recorder. My client got the confession she wanted. Too bad for Micky, I'm not done with him.

"No," I say, "it's not." Those few people who know me well enough would recognize my tone's changed.

Again his brows draw together as his confusion peeks through.

I touch his lapel. "This suit is nice—really nice. And your watch—Rolexes aren't cheap, are they?"

The glamour makes him shake his head.

"No," I agree. "See, for men like you, money doesn't just vanish. It goes toward…what did you call it?" I look around for the word before snapping my fingers. "*Investments*. It moves around a bit, but that's all." I lean in close. "We're going to move it around a little more."

His eyes widen. Now I see Micky—not the puppet controlled by my magic but the Micky he was before I walked into this room. Someone shrewd, someone weak. He's fully aware of what's happening.

"Wh-who are you?"

Oh, the fear in his eyes. The siren can't resist that. I reach over and pet his cheek.

"I–I'm going to—"

"You're going to sit back and listen, Micky," I say, "and that's all you're going to do, because right now, you—are—*powerless*."

11

CHAPTER 2

May, eight years ago

The air wavers in my kitchen, like I'm staring at a mirage, then suddenly, he's here, filling the room like he owns it.

The Bargainer.

Holy shit, it worked.

All I can see of him is a good six feet of man and a whole lot of white-blond hair tied together in a leather thong. The Bargainer's back is to me.

A whistle breaks the silence. "That is one dead man," he says, staring at my handiwork. His heavy boots thunk as he approaches the body. He wears black on black, his shirt stretched tight over his wide shoulders. My eyes drop to his left arm, which is covered in tattoos.

Callie, what did you get yourself into?

The toe of the Bargainer's boot nudges the corpse. "Hmm, I stand corrected. Mostly dead."

That snaps me out of it.

"*What*?" He can't be alive. The fear that thrums through my veins is a living, breathing thing.

"It will cost you probably more than you're willing to offer, but I can still revive him."

Revive him? What is this dude smoking?

"I don't want him *alive*," I say.

The Bargainer turns, and for the first time ever, I get a good look at him.

I just stare and stare. I'd imagined a creep, but wicked though the man in front of me might be, he is no creep.

Not even close.

The Bargainer is gorgeous in a way that only a few rare men are. He's not rugged, despite the strong jaw and hard gleam in his eyes. There's a symmetry to his face, a lushness in each one of his features that I've seen more often in women than men. High, prominent cheekbones, wicked, curving lips, gleaming silver eyes. Not that he looks feminine. That's impossible with his broad, muscular frame and shit-kicking attire.

He's simply a pretty man.

A *really* pretty man.

He sizes me up. "No."

I stare at him quizzically. "No what?"

"I don't do business with minors."

The air shimmers and, *oh my God*, he's leaving.

"Wait! Wait!" I reach out. Now it's not just the air that shimmers. It's my skin. It's been doing that a lot lately—glowing softly.

He pauses to stare at my arm. Something passes through those eyes of his, something wilder than shock, something more untamed than excitement. The room around him seems to darken, and at his back, I swear I catch sight of something large and sinuous.

As quickly as the moment comes, it's gone.

His eyes narrow. "What are you?"

My hand drops. "*Please,*" I beg. "I really need to make a deal."

The Bargainer sighs, sounding all sorts of put out. "Listen, I don't make deals with minors. Go to the police." Despite his tone, he's still staring at my hand, now wearing a distant, troubled expression.

"I *can't.*" If only he knew. "Please, help me."

His gaze moves from my hand to my face.

The Bargainer gnashes his teeth together, scowling like he smells something bad. He stares at me in all my bloody, disheveled glory. More teeth gnashing.

His eyes sweep the room, lingering on my stepfather. What does he see? Can he tell it was an accident?

My teeth begin to chatter. I hug my arms tightly to my chest.

In spite of himself, his eyes return to me, his gaze briefly softening before it hardens all over again.

"Who is he?"

I swallow.

"Who. Is. He?" the Bargainer repeats.

"My stepfather," I croak.

He stares at me, his gaze unflinching. "Did he deserve it?"

I release a shuddering breath, a tear slipping out in spite of myself. Wordlessly, I nod.

The Bargainer scrutinizes me for a long time, his gaze moving to the tear sliding down my cheek.

He glances away, grimacing. The man rubs a hand over his mouth, paces two steps away before turning back to me.

"*Fine*," he rasps. "I'll help you at"—more teeth gnashing and another raking gaze that pauses on the tear on my cheek—"*no cost*." He practically chokes on the words. "Just this once. Consider this my pro bono for the century."

I open my mouth to thank him, but he raises his hand, his eyes pinching shut. "*Don't*."

When he opens his eyes, they pass over the room. I feel the magic pulse out of him. I know about this side of our world—the supernatural side. My stepfather built his empire on his magical ability.

However, I've never seen *this* kind of magic in action—magic that can make things inexplicably occur. I gasp as the blood dissolves from the floor, then the countertop, and then my clothes, hair, and hands.

The broken bottle follows. One moment, it's there, and the next, it vanishes. Whatever enchantment this is, it tickles my skin as it passes through the room.

Once he's done with the crime scene, the Bargainer heads toward the body.

He pauses when he gets there, peering curiously down at the dead man. Then he stills. "Is that who I think it is?"

Now is probably not a good time to tell the Bargainer that I offed *the* Hugh Anders, the most powerful stock market analyst out there and the man who, for the right price, could tell someone just about anything they wanted to know concerning the future. When a drug deal was going to go down, whether the threat on their life was harmless or real, if they were going to get caught for the death of an enemy. If Hugh wasn't the world's best seer, he was at least one of the richest. Not that it saved him from death.

Oh, the irony.

The Bargainer lets loose a string of curses.

"Fucking cursed sirens," he mutters. "Your bad luck's rubbing off on me."

I flinch, well acquainted with sirens' predisposition for misfortune. It's what landed my mother an unwanted pregnancy and an early death.

"Have any relatives?" he asks.

I bite my lower lip and shake my head, hugging myself tighter. It's just me in the world.

He swears again.

"How old *are* you?"

"I'll be sixteen in two weeks." The birthday I'd been waiting *years* for. In the supernatural community, sixteen is the legal age of adulthood. But now that very fact could be used against me. Once I hit that magical number, I could be tried as an adult.

I'd been two weeks away from freedom. *Two weeks*. And then this happened.

"Finally," he sighs, "*some* good news. Pack your bags. Tomorrow, you're moving to the Isle of Man."

I blink, my mind slow to catch up. "What? Wait— *tomorrow?*" I'd be moving? And so soon? My head spins at the thought.

"Peel Academy has summer sessions starting in a couple weeks," he says.

Located on the Isle of Man, an island smack-dab between Ireland and Great Britain, Peel Academy is *the* premier supernatural boarding school. I'd been dreaming of going for so long. And now I would be.

"You're going to attend classes starting then, and you're not going to tell anyone that you killed Hugh fucking Anders."

I flinch at that.

"Unless," he adds, "you'd prefer that I leave you here with this mess."

Oh God. "No, please stay!"

Another long-suffering sigh. "I'll deal with the body and the authorities. If anyone asks, he had a heart attack."

The Bargainer eyes me curiously before remembering that he's annoyed with me. He snaps his fingers, and the body levitates. It takes several seconds to process the fact that a corpse is floating in my kitchen.

The Bargainer looks unfazed. "There's something you should know."

"Uh-huh?" My gaze is fixed on the floating body. So creepy.

"Eyes on me," the Bargainer says.

My attention snaps to him.

"There's a chance my magic will wear off over time. I might be powerful, but that pretty little curse all you sirens have hanging over your heads might override even my magic." Somehow he manages to come off as arrogant even as he's telling me his powers might be inadequate.

"What happens if that's the case?" I ask.

The Bargainer smirks. Huge asshole. I've already got him profiled.

"Then you best start utilizing your glamour, cherub," he says, his eyes flicking over me. "You'll be needing it."

With that parting line, the Bargainer disappears, along with the man I killed.

Present

Power.

That is the heart of my addiction. Power. I was once

crushed under the weight of it, and it almost swallowed me whole.

But that was a long time ago. And now I'm the formidable force.

The restaurant's private room glows softly under the candlelight. I lean in close to Micky. "So this is what's going to happen. You are going to return that money you embezzled to your mother."

His previously vacant eyes focus on me. If looks could kill…

"Fuck. You."

I smile, and I know I look predatory.

"Listen closely, because this is the only warning I'm going to give you: I know you have no idea what I am. But I assure you, I can ruin your life, and I'm just enough of an asshole to consider it. So unless you want to lose everything you care about, you are going to be respectful."

Regular mortals know that supernaturals exist, but we like to separate ourselves from those who aren't magically gifted, simple reason being that fun shit like witch hunts tend to pop up when mortals get too intimidated by us.

I reach for my purse.

"Now, because you can't be a good son on your own, I'm going to help you," I say conversationally. I pull a pen and a series of documents my client gave me out of my bag. Shoving Micky's plate out of the way, I lay them out in front of him.

One is a written confession of guilt, and the other is a promissory note, both documents drafted by my client's lawyer.

"You're going to repay every penny you stole—*with* ten percent interest."

Micky makes a small noise.

"Was that fifteen percent interest I heard?"

He shakes his head furiously.

"That's what I thought. Now, I'll give you ten minutes to flip through the document, and then you're going to sign it."

I spend those ten minutes sampling the wine and food that Micky's guests left behind, kicking my heels up because, ugh, *stilettos*.

When the time's up, I collect the documents from Micky. As I flip through them, I peek over at the man himself. His face is now coated with an unhealthy sheen of sweat, and I bet if he removed his dinner jacket, I'd see huge rings of it beneath his armpits.

I finish flipping through the documents. Once I'm done, I slide them back in my purse.

"We're almost done here."

"Almost?" He says the word like he's never heard of it.

"You didn't think I'd leave you to just a few paltry signatures, did you?" I shake my head, and now my skin is doing more to illuminate the room than the low lighting is. The siren in me loves this. Toying with her victim. "Oh, Micky, no no no." And this is where I stop toying with Micky and go in for the kill. I lean forward, putting as much power into my voice as I can manage. "You are going to right your wrongs. You're never going to do this ever again, and you are going to spend the rest of your life working to be a better person and earn your mother's forgiveness."

He nods.

I grab my purse. "Be a good son. If I hear you haven't been—if I hear anything at all that reflects poorly on you—you'll be seeing me again, and you don't want that."

He shakes his head, his expression vacant.

I stand. My work here is done.

A single command is all it takes.

Forget I exist. Poof, your memory scrubs away my existence.

Look away. Your eyes move everywhere but me.

Tell me your darkest secret. Your mouth and mind betray you.

Give me your riches. You'll clean out our bank account in an instant.

Drown.

Drown. Drown. Drown. You die.

That was someone's favorite back when the world was young, back when sirens got their reputation for coaxing sailors to their deaths.

Drown.

Sometimes, when I'm left alone to my own thoughts—which is fairly often—I wonder about those women, the ones who hung out on the rocks, calling out to sailors and coaxing them to their deaths. Did it really happen that way? Did they want them to die? Why did they prey on those particular men? The myths never say.

I wonder if any of them were like me—whether their beauty made them victims long before it gave them power. Whether some sailor somewhere abused those women before they had a voice at all. Whether they grew angry and jaded like me and used their power to punish the guilty as payback.

I wonder how much of the tale is true and how many of their victims were innocent.

I prey on bad men. This is my vendetta. My addiction.

———

I climb the staircase to my Malibu beach house, my feet sore from the hours spent standing in heels. In front of me, the slate-gray paint of my house peels away from the wooden slats. Bright green mold grows along the roof's shingles. This is my perfectly imperfect home.

I step inside, and in here, the air smells like the ocean. My home is simple. It has three bedrooms, the tile counter-tops are chipped, and if you walk through it barefoot, you'll get sand between your toes. The living room and bedroom face the ocean, and the entire back wall in both rooms is nothing more than giant sliding glass doors that can open completely onto the backyard.

Beyond my small backyard, the world drops away. A wooden staircase winds its way down the coastal cliff my house is perched on, and at the bottom of it, the icy Pacific Ocean kisses the sandy California shore—and my feet, if I let it.

This place is my sanctuary. I knew it the moment the real estate agent showed it to me two years ago.

I walk through my house in the dark, not bothering to flip on the lights as I strip my clothes off piece by piece. I leave them where they fall. Tomorrow, I'll pick them up, but tonight, I have a date with the sea and then my bed.

Through my living room windows, the moon shines brightly, and my heart is filled with such unending longing.

I've secretly been glad that Eli has to keep away from me until the full moon passes. As a lycanthrope, he has to stay away during the Sacred Seven, the week surrounding the full moon when he can't control his shift from man to wolf.

I have my own reasons for wanting to be alone around this time, reasons that have nothing to do with Eli and every-thing to do with my past.

I step out of my jeans as I enter my bedroom to grab my swimsuit. Just as I reach back to unclasp my bra, a shadow darker than the rest moves.

I stifle the shriek bubbling up in my throat. My hand gropes against the wall next to me until I find the light switch. I flip on the bedroom lights.

In front of me, lounging on my bed, is the Bargainer.

CHAPTER 3

October, eight years ago

"Hi, this is Inspector Garrett Wade with the Politia. I'd like *to ask you some questions regarding your father's death…"*

My hands begin to shake as I listen to the message. The Politia is looking into this? They're like the supernatural version of the FBI. Only scarier.

There were supposed to be no questions. The authorities were supposed to stay away. The Bargainer had made sure of that.

That pretty little curse all you sirens have hanging over your heads might override even my magic.

I sit heavily on my bed and rub my temples, phone clutched in my hand. Rain pelts against my dorm room window, obscuring my view of Peel Castle, the castle-turned-academy where all my classes are held.

It's only been five months since that fateful night. *Five months.* Too short to enjoy my freedom, but too long to ever appear innocent to the authorities again.

I missed my opportunity the moment I took the Bargainer up on his offer.

Peel Academy and the life I've made here could be taken from me. All in an instant.

I take a deep breath.

The way I see it, I have three options. One, I can run away and give up the life I've made for myself. Two, I can call the officer back, go in for questioning, and hope for the best.

Or three, I can contact the Bargainer and have him fix this. Only this time, I'd owe him a debt.

It's an easy choice.

I push off my bed and head to my closet. I pull out a shoebox from the top shelf and open it. The Bargainer's black business card lies hidden under other odds and ends, the bronze lettering somewhat faded since the first time I held it.

Lifting it out of the box, I flip the card over and over in my hand. Seeing it brings that night back in all its gory detail.

Can't believe it's only been five months.

My life is so different now. I've worked hard to bury my past, and I've gotten comfortable with my glamour.

Where once I was weak, now I am powerful. A siren who can bend a person's will—who can even break it if I so desire. That knowledge is a kind of armor that I put on every morning I wake up. It only comes off late at night when my memories get the better of me.

I run my thumb over the card. I don't need to do this. I promised myself I wouldn't contact him again. I got away with murder—literally—last time I met him. I won't be that lucky twice.

But this is the best of three bad options.

So, for the second time in my life, I call the Bargainer.

Present

I freeze in the doorway.

The Bargainer reclines against my headboard, looking for all the world like a predator. Sleek, caged power and dangerous eyes. He also appears far too comfortable in my bed.

Seven years. Seven long years have passed since he exited my life. And now here he is, lounging on my bed as though nearly a decade didn't come between us. And I have no fucking clue how I'm supposed to react.

His eyes move over me lazily. "You've upgraded your lingerie since I last saw you."

Jesus, talk about getting caught with your pants down.

I ignore the way his words cut into me. The last time he saw me, I was a lovesick teenager, and he wanted nothing to do with me.

"Hello, Desmond Flynn," I say, invoking his full name. I'm fairly certain I'm one of only a few people who know it, and that information makes him vulnerable. And right now, as I stand clad in nothing but my lingerie and come to grips with the fact that *the Bargainer is in my room*, I need him vulnerable.

He gives me a slow, smoldering smile that tightens my stomach even as it constricts my heart. "I didn't realize you wanted to spill secrets tonight, Callypso Lillis," he says.

The Bargainer's eyes devour my exposed skin, and I feel like that fumbling teenager all over again. I take a deep breath. I'm no longer that girl, even if the man in front of me looks exactly the same as he did in my youth.

Same black-on-black clothing, same imposing frame, same stunning face.

I cross the room and grab my cotton robe from where

it hangs on the back of the bathroom door. The entire time, I can feel his eyes on me. I turn away from him to slip it on.

Seven years.

"What do you want, Des?" I ask, cinching the robe at my waist.

I pretend like this is normal. That him being in my house is normal, when it's not. God, is it not.

"Demanding as always, I see."

I yelp as his breath tickles my ear. I swivel around to face him.

The Bargainer stands not even a foot away from me, so close I can feel his body heat. I didn't hear him get up from the bed and cross the room. Not that I should be surprised. The magic he uses is subtle; most of the time, if you aren't looking for it, you won't notice it.

"Odd character flaw of yours," he continues, his eyes narrowed, "considering how much *you* owe *me*." His voice is husky and low.

This close to him, I can see every complex facet of his face. High cheekbones, aristocratic nose, sensual lips, chiseled jaw. Hair so pale that it appears white. He's still far too pretty for a man. So pretty, I can't seem to look away when I know I should.

It's his eyes that have always captivated me the most. They're every shade of silver, darkest at their edges where a thick band of charcoal gray rings them and lightest near their centers. The color of shadows and moonbeams.

It hurts to look at him, not just because he is inhumanly beautiful but because he shredded my fragile heart a long time ago.

The Bargainer takes my hand in his, and for the first

time in seven years, I come face-to-face with the sleeve of tattoos he sports.

I glance down at our entwined hands as he pushes the sleeve of my robe up, exposing my onyx bracelet.

My bracelet covers most of my forearm, each bead a magical IOU for a favor I've bought off the Bargainer.

He twists my wrist back and forth, assessing his work. I try to pull my hand away, but he won't let go. "My bracelet still looks good on you, cherub," he states.

His bracelet. The one piece of jewelry I can't remove. Even if it weren't strung with spider silk and thus too strong to cut off, the magic that binds it to my wrist prevents me from removing it until I pay off my debts.

The Bargainer's hand tightens on mine. "Callie, you owe me a lot of favors."

My breath catches in my throat as my gaze meets his. The way he looks at me, the way his thumb is rubbing circles into the soft skin of my hand…I know why he's here. On some level, I knew it since I first caught sight of him on my bed. This is it, the moment I've been waiting seven years for.

I exhale. "You're finally here to collect."

Instead of answering me, the Bargainer's other hand glides up my captive wrist, over all seventeen rows of my bracelet, not stopping until he gets to the very end of it, until his fingers grasp the last of my 322 beads.

"We're going to play a little game of truth or dare," he says. His eyes flick to mine, and they gleam with mischief.

My heart slams into my chest. *He's finally collecting his payment.* I can't seem to wrap my mind around it.

His mouth curls seductively. "What will it be, Callie? Truth or dare?"

I blink a few times, still stunned. Ten minutes ago, I

would've laughed if someone told me Desmond Flynn was waiting for me to come home so that he could collect on my debts.

"A dare it is," he says gleefully, filling in my silence for me.

Fear grips my heart. The Bargainer is infamous for his steep payments. And it's rarely money he asks for; he has no need for it. No, he usually takes something more personal, and every repayment comes with added interest. Considering I have 322 unpaid favors, the man essentially owns my ass. If he wanted to, he could order me to wipe out a small village, and I'd be magically bound to until each and every bead winked out of existence.

He's a dangerous man, and at the moment, he's rolling a bead between his fingers and watching me with those calculating eyes.

I clear my throat. "What's the dare?"

Instead of answering me, he lets go of my wrist and steps into my personal space. Never taking his eyes off mine, he tilts my head back and cradles it.

What is he doing?

I stare up at him. A small smile dances along his lips, and I notice his gaze deepens the moment before he leans in.

I stiffen as his lips brush mine, and then my body relaxes as his mouth glides against them. Immediately my skin illuminates as the siren awakens. Sex and blood, that's what she thrives on.

I wrap a hand around the arm that cradles my head. My fingers press against the warm skin of his wrist. Beneath it, I can feel Des's unyielding muscle.

He's real. This is real. That's all I have time to think about before the kiss ends and he pulls away.

He glances down at my wrist, and I follow his gaze. The

very last bead on my bracelet shimmers for a moment, then fades away. The kiss had been my dare, the first payment the Bargainer collected.

I touch my fingers to my lips, the taste of him still on my skin. "But you don't like me," I whisper, confused.

He reaches up to my face to trail his fingers over my glowing skin. If he were a man, he'd be completely under my spell at the moment. But he's something else entirely.

The Bargainer's eyes glitter, full of emotions I spent a year memorizing and then seven years trying to forget.

"I'll be back tomorrow evening." His gaze sweeps over me again, and he raises an eyebrow. "Consider the following advice a favor free of charge: be prepared for more than just a kiss."

At sunrise, I'm still awake, still in my robe, and I still have no clue what the hell is going on. I sit on the grass at the edge of my property, breathing in the salty sea air. My knees are pulled up to my chest, and a mostly empty bottle of wine rests next to me.

I already called Temper and told her I wouldn't be in the office today. The nice thing about running your own business? You get to pull your own hours.

I watch the stars dim and the Bargainer's kingdom close as the sky slowly lightens.

I glance down at my wrist. I could swear it feels different now that one bead is gone. Only 321 favors left, and the rest are guaranteed to be far more painful than the first.

I trace my lips with a finger. I was wrong earlier. At one point in time, Des *had* liked me. But not like I had liked him—like he had hung the very moon itself. The day he left me ripped my heart out, and it never healed right, and no amount of booze, men, or work could ever patch it up.

Despite the enormous debt I still owe him, I don't regret buying the favors, not one bit. They took me away from a monster; I would've sold my soul for that. But unease slithers through me at the price I might have to pay. It could be anything.

I need to call Eli. It's time to end things.

————

"Hey, babe," Eli answers the phone, his voice low and gravelly. He's a man of few words and even fewer secrets, and the latter is becoming an increasingly bigger problem for me. I have nearly as many secrets as the Bargainer, a man who makes a living off gathering them.

Eli's aware that there's a lot I don't share, and the alpha in him has been pushing me to be more open. Shifters are just so damn frank. They operate under that whole sharing-is-caring principle.

I lean on my counter. "Eli…" That's about all I can get out before I scrub my face. I'd prepared myself for this day a long time ago, but that doesn't make it any easier. I try again. "Eli, I need to tell you something about myself that you're not going to want to hear."

This should've been a fast conversation—dump him, then end the call. And I considered doing just that. But breaking up with him over the phone is shitty enough. The least I could do is give the man an explanation.

"Is everything all right?" There's a lethal edge to his voice. The wolf is riding it. Now is not the time to be dropping this bomb.

Should've told him months ago. Months ago, when we

were what to each other? Friends with benefits? Colleagues working after hours together?

In no version of my life would I have spilled my secrets to Eli, the upstanding shifter who upheld supernatural law during his day job and who *was* the law in his pack. No, most of my secrets would land me in lots and lots of trouble.

"I'm fine, just… You know the bracelet I wear?"

God, this is it. Moment of reckoning.

"Yeah," he rumbles.

"That bracelet isn't just a piece of jewelry."

A pause. Then, "Callie, can we talk about this when I get back? Now's not a great time—"

"Every bead is a favor I owe the Bargainer," I rush to explain. The secret burns leaving my throat.

For most of the supernatural world, the Bargainer is more myth than man. And those who do know a bit about him know that he doesn't let any of his clients buy more than two or three favors at a time, and he never waits this long to collect his dues.

The other end of the line is quiet, which is not a good sign. Finally Eli says, "Tell me you're kidding, Callypso." A low growl enters his voice.

"I'm not," I say softly.

His growl intensifies. "The man's a wanted criminal."

As if I'm not aware of that little fact.

"It happened a long time ago." I don't know why I even bother defending myself.

"Why are you just now telling me this?" The wolf in him has almost drowned out his words.

I take a deep breath. "Because he visited last night," I say.

"He…visited you? Last night? Where?" he demands.

I close my eyes. This call is only going to get worse.

"My house."

"Tell me what happened." Judging from the way Eli's voice is rumbling, I doubt he's going to hold on to the phone conversation for much longer.

I look down at the chipped polish of my nails.

Just say it.

The only other person besides Des who knows about my debts is Temper. "I had three hundred and twenty-two favors I owed him. Now I have one less. He's going to collect the rest starting tonight."

"*Three hundred and twenty-two favors?*" Eli repeats. "Callie, the Bargainer would never—"

"He would. He *did*," I insist.

The silence on the other end of the line is ominous.

He must be wondering what would make the Bargainer part from his business practices so thoroughly. And I know the moment he comes to his own conclusion.

I pull the phone away from my ear as Eli roars, and I hear something smash. "What were you thinking, making deals with the King of the Night?"

The King of the Night. Being the Bargainer is just a side gig for Des.

I don't answer Eli. I can't explain myself, not without unleashing more terrible secrets.

"What did he make you do?" A growl drowns out most of his words.

My dread mounts. My life is about to be flipped on its head. Knowing the Bargainer, whatever repayment he asks of me, it's going to involve breaking the law at the very least.

Eli would never stand for that.

I have to tell him.

"Eli, I can't be with you," I whisper. The words have

been echoing in my mind from the very beginning of our relationship. I'd just had so many reasons not to say them that I ignored the truth.

And now that they're out in the open, relief washes through me. It's the wrong reaction. Ending a relationship is sad; I should feel sad, not...*free*. But I do feel free. I've been leading this poor man along, desperately trying to fix my scarred, broken heart in the arms of someone who isn't right for me.

"Callie, you're not serious, are you?" The wolf in him lets out a whine.

I close my eyes against the heartache I hear over the line; it's a painful, broken sound, and it matches his voice.

Better this way.

"Eli," I continue, "I don't know what the Bargainer is going to ask me to do, and I have over three hundred favors I owe him." My voice breaks.

I'm leaving Eli for what? Memories and dust. The man who broke my heart long ago will make me do things at his behest, and the entire time, I'll have to remember that I brought this upon myself.

Long ago, I thought he was my savior, and like a fool, I bought favor after favor from him, determined to keep him in my life, all the while falling for him.

I traded my life for a love that was nothing more than shadows and smoke screens.

"Callie, I'm not leaving you just because—"

"He kissed me," I cut him off. "Last night, the Bargainer *kissed* me. That was the first debt he made me pay off."

I meant to spare Eli's feelings as much as possible because he's a good man, but I also need him to stay away. I know the pack leader wants to protect me—to *save* me. And if he believes I want that as well, he will hunt Des down to the edges of the earth, and it won't end until one of the two men is dead.

I can't have that. Not when this situation is my fault and these debts are my burden.

I force the rest of my words out. "I don't know what he'll ask of me tonight, but whatever it is, I'll have to do it. I'm so sorry," I say. "I never meant for this to happen."

I hear something like a whine from the other side of the receiver. Eli still hasn't spoken, and I get the impression it's because he *can't*.

I pinch the bridge of my nose. Now for the especially unpleasant part.

"Eli," I say, "if he makes me do something illegal, something that hurts someone, you might have to..." I trail off and rub my forehead.

As a supernatural bounty hunter, part of Eli's job is to make paranormal bad guys disappear. And now I might become one of those bad guys.

"I don't think you need to worry about hurting anyone," Eli says, his voice rumbling menacingly. "The bastard has something else in store for you."

CHAPTER 4

October, eight years ago

"Not you again," the Bargainer says when he manifests in my dorm room.

I stumble back at the sight of him. This is the second time I've called on him, and I shouldn't still be surprised that he can just appear at will, but I am.

I straighten. "Your magic is failing." It's supposed to sound like an accusation, but it comes out like a plea.

He eyes my cramped quarters. "I warned you it might," he says, moving over to the window and glancing out at the rainy night.

I've already lost his attention.

"I want to ensure that it doesn't."

The Bargainer turns and assesses me. "So Baby Siren wants to make another deal?" he says, crossing his arms. "I didn't manage to spook you enough the first time?"

My eyes move over his white hair and large, sculpted arms.

He spooked me all right. There's something about him that looks a little feral. Feral and strange. But desperate times call for desperate measures.

"What would you be willing to give me?" he says, prowling toward me. "What dark and terrible secrets would you share?" he asks, moving in even closer. "You've heard that secrets are my favorite, haven't you?"

I want to back up, but a primal sort of fear roots me in place.

His eyes rove over me. "But for a siren…oh, I would make an exception. Anything I want, you would have to give to me. Tell me, cherub, could you give me *anything* I wanted?"

I swallow as he steps in close.

"Could you kill for me?" he asks, his voice low. His lips brush my ear. "Could you give your body to me?"

Oh God, is he telling the truth? Could he really make me do those things?

He runs his nose down my cheek and laughs at my obvious fear.

Stepping away from me, he says, "Like I told you before, I don't bargain with minors. Don't ruin your life owing me."

The air shimmers.

He might've scared the shit out of me, but at this point, I'm too far gone. I can't let him leave. It's as simple as that.

The siren surfaces, stretching out just beneath my skin. I lunge for him and catch his wrist, my hand glowing. "Make a deal with me," I say, putting as much glamour into my voice as possible. "I'm not a minor."

I'm really not. In the supernatural community, the legal age of adulthood is sixteen. And God knows with what I've done and experienced, I don't feel like a minor.

And right now, I am not complaining.

The Bargainer stares down at my hand, like he can't believe what's happening, and I feel an instant's worth of remorse. It's crappy to take away someone's free will.

Desperate times.

His features sharpen, his brows knitting, the rest of his face turning, in one word, *sinister.*

He rips his arm out of my hand. "You *dare* to glamour me?" Power rides his voice, and it's petrifying, filling the whole room.

I step back. Okay, glamouring him might've been a shit idea.

"It doesn't work on you?" What kind of supernatural is immune to glamour?

The Bargainer eases closer to me, his boots clinking ominously. He's furious, that much is obvious.

He leans in so close that several strands of his white-blond hair tickle my cheeks. "You want to piss your life away by making a deal?" His mouth curves up ever so slightly, his eyes sparking with interest. "Fine, let's make a deal."

Present

"I have to say, sleep does not become you."

I roll over in bed and rub my eyes. When I pull my hand away, I see the Bargainer standing off to the side of the bed, his arms folded and his head cocked. He's studying me like I'm an exotic bird, which technically, I sort of am.

"What are you doing here?" I ask, still groggy from sleep.

"In case you've missed it, the day is done. I'm here to collect more of my payment." The way he says *payment* sends shivers up my arms. Behind him, the moon shines brightly into the room.

I groan. I slept the entire day away. Ever since that phone call…

He snaps his fingers, and the blankets that cover me slide off.

"Des, what are you—?"

He *tsks*, interrupting me. "Your pajamas don't become you either, cherub. I was hoping those would improve with age as well."

I stifle a yawn and push myself off the bed. "Because I care what you think," I mumble, padding past him. Where yesterday his presence filled me with old pain, tonight all I feel is annoyance. Well, and a little lust, and a shit ton of heartache. But right now I'm focusing on annoyance.

I make my way to the bathroom, discreetly wiping away a bit of drool from my mouth.

The Bargainer follows me, enjoying just how much he's ruining my evening. "Oh, but I think you do," he says.

In response, I slam my door shut in his face. Probably not the wisest way to deal with the King of the Night, but right now I don't really care too much.

I take two steps away from the bathroom door, and it blasts open behind me. I spin around and stare at the Bargainer, his body filling up the space. My door hangs off its hinges at a funny angle.

"I wasn't finished," he says calmly. His eyes glint as they watch me; he's beautiful and terrible to behold.

"You owe me a new door," I respond.

He chuckles, and it's full of dark promise. "Why don't we work on paying off your current debts before you talk about what I owe you?"

I glare at him, because he has me. I have always been fully aware of the repercussions of those deals I made long ago. I cannot pretend otherwise.

Doesn't mean I have to like it.

"What was so important that you had to blow off my door to tell me?" I ask, folding my arms across my chest.

A watch forms over his tatted wrist and he taps the face of it. "Time, Callie, time. I have some important appointments to keep. You need to be ready in twenty minutes."

"Fine." I walk over to my shower and turn on the faucet. This will have to be a fast shower.

When I turn back around, the Bargainer has made himself comfortable on my bathroom's tile countertop. He leans against the wall next to the mirror, one of his leather-clad legs stretched out in front of him, his other leg bent at the knee.

"Get out," I say.

He gives me a lazy smile. "No."

"I'm not kidding."

One of his eyebrows quirks up. "Nor am I."

I run a hand through my hair. "I'm not getting naked in front of you."

"That's fine with me," he says. "Shower with your clothes on."

Oh, because *that's* reasonable. "If you're not going to leave the room, then I'll go somewhere else."

"The faucet in your guest bathroom doesn't work," he says, calling my bluff. My eyes widen before I remember that it's his business to know secrets.

He's not leaving.

My siren is thrilled at the prospect. There's another heartsick part of me that wouldn't mind him seeing what he gave up on long ago.

"Fine," I say, taking off my T-shirt. "Enjoy the peep show. That's all you'll be getting from me."

His laughter skitters up my arm. "Don't delude yourself, cherub. You have a wrist full of debt, and I have many, many demands."

I flash him another nasty look as I step into the shower to remove the rest of my clothing, uncaring that the water is quickly drenching the material. The shower curtain completely hides me from him.

I step out of my pajama bottoms, making sure that when I toss them over the curtain rod, I aim right for Des's perch.

He chuckles sinisterly, and I know without looking he stopped the clothing from hitting him. "Throwing things isn't going to change your fate, Callie."

But it does feel damn good. I chuck my sports bra, then my panties at him. Several seconds after I throw them, I hear them fall uselessly to the ground with a dull plop.

"Seems your pajamas are no better wet than they are dry. Shame."

"Seems you still think I care," I fire back.

He doesn't respond, and the bathroom quickly falls to silence.

This isn't immensely awkward or anything, I think as I begin to rinse off.

"Why are you here, Des?"

"You already know why," he says.

To collect.

"I mean, why now? It's been seven years."

Seven years of radio silence. And to think this man and I were once nearly inseparable...

"You counted our years apart?" Des says with mock

40

surprise. "If I didn't know better, I'd say you missed me." A faint trace of bitterness laces his words.

I turn off the water, snaking an arm around the curtain to grab a towel. "But you do know better." I wrap the towel around me and step out.

"Sticks and stones, cherub," he says, hopping off the counter. "Now, chop-chop. We've got people to see, places to go." And with that, he leaves the room.

I'm just stepping into my pants, my shitty lingerie on full display, when the Bargainer glances at his watch.

Ever since he left my bathroom, he's been lounging on a side chair in my bedroom, waiting for me to finish getting ready. One leather-clad leg jiggles as he waits. I can't help but feel that he's making sure I don't try to run.

As if, of the two of us, I'm the one known for running.

"Time's up, Callie." He pushes himself out of my chair and strides toward me. There's something predatory about the way he moves.

"Wait—" I back up and bump into my dresser. My hair is still dripping wet, and my feet are bare.

"No," he says just as he closes in on me.

I manage to open my dresser drawer and snatch a pair of socks from it before he scoops me into his arms. He used to hold me like this before he left. He'd press me close against him and rock me in his arms as I cried my heart out. And when I fell asleep, he'd lie next to me for hours, just so he could wake me from my nightmares.

But he'd never kissed me then—he'd never even tried to. Not until that last night, and then, it had still been all me.

"Is this really necessary?" I ask, referring to my position

41

in his arms. I push down a shudder. His body still feels like home, just as it did when I was a teenager, and I hate that.

I've never been free of him. When the sun hits my face, it's his shadow I see on the pavement. When the night closes in on me, it's his darkness that blankets my room. When I fall asleep, it's his face that haunts my dreams.

He's everywhere and in everything, and no number of lovers can make my heart forget.

Des glances down at me, his silver eyes softening just a smidge. Perhaps he's also remembering all the other times his skin pressed against mine. "Yes" is all he says.

Awkwardly I pull one sock over my foot. The other sock slips from my grasp, and I curse as it falls.

A moment later, the sock flutters up next to us and lands on my stomach.

"Can you grab my shoes?" I ask.

The Bargainer's eyes move to the boots resting next to the sliding glass door of my bedroom. As I watch, they lift off the ground and float toward me. I catch them in midair.

"Thanks," I say, giving him a genuine smile. I've watched him do this little parlor trick a hundred times, and I'm always enchanted by it.

For just a split second, his steps falter. He frowns as he looks down at me, his brows pinching together. And then he resumes walking again.

The sliding glass door unlocks and glides open. Cool night air hits me as the Bargainer steps outside.

"Truth or dare?" he says just as I finish putting my boots on.

My limbs lock up. Repayment is beginning.

Earlier today, I had been ready for it, but now I'm not. He still hasn't answered why, after all this time, he chose this moment to come back into my life. Or why he left it in the first place. But I know better than to expect an explanation. Getting secrets out of him is harder than bathing a cat.

"Truth."

"Did you say dare?" he asks, raising his eyebrows as he looks down at me. His hair isn't tied back today, and the white strands of it frame his face. "You sirens always *do* know how to spice things up."

I don't bother responding. The Bargainer is crooked through and through, so his words don't surprise me in the least.

But what he does next does.

The air behind him shimmers and coalesces until a set of folded wings appears, rising above his shoulder blades.

My breath catches in my throat.

All my animosity, all my hurt, all my pain—it all quiets as I stare at those wings.

Dark, silvery skin stretches over bone, so thin in certain areas that I can see the delicate veins beneath. His wings are tipped with bone-white talons, the biggest of them nearly the size of my hand.

I've only ever seen Des's wings once before, and then it was because he lost control of his magic. This doesn't seem spontaneous; this seems deliberate. I can't imagine why now of all times he's decided to unveil them, and to me of all people.

I reach over his shoulder and run my fingers across the smooth skin of one. His arms tense around me, and I can feel his breathing still.

"They're beautiful," I say. I'd meant to tell him this a long time ago; I just never got the chance.

The Bargainer's eyes travel down my face to my lips. He stares at them for a beat. "I'm glad you like them. You're going to be staring at them quite a bit tonight."

CHAPTER 5

October, eight years ago

I twist my bracelet round and round my wrist, anxiously playing with the single black bead strung along it, an IOU to the Bargainer for getting the authorities off my back.

Ahead of me, the man himself appears for the second time in my dorm room. He's clad from head to toe in black, the vintage AC/DC T-shirt he wears hugging his sculpted shoulders and broad back.

As soon as he sees me, he folds his arms over his chest. "My magic is still holding strong," he says, "so what else could you possibly need from me?"

I twist the bracelet around my wrist again, my heart thumping like mad at the sight of him. "I want to make another deal."

He narrows his eyes at me.

I wait for him to say something, but he doesn't.

Time to soldier on. "I…uh…"

He raises an eyebrow.

Just spit it out, Callie. "…want to buy you for a night."

Oh. My. Sweet. Lord.

Fuck you, mouth. Fuck you to the fiery pits of hell.

All expression wipes clean from the Bargainer's face. "I'm sorry, *what?*"

My cheeks and neck flush. I'm going to die of embarrassment. Scratch that, I wish I *could* die of embarrassment. Better than just standing here, my mouth opening and closing like a gaping fish.

The Bargainer begins to smirk, and somehow that makes this all even worse.

Should never have done this.

"I just want to hang out with you," I rush in to say. "It would be completely platonic."

Ugh, and now I sound desperate. But who am I kidding? I *am* desperate, desperate for companionship. When I came to Peel Academy, I thought I'd fit in and make friends, but it hasn't yet happened. And I'm so lonely.

"That's too bad, cherub," he says, beginning to poke around my room. "I was liking your offer better when it wasn't platonic."

I swear my cheeks burn even hotter, my eyes suddenly drawn to the Bargainer's built torso.

His gaze slides to mine, and now his smirk widens, his eyes glinting mischievously.

He knows exactly where my mind is.

"It would just be for an evening," I say, watching him as he idly picks up a perfume bottle from the top of my dresser and sniffs it. He winces at the smell, hastily putting it back where he found it.

"I have work," he says. And yet he doesn't leave.

He's willing to be convinced.

But how to convince him? The last time I glamoured him, it only served to piss him off. I don't think logic would sway him, and besides, there's no logic to this. If anything, me wanting to hang out with him for an evening is madness.

The first time I had convinced him to help me, what had I done?

My eyes widen when I remember.

"Bargainer," I say, heading over to where he stands eyeing my *Keep Calm and Read On* poster. When I'm close enough, I reach out and touch his forearm, my stomach tightening at the contact. "Please?"

I swear I feel his body shiver under my hand. He looks down at where our skin meets, my hand covering some of his tattoos.

The first time I had convinced him, it hadn't been my words so much as my touch. It's a real and vulnerable plea, and I think he knows it.

When his silver eyes find mine again, I swear something devious sparkles in them. "You're pushing your luck, baby siren." His fingers brush over my knuckles. "One night," he says.

I nod. "Just one night."

———

Present

Near the edge of my property, the Bargainer stops walking, but he doesn't put me down. Far below us lies the ocean, and nothing but a forty-foot drop separates here from there.

His wings stretch out behind him, and I suck in a breath

at the sight. His wingspan is incredible—nearly twenty feet across—and except for their silver hue, they look a lot like bat wings.

I meet his eyes; I know what he's about to do. "Des, no—"

He flashes me a wicked smile. "Hold on tight, Callie."

I bite my lip to stifle my scream as he jumps from the cliff. For a second, we drop, and my stomach somersaults. Then the Bargainer's wings catch the wind, and the air current pulls us up.

I wrap my hands around his neck and bury my face against his chest. All that's keeping me from plunging to my death are two sets of arms.

My wet hair whips about my face, the strands now icy cold as we rise in elevation.

"You're missing the view, cherub," he says over the howl of wind.

"I'm trying not to barf," I say, not sure he can even hear me.

It's not that I'm afraid of heights—I mean, my house rests on a *cliff*—but being carried through the air by a fairy is not on my short list of fun activities.

But eventually I do lift my head and look down. The water glitters far below us, and ahead of us, the rest of Los Angeles beckons, the land lit up like a Christmas tree.

The higher we rise, the colder it gets. I shiver against Des, and his grip tightens. He adjusts me slightly so that more of my body is pressed against his.

Just as I feared, being this close to him is reminding me of all those other times he held me close.

"Where are we going?" I yell over the wind.

"…location of your second dare." The constant shriek of the wind snatches away most of the Bargainer's words but not the important ones. I sort of wish it had.

I can't imagine what's in store for me, and considering my sordid past, that's not a good thing.

Not at all.

"You have *got* to be kidding me." I fold my arms, taking in the parking lot we landed in and the building beyond it. "This is what you blew off my door for?" I say, my eyes moving over the couches and tables on display in the store's windows. "A *furniture store?*"

His mouth twitches. "I'm redesigning my guest bedroom—or, rather, you are."

I roll my eyes. Picking out furniture, that's my dare.

"The place closes in fifteen minutes," the Bargainer says. "I expect you to choose and purchase the appropriate furnishings for a bedroom before then."

As soon as he finishes speaking, I feel the cloak of his magic settle on my shoulders like a weight, compelling me to action.

I begin moving, grumbling to myself. Of all the dumb, inane tasks, he gives me this one. This is what the internet is for.

I shouldn't complain; it could be worse.

It *should* be worse. I've seen enough of Des's bargains to know what repayment involves. It's never this effortless.

The Bargainer falls into step beside me, his wings shimmering out of existence. It's all I can do not to look at him. The man is nothing but a will-o'-the-wisp; the closer I think I get to him, the further out of reach he seems.

I pull open the door and head inside the store. Spread out before me is a sea of furniture. Fifteen minutes is not nearly enough time to see even half of what's in here.

Des's magic coils around my stomach, the sensation foreign and uncomfortable.

"What furniture do you want?" I ask, even as the spell Des has put on me tugs me forward.

The Bargainer shoves his hands in his pockets, wandering over to a table and peering at the place settings. He looks comically out of place with his big, manly muscles and the faded Iron Maiden shirt he wears.

"That, cherub, is for you to decide."

Fuck it. I don't have time to worry about this man's tastes. No sooner does the thought cross my mind than I feel an insistent tug from the magic, making my insides squirm.

Des flashes me a wicked smile from where he lies sprawled out on one of the couches, and I realize I should be more worried about this task than him.

This favor is a far cry from the kiss last night. Then, I didn't feel the magic. But perhaps I only feel the pull when I resist it. The thought makes me disgusted with myself. Last night I should've fought against that kiss more.

I move down the aisles, going for the ugliest pieces of furniture I can find. My little act of rebellion. This is what happens when you don't give good instructions.

I dart a quick glance at the Bargainer, and he watches me raptly.

He definitely has something else up his sleeve.

Don't focus on that now.

As fast as I can manage, I snatch up the price tags on the pieces I decide on and head to the cash register. The magic is an insistent drumbeat in my veins, quickening by the minute.

The entire time, the Bargainer's eyes are still on me. I know he's enjoying himself. Bastard.

God, his magic feels so invasive. Like an itch beneath my skin. And while a small, sick part of me thrills at the feel of his magic on me and in me, the bigger, more practical part finds it disturbing as hell.

The woman working at the register looks alarmed when I dump the price tags at her register. "Ma'am, you're not supposed to remove the tags from the furniture."

My skin glows lightly. "It's fine. Nothing to worry about," I say, using the siren in me to compel the store clerk.

She nods dumbly and begins scanning the barcodes. Behind me I hear the Bargainer's rumbly laughter.

"Hmm." The woman at the register stares at her computer and her brows furrow. "That's weird."

"What?" I say, immediately knowing this is going to be more difficult than I'd hoped.

"I could've sworn we just got a new shipment of these on Thursday, but it says we're all sold out." The item she's referring to is a hot-pink, leopard-print chair. She sets the price tag aside. "Let me ring up the rest of your items, and then I'll try checking the storeroom for this one."

"Forget about it." The magic's starting to breathe down my neck. I doubt I'll have time for the clerk to check the storeroom.

She gives me a strange look before her eyes move to the clock mounted to the wall on my left. I know she must be thinking how close her shift is to being over. "If you're sure…"

"I am," I rush to say. I grabbed enough price tags to still fully furnish the Bargainer's room.

She scans the next barcode—for a couch upholstered in a repeating pattern of roses and sickly sweet bows—and the same issue comes up.

My eyes thin, and I glance back at the Bargainer. He holds up his wrist and taps the face of the watch. The magic constricts around my innards, and before I can help it, I fold in on myself. The magic's becoming more than unpleasant.

I hold up a shaky hand and flip him the bird before returning my attention to the woman.

Every other item she rings up runs into the same mysterious problem. A problem I know better as Desmond Flynn.

The magic is making my heart race, and it's getting worse with each passing second. It's clear that in addition to the store closing, the Bargainer has imposed a time limit of his own.

This stupid task.

I lean over the counter and swallow. "What in your system *is* currently available for purchase?"

The cashier types something into her computer. Her brows furrow. "At the moment, it looks like we only have a four-poster bed, a wrought iron chandelier, a love seat, and a gilded mirror." She sounds hopelessly confused.

"I'll take one of each," I say, shoving my credit card at her, my hand beginning to shake. Sweat beads along my forehead.

I would *not* be killed by some ugly furniture.

Startled, she takes it. "But, ma'am…"

"*Please*," I practically beg. The magic is starting to seize up my lungs. Again, I feel the Bargainer's laughter at my back.

The cashier looks at me like I've lost it. Then her head tilts. "Hey, are you that actress…you know from—"

"*For the love of all that is sacred*, please ring me up!" The magic is twisting its way around my innards. I'm going to pass out if I don't complete this soon.

She flinches as though I slapped her. If I wasn't in physical pain, I'd feel bad for hurting her feelings. But all I can think of right now is how the magic seems to be doubling on itself.

She sniffs and shakes her head but does as I ask. An agonizing minute passes when she goes over delivery methods and shipping times, but then she swipes the card through the system.

I sigh as the magic releases me and I collapse against the counter. I glance down at my wrist in time to see two beads vanish.

I'm going to kill him.

"Ran into trouble?" the Bargainer asks innocently, standing up from the couch.

I stride past him and out of the store.

In the dark parking lot, he materializes in front of me, arms folded. Naturally, no one notices that he can appear and disappear at will.

As I try to pass him, his arm shoots out and catches my wrist.

I twist to face him. "*Two?*" I practically yell. "You make me redecorate your stupid bedroom in under twenty minutes, I nearly die, and that only eliminates *two* beads?"

I shouldn't be this upset. He hasn't yet asked anything truly awful of me, but the feeling of magical fingers squeezing my organs has almost undone me.

The Bargainer steps into my personal space. "Didn't like that task too much?" he asks, his voice low. His eyes glint in the moonlight.

I'm smart enough to keep quiet. He looks especially predatory right now, and when he's like this, I know better than to provoke him.

He steps in even closer. "I had more tasks like this one planned, but if you really hated it, then perhaps we can do something that's a bit more…comfortable."

The moment the words are out of his mouth, I realize I just messed up big time. I played right into his hands.

The Bargainer wraps his arms around me, his gaze lingering on my lips.

Eli was right.

The bastard has something else in mind for me.

But just when I think he's going to kiss me, his wings unfurl. And then we're rising, heading back into the night.

Twenty minutes later, the Bargainer lands gracefully in my backyard, holding me in his arms. His enormous silver wings fold up as soon as we touch ground, and a moment later, they shimmer out of existence.

Wordlessly, the Bargainer carries me to my sliding glass door. Without prompting, it slides open, and he steps inside.

It shuts behind us, and the Bargainer places me on my bed and crouches before me. His eyes never leave mine as his hands move to my ankles.

I'm beginning to get nervous. Just what else is he going to demand of me tonight? The man's never even seen me naked. Besides, I *know* the Bargainer wouldn't make me pay him back in sex unless I was already on board with the idea.

And I'm not.

Right?

Des removes first one boot, then the other. He tosses them aside and peels off my socks one at a time. "Tell me, Callie," he says, his gaze sliding to me, "are you nervous?"

He's not exacting repayment right now, so I don't need to answer him. But I find myself reluctantly nodding anyway.

"So you have not forgotten everything about me," he says. "Good." He clutches one of my feet in his hands, and he places a tender kiss on my ankle. "Truth or dare?"

My breath catches.

"Truth."

His grip on my ankle tightens. "Why do you think I left you all those years ago?" he asks.

He had to go straight for the killing blow. My heart feels like it's at the back of my throat, and I swallow down my emotion.

I draw in a ragged breath. The past can't hurt me anymore. None of it. It only exists in my memory.

"Des, what does it matter?"

His magic flares up in my throat, though it's not painful like it was before. Just a reminder to answer his question.

He waits, letting his rising magic speak for him.

My fingers pluck at a loose thread of my comforter. "I forced your hand." I lift my gaze. "I pushed you too far and made you leave." I feel the spell release me as soon as the words are out of my throat.

The past might not be able to hurt me, but it sure feels like a living, breathing thing. Amazing that something and someone who entered and exited my life close to a decade ago can still have this kind of hold on me.

The Bargainer's eyes search mine, the silver of them glinting in the moonlight. I can't read his expression, but it makes my stomach clench uncomfortably.

He nods once and stands. The man is almost to the balcony door before I realize he's leaving.

That thought sends a stab of pain through me. I am so damn fed up with my stupid heart. If I could, I'd break it myself simply for being foolish enough to soften for this man when my mind wants to push him as far away as possible.

"Really, Des?" I call out. "Running again?"

His eyes flash as he swivels to face me, one hand on my sliding glass door. "You're righter than you know, cherub.

You did force me to leave you. Seven years is a long time to wait, especially for someone like me. A word of caution: I'm not leaving again."

CHAPTER 6

November, eight years ago

One wish becomes two, two wishes become four, four become eight…until somehow a whole row of beads circle my wrist.

It was just supposed to be one evening. But like an addict, I came right back to him for more. More nights, more companionship. I don't know what the Bargainer's story is. He has no reason to keep indulging me.

And yet he does…

I look at my beads and remember the Bargainer's warnings.

Anything I want, you would have to give to me. Tell me, cherub, could you give me anything I wanted?

Could you give your body to me?

I should be afraid of that threat. Instead, a restless sort of anticipation gnaws away at me.

I am not right in the head.

"What are you thinking about, cherub?" he asks.

Tonight, the Bargainer makes himself comfortable on my

bed, his body so large his feet hang over the edge. The sight of him lounging there, combined with the train of my thoughts…

I feel heat crawl up my cheeks.

"Oh, *definitely* something inappropriate." He settles himself against my pillow, sliding his hands behind his head.

Just when I think he's going to taunt me about it, the Bargainer's eyes move over my room. My gaze follows his, sliding over the rack of my cheap jewelry and the bag of makeup sitting on top of my dresser. I take in the posters hanging on my wall—one of the Beatles, another a black-and-white picture of the Eiffel Tower, and that dumb *Keep Calm and Read On* poster. My textbooks are piled on my desk, alongside my mug and cans of tea bags.

Dog-eared books, clothes, and shoes litter my floor.

I feel young all of a sudden. Young and inexperienced. I can't imagine how many women the Bargainer has visited, but I bet their rooms looked far more mature than mine, with my thumbtacked posters and sad little tea set.

"No roommate?" he asks, noticing the foldout chair I have situated where another bed should be.

"Not anymore."

She moved in with her friend, who'd been placed in a single and wanted a roommate. I was both disappointed and relieved to see her go. I liked the companionship, but the two of us hadn't really hit it off. She'd been funny and chirpy, and I was…*troubled*.

The Bargainer gives me a pitiful look. "Struggling to make friends, cherub?" he asks.

I wince. "Stop calling me that," I say, sliding into my computer chair and kicking my legs up on my desk.

Cherub. It makes me think of fat baby angels. That makes me feel even younger.

He just smiles at me, really making himself comfortable.

"What even is your name?" I say.

"Not going to address the friends' issue?" he asks.

"It's called deflecting," I say, tipping my chair back as I talk to him, "and you're doing it too."

His eyes dance. I doubt he'll ever admit it, but I'm beginning to believe he likes visiting me. I know I like having him around. It keeps my demons at bay for just a little bit longer than it otherwise would.

"You really think I just give clients my name, *cherub*?" He picks up a stray piece of paper from my bedside table.

"Stop. Calling. Me. That."

"Who's George?" he asks, reading off the paper.

And now I want to die. I snatch the note from him, crumpling it up and throwing it in the trash.

"Oh my. *George*." Just the way he says that is enough for me to fight off another blush. "Is he the one you're thinking inappropriate thoughts of?"

If only.

"Why do you care?" I ask.

"When a boy gives you his number, it's because he likes you. And you kept it. On your nightstand." The Bargainer says that like the nightstand is the clincher.

What am I supposed to say to him? That the only guy I'm fixating on at the moment is the Bargainer himself?

No thank you.

"It's not like he and I are going to date," I mumble. "His sister is friends with a girl who doesn't like me."

I don't have to spell out the rest. The Bargainer raises his eyebrows. "Ah." I can feel his gaze dissecting my body language.

What does he see? My embarrassment? My frustration? My humiliation?

He swings his legs off the bed, the sudden action startling me. He reaches out a hand and pulls me to my feet. "Grab a coat."

"Why?"

"Because we're going out."

Present

In the morning before I head off to work, I pad over to my bathroom and inspect my broken door.

Fixed. The Bargainer repaired it without making a deal. My heart pounds harder at this realization. The Bargainer's a trickster; everything comes at a price. So why not this?

And the Bargainer's parting lines. I squeeze my eyes shut. Something he said stuck in my mind.

Seven years is a long time to wait, especially for someone like me.

The Bargainer waits for no one, especially not a lovestruck client who was once only too eager to pay back all her favors. But it sounds as though that's exactly what he did—he waited. It makes no sense.

I roll my bracelet round and round my wrist, counting, then recounting my beads.

Three hundred and sixteen of them are left. That means that the Bargainer removed some *after* I bought his precious furniture. Several beads in exchange for the secret I revealed.

I scrub my face.

Right now, more than ever, I think I hate the Bargainer. Hate that he came barging into my life when I was really making something of it. Hate that I had to break up with Eli *over the phone* because I didn't know what tasks Des would ask of me. But most of all, I hate him because he is easier to hate than myself.

I shuffle into West Coast Investigations twenty minutes late, a pink cardboard box tucked under my arm.

For the last six years, Temper and I have been in the PI business, though what we do is a bit more questionably legal than what the job entails. West Coast Investigations can procure just about anything for you—a missing person, a confession, proof of a crime.

"Hey," I call out from our reception area, "I got us breakfast."

The typing in Temper's office pauses.

"Doughnuts?" she calls out hopefully.

"Nah, I picked us up some fruit. Thought today would be a good day to start working on our swimsuit figures," I say, dropping the box of doughnuts on a table in our waiting room, a little cloud of dust billowing out around it.

Reminder: Need to wipe down the sitting area.

"Swimsuit figures?" Temper strides out of her office, giving me a look like I blasphemed. "Are you insinuating—"

Her eyes land on the box of doughnuts.

"I got us blueberry old-fashioned and jelly-filled," I say, handing her coffee as well. "Boom—fruit."

She guffaws, then begins to laugh in earnest. "That was a messed-up joke. I almost had an aneurysm." She opens the box, making a happy humming sound as she pulls out one of the old-fashioned doughnuts. She takes a bite and moans a little. "So good. Thanks for these."

I nod. "How's it going?"

"Work?" She smiles around another bite of doughnut. "You know work is always good."

That's the perk of doing what you love.

"Get out of here, Temper. You know I wasn't asking about *work*," I say.

"You're going to make me talk about my personal life before I've even had my second coffee?" she says, lifting said coffee to her lips.

Rather than responding, I just wait, leaning my hip against the table.

She exhales, and I raise my eyebrows.

"It's that bad?" I say. Temper is usually unflappable when it comes to her personal life.

"Eh." She lifts a shoulder. "It's fine. My parents have stopped reaching out for the time being, thank fuck, but Leo—" She makes a face at the name, and it takes me a second to remember.

"Wait, are you talking about *Leo* as in Leonard Fortuna?" I say.

She grimaces again. "That's the one."

Long, long ago, Temper's and Leonard Fortuna's parents had gotten together and promised to join their houses through the marriage of their children. Really archaic shit. Temper is still dealing with the fallout from it.

"Why is he contacting you?" I ask.

Temper takes another sip of her coffee. "He still wants it to work out between us." She shakes her head. "He seems to think if he's nice to me, I'll forget he's a monster."

As long as I've known Temper, Leonard Fortuna has always been the fate she escaped—nothing more.

But now that he's reaching out...

"I've told him to beat off," Temper says. She frowns at her doughnut. "Not that it did anything at all. If anything, Leo sounds like he might be planning a visit to LA soon."

My eyes widen. Contacting my friend is bad enough, but the idea that Leonard Fortuna might be coming to our city…that he could actually get close enough to nab Temper if his blackened heart so desired…

"Shit," I breathe. "Do you want me to glamour him?"

I suppress a shiver at the thought of doing such a thing, even if my siren preens at the thought of making a bad man *succumb* to her.

The entire Fortuna family is nothing but bad news—rich, powerful, bad news. And from everything I've heard about him, Leonard Fortuna is one of the worst of the lot, despite his young age. I wouldn't want a man like that to even be aware of my existence.

My friend shakes her head and uses her doughnut to wave away my concern. "I have it handled."

I stare at her a second longer, worrying my lower lip. Temper has been strong and independent for as long as I've known her—her circumstances growing up have forced her to be—but because of that, I can never tell when she really does need my help.

She sees my look. "I *promise*," she insists. "Now go get to work so I can covertly eat the rest of these doughnuts while you're distracted."

I grab a maple bar. "Fine, I'm going." I head into my office.

These are the same offices we moved into five years ago when, on graduation night, we packed up and all but fled Peel Academy for something better. Our office space still holds that same excited, desperate feel it did then, back when the two of us were running—me from my past, and Temper from her destiny—and eager to make something new for ourselves.

I smile around a bite of my doughnut when I see the check from my last assignment on my desk. I polish off the rest of the pastry, then slide into my chair and grab the check, stuffing it into my purse. I hope Micky, the shitty son, is treating his mother right. It's a privilege to have one at all.

Kicking my heels up on my desk, I turn on my computer. While I wait for it to come to life, I flip through messages on my office phone.

One is from a former target, a stalker by the name of Sean who'd been following one of my clients home. Both Temper and I had to get involved in the case, and we clearly left a lasting impression, judging by all his colorful language. I delete the message and move on to the next.

The following three messages are from potential clients. I slide a legal pad over to me and grab a pen, jotting down the names and contact information they leave behind.

And then there's the final message.

My muscles seize up when I hear the warm, gravelly voice. "Baby girl, I'm not breaking up with you. Not over this. When I get back, we'll talk about it."

My back goes ramrod straight.

No, no, *no*.

"Until then," the message continues, "I've pulled some strings and moved the Bargainer up on the wanted list to top priority." In other words, top ten.

Shit.

This is exactly what I didn't want to happen. Eli taking my mess and making it his own.

As soon as my computer loads, I open up the Politia's website, clicking to their most wanted list.

The list goes all the way down to a hundred, but the top ten most wanted criminals are front and center, their photos right next to their names.

Coming in at number three on the list: *The Bargainer (real name unknown)*.

"Motherfucker," I mutter, kicking the file cabinet next to me.

I don't know why I'm so bothered. The Bargainer can handle his own shit, and I can handle *my* own shit. Or I could until I got involved with an alpha fucking werewolf.

My eyes move to the sketch of Des's face. The Politia doesn't even have a photo of him, and the picture itself...he could be anyone. The only thing they got right are his silver eyes and white hair. Which, to be fair, is enough.

I click on the link, wondering just how many female officers Eli had to butter up for the Bargainer to make the top ten. Des has always been on the wanted list, but I don't know if I've ever seen him make it this high.

The page that opens is full of his stats and a more detailed description. And unlike the drawing of Des, these seem to be accurate, down to his sleeve of tattoos. They didn't, however, mention his pointed ears or his wings.

They don't know he's a fairy.

But still, what they do have is damning.

I open the bottom drawer of my desk and pull out the bottle of Johnnie Walker.

It doesn't matter that it isn't even noon or that I've just finished breakfast. Today is one of those days.

Temper comes in five minutes later. When she sees me drinking, she motions for the bottle. Reluctantly, I slide it across the desk.

"What's going on, chick?" She knows that when Johnnie comes out, something bad has happened. Temper takes a drink, then makes a face. "Ugh, that mixes horribly with doughnuts."

I'd laugh if I weren't so on edge. Instead, I suck on my teeth and shake my head at her question.

I glance down at my bracelet. "My past caught up with me."

She slides the bottle back my way. "Need me to hurt someone?" she asks, dead serious. It's an echo of my own earlier offer.

She and I are as close as friends come, and we have been since senior year of high school. At the core of our friendship is a pact of sorts: nothing's going to drag her toward the future she doesn't want, and nothing's going drag me back into the past I've worked to forget.

Nothing.

I huff out a laugh. "Eli's already beaten you to it."

"Eli?" she says, raising an eyebrow.

"I didn't ask him to get involved," I explain. "I broke up with him, and then he got involved—"

"*What!*" She grabs the table. "You broke up with him? When were you going to tell me?"

"Today. I was going to tell you today."

She's shaking her head. "You should've called me."

"I was busy ending a relationship."

She falls back into her seat and rubs her forehead. "Damn, now Eli's going to stop giving us a discount."

"*That's* what your most upset by?" I say, taking another swig of whiskey.

"No," she says. "I'm happy you grew a vagina and broke up with him. He deserves better."

"I'm going to throw this bottle of whiskey at you."

She holds her hands up to placate me. "I'm *kidding*. But seriously, are you okay?"

I barely stop myself from looking at my computer screen again.

I exhale. "Honestly? I have no fucking clue."

I'm taking a healthy swig of wine when my back door opens and the Bargainer walks in.

"Trying to drink your feelings away again, cherub?"

My heart gallops at the sight of him in his black fitted shirt and faded jeans.

I set down my wineglass and the book I was reading. "*Again?*" I say, raising an eyebrow. "How would you know how I cope?"

"Rumors," he says blandly.

I narrow my eyes. "Have you been keeping tabs on—"

My voice cuts off as the Bargainer crosses the room, grabs my glass of wine, and makes his way to the kitchen sink. He dumps its contents down the drain.

"Hey!" I say, "That's expensive burgundy."

"I'm sure your pocketbook is suffering," he says. There's not an ounce of remorse in his voice.

I follow him into my kitchen. "You shouldn't waste good wine on principle."

He moves away from the sink, and I gasp when I see my bottle of wine levitate off my coffee table and cross the living room and into the kitchen, landing in the Bargainer's waiting hand.

He turns the bottle on its head, and I hear the sound of precious wine chugging out of it and into the porcelain basin of my sink.

"What are you *doing*?" I'm too shocked at his audacity to do more than gape as the last of the wine swirls down the drain.

"This is not how you solve your problems," the Bargainer says, shaking the now-empty wine bottle at me.

The first flare of righteous indignation replaces my

shock. "I was drinking a glass of wine, you psycho, not the whole damn bottle."

He drops the bottle into the sink, and I jump when I hear glass shatter. "You're in denial." Des's eyes are angry. He grabs my wrist roughly, never taking his eyes off me.

He fingers a bead.

"What are you doing?" The first stirrings of trepidation speed up my heart rate.

"Taking care of you," he says, staring at me with the same intensity.

I can't help it. I glance down at his hands, because his expression is making me squirm. Beneath his fingers, a bead disappears.

I raise my eyebrows. Whatever repayment he just asked for, I know I'm not going to like it.

"Are you going to tell me what that bead just cost me?"

"You'll figure it out soon enough."

CHAPTER 7

November, eight years ago

Ever since the Bargainer took me out last week—for coffee and pastries of all things—we've spent half of our evenings in my dorm and the other half inside a bakery on the other side of the Isle of Man.

He's been careful to keep things platonic, despite the fact that he's been paying for the coffee and French macarons I order every time we visit Douglas Café, the Isle of Man's best bakery. Or that he's spent most nights over the last month hanging with me.

This situation isn't right.

But I don't want it to change.

"So what's your real name?" I pester him for the hundredth time.

Tonight we're hanging in my room. I'm lying in my bed, the credits of the movie we watched rolling down my laptop screen, which is situated next to me.

A part of me dreads turning and seeing the Bargainer's face. He has to be bored, sitting in my uncomfortable foldout chair and watching *The Mummy* on a tiny screen between us.

But when I turn, I don't see a bored man. I see a confused one. His brows are pinched, and his lips form a thin line.

"Bargainer?"

"Why did you kill your stepfather?" he asks, his gaze moving to mine.

I sit straight up, my reaction immediate. Old fear pounds through me, accompanied by unwanted memories. My stepfather's sour breath, the smell of his expensive cologne.

"Why would you ask me that?" I don't quite manage to keep the emotion out of my voice.

He leans back in my chair, threading his hands behind his head. One of his feet rests on his other thigh. The man doesn't look like he's going anywhere anytime soon.

"I think I'm entitled to some sort of explanation," he says, "seeing as how I'm your accomplice."

I swallow. I never should've bargained for this man's presence.

I'm a stupid, stupid girl.

"You're not going to get one," I say. It's not that I don't trust him—because I do, even though I shouldn't.

But the idea of sharing that part of my past with the Bargainer…I feel queasy at the mere thought.

He watches me for a long moment, then his lips curl into a smile. "Tell me, little siren, are you getting a taste for secrets?" He looks almost proud.

But then it evaporates, and he turns serious again.

He leans those scary, ripped arms of his on his thighs. "Whatever he did to you, it's—"

"*Stop it*. Stop talking." I stand, my laptop nearly falling off my bed in my mad dash to get off the mattress.

The Bargainer *knows*. Not that it would take a genius to figure out why a seemingly innocent teen would attack her stepfather.

I silently beg him not to push any further. I know I'm wearing my heart on my sleeve, that my broken, battered soul is staring out through my eyes.

The Bargainer's form blurs. At some point, I must've started crying, but I only notice it now, when I can no longer clearly see him.

He curses under his breath, shakes his head. "I need to go."

I blink away the moisture in my eyes.

He's leaving? Why do I feel so desolate at that thought when a moment ago, I was wishing just the opposite?

As he gets up, the Bargainer's gaze follows the tears that slip down my cheeks, and I can see his regret. That eases my pain. Somewhat.

Just when I think he's going to apologize, he doesn't.

He says something better.

"Desmond Flynn."

"What?" I say.

The air is already moving, shifting as his magic takes hold. "My name."

It's only after he leaves that I realize he never added a bead for the information.

Present

Des doesn't tell me where he's taking me, nor what task he has in mind for tonight. As the two of us soar over the ocean, all I know is that he's heading down the coast rather than inland.

Now that I've gotten somewhat used to flying in the Bargainer's arms, I stare out at the glittering sea and the twinkling stars. Dark though it is, the view is something to behold. I can smell the salt in the air, and the wind weaves through my hair. It makes me yearn for something I've forgotten—or lost.

I turn my head inward, my eyes falling to the column of Des's throat and the underside of his strong jaw.

A fairy is carrying me off into the night. That sounds like all the stories I've ever read of them.

Up my eyes climb, to those beautiful, familiar features of his. He glances down, catching me staring at him. His eyes are sly, but whatever he sees in mine causes them to soften.

My heart lodges in my throat. I tear my gaze away before that look can get under my skin.

We turn away from the coast, heading out to sea.

What could possibly be out there for us?

I find out a short while later, when out of the coastal mist, Catalina Island comes into view. Sitting off the coast of LA, Catalina is a place where locals go for weekend vacations. Most of the island is uninhabited.

We pass Avalon, the island's main city, moving along the edge of Catalina's coastline. We curve around the bend in the cliffs, and a white stone house comes into view, lit up amid the darkness. It becomes clear by the way the Bargainer maneuvers us in the air that this is our destination.

I drink in the sight of it. It's perched near a cliff's edge, much like mine, the back of the house giving way to a terraced yard that ends right at the edge of the property.

The closer we get, the more magnificent the place appears. It's made of glass and white stone, and as we circle to the front, I catch a brief glimpse of the elaborate gardens that surround it.

The Bargainer glides over the front lawn, and with one final dip, we touch down.

I step out of his arms and look around. "What is this place?" It looks like something out of a dream. A palatial house set at the edge of the world.

"Welcome to my home," Des says.

"Your *home*?" I say, incredulous. "You live here?"

"From time to time."

I never thought of the Bargainer as having a place of his own, but of course he does. He visits this realm often enough.

I take in the climbing bougainvillea and the gurgling fountain set in the front yard. Beyond it, his house stands majestic.

"This place is unbelievable," I say. Suddenly my little home seems dingy and dilapidated by comparison.

He glances around, and I get the impression he's trying to see his house through my eyes. "I'm glad you like it. You're my first guest."

I balk at this. "Really?"

First he shows me his wings. Now he shows me his hideaway. Both of these revelations are obviously important, but I can't figure out the Bargainer's motives.

"Does that make you uncomfortable?" he asks, his voice dropping low. "My bringing you here to my home?"

I get the distinct impression that he wants me to be uncomfortable.

He's doing a good job of it too.

"Curious, not uncomfortable," I say, challenging him with my eyes. After all, he'd been in my home hundreds of times when I was younger.

The corner of his lips quirks, his eyes darkening with whatever schemes are brewing in that mind of his. He extends a hand forward. "Then come inside. We have much to discuss."

I move through his entryway slowly, taking in the polished wooden floorboards and gleaming metal wall fixtures. No iron, I notice.

My brows furrow when I see two Venetian masks hanging along the wall. I used to have an identical pair back at Peel Academy. I feel goose bumps break out along my skin.

It means nothing.

A series of panoramic photographs line the entryway and spill into the living room, each one taken from a different corner of the world. The bright bazaars of Morocco, the austere mountains of Tibet, the red tile roofs of Cuzco. I've seen them all in person, thanks to the man at my side.

I can feel Des's eyes on me, watching my every reaction.

Tentatively, I make my way into the living room, where a worn leather couch rests on a shaggy fur rug. His coffee table is a giant wooden chest, the brass buckles dull with age.

"Tell me what you're thinking, Callie."

I love your place.

I want to bury my bare feet in that shaggy rug and feel the fur tickle my toes. I want to sprawl out on his couch and hang out with the Bargainer like we used to.

"I never realized how close you lived," I say instead.

His eyes narrow, like he knows I didn't speak my mind.

I crane my neck and try to peer down a darkened hallway.

"Want a tour of the place?" he asks, leaning against one of his walls. With his low-slung jeans and windswept hair, he looks like he invented the word *sexiness*, which is really annoying when you're determined to harden your heart against someone.

I'm nodding before I think better of it.

So much for hardening my heart.

And so the Bargainer shows me his house, from the fancy kitchen to the guestroom I so recently furnished. The only two rooms he doesn't show me are the room that contains a portal to the Otherworld—the land of the fae—and his bedroom, a.k.a. the two most interesting rooms in his house.

We end up back in his kitchen, an area of his house that, while much more polished than mine, is nonetheless a place you want to linger.

"Why did you bring me here?" I ask, idly opening a copper canister he has sitting against the wall. At first I think I'm staring at flour, but when it catches the light, it shimmers.

Fairy dust?

Instead of answering, Des sets the canister I hold aside and grabs my wrist. He runs a hand over my bracelet. "Tonight I want a truth from you," he says, his eyes twinkling with mischief. "Tell me, cherub, what have you been up to in the last seven years?"

As soon as the words are out of his mouth, I can feel the magic compelling me to talk. It's not pushy like it was last night, because there is no time limit to this, but it does coat my tongue, beckoning me to speak.

"I went to Peel Academy for one more year," I begin, "and that's when I met my best friend, Temper."

I swear I see him react to even that one little detail. He once held the prize position of my best friend, odd match though we were.

"She got me through that last year." I don't need to

elaborate for him to understand that the thing I was *getting through* was him.

The hand that still holds my wrist now tightens.

"On graduation night, Temper and I left the UK. We moved to LA and started our own business."

"Ah, yes, West Coast Investigations, is it?" he says.

My eyes widen before I can help it. "You know about it?"

He releases my hand. "I'm the Bargainer. I know all about your little business." He says that like he keeps tabs on everyone. "Seems I'm not the only one extracting secrets these days."

I can't tell whether he's pleased or annoyed.

"Does that bother you?" I ask.

"It pleases me. And it *angers* me that it pleases me." He frowns, folding his arms over his chest. "I never wanted you to end up like me." All the trickery is gone from his voice when he says that.

"I didn't realize that you cared one way or another." Is that bitterness in my voice? I think it is.

He gives me a rueful smile. "Tell me about your business." He says this innocently enough, but I still feel his magic on my tongue, forcing me to answer.

"Temper and I are in private investigation. She uses her spells to catch criminals, find missing persons, and"— scare the living crap out of bad guys—"*other things*. I use my glamour to compel people to confess or to act against their base nature." I think of Micky, my last client, as I say this.

Des clicks his tongue. "Callie, Callie, making a business of breaking the law. *My*, how this is sounding familiar."

So I modeled my business after his. Big deal.

"Copying is the sincerest form of flattery," I say.

The Bargainer leans forward. "Cherub, this is perhaps

too sincere. Though, like I said, it *does* please me… You are taking precautions to guard yourself against the authorities, aren't you?"

In other words, *you're not going to get caught anytime soon, are you?*

I swear it sounds like he actually cares. All this coming from the third most wanted man in the supernatural world.

"I'm fine." I pull out one of the barstools in his kitchen and sit down. "That's what I've been up to for the last seven years."

I spin myself on his barstool.

"You're omitting some details," he says, rounding to the other side of the bar where I sit.

He doesn't need to tell me that for me to feel the magic pressing down on me, demanding I say more.

"What have I missed?"

Des leans against the island in his kitchen, his eyes unwavering. "Your personal life."

I can feel my face flushing even as I give him a strange look. Why would he, someone who spurned me long ago, care about my personal life? I'm just a client.

It's the magic that compels me to speak. "You want me to tell you about all the relationships I've had within the last seven years? There's nothing to tell."

He raises an eyebrow. "You've been with no one in all that time?"

This is the sort of history you discuss with a significant other, but I don't think the Bargainer is interested in a relationship. And thinking otherwise would just set me up for inevitable heartbreak. Again.

"What about you?" I demand. "Who've you been with?"

"I'm not asking about me, and you still need to answer the question."

The magic sinks its talons in, tightening my throat.

"Eight. Okay? I've been in eight 'relationships.'" I air quote the word, because my idea of a relationship really is a joke. None have lasted longer than six months.

I have commitment issues.

Des's magic still has me in its grip.

"And some flings here and there in between," I say, my face heating as I speak.

God, this is embarrassing, considering I'm telling this to the object of my teenage infatuation. And the longer I'm around him, the more I think he wasn't strictly a teenage infatuation. No, the more he stares at me with those bedroom eyes of his, the more I feel the armor around my heart crumbling away, like it was made of nothing more than papier-mâché.

As I talk, Des's face hardens. I get a little thrill at the possibility that he's actually upset at the idea of me being in a relationship.

"Did you love any of them?" he asks.

I tilt my head at him. "That's none of your business," I say, more confused than anything.

"Au contraire, so long as you owe me, it *is* my business."

"You're really going to make me say this?" It's a rhetorical question; I can feel the magic dragging my answer up my throat. "No, I didn't love any of them." *Finally* the magic releases me. "Are you happy?"

"No, cherub," he says, his expression flinty. "I'm not."

I eye him up and down. This entire repayment has been a farce. A kiss, some furniture, and a couple of confessions. That's all he's asked for so far.

I've seen this man single-handedly force a politician to change supernatural law as repayment. I've seen him drag secrets out of men who would rather die than confess.

I lean my elbows against the granite countertop. "Why have you come back into my life? And don't tell me it's just because you randomly decided I needed to pay my debts."

He leans forward as well, our faces no more than a foot apart. "I didn't randomly decide that, Callie. That was very, very deliberate." He says this like the words themselves are weighty.

I search his face. "Why, Des?"

He hesitates, and I see the first crack in his façade, something that's not angry or bitter or aloof. Something… vulnerable.

"I need your help," he finally admits.

Des has made an empire on secrets and favors. Surely I can't offer anything he can't already get elsewhere?

"The infamous Bargainer needs my help?" I say this sarcastically, but I'm intrigued.

"There's something happening in the Otherworld," he explains. "Something even my secrets can't uncover."

Otherworld. Just the mention of it raises my gooseflesh. It's the realm of fairies and other creatures too cruel for earth. All supernaturals know of it, and those with a lick of sense fear it.

"How can I possibly help?" I ask as his fridge opens behind him. Already I'm dreading what he might say.

A bottle of sparkling cider floats out from the fridge. Just as the door closes behind it, a bottle of wine slides off the far countertop. A moment later, a cupboard opens and two wineglasses levitate out of it. All four items land in front of the Bargainer, who then begins to pour us drinks.

"I need you to get some information out of a few of my subjects."

He slides a glass of sparkling cider across to me. I frown at it but take a tentative sip of it anyway.

"And you can't?" I ask, my eyebrows rising.

He shakes his head, his eyes far away. "I can, to a point. Beyond that point…they die."

"They *die*?"

Jesus. What is this man talking about?

"Like you, I can compel people. But there is one key difference between our two abilities."

There was a whole lot more than one key difference between our abilities. Des didn't happen to glow every time he used them, nor did he try to dry hump the object of his glamour like the siren in me did, that horny bitch.

"Your glamour doesn't give your target the ability to refuse orders," he continues. "You want them to talk, they talk. You want them to dance naked in the streets, they dance naked in the streets. There is no other option." He slides his wineglass back and forth between his hands. "With *my* power," he says, "a person can choose not to be compelled, but it will kill them. So if they wish, they can choose to die fully clothed rather than dance naked in the streets. Or they can choose to die silent rather than spill a secret."

I'd never realized…

"But you get everyone to talk," I say.

The Bargainer takes a long drink of his wine before he answers. "Most people want to live."

I let that revelation sink in. "So your subjects are choosing death rather than sharing information?"

He nods, staring at his glass.

Yikes. I can't imagine what secret would be worth dying for.

"There's one thing wrong with your plan," I say. "I can't glamour fairies."

His eyes rise to mine. "I'm not asking you to glamour fairies."

That gives me pause. "Then what are you asking?"

His moonlit eyes are just as mysterious as they've always been. Making some sort of decision, he rounds the bar and, grabbing another barstool, pulls it up close.

"Things in the Otherworld are...amiss." His voice is softer, like he needs to gently ease the words out. "My kingdom is restless, as are the others. There have been disappearances—many, many disappearances. Soldiers vanishing without a trace. Only the women have returned. I need to find out what's happened to them."

"Why don't the women just tell you themselves?" I ask.

"They can't." Des's expression is agonized.

"They're dead?"

He shakes his head. "Not quite. They are neither alive nor dead."

I swirl my glass of sparkling cider. "I still don't understand. What do you want me to do, Des?"

"The fae won't talk to me." He chooses his next words carefully. "But fae aren't the only ones who live in the Otherworld."

All at once, I understand.

"The changelings," I breathe. Humans snatched up by fairies and taken to the Otherworld. Most lived there as slaves.

"I need to protect my kingdom."

I stiffen. It's rare to get Des to talk about the other half of his life, the half where he's not just some phantom in the night. The half where he is actually a king, one who rules over all those creatures that go bump in the night.

"So you want to take me into your world," I say. "And you want me to glamour your slaves—"

"They're not slaves," he growls.

"Don't play me for a fool, Des. Just because it's all they've ever known doesn't mean they'd choose that life if they could."

"None of us get to choose our lives," he says, and his eyes are a little too penetrating.

"You want me to force the truth out of the humans who live in your kingdom, even though it's unethical and it will probably get them worse than killed."

"You've never cared about the ethics of your glamour before," he says.

"Because none of the people I've glamoured have been victims." They'd all been criminals of one sort or another. I continue. "Haven't you ever considered that if the King of the Night, with all his tricks and promises, can't get these people to talk, we should leave them alone?"

"Callie," Des says, leaning forward, "fairies are dying. Humans are dying. Something's happening to the Otherworld, and it's happening right under my nose."

"What if I told you no, that I wouldn't do this?" I say.

He studies me for several seconds, his jaw tightening. "I would make you do it, regardless."

That's what I thought. He'd prefer my permission, but he'd use my abilities either way.

"Then it's no choice at all," I say. "I'll do it."

And just like that, I'm back to working alongside the Bargainer.

CHAPTER 8

December, eight years ago

"So what do you do when you're not making bargains?" I ask Des, who is sprawled out on my floor, flipping through one of my textbooks.

He has a pen in hand, and I've seen him scribbling stuff in the margins. I'm seriously afraid he's drawn dicks inside my textbook, but when I take a peek, I see myself instead. He's drawn a sliver of my face, and damn, he's a really good artist on top of everything else.

"Besides ruining the mind of a little siren?" he says.

"Besides that," I say, smiling softly.

In the hall outside my room, I hear some of my floor-mates laughing as they run off to dinner. They knock on the door next to mine, inviting Shelly and Trisha to dinner with them. I hear their footsteps coming toward my room, and a small part of me hopes they'll knock on my door, even though Des is here.

Their footsteps pass my door without pause.

"They can't hear us, you know," Des says, not looking up from his work.

I *didn't* know, but I had wondered why no one on my floor had asked about the masculine voice coming from my room. The walls here are paper thin.

"That was kind of you, Des," I say.

"I like my privacy. It had nothing to do with you."

"Right." God forbid the Bargainer actually gets a reputation for kindness.

"And my name is Desmond, not...*Des*." His voice drips with disdain.

So the name bugs him? Goody.

"I'll stop calling you Des as soon as you stop calling me cherub."

He grumbles at that.

I take a seat at my computer chair and watch him work for several seconds. And as I sit there, staring at him, I feel my stomach flutter.

If I close my eyes, I can pretend that we're not in my shady dorm room, that I'm not paying the Bargainer off to keep me company, that Des likes me every bit as much as I like him.

But then I remember that I get to hang out with him for no more than four hours of his day. I live for those four hours, but what about him? I'm probably just his equivalent of paid vacation.

What *does* he do when he's not stealing secrets or collecting debt? What is this man's idea of fun?

Probably stealing candy from babies or something awful like that.

"What do you do in your free time?" I ask again.

He flips another page of my textbook. "This will cost you," he says.

I shrug. I already have two rows of beads. What was one more? "Add a bead."

I catch sight of my wrist just as another dull, black bead forms.

"I rule." He doesn't even look up when says it.

I wait for more, but it never comes.

"Oh, c'mon. That's it?" I say. "That answer was two words." I deserve a better answer than that, considering the price I will eventually have to pay for the favor. In all likelihood, someday this bracelet of beads will turn into a very real version of fuck-marry-kill.

"So was my name. You didn't complain then." He begins drawing in my mouth.

"You didn't add a bead for that answer," I say.

"A generosity I'm not interested in repeating." His words are clipped.

I grind my teeth together.

Dropping down to the floor next to him, I snatch the pen from his hand. "What exactly do you rule?" I demand.

The Bargainer rolls onto his side, propping his head up with a hand, a smirk on his face, a wisp of white-blond hair falling into his eyes. He studies me for a second, then gives in. "I'm the King of the Night."

"The King of the Night?" I repeat dumbly.

What kind of title is that?

"In the Otherworld," he elaborates, taking the pen back from me.

The Otherworld.

I stare at him.

The Otherworld.

Holy crap, this dude is a fairy. No, not just a fairy, a fae *king*. A leader of one of the most ruthless races of beings.

And I've been *mean* to him.

"So you're...really important," I say.

He inclines his head slightly, still looking amused. "A bit."

Well, fuck me good, I hadn't realized.

I take in his unruly white hair, his staggering frame, tatted arm, and black-on-black attire.

"You don't *look* like a king," I say.

"And you don't *look* like the kind of girl who makes deals with the Bargainer, cherub. Your point?"

He has me there.

King of the Night. Just the name sounds badass.

"Where are your wings?" I ask.

He levels me an annoyed look. "Away."

Des must realize I'm going to keep pestering him because he closes my textbook and sets it aside.

Having the Bargainer's full attention is like catching a tiger's eye. All you wanted to do was pet the creature, but as soon as it turns its gaze on you, you realize it's simply going to tear you apart.

"Tell me, cherub, would you like to visit my kingdom one day?" he asks, his voice soft like velvet.

Is this a trick question? I feel as though I'm about to walk into a trap.

"You'd take me?" I ask. I try not to sound too excited, or frightened for that matter. Everything I've learned about the Otherworld terrifies me. But the idea of the King of the Night giving me a guided tour of his realm is impossibly appealing.

"Oh, I'll take you," he promises, a wicked glint in his eyes. "One day, I won't give you a choice."

Present

Shortly after I agree to help Des, he returns me home for the night. Now that I'm on board, he has preparations to make on his own end. Tomorrow, we'll be going over the disappearances. The day after, I'll be interviewing the changelings. That means visiting the Otherworld and seeing for the first time in my life the kingdom Des rules.

I stand outside in my backyard, watching the Bargainer fly back into the night, a large part of me wanting to follow him.

Tonight, he didn't need to show me his place, but he did. Just as he didn't need to show me his wings, but he also did. If he's trying to confuse me, he's doing a good job of it.

Once Des fades out of sight, I slip inside and head into the kitchen. Earlier, he'd taken a bead from me shortly after he caught me drinking wine. He never explained what exactly he took the bead for, though I have my suspicions.

Now my curiosity gets the best of me. Time to test my theory and hope to God I'm wrong.

Grabbing a bottle of Jameson whiskey from my cupboard, I unscrew the cap, catching the first whiffs of the liquor. I pause for a second. If his earlier repayment is what I think it is, this might be unpleasant. That niggling worry stills my hand only for a moment, and then I tip the bottle back and take a long, deep swig from it.

The whiskey is like liquid amber going down; I can already feel it burning away my nerves. I close my eyes and enjoy the initial sting of it at the back of my throat and the warmth that curls inside my stomach.

A moment later, I relax.

I thought he'd banned me from drinking alcohol, but obviously my theory was wrong.

I put the whiskey away, relieved.

It's only as I'm padding back to my bedroom that I feel it. My stomach lurches. I swallow and pause. The sensation fades and I begin walking again. Three steps later, my stomach convulses. The sensation ripples up my torso and I nearly fall to my knees; I can feel it all the way up to my throat.

That evil bastard.

I run to the bathroom and barely make it in time. My entire body spasms as I vomit up the whiskey. I can feel the threads of magic forcing my insides to rid themselves completely of the alcohol, and it's just as invasive as it was the first time I'd felt his magic stir inside me.

My knuckles go white as my grip on the porcelain tightens. Now I know what Des cashed that one particular bead in for.

Sobriety.

Forget the supernatural bounty hunters that are after him; that fucker is mine.

The next night, when Desmond Flynn opens the sliding glass door and saunters into my living room like he owns the place, I'm ready for him.

"I." I chuck a whiskey bottle at the Bargainer's head. "Hate." Now a wineglass. "You." Now a beer bottle.

The Bargainer's form disappears the moment each item should come in contact with him. A moment later, he reappears, his body flickering in and out of existence as he heads toward me. Each glass container smashes against the wall behind him, amber and maroon liquid splashing against it and dripping down to the wooden floorboards below.

"That's not nice," he growls.

I go to grab more ammunition. My complete supply lines the counters. I've decided to use it as target practice since it's clear I won't have any other use for it now.

The Bargainer disappears again, and when he reappears, he's in front of me.

"We have work to do today."

"You can take your work," I growl, "and shove it—"

"Ah, ah, ah," he says, catching my jaw and pressing me back up against the counter. "Be careful what you wish for around me. I'd like nothing more than to take my work and shove it somewhere the sun can never reach."

I know from past experience that when he's in a bad mood, the Bargainer loves twisting his clients' words. The thought makes the siren in me sing. The rest of me is madder than hell.

The Bargainer seems to be aware of my conflicted reaction because his pupils dilate. "Time to go."

"No," I say obstinately.

"I wasn't asking." He drags me away from the counter and walks us across my living room to the back door.

Shards of glass and droplets of alcohol lift from the walls and the ground, the liquid making a path to the sink and the glass to the trash. He's cleaning up for me again.

I yank against his hold of my wrist, fighting him the whole way. "Des-*mond*. Let me go. *Now*." My siren has taken over my voice, making my angry command sound seductive.

Instead of letting me go, Des throws me over his shoulder.

"Keep talking to me like that, cherub," the Bargainer says. "You don't know how much it turns me on." He pats my ass, and I see red.

"Put me down, you prick!"

But instead of putting me down, he rearranges me so that my legs are wrapped around his waist and my arms around his neck. I try to squirm free, but his hold is like a cage, keeping me in place.

I pinch his back. He swears, and the glass and liquid he's cleaning up behind us drops to the ground.

"Damn it, Callie," he says, "don't make me waste one of your beads on immobilizing you."

I stare him in the eye as he carries me outside. "I dare you to fucking do it, Des."

His eyes flash. "Don't test me. I will, and I'll enjoy feeling every inch of your skin while you're forced to sit still."

I settle for glaring at him. "That was wrong of you," I say, "to take away my ability to drink."

"It's not the worst thing I've done, cherub," he says. "And it's not permanent if you learn how to drink responsibly."

The cojones of this man. How can I even learn to drink responsibly if I *can't drink*?

I tighten my hold on him as his wings materialize. "I was doing just fine before you meddled in my life."

He gives a derisive snort. "That's debatable."

Before I can retort, he launches us into the air. I let out a yelp of surprise, and he rubs small circles into my back, probably in an attempt to reassure me. I want to swat that hand away, but short of letting go of his neck, I can't.

Instead, I fix my eyes on the sky above me, determined to recite constellations in an effort to ignore the man who both angers me and confuses me.

And naturally, I see a whopping three stars in the sky—and one of them might be a plane. So I settle on simply ignoring Des, which proves to be nearly impossible. I'm breathing in the smell of him, his hair is tickling the backs of my hands, and all I can see besides the dark night is the menacing arc of his wings.

Something like ten minutes in, I give up and rest my head in the crook between his neck and shoulder.

The Bargainer tightens his hold on me, and I feel the rough brush of his cheek as he nuzzles me. I'm starting to notice a pattern; he gets affectionate when I'm in his arms.

I'm not sure how long we stay like that, but eventually I feel us begin to descend. I peek at the world beneath us and watch as Catalina Island gets larger and the Bargainer's house comes into view.

Fifteen minutes later, we enter his living room. Today, sheets and sheets of handwritten notes and sketches cover his coffee table. I lean in to get a good look at them. I've worked enough jobs as a PI to recognize a case file when I see one.

I pick up one of the sketches, immediately recognizing Des's handiwork. He used to draw portraits and landscapes back in my dorm room at Peel Academy. Though none quite like this.

In the sketch, rows and rows of women lie in what appear to be caskets, their eyes shut, their arms folded over their chests.

Holy shit.

"These are…the women?"

I feel the air stir; a moment later, Des is at my back, looking over my shoulder, and I'm so very aware of him.

"They are. Each is returned in a glass coffin."

Last night, Des told me these women weren't dead, but they *look* dead.

He leans around me and pulls out another image, this one of a single coffin sitting in what looks like a great hall.

Des's palace. It's such a strange thought.

My attention turns to the sleeping woman, wearing her battle leathers. In one hand, she holds a weapon, and in the other—

My eyes must be deceiving me. "Is that…?"

"Yes. It's a child."

I stare at the drawing.

Child is not the correct word for the tiny life cradled to the chest of the sleeping fae warrior.

Infant. *Baby.*

Held in the arms of a woman who might as well be dead.

Being a private investigator, I've seen and heard my fair share of twisted shit.

Fairies always manage to top it.

"Is the baby dead?" I ask.

"Oh no." The way Des says that has me turning to look toward him.

"So it's alive?" I probe.

"Very much so. The humans you will be interviewing? They are wet nurses to some of these children."

My eyebrows knit together. What could a bunch of wet nurses know?

I slide a glance to his notes, written in his looping scrawl.

…Male warriors still missing…

…goes by the name "Thief of Souls"…

That name sounds familiar. It takes me a moment to remember why.

Seven years ago, a man owed the Bargainer a debt, and I was along for the ride. Des had been questioning him about someone, but it was me who pried the name from the man's unwilling lips.

The Thief of Souls.

I suck in a breath. "Is this the same bastard you were looking for all those years ago?"

Des's jaw is tight, his expression grim. He gives a curt nod.

I try to wrap my mind around the fact that in all that time, not even the Bargainer has been able to close in on this monster. And I try not to feel intimidated at my task—to uncover what Des cannot.

He takes the sketches out of my hands. "In order to assist me, you first need to learn about the Otherworld— even before you learn the ins and outs of this particular mystery. Ignorance, you see, will get you killed in my world."

I stifle a shudder. Already the Otherworld sounds worse than I feared.

I sit down on his couch. "I'm all ears, Des."

He takes a heavy seat next to me. From the pile of notes spread out before us, he produces a pen and a blank sheet of paper. "Here are the basics. The world of the fae is one huge hierarchy." He draws a pyramid. "The power players are at the top, none as powerful as the Queen and King of Fae—Titania and her king consort, Oberon, or the Mother and the Father, as we call them. They're some of the oldest ancients still living. You don't need to worry too much about them. Both have gone far under the mountain, and they have taken the undying sleep."

"Um, in English," I say.

"They're in a coma-like state. Not sentient, but not dead."

"A bit like the female warriors," I say.

Des gives me a sharp look. "Yes," he says slowly, "a bit like them, I suppose." His hand slides farther down the pyramid, and he draws another line. "Beneath them are the four biggest kingdoms: Night, Day, Flora, and Fauna."

I recognize Des's house immediately, and once again I'm struck by how powerful this man is.

"There are two additional houses that usually go unrecognized but are equally powerful—the Kingdom of Mar, which reigns over all bodies of water, and the Kingdom of Death and Deep Earth. These two houses keep themselves apart. Death doesn't like to dabble in the land of the living, and the Kingdom of Mar likes to stay in its watery depths for the most part.

"As for the four houses, I rule the Kingdom of Night. My people know me alternately as His Majesty Desmond Flynn, Emperor of the Evening Stars, Lord of Secrets, Master of Shadows, and King of Chaos."

I raise an eyebrow. "No one calls you Bargainer?"

I don't mention this strange ache I feel to learn about Des's other life. The more he tells me, the more I realize how little I actually know of him.

"Not in the Otherworld, no." Turning back to his work, Des begins writing again. "In direct opposition to the Kingdom of Night is the Kingdom of Day. Ruled by Janus, Lord of Passages, King of Order, Truth Teller, Bringer of Light, asshole supreme."

I almost miss the jab. A surprised laugh trickles out. "Don't like the guy?" I ask.

Des doesn't laugh with me. "He's the light to my dark. The good to my evil. The truth and beauty to my deception and wickedness. He is my opposite; I was made to dislike him," he says. "Not that you should share my opinion," he adds. "If you met him, you would probably like him. Everyone does."

I glance over at Des as he stares at the people he's drawn, and I notice something on his face. Envy? Regret? *Longing*?

Again, I feel a strange ache, this time for this man.

I place a hand on his leg, drawing Des's attention. "Perhaps I'd like him—and perhaps not. My appreciation for truth and beauty died long ago."

Des glances over at me, and a whisper of a smile lifts the corner of his mouth before he returns his attention to the sheet of paper.

"The Kingdom of Flora is ruled by Mara, Queen of All That Grows, and her consort king, the Green Man. She rules over all plant life." He writes their names out on the sheet of paper. "And lastly, there's the Kingdom of Fauna, ruled by Karnon, Master of Animals, Lord of the Wild Heart, King of Claws and Talons. Also known in certain parts as the mad king for his reclusive tendencies and his…eccentricities.

"While you're in my kingdom, you must follow my land's rules. When you're in the Kingdom of Day, you must follow theirs. Even I, a king, must abide by their rules."

Whoa, whoa, whoa. "I'm not going to be in the Kingdom of Day or any others, right?" Because I don't have enough time to learn the laws and etiquette of all the different fae kingdoms. Not if Des and I are going to visit the Otherworld tomorrow.

"You'll be in my kingdom and mine alone, and there you have my absolute protection."

I hear the hard edge of a ruler in his voice.

"That's all you need to know about the Otherworld—for now." He slides his drawing of the pyramid aside, his attention drifting back to his scattered notes.

My eyes unwillingly move back to the picture of the sleeping woman holding a baby against her breast. "So all the women come back with children?" I ask.

Des nods, his fingers trailing over the drawing.

"Whose children are they?" I ask. Fairies have a bad habit of taking kids that aren't their own.

"They've come from these women's wombs," Des affirms.

Not going to ask how they figure that one out.

"And the father?" I ask.

The beginnings of a wry smile spread across the Bargainer's lips, but then it turns into a grimace.

"Just one more mystery," he says. He shuffles the papers into a neat stack. "For right now, none of this matters except"—he draws a sheet of paper from the pile—"*this.*"

I take it from him, looking it over. A list of questions spans nearly the length of the page, each one odder than the last. "What is this?"

"Those, cherub, are the questions you'll be asking tomorrow."

Even after Des has set aside the case notes and I've tucked my sheet of questions away, he doesn't make a move to end the evening. Instead, a spread of cheese and crackers drifts into the living room from the kitchen, a set of glasses and drinks on its heels.

I catch the Coke that floats just above my lap, while the Bargainer pops the lid on his beer, taking a healthy swig.

I give him the stink eye, remembering all over again that I can't drink liquor alongside him, before I begin drinking my soda.

Des settles into the couch, his shirt riding up as he drapes his arm across the seat back.

He takes a swig of his beer, eyeing me over the rim and looking as sinful as all get-out.

This doesn't feel like the end of an evening; it feels like the beginning. It also doesn't feel like repayment.

The whole thing is a bit too intimate for that.

"What, pray tell, is going on in my little siren's mind?" he says, his eyes moving over me.

My little siren.

"I'm not your anything," I say.

He takes another swig of his beer, smiling around the rim. Once he brings the drink away, he swirls the amber liquid inside its bottle. "You were once my client," he says, "and then you were my friend, and now..." His lips curve up almost nefariously, his silver eyes glittering. "Perhaps we won't put a label on what we are now."

The atmosphere in the room changes, becoming heavy, almost sultry. I don't know whether it's his magic or just Des's natural magnetism, but it has me shifting in my seat.

"Why come to earth?" I ask, desperate to get the focus off our relationship—or lack thereof. "Why do any of this if you're a king?"

Some of the heat in the room dissipates. He takes another swig of his drink before answering. "Do you want the appropriate explanation or the real one?"

"Both," I say, kicking my shoes off so that I can better curl up on his couch.

Des notices the action, his expression becoming almost pleased.

"The appropriate answer is that I have time for it. Laws and politics aside, my kingdom does my most important job on its own," he says, kicking his own booted feet up onto the coffee table and crossing them at the ankles. "It drags the night across the Otherworld. Another part of my job as King of the Night is to make sure that chaos exists, and chaos is the natural state of things, even here on earth. Again, the universe does my job for me. Then there are those other deeds that best happen under the cloak of darkness. Violence, sleep, and"—he runs his gaze down one of my arms, and I feel a phantom finger trailing down my skin—"*sex*."

My siren stirs.

"Let's call them *baser impulses*. And again, those don't need much management."

Am I hearing him correctly?

I set my drink down on the coffee table. "So you encourage people…to get it on?" I can't believe we've never talked about this. He always acted like a nun around me. I never would've guessed this would be part of his job.

One of his eyebrows arches. "Would you like a demonstration?"

The siren in me is waking up. All the things he rules, she feeds off. Violence, chaos…*sex*.

She would gladly take a whole armful of beads for such a demonstration.

He sees my silence for what it is—consideration. One moment, he's sprawled on his end of the couch, setting his drink down; the next, he disappears. I jolt when he reappears next to me on the couch.

"You would enjoy yourself, Callie," he says, leaning in. This close to me, his presence is overwhelming. His lips brush my ear. "I would make sure of that."

He was never like this with me before. Only now am I learning that he fought his most innate nature to be appropriate with me. Even when I put all the moves on him I could think of.

I clear my throat. "*Des*." I'm drowning in *years* of desire for this man.

"Think about it." He pulls away. "Nothing would please me more."

My heart's thundering, the siren desperately trying to claw her way out the longer I stare at him.

"You were mentioning your reasons for visiting earth?" My voice is hoarse as I force the question out. It's a last-ditch effort to stop whatever's going on from continuing.

His mood shifts, his eyes shuttering as he returns to his corner of the couch. "Ah yes, the *official* reason. The duties I have running my kingdom still leave me with plenty of time to work on international—interworldly, really—relations. As the Bargainer, that's what I'm doing. I mingle with supernaturals here, use my magic to grant them petty favors"— favors like mine—"and I collect repayment with interest. These things make my kingdom richer, safer."

He picks his beer back up and takes another swallow.

"And what's the unofficial reason?" I ask.

He stares at me for a long time, his eyes growing distant. "I've been pulled here for reasons that have long mystified me."

The eternal wanderer.

His eyes move over his living room, his gaze still unfocused. Wherever his mind drifted to, it's not here.

"Do they still?"

His attention snaps back to me. "Still what?"

"Mystify you."

A muscle in his cheek jumps. "No, cherub, they don't."

CHAPTER 9

December, eight years ago

Des and I stand in a dark corner of campus, where a low-lying stone wall separates the grounds of Peel Academy from the edge of the cliffs that border this area of the Isle of Man. Far below us, the ocean churns as it crashes against the rocks. I swear I can hear that water whispering to me, begging me to come closer. It's not a stretch to believe that the sea birthed sirens. It calls to my dark, inner self the way my voice calls to men.

Well, *mortal* men, anyway.

I had wondered what kind of supernatural was immune to my glamour. Now I had my answer.

Fairies. Creatures that are not of this world.

I look over at the campus grounds, where students bustle between Peel Castle to my left—which houses the school's classrooms, dining halls, and libraries—and the dormitories to my right. The place is lit up by lamps, but even so, between the coastal fog and the evening darkness, it's hard to make people out.

"They can't see us," Des says. He steps in close, and the heat of his magic brushes against me. "But it wouldn't matter anyway, would it?" he says.

I take a step away from him. "What's that supposed to mean?"

Des moves forward. "Poor Callie. Always on the outside, always looking in."

I frown, my eyes returning to the groups of students that cross the lawn. Even from here, I can hear their laughter and bits of their conversation.

"Tell me, cherub," he continues, "how does someone like you"—his eyes move pointedly over me—"end up being an outcast?"

Briefly my gaze drops to my ripped jeans and ankle boots, then to my leather jacket and the scarf that rings my neck. Physically, I fit in. It's everything beneath my skin that sets me apart.

"Why are we even talking about me?" I ask, tucking a strand of hair behind my ear.

His gaze follows my hand. "Because sometimes you fascinate me."

My heart skips a beat. I'd all but assumed that the interest went one way.

He's still staring at me, waiting for his answer.

"It's not them, it's me."

His brows pull together.

I glance back down at my boots and kick at a patch of grass. "It's hard pretending to be normal after…you know." *After you off someone.* I exhale. "I think I have to put myself back together before I make friends. Real friends."

I can't believe I just admitted that. I rarely admit these things even to myself.

Des tips my chin up, his face serious. He doesn't say anything for a long time, though I'm sure a million different things are going on in his devious mind.

"How about I make you a queen for a night?" he finally says.

I give him a queer look. But before I can read into his intentions, a line of small, twinkling lights appear over his shoulder. As they get closer, I hear the buzzing of their wings.

Fireflies. A whole group of them. They fly in one single, orderly line.

My eyes cut to Des, who's smiling softly. This is clearly his work.

The twinkling fireflies circle me before—horror of horrors—they descend on top of my head.

"I have bugs in my hair," I tell him, my shoulders tense.

"You have a crown," he corrects, smirking and leaning against the stone wall.

This is his idea of a crown? I can feel them moving about my hair, and it takes everything in me not to swat them all away.

I'm not really a bug person.

One of the fireflies tumbles off, landing on my scarf. It then proceeds to crawl beneath my scarf and down my shirt.

"*Oh my God!*" I squeal.

"Naughty bugs," Des chastises, coming over and helping me scoop the firefly up.

The Bargainer captures the bug in his fist, his knuckles grazing my skin. He steps away from me and, opening his palm, releases the glowing critter. The two of us watch it drunkenly canter back to my hair.

I can just barely make out their luminescent bodies flickering above me. The whole thing is so ridiculous and strange that I begin to laugh. "Des, are you trying to cheer me up?"

But when I get a good look at him, he's not laughing. The insects' light dances in his eyes as he stares at me, lips parted.

Des blinks, and it's like he's returning from wherever his mind drifted.

He takes my hand. "Let's get out of here. You hungry?" he asks. "Dinner's on me."

I squeeze his palm, feeling like something between us changed for the better. But I don't address it; there's nothing like a good confession to scare the Bargainer away.

"Dinner's *on* you?" I say instead. "Now that sounds interesting…"

He flashes me a wicked smile, his eyes twinkling. "Cherub, I may make a fairy out of you yet."

––––––––––––

Present

I'm already elbow deep into my work by the time Temper saunters into West Coast Investigations, slamming open the door to her office. That woman is a force of nature when she wants to be.

I hear her click on her message machine and then, a moment later, I hear the tinny sound of a message.

Sipping my coffee, I once again check the most wanted list.

The Bargainer is still listed as the third most wanted criminal in the supernatural world. Whatever strings Eli pulled, they're still holding.

I suppose if the Politia catches me and the Bargainer together, I'll be viewed as an accomplice.

Motherfuckery.

This is *precisely* why I keep secrets. The law and I don't quite see eye to eye.

"*Ho-ly*—" Temper whoops from the other room. I hear the click of her shoes as she jogs over to my room. "Callie," she says, pausing dramatically in my doorway. Today, her hair falls in loose waves around her shoulders. "Did you hear—"

"—about the hundred-K client?" I finish for her. I swivel in my chair, the heels of my boots scraping across the top of the desk. "Yeah, I already got a file written up for him."

The client in question had also called my phone, specifically requesting to work with me. What he needed my help with wasn't clear, only that he was willing to pay a king's ransom for it.

I finger the file I created for him. "Seems a little sketchy," I admit. Not sketchy enough to turn down, but enough to raise red flags.

Temper huffs out a breath. "If you don't take it, *I* will. I've got a kitchen to remodel."

"I'll take it, I'll take it," I grumble. "By the way." I grab a stack of files to my left and toss them to her. "These are officially yours."

She grabs the folders and flips through them. "Excellent. Oh, look at this precious gem—an abusive husband I get to hex. Poor baby, he has *no idea*." Temper slides out of her chair. "All right, I better get to work. So many criminals, so little time." She pauses when she catches sight of my face. "Hey, how are you holding up?"

Whatever she sees in my expression must be giving away

some of my inner turmoil. My personal life is never very great, but right now it's at an all-time low.

I lift a shoulder. "Meh."

"Meh good, or meh bad?"

"Meh I'm not sure?" I answer.

She leans across the table and places her hand over mine. "I'm sorry. I assumed that thing with Eli...that it was just a fling."

I slide my hand out from under hers and wave her off. "Stop being a sap. This isn't about Eli."

"Oh *good*." She relaxes, straightening. "I was about to feel massively guilty about ribbing you for it the other day." She frowns as she takes me in again. "So what *is* wrong?"

I set down my coffee and scrub my face. "My past."

"Ah," Temper says, "the mysterious past you still haven't told me about."

"I will," I insist, "I just..."

Would you like a demonstration?

You would enjoy yourself, Callie. I would make sure of that.

Des might as well be in the room, I can hear his voice so clearly right now.

"...don't know how I feel about it at the moment," I finish.

Temper nods sympathetically. I mean, if anyone understands, it's her. There's so much about Leo, her would-be fiancé, and the rest of her family that she has never told me about. Some things about our pasts are better left unsaid.

Speaking of that dude—

I wave away the conversation. "Have there been any updates on Leo?"

"Ugh." She blows out a breath. "None worth mentioning." After a pause, she says, "You know what? Screw talking about any of this. Want to grab drinks tonight, piss off a bartender for being rowdy, and pick up some eligible bachelors?"

"Um, rain check." There'd be no drinking and dating in the near future for me.

"Hmm," she says, eyeing me over, as though she can sense my thoughts. "Well, you'll let me know if everything isn't okay, won't you?" she asks.

No.

"Of course."

"You're such a goddamn liar, Callie," she says, shaking her head. "Fine, tell me when you're ready."

But when it comes to the Bargainer, that's the thing: I'm not sure I'll ever be.

I spend the next hour taking care of several odds and ends, including leaving a message for the client who wants to work with me and memorizing the list of interview questions the Bargainer gave me last night. After that, I leave the office and head out to interview the primary person of interest in one of the cases I'm working. Most of my job is simply this: cornering people, glamouring them, and forcing them to confess whatever they know.

Today it's about a client's missing daughter.

"Where is she?" I demand, crossing my arms.

The suspect: twenty-four-year-old Tommy Weisel, local drug dealer, community college dropout, and ex-boyfriend of sixteen-year-old Kristin Scott, who's currently missing.

Tommy sits in one of his kitchen chairs, pinned in place by my glamour. He squirms in his seat, unable to stand, his throat working as he tries to suppress his answer.

As usual, it's all in vain.

"She-she's in the basement," he says, his upper lip

quivering. Once the words are out, he scowls at me. "You coc—" The rest of the sentence dies in his throat.

Another order I gave him: no swearing and no put-downs. It's really for his own good. The siren in me loves nothing better than to reward hate with cruelty.

"How did Kristin get into your basement?" I ask.

Tommy licks his lips, his gaze darting to my phone, which is just out of his reach and currently capturing this all on video.

"I...*led* her there," he says.

The side of my mouth curves up, and I prowl closer to him, stroking his face with the back of my glowing hand. "*Led?* Is that you trying to be clever?" I *tsk*, shaking my head. "It was a good try. Let me rephrase: is Kristin there against her will?"

He squeezes his eyes shut as sweat beads on his forehead. "Answer me."

"Yeeeeeessss." The word hisses out of him, and then he's panting, trying to catch his breath. His shoes slam against the linoleum floors, and he screams out in frustration. "You motherfu—" His voice cuts off in a gurgle.

I lean in close to him, ignoring his oily hair and the smell of stale BO wafting off his clothes. "This is what you're going to do," I say. "You're going to release Kristin, then you're going to turn yourself in and confess to everything you're guilty of, and you're going to work with the police to prove your guilt. And you are never, ever going to harm Kristin, her family, or any other girlfriends or exes you have ever again."

He shudders as my glamour takes hold of him.

"Now get up and release your ex-girlfriend."

Without any further prodding, Tommy leads me to Kristin, who's cowering in his basement.

Several minutes later, a crying Kristin and I are in the foyer of Tommy's house.

The drug dealer looks scared and angry as he watches us, forced to stand over ten feet away from me and Kristin thanks to another order I gave him.

I lead Kristin to the front door, using my jacket to turn the knob. One can never be too careful about leaving finger-prints behind. Guys like Tommy are sometimes wilier than they appear.

I usher Kristin out, then pause, glancing back at Tommy, who's glaring at me.

"Remember," I say, "you're going to turn yourself in right after this." I begin to close the door before I pause again. "Oh, and I was never here."

<hr />

As soon as I get home, I drop my things and head for my bedroom to fetch my swimsuit. Today, I'm getting in the ocean.

Now that I'm officially not drinking, swimming is one of the only other ways that I relieve tension. And interacting day in and day out with some of the greediest, least scrupu-lous people in LA, I have *a lot* of tension to relieve.

I never make it past my living room.

My front door rattles, then metal groans as someone breaks apart my doorknob. A moment later, the door bangs open.

I only have enough time to call the siren to the surface.

Instead, a familiar form comes storming in.

I clutch my chest. "Crap, Eli," I say, my voice ethereal, "you scared me." And then I realize Eli just broke into my house. I glance back at the door. "Were you...waiting for me?"

He doesn't respond, and there's an intensity to his features that makes me tense up.

He crosses the foyer, his attention focused wholly on me. Without speaking, he closes the last of the distance between us and pulls me into his arms, kissing me hard.

"Whoa," I say, managing to break my lips away. The rest of me is still crushed to him. "What's going on?"

My mind is having trouble catching up.

Eli's in my home. Eli's holding me.

"I had to see you, baby." He's back to kissing me, and I am so confused.

I rip my head away to glance at the calendar I have up.

The full moon...

"Eli, you shouldn't be here."

It's only been a day since the full moon, and the closer to the full moon it is, the more a shifter's human side gives way to the animal. It's dangerous for nonshifters to be around them.

"I couldn't stay away." His lips are back on mine, and I'm trying really hard not to freak the fuck out, but his hands are shaking, and I can feel Eli fighting to keep this form.

"Why didn't anyone stop you from leaving?"

"No one gets in the way of mate business," he says, doing everything he physically can to get close to me.

Mate business.

Mate. Business.

Nope.

Nope, nope, nope.

I think I'm beginning to hyperventilate. All I wanted was to go for a swim, and instead...this steaming pile of horseshit.

"But I'm not...I'm not your mate," I say. I'm not even his girlfriend. Not anymore.

I can hear him growl low in his chest. "I was going to ask. Once I got back, I was going to ask."

Uh-oh.

"Ask me what?"

Please don't ask me what I think's on your mind.

We'd been together a whopping six months. I'm still getting used to the fact that he has a toothbrush in my bathroom.

This entire relationship, he's been pushing. Pushing for more touching, more intimacy, more openness—just *more*.

He pauses long enough to look me in the eye. "For you to be my mate."

I might be the most awful person in the world because at his words, I shudder. Not the good kind of shudder either.

"Um." I can't edge away from him, caught in his arms as I am. He's not even acting human at the moment. Eli's touchy-feely in general, but he's never like this—never crazed with the need to mark and claim me as his. My eyes slide to the window, where dusk is setting in. "We should talk about this when we aren't close to the full moon." *When I know you're not going to go big bad wolf on me.*

His chest rumbles with his disapproval. "I don't want to talk about this, Callie. I don't want to analyze what I feel for you. I want you to say yes, and then I want to fuck you until you're saying my name like a mantra."

That right there is how this man managed to end up in my bed in the first place. He knows exactly how to win over my siren.

"I have a ring," he says, kissing my jaw, his fingernails shifting into claws, then back to human nails. "Shit," he says, a bit of his human side peeking out. "None of this is coming out right. Just, be mine."

A grown man as sexy as Eli can't just say stuff like that. My lady bits want to overthrow my brain.

"Please, Eli," I say as he rubs his cheek against mine, masking me in his scent. "We need to talk about this."

Wait. What am I saying?

This isn't a negotiation. There's nothing to talk about. When you end a relationship, you don't owe the other person an explanation, crappy though that may be.

Besides, I already gave him one.

His chest rumbles. "Fine, we'll talk later."

He resumes kissing me with the same animalistic passion he entered my home with. Only now, it's even sharper than usual. The man's giving way to the beast even as the sun sets.

I don't know what to do. I ended my relationship with this man. He's acting like our conversation never happened.

I pull away long enough to say, "We broke up."

"I thought about it after we talked." He kisses me, then pulls away again. "What kind of mate would I be if I didn't stand by you when you needed me?"

The alpha in him is telling me that that's the end of the conversation, and for a few moments, I get dragged under.

I blink through the haze of his dominance, the same dominance he's been throwing around since he swept me up in his arms. I just hadn't noticed it then.

He doesn't get to decide we're back together. And even if he's okay with me receiving attention from two men at the same time—and an alpha would never settle for being second fiddle—*I'm* not.

His hands are beginning to roam. This is escalating *way* too quickly.

"Wait, Eli," I say. But the wolf in him is calling to my siren. "Eli," I say again, even as that very siren surfaces.

His hand dips into my pants and—

"*Eli, stop.*" My voice hits multiple notes as I force the siren into it.

Eli stills, obeying the command in my voice.

I bent an alpha to my will. Not good, not good, not good.

But more than that, I just glamoured Eli, the man who proclaimed to love me. A bounty hunter who works on the right side of the law.

I'm fucked in every way but the one I'd actually enjoy.

"Did you…glamour me?" His voice becomes so gravelly as the predator tries to take over.

I swallow.

I've glamoured Eli before. There are certain *situations* where that's inevitable. But I'm always careful to avoid taking away his will. And a second ago, his will was gone.

Behind me, the glass doors out to my balcony shatter, and the night sweeps in, darkening the room. With it comes a wave of menace so palpable my hair stands on end.

Des steps out of the shadows, every line of his body tense. "Well, doesn't this look cozy," he says, taking in the two of us.

Eli begins to growl, something so deep and sinister that my hair stands on end, and it's not even directed at me. "*You,*" he says.

"Me what, dog?" Des responds, crossing his arms.

Dog? Did the Bargainer just guess that Eli was a shifter, or had he known? I hadn't told him about Eli when he asked about my relationships…

"*Des,*" I warn.

Eli pushes me behind him, like the Bargainer is the one we should all be worried about right now. "Stay out of this, Callie," he orders.

See, now *that*—that was what was always wrong with our relationship. Eli taking command and assuming I'd fall in line. Which was about the equivalent of him poking a hornet's nest with a stick.

"I don't think you're in any position to give her orders," Des says. He cocks his head. "Did you really think someone like Callypso would actually want more from you than your dick?" he says, stepping forward, bringing the night at his back in with him.

I can feel the tug of Des's magic luring me out from behind Eli, whose growl is getting louder with every passing second.

"What can you give her besides that?" the Bargainer continues. "Intellectually stimulating conversations?" His eyes flick over all six plus feet of hulking, barely contained shifter. "That's a definite no. I'm sure she's been getting *that* need fulfilled elsewhere."

Eli's growl is so loud, I swear the house is vibrating with it.

"If you touch her..." Eli can barely get the words out. "If you lay one hand—"

Des flashes a sinister smile. "I have already laid a hand on her. And my mouth. And all sorts of other things—"

Eli lets out a roar, his muscles tensing. I think he's going to rush the Bargainer, but instead, he takes a staggering step forward, his skin rippling.

I've never seen the change happen in person, but oh my sweet baby Jesus, I'm about to. In less than a minute, Des and I will be trapped in a room with a werewolf.

This is why shifters stay away from nonshifters during the full moon.

Unless, of course, they want to turn a particular nonshifter into a shifter.

That couldn't be why Eli's here, could it?

Eli knew I didn't want to change, and even if I did, a witch should always be close at hand, just in case the change didn't take, or the body became too weak, or any other sort of complications arose.

But Eli hasn't been in the right frame of mind since he arrived, his brain already more wolf than man.

"*You won't change,*" Des's voice resonates throughout the room, and I feel the magic brush past me, forcing itself on Eli. "Not in this house, not so close to one whom you consider your…mate."

How much had he heard of our conversation?

How much had he already known?

A whine interrupts the string of deep growls coming from Eli. He turns to me, his eyes already amber. There's nothing of the man I cared for in them. Just the feral eyes of a wolf. Yet I don't fear him. Eli's protective instinct is innate, and I'm part of his pack.

But he will hurt Des. Des, who is competition. Des, who is in his territory, exerting control on his—ugh—*mate*. Des, who I can feel staring at me. I can sense his growing need to take me away.

"Eli," I say quietly. I hold his gaze as shades of brown start to bleed back into his irises.

I begin to relax, especially when he straightens.

Then Eli's head swings toward Des, and the growl erupts in his chest all over again.

And then something makes him snap. Letting out a snarl, he charges Des.

My heart nearly stops.

Fear, the likes of which I haven't felt in a long time, courses through me.

"*Eli, don't touch him.*" This time, when I use the glamour, I know what I'm doing. My voice is strong and unwavering.

Eli stops just short of Des, bound by my magic.

I crossed a line. I know I did.

I don't care. That's the truly frightening part. I took away Eli's free will, and all I feel is relief that Des is unharmed.

The panic I felt, the utter terror...

My eyes meet the Bargainer's. His are unreadable.

"It's time to go, cherub," he says while Eli chuffs in confusion mere feet away.

I give the shifter a worried look. Eli might've forgiven me using glamour on him once. But twice?

No way.

He makes a baying sound, something that cuts me deep. "Callie, no," he says. He's beginning to hunch over again, his brown eyes bleeding to gold. Not even the Bargainer's magic can hold the change back for long.

I hesitate, realizing what this is—a crossroads. Down one path is Eli and everything he represents; down the other is Des.

If Eli killed the Bargainer, I'd be released from my debts. Des probably deserves death. And with the Bargainer gone, I'd get another chance at life with Eli. And eventually I would become his mate. It would be so easy to just say yes, to give in to a life that a thousand other women would want.

But eventually Eli would want me to make the change. Eli had already started bringing that up—that and...*pups*. Shifters were big family people. I'd be his wife, mother of his many children.

I couldn't just be Callie; I'd have to be *his* Callie. I'd have to come to heel, be subservient to him, as the rest of his pack was. I'd have to put the pack first before my needs.

Or I could leave with Des. Des, who guarantees nothing. Des, who left me all those years ago only to come roaring back into my life. Des, who doesn't want to change me.

Des, who's offered me nothing but hope and heartache. Des, my friend. Des, my mystery.

Des.

Des.

And there is my answer.

Eli is someone's dream, but…but he isn't mine.

"I will always care for you, Eli," I say, "but you need to go back to your people."

"*Callie.*" His voice breaks.

His pain's shattering me. I don't want him to hurt.

Shadows gather around me. Suddenly, Des is wrapping his arm around my waist. "Cherub, we *need* to go."

Seeing us together is Eli's final straw. His eyes become wholly golden, and they lose their spark of human intelligence. Hair sprouts along his skin. His back bows, his muscles rippling. He throws his head into the air and howls, the sound making every nerve of mine stand on end.

Night air swirls around me as Des tugs me toward my backyard.

When Eli drops to all fours, I throw caution to the wind and run, grabbing Des's hand and hauling him with me.

The Bargainer scoops me into his arms just as a spine-chilling howl fills the air behind us.

"Hold on," Des says as Eli lopes toward us.

Geez, that is a big fucking wolf.

The Bargainer's body tenses, and then he pushes off the ground.

I catch a glimpse of Eli's wolf lunging after us, his teeth snapping at empty air where a second ago Des's ankle was.

I hear the mournful howls long after we're airborne, the sound haunting.

I lean my head into Des's chest, feeling his hands tighten around me.

For better or for worse, I'd chosen him.

And I still don't regret it.

CHAPTER 10

January, seven years ago

"Why don't you take me with you?" I ask.

The Bargainer and I sit inside Douglas Café, the warm light illuminating our surroundings. Outside, it's begun to snow.

Des leans back in his seat, stirring his coffee idly. "To collect payment from my clients?" He raises his eyebrows. "Not going to happen."

"Why not?" I ask. Or I try to ask—it comes out more like a whine. I have to stifle a wince. The last thing I want is for him to think I'm immature.

"Cherub, have you ever considered the possibility that there are things about me I don't want you to see?"

"I'm not innocent, Des," I say. "I already know what you do." I'd seen it firsthand the first time I called on him. "Add a bead. Let me come along."

He leans forward, jostling the table as he does so. "You

foolish girl," he growls as I reach forward and steady my cup. "Those beads aren't a joke."

"If you're so against them, then stop handing them out like candy." I know my words will just bait him, but part of me—the wilder, cursed part—wants to see Des lose control.

Des's face sharpens. "You want to know what my favors will eventually cost you? Fine. I'll show you. Maybe then you'll stay far away." He downs the rest of his coffee and stands, his chair screeching behind him as he does so.

Wait? We're doing this now?

When I don't immediately get out of my seat, he waves his hand.

My chair begins to tilt, forcing me to stand. Around us, no one notices.

I barely have time to grab my coat and the last of my macarons before he takes my hand and drags me out of there.

Outside, snow catches in my hair as we head down the street. Almost immediately, the cold seeps into my clothes. Perhaps this was a bad idea.

Shadows of Des's making curl around us like smoke.

He doesn't speak to me the entire walk back to Douglas Cemetery, where the closest entrance to the ley lines is.

Ley lines are essentially supernatural highways. Across the world, there are certain wrinkles and tears in the fabric of our world, which are entry points, or portals, onto these ley lines. From there, if you were a certain type of creature— say a fairy or demon—who knew how to manipulate these ley lines, you could move through worlds and *between* worlds. That last bit is precisely how Des could be a king in the Otherworld, then come to earth and bargain with mortals.

When we get to a particularly old section of the cemetery, the headstones so old and weathered most of the names and dates have been worn away, he pulls me close, his jaw clenched. His stormy eyes stare down at me. "Don't make me regret this."

Before I have a chance to say anything, our surroundings disappear. A moment later, buildings and canals replace tombstones.

I stare around us with wonder. "Venice," I breathe.

I always wanted to visit. And at the snap of the Bargainer's fingers, we're here.

Perks of being friends with a fae king.

"Stay close," he warns.

"It's not like I'm going anywhere," I mumble, trailing after him. He practically has my hand in a chokehold.

The two of us wind through back alleys, and I wrinkle my nose at the smell of sewage. When we get to a small, weather-worn door, Des stops.

I glance over at him. His jaw's clenched, his silver eyes icy. Still pissed.

Moody fairy. It's not like he had to take me. He's a king, for Christ's sake; I'm sure *no* is the first word in his vocabulary.

I hear a lock tumble, pulling me out of my thoughts, and then the door in front of us swings open of its own accord.

Beyond it is a dark hallway. Exactly the kind of place you don't visit if you want to stay out of trouble. Which I guess is why the Bargainer's decided to come here.

Des steps into the hallway, pulling me in after him. Behind us, the door clicks shut.

"Well, this is cozy," I say.

"Shh, cherub," he says. "And while we're on the subject, try not to talk."

I stick my tongue out at him.

"I saw that," he says, not turning around.

Eyes at the back of his head, this one.

We move deep inside the building, heading down a flight of stairs until we come to a dimly lit area that is really nothing more than a grid of pylons, cement walkways, and large, barrel-like buoys. And between the walkways and beneath the buoys is water.

Lots and lots of water.

Venice is sinking, I remember.

A slick-looking man with receding hair and a paunch steps out from the shadows.

"I called you an hour ago," he says, his Scandinavian accent thick. He flicks the Bargainer's business card out of his hand.

Des watches it hit the ground. "I'm not your lapdog," Des says. "Don't like my methods, call someone else."

The Bargainer makes his clients wait? I sort of got the impression that he was as prompt with everyone else as he was with me.

Now I feel like a special snowflake.

The man jerks his chin to me. "Who's the girl?" he asks.

"Doesn't fucking matter. Don't look at her," the Bargainer says.

But the man can't help himself. I'm a siren. I'm made to be distracting. His eyes move over me, his expression turning hungry.

Next to me, I feel the air begin to vibrate with Des's power. Darkness begins to creep in the corners of the room. I don't need to look at him to know that he's tense.

"Listen to what the Bargainer tells you," I say to the man, putting power into my voice.

Reluctantly, his eyes leave me.

And now I feel like I need to wash my skin.

"What do you want?" Des asks, crossing his arms.

"I want my daughter to get into the Royal Academy of Arts."

A.k.a. the supernatural equivalent of Juilliard. It's a performing arts school that caters to students with *special* abilities.

The Bargainer whistles. "Last I heard, almost all the slots for next year's incoming class were full. I'd have to pull a lot of strings…"

"You know I'm good for it," the man says.

I hear the gentle lap of water as it brushes against the buoys and the walkways down here.

"And what will you give me?" the Bargainer asks.

The man clears his throat. "I have information on a series of ley line entrances that the House of Keys is considering destroying."

The House of Keys is the supernatural world's government. It doesn't matter if you are American or Argentinian or Australian; so long as you are a supernatural, you have to follow their laws first and foremost.

"Mmm," the Bargainer says, "I need you to do better than that if you want the deal. I need you to prevent that legislation from getting passed in the first place."

"There's no way," the man says. "It's public sentiment. People are worried about their homes, their neighborhoods. There's been a rise in the changeling population—"

"Best of luck with your daughter's future." The Bargainer places a hand on my back and begins to steer us out of there.

I guess shutting a bargain down is as simple as that.

Behind us, the man blubbers out some more excuses and explanations.

We're almost to the stairway when we hear it.

"Wait, wait! Fine, I'll do it."

I cast a side glance at Des. A nefarious smile spreads across his face.

"Then we have a deal," the Bargainer says, not bothering to look over his shoulder. "Make sure that legislation doesn't pass. It would be a shame if your daughter didn't get in to *any* of the schools she applied for."

And with that, the two of us leave.

Back out on the streets of Venice, I reappraise Des. "That was pretty cold," I say as we begin to walk, my boots clicking against the cobblestones.

"That was business, cherub. If you want to come along with me, you better get used to it—and worse."

"Yeah, yeah, you're a bad dude."

He nods to my bracelet. "One day, you'll have to pay all those back. Are you scared now?"

A little.

But when I look in Des's eyes, I get the distinct impression that he doesn't want me to be scared. That despite trying to frighten me, he doesn't want to push me away.

I guess that makes two of us.

"I would be if you weren't wearing your hair in a girly little ponytail," I say, reaching for the ends of his white hair.

He catches my hand. "It's not good manners to taunt a fairy. We have notoriously thin skin." Despite the threat, his eyes spark with excitement.

"I'm sorry," I say. "Your ponytail is very masculine. I feel like I'm going to grow a beard just looking at it"

"Mouthy thing," he says endearingly.

We walk along the Grand Canal, passing tourists as we go. I watch boats move down the canal. Looking out over it are gift shops and restaurants, their warm light spilling out onto the streets.

Venice. It's even more wonderful than I imagined it would be.

"Before we go, can we take a gondola ride?" I ask.

The Bargainer's upper lip curls when he sees one such boat pass by us. "Why would I ever—?"

"And can we swing by one of those gift shops so I can get a mask?"

I'd also like some gelato—and perhaps a blown glass bottle—but I won't push my luck too far.

He groans. "Haven't you ever heard the expression 'Don't mix business with pleasure'?"

A sly smile spreads across my face. "Aww, are you suggesting I'm the pleasure?" My heart is thumping way too loud.

He frowns severely at me. "I'm definitely rubbing off on you."

He really is.

"C'mon, it'll be fun," I say, grabbing his hand and tugging him toward a little area along the canal where several gondolas wait.

Behind me, the Bargainer says, "I'll only agree to this if you do me one favor."

Me do him a favor? "Yeah, anything."

"Please give me my balls back at the end of the evening."

———

Present

Even after we land in front of Des's home and Eli is a whole body of water away from us, the Bargainer doesn't immediately release me. Instead, his claw-tipped wings brush against my hair as they wrap around us protectively.

"Des?"

His wings twitch, and he lets out a shuddering sigh. "I kept thinking that something was going to happen to you," he whispers, his voice hoarse. "I kept seeing that animal turning on you. I feared I wouldn't get to you in time." His entire body trembles.

Right now, I feel oddly vulnerable with him. Maybe it's the raw honesty in his words; Des has always been careful to bury his feelings under wit and wiliness. Maybe it's that I felt that same fear when I saw Eli lunging for him. And maybe it's simply being held in his arms after choosing this life and not the one I left back at my house.

I lean my forehead against his, placing my hand against his cheek. "Thank you for coming for me," I say.

I fear what would've happened if he hadn't.

"Cherub," he says, his voice serious, "I will *always* come for you."

We stay like that for another minute, unmoving. It's actually kind of nice under these wings of his, but eventually I get antsy to put my own two feet back on the ground.

"Des," I say, "you can put me down."

Reluctantly, he releases my legs, letting me stand, but he keeps my upper half still caught up in his arms. His wings pull back, but they won't fold nicely behind him. Instead, they keep spreading and retracting, spreading and retracting, looking agitated.

"He visited you during one of the Sacred Seven," Des says. "He thought of you as his mate, and *he knowingly put you in danger*." Now his wings billow out around him, flapping angrily, those talons of his looking particularly sharp. Des releases me. "He is no true mate if he thought to do that."

Des is right of course, but I'm not even thinking about

me at the moment. All I can see when I close my eyes is Eli charging at Des. He would've killed him.

And then another thought strikes me.

"Oh God," I say quietly. "We left a fully shifted werewolf in a residential neighborhood."

"I already contained him. He can't venture beyond your property for the night. Hopefully by morning, he'll have gotten control of himself." Des looks at me apologetically. "I'm sorry about your house."

I'm just relieved he can't hurt anyone else for the moment.

And then another horrifying thought hits me.

I won't be able to go back home tonight.

Not unless I want to chance another encounter with an angry werewolf.

I rub my face. I glamoured and then spurned an alpha werewolf.

Once he is back in his right frame of mind, he could put out a warrant for my arrest. Even if he decides not to press charges, he'd do something to punish me for glamouring him, spurning him, *humiliating* him. The alpha in him would demand nothing less.

He knows exactly where I live, and earlier he made it more than clear that a locked door wouldn't stop him from entering.

Tonight, I can't go back, but could I go back tomorrow? Or the next night? Or the next? Would I feel safe knowing how easily he broke in and how quickly he shifted?

Des's eyes are sad. "Cherub, my home is your home," he says, reading my thoughts, "for as long as you need it."

I look over my shoulder at the sprawling house behind me. All that furniture Des had me purchase, it had all been to furnish a single guestroom in his house.

A room I'd now likely stay in.

And when he confronted Eli, Des hadn't acted surprised or confused by any of what happened back at my home. And the only reason for that would be...

I swivel back to him. "You *knew*," I say, remembering how he taunted my ex earlier. "You kissed me that first night knowing I was with Eli."

My anger rises.

The Bargainer knows my heart; he knew I'd never agree to being romantic with two men at once. All he had to do was plant the seed—brush a chaste kiss along my lips and suggest that he and I would be intimate. Easier than snapping his fingers, I'd broken up with Eli.

And now there's a room in Des's home just waiting for me.

I feel like a fly caught in the Bargainer's web. I'm playing right into his hand.

I went from a controlling man to a scheming one.

Des's jaw tightens. "Callie—"

"Do you do this for all your clients? Force them to break ties with their boyfriends? Furnish a room in your house just for them?"

He steps up to me, his eyes bright with life. "I'm not doing this with you. Not tonight."

"No, you won't, will you?" I challenge. There's fire in my veins, fire that's been building from the moment Des reentered my life. "You'll just run like you always do."

He catches my face. "Does it look like I'm running, Callie? Does it look like I'm trying to leave your side?"

"But you will," I say fervently.

How did this conversation become me airing my own insecurities?

"You want to speak truths," he says hotly, "here's one for you: this isn't about the dog. This is about us."

"Will you stop calling Eli that?" I say.

The Bargainer releases my face and squints down at me. "You defend him even now?"

"He still means something to me." And I hurt him. Deeply.

A muscle in Des's cheek feathers. The Bargainer steps in close, his lips curling up in a sardonic smile. "You have over three hundred favors to repay me. By the time we're done, you will realize that Eli and all those other men were just a dissatisfying dream. That this, *and only this*, is real."

CHAPTER 11

I lie back on my bed and play with my bracelet. "Do all your clients get bracelets?" I ask the Bargainer. I smirk at the thought of some criminal with his dainty string of black beads.

Leaning his back against the foot of my bed, Des flips through the *Magic & Science* magazine he picked up from my bedside table.

"Nope."

I hold my wrist up to the light, twisting it this way and that, trying to get my overhead light to reflect against the polished beads; it seems instead like the beads absorb the light deep into them.

"What do your other clients get?" I ask.

Des flips another page. "Tats."

I sit up. "*Tats?* They get *tats*?" Absently my eyes move to the two Venetian masks hanging on my wall that Des and I picked out in Venice—one with the beaked bill of a plague doctor and the other with the painted face of a harlequin. "Why didn't I get a tattoo?" I ask. The bracelet that a moment ago I thought was so cool now seems like a lame substitute.

The Bargainer closes the magazine and set it aside. "Do you want a tattoo instead?"

"Of course," I say absently, missing the warning note in his voice.

A tattoo would be so much edgier than a flimsy bead.

Des turns himself so that he's facing me at the foot of my bed. And then he climbs onto it.

The Bargainer is prowling up my bed—and up me while he's at it.

I can't breathe. I legit don't think I can breathe.

The dangerous look in his eyes shuts down all coherent thought. This might be the moment when our relationship goes from a strange sort of friendship to something more.

I'm so frightened of that possibility. I'm so eager for it.

He straddles my waist, his powerful, leather-clad thighs trapping me beneath him. Leaning down, he takes my hand, the one that isn't wearing the bracelet.

My heart's going to escape my chest. It's galloping away like crazy. I've never been this close to Des. And now I'm pretty sure I'm never going to be satisfied until it's natural to be this close with him.

My skin begins to glow, and Des is kind enough to ignore the fact that I'm pretty much turned way the hell on.

He runs a palm along my wrist and my forearm. Beneath his touch, inked tally marks appear on my skin, rows and rows of them. "You would rather have this than beads?" he asks.

I drag my attention away from Des to get a better look at the markings.

They're…ugly. Vile in a way I've never considered a tattoo to be.

"You can wear my ink on your skin," he says, his voice coaxing. "Just say the word, and I'll transfer it all over. It won't even cost you a bead."

Des waits for me to answer. When I don't, the markings fade until they disappear altogether.

"That's what I thought." He releases my hand and pivots himself off me. Resituating himself against the foot of my bed once more, he picks up the magazine and resumes flipping through it. "I'm not going to mark you up like some common criminal," he says over his shoulder, "and you shouldn't want that anyway. The Politia looks for that kind of thing. They'd have an aneurysm if they saw a teenage girl with over a hundred marks."

"Why?" I ask, holding the wrist he just touched. "Is that unusual?"

He doesn't answer for a moment, but I can tell by his stillness that he's no longer reading.

Finally, he tosses the magazine aside and stands. He runs a hand through his hair, avoiding my eyes. "I need to go."

That's all the warning I get before he turns on his heel and heads to my door.

"Wait!" I scramble to my feet and grab his arm. As usual, a small thrill runs through me at the contact. "Don't go, please." Without meaning to, I've begun to glow in earnest now, my glamour accidentally slipping into my voice.

Des's eyes are on my hand, my hand that's really fucking enjoying the feel of his corded arm.

"Cherub, you're surrounded by over a thousand people your age. I need to work and you need to get better friends than me."

"I just want to be around you."

"Why?" he says, his eyes searching mine.

Because I can't control you. Because you know my secrets. Because you make me feel normal.

Because in spite of all logic and reason, I think I might be in love with you.

"Please," I say.

But it's not enough. Gently, Des pries my hand off his arm, and then he's gone.

Present

Just when I think the Bargainer is going to proclaim his true feelings for me, his face shuts down.

He leads me inside, the two of us tense. I'm rattled by Eli, by this evening, but most of all by Des.

I walk ahead of him, plopping down on one of his barstools. "So I'm staying here for the night?"

Des saunters in after me, leaning against one of his cupboards. "Unless you'd prefer I drop you back off at the dog run your house has turned into."

I give him a look. He returns it, his heated gaze moving over me. His wings are still out. The siren in me really likes that. So does the woman.

I slide off the barstool and open his refrigerator. "So when are we—" I let out a little noise, distracted by the food in the fridge.

The thing's filled with all my favorites—samosas, pizza, pasta, pie, fried rice, macaroni salad. Out of curiosity, I open the freezer.

Ice cream, mini quiches, ice cream cake—*what?*—taquitos.

I throw the Bargainer a squinty glance. "You *so* prepared for this."

He lifts a shoulder, but his eyes are laughing.

I turn back to the fridge and grab the container of cookie dough ice cream. Pulling it out, I set it on the island bar. "Spoon?"

He opens the drawer next to him and tosses one to me. I barely manage to catch the thing before it takes out an eyeball.

I'm about to scoop out a bite of the ice cream when I catch sight of a white paper bag next to him.

No. Effing. Way. "Are those…?" I can't even ask it.

"French macarons from Douglas Café," he finishes for me.

Forgetting about the ice cream, I get up and head over to Des. "Douglas is far away." Half a world away.

"Ley lines, cherub," he says.

"Can I?" I ask, indicating the bag.

"They're for you." He watches me as I reach around him.

He *so* planned on me being here tonight. I wonder if he planned on the evening turning out the way it had or if he had something else entirely up his sleeve. Knowing what a trickster he is, I wouldn't be surprised on the latter.

His eyes flick to the ice cream. It lifts off the table, floating toward the freezer. One of the sleek, stainless steel refrigerator doors open, and the ice cream slides in. The spoon soars back across the room, the drawer opening in time for it to clatter inside.

Seeing all this brings a cozy warmth to the pit of my stomach, the kind that comes with happy, familiar memories.

I pull out a pink macaron and take a bite into it.

I let out a long, deep moan.

It's perfect.

"Des, you are a god," I say in between bites. It's been years since I've had any macarons at all, and Douglas Café's were always the best.

"*King*," he corrects. His lips have quirked, lightening that stare of his. It's turning mischievous.

He steps in close, taking the paper bag from me and setting it aside, along with the partially eaten macaron. "You've had a trying evening, Callie."

I stare at him warily, feeling like that little bug trapped in a spider's web all over again.

"How would you like to postpone going to the Otherworld until morning?" I feel his breath against my skin. "What if tonight we just had a little fun?"

My pulse begins to pound.

Be prepared for more than just a kiss.

"What did you have in mind?"

But it's already too late. He grabs my wrist, his fingers grazing over all his beads.

"Time for a truth, cherub: What would you most like to do tonight?"

The magic wraps around my throat, tugging at my windpipe. There are a million things my dirty mind would be quite happy doing, so I'm surprised when I say, "I want to swim in the ocean."

I guess it's really that simple.

Des smiles at me, and for once it's genuine. "All right, let's take you to the ocean then."

He leads me back outside and then, wrapping me up in his arms, he flies us down the cliffs behind his home to a tiny little cove of a beach.

I step out of his arms, listening to the crash of the waves. It calls to me, each slick splash of the water beckoning me

133

closer and closer. Absently, I kick off my shoes and pull off my socks.

I still sense the Bargainer behind me, but I might as well be alone right now. I wade into the water, wincing just slightly at the frigid temperature.

The sound, the smell, the feel of the ocean all steady my pulse.

I am home.

Clothes and all, I dive into the sea. I surface only to dive back under again. Down here in the sea's watery depths, there's a quiet peace. Second by second, I feel my worries and insecurities wash away. There's just me, the night, and the ocean.

The next time I surface, I look to the beach. Des watches me from shore, several strands of his white hair whipping about his cheeks. The expression on his face is so familiar; I've seen it on mine a thousand times. An outsider's expression.

I swim to shore, dragging myself out of the ocean. He steps forward, probably thinking I'm ready to go back. Instead, I grab his hand, tugging him back toward the frigid water.

Des stares at me, looking bewitched, as I drag him into the waves. And he doesn't resist. That's the oddest part of all.

The ocean has always been the place where sirens kill men.

"Callie, what are you doing?" he finally says when the water rises above his waist.

Isn't it obvious? "Making you join me."

We move out far enough that our toes no longer touch the seafloor. Des dips his head underwater and slicks his hair back.

We tread water like that for almost a minute, neither of

us saying anything. I drift to my back and stare up at the dim stars. His world is above us, and mine is below. There's something very satisfying about that.

"You know," I say, "I missed you. Every day." It was an ache that lasted seven years. It should've dulled, but it never did.

He's quiet for a long time. Finally, he confesses, "I missed you too."

It's not until late that evening that, soaked to our bones, we make it back inside. The Bargainer leads me to my room, and when I see the giant four-poster bed waiting for me, I belly flop onto it, quickly ruining the sheets with sand and ocean water.

"You continually disprove the theory that sirens are graceful creatures," Des says from behind me.

I bury my face in the sheets. "I have no clothes."

"I have a pretty loose no-clothes policy," he replies.

"*Des.*" My voice is muffled by the sheets.

He gives a rumbly laugh, then comes over, dropping a large faded Kiss T-shirt and a pair of boxer briefs next to me. "You can wear these, or..."

I reach for them before I can help myself. The shirt is soft, worn from years of use. I'm trying to act like it's no big deal that Des offered me one of his favorite shirts. But even after all this time apart, it still is a big deal. I feel like I've been given permission to step into Des's skin with these clothes.

He places a hand on my back, and every single cell is aware of that touch.

Des leans in close to my ear. "Shower quickly enough,

135

and I might just tuck you into bed." He punctuates the thought by nipping my ear.

I give him an annoyed look, but it's no use; my skin's glowing like it used to when I was a teenager and my hormones ran wild.

"Only if you take away a bead."

"Callie, Callie, Callie," he *tsks*. "I thought we were beyond paying for each other's company."

I grimace, remembering all those days I bought his presence, using him to drive away my loneliness.

"Try to stay out of the bathroom this time," I say, sliding off the bed and heading over to the room in question.

"Try not to think about me," he says.

I flip him the bird over my shoulder.

Twenty minutes later, the Bargainer manages to stay out of the bathroom.

I don't manage to avoid thinking about him.

Toweling off, I slip into the shirt and boxer briefs Des gave me. They smell like him. I hadn't realized he had a smell, but he does. It's smoky, like wood fire, and masculine.

When I walk back into the bedroom, the Bargainer has already made himself comfortable on my bed. He catches sight of me, and the shadows in the room deepen. Amid them, his eyes glint.

There was a time when I would've happily given away my firstborn to see him give me that look from my bed.

Now I'm slightly scared.

And with that hungry look on his face, I know where his thoughts are. It's not that I'm against doing more with him. It's that I'm really *not* against it, and I should be. I can be intimate with most men and feel nothing. But not with the Bargainer.

Not with Des.

"I don't bite, cherub," he says, noticing my hesitancy. He pats the space next to him. "I even left you room."

Warily, I climb onto the bed. I lie on my side, facing him. "I thought you were big on not crossing boundaries, Des."

He wraps an arm around my waist and pulls me in close. "When you were sixteen. Now—" He runs his hand down my arm. "I'm looking to expand my territory with you."

My breath catches. "Are you saying...?"

He leans in close, brushing a kiss against my forehead, and steps off the bed. "Good night, sleep tight, and don't let any monsters bite."

And with that, the Bargainer leaves.

The next morning, I pad into Des's kitchen, rubbing sleep from my eyes.

"Morning, cherub."

I shriek like a banshee at the Bargainer's voice, clutching my heart. My skin glows, making the tail end of my shout harmonize as the siren slips in.

The fae king leans back in one of his kitchen chairs, sipping coffee. His shirt's gone, and I clearly see his sleeve of tattoos that runs the length of his left arm.

He raises his eyebrows at me like I'm insane.

I finally catch my breath. "You-you scared me."

"Clearly." His mouth twitches.

"*Don't* laugh." I pat my hair absently. It feels like it's defying gravity at the moment.

"I wouldn't dare," Des says. His eyes move over the shirt and the boxer briefs I wear, and his expression heats.

When he looks at me like that, the siren refuses to go away.

"*Des.*" I'm supposed to say his name like a warning, but instead, it comes out like a purr.

Fuck. Pre-coffee, my hold on my siren is not so great.

"Why, hello, love," he says, giving me a smile that he saves for just my siren. These two have a major thing for each other. Even when I was a teenager and Des made it clear he didn't go there, he was extra indulgent with her.

And now my hold on her is slipping...slipping...

Gone.

I walk over to him, swaying my hips a little, my skin glowing. I don't stop until I'm climbing into his lap, my legs straddling him.

I take the mug he's holding and toss it over my shoulder. He lifts a hand, presumably to stop it and the coffee inside it from crashing against the floor.

I lean in close to his ear, shifting my hips until I hear him groan. "Seven years, you fucker," I say—or rather, the siren says, since she's leading the show at this point.

His hands fall to my waist. "The best things are worth waiting for, Callie."

I wind my arms behind his neck. "Truth or dare?"

His eyes are heated, a smirk spreading across his lips. "Trying to play my—"

"Truth: had you bothered to stick around, I would have given you every single one of your *wickedest* desires." I move my hips against him to punctuate my words.

I feel him react, something that brings me no little amount of pleasure.

Leaning in extra close, my tongue tastes the shell of his ear. "And I know my dark king has *many* wicked desires," I whisper.

I turn his face to mine, pulling it to me until only the barest bit of distance separates our lips.

But instead of kissing him, I say, "I'm going to make you ache and ache and ache, and I will do *nothing* to alleviate it. I'm going to make you pay for leaving me."

I step off him and saunter away.

"Cherub," Des says to my back, "I will enjoy every sweet second of it."

———

It's not until I get several good swallows of coffee in me that the siren goes away completely.

"Gods, did I miss your siren," Des says.

Typical that a fairy would miss the most sinister, mischievous part of me.

I grumble as I make myself at home in his kitchen, toasting some mini waffles and searching the cupboards for syrup.

He really does know my favorite foods.

The cupboard above me opens, and the syrup floats out. I catch it.

"Thanks," I say over my shoulder.

"Mmm."

I'm playing house with the Bargainer. And it feels so...*normal.*

Once I finish preparing my waffles, I head back over to the table.

"Now both of our names are on the wanted list," Des says when I sit down next to him.

It takes a second for that to compute. "Wait, I'm on the wanted list?"

Des passes me his tablet, and sure enough, there I am. Number eighty-six.

I feel my jaw hanging open. "Seriously, what the actual fuck?"

Eli has lost his damn mind. He broke into my house and shifted, placing me and Des in mortal danger. And the asshole has the audacity to put *me* on the wanted list?

A second later, I realize that Temper has surely seen the list, which means she must be going ballistic. I reach for my phone, only to remember that I never had a chance to grab it last night.

I turn my attention back to my listing, tapping on the link. The charges include illegally using glamour and consorting with the Bargainer. It's the latter charge that got me on the list, of that I'm sure.

My gaze rises to Des as I hand his tablet back to him. There's murder in his eyes.

I know that look. Fae vengeance.

Over the years, Des has left a trail of mangled bodies in his wake, from clients that tried to cross him to enemies that tried to kill him. He's even disfigured at least one man who tried to harm me on my behalf.

"Whatever you're thinking," I say, "don't, Des. *Please.*"

His hand tightens on his tablet. "You plead for that dog even now?"

"I'd prefer not to find him chopped up into tiny little bits."

"That's too good a death for the bastard," the Bargainer says darkly, tossing his tablet onto the table.

"Des, you are *not* killing him." Of all the conversations I imagined having today, this wasn't one of them.

He leans forward, wisps of shadow curling around him. "It is not in my nature to be lenient," he says, his voice low. "So if you want to ensure his safety, you're going to have grant me a favor."

"What do you want?" I ask, shoving a slice of waffle into my mouth.

He just stares and stares. "I think you already know."

The waffle gets lodged in my throat.

Give me a chance, his eyes plead.

He really does want more than just a kiss.

"Why, Des?" The question I always come back to.

He studies me for a long moment. "Eventually, I will tell you," he admits. "But not today." He takes a satisfied sip of coffee.

I eye him. "You're so lucky my glamour doesn't work on you."

He sets his cup down, and I try to ignore the way his arms tighten at the motion.

"You would use it on me?" he asks.

"Absolutely."

Now he smiles, the look almost feral. "That pleases me greatly, cherub."

It's responses like that that make me worried.

"So," I say between bites of waffle, "you're here and it's daylight."

"And?"

I glance up and stare directly at his abs. He needs to put a shirt on really effing badly.

"Isn't there some rule against showing up during the day?"

He picks his coffee back up. "I'm not a vampire. I'm not just going to melt the moment the sun hits me." Pushing his chair out, he stands. "Finish those waffles. It's time to get to work."

My plate begins to levitate, and I have to snatch it out of the air.

I glare at him. "Just for that, I'm going to eat this twice as slow."

The Bargainer smiles, and the plate lifts into the air again. This time when I grab for it, it resists, and I have to settle for snatching the waffles off the plate.

"You are a vindictive little shit," I say, glowering at him.

"*Little?*" He gives me a precious smile. "Let's not use adjectives improperly now." He takes a final sip of his coffee and sets it in his sink.

Meanwhile, I'm dealing with the clusterfuck that is currently my breakfast. I shove the last bits of waffle into my mouth, my hands covered in syrup.

I make my way over to him, turning on the sink faucet and rinsing my sticky hands off.

His eyes flick over me again. "Much as I like you in my clothes," he says, "you need to change. There are outfits in your closet."

"Seriously? Did you just stock it?" I ask, trying to figure out when he could have slipped the clothes by me.

"Naw," he says, walking out of the kitchen. "The clothes were always there waiting for you. Last night, I just wanted to see you in mine."

Wily bastard.

"I hope you're ready to glamour some people," he says over his shoulder. "In an hour, we're leaving for the Otherworld."

———

I take a deep breath as I head to Des's portal room, girding myself for the trip to the Otherworld.

My glamour only works on earthly beings. Once we cross over, I'm as good as defanged.

It's just a visit. We're not staying.

I glance down at the shimmery fae gown. The material

parts as I walk, revealing the crisscrossing ribbons of my sandals that tie high up on my thighs. As soon as I opened the door to my temporary closet, the outfit floated out, landing on the bed.

Hint taken.

I will say this for the fae—they may be heartless sons of bitches, but they have seriously good taste in fashion.

The Bargainer waits for me in front of his portal room, one of the two rooms in his home I've yet to see. I've never seen Des in anything but the T-shirt and pants combo he always wears—until now.

The black, sleeveless tunic he wears hugs his torso. Beneath it, his black breeches are tucked into dark riding boots. A low-slung leather belt is strapped loosely around his waist.

Jesus. He looks like an assassin—a bangable one.

Behind him, an assortment of locks lines the door, and I bet there's even more magical ones I can't see. I don't know whether to feel reassured or worried by the extensive security measures.

Still facing me, Des raps his knuckles on the door at his back. "On the other side of this door, there's an active portal," he says. He extends his arm. "You're going to want to hold on to me until we step off the ley line."

He doesn't need to warn me twice. I take his hand, enjoying the warm feel of his skin against mine.

One by one, the locks tumble, each ratcheting up my unease.

All the old stories of fairies come back to me. Monsters that lurk under mountains. The tooth fairy that built herself a palace of children's teeth. The wild fae that, with one look, can enslave their prey.

And then there are the fae that aren't so humanlike. Things that eat humans whole and wear their innards like jewelry.

All that is waiting for me on the other side of this portal.

The door opens, and Des and I step into a circular room, my sandals squishing into bright green grass, tiny white and pink flowers speckled among the ground cover.

Crisscrossing vines of wisteria cover the walls and ceiling. Where the wall meets the floor, there is a ring of mushrooms circling the room.

The grass sways back and forth, and the leaves of the vines shiver as some phantom breeze blows against them.

Like most portal sites, the laws of nature don't really apply here.

Des turns, assessing me. "Ready, cherub?" he asks.

Shit, I'm really doing this.

I nod. I let him lead me forward, toward the middle of the room. The air feels thicker with each step, and I swear I hear music, but it's so soft that I can't be sure that my ears aren't just playing tricks on me.

With a poignant look, the Bargainer drags me into his arms, and our surroundings disappear.

CHAPTER 12

January, seven years ago

When Des appears in front of me, I'm a fucking mess. A handful of tissues are spread out around me. My face is wet and my eyes are swollen.

I look up at the Bargainer miserably, my entire body trembling.

He crosses his arms, his leather jacket groaning. "Who do I have to hurt?"

I shake my head, dropping my gaze. I don't know why I called him. I don't let other people see me when I'm like this. But I'm so tired of being alone.

Today was…today was a bad day.

"Give me a name, cherub."

I wipe my eyes. I'm not done crying, but for the moment, the tears have stopped.

When I finally meet Des's eyes, I see he's serious. It

takes me a moment to realize that the Bargainer is *pissed* and another moment to realize he's pissed *on my behalf.*

And I'm codependent enough to actually feel better because of this reaction. "He's an instructor," I whisper, my voice hoarse.

Des sits down next to me, one of his wide shoulders brushing mine before he wraps his arm around me and pulls me in close. For the next five minutes, he lets me just cry and make a mess of his leather jacket, my head tucked beneath his. His hand moves up and down my arm reassuringly, but the action is somewhat ruined by how menacing his presence feels.

Finally I manage to pull myself together, my body not shaking quite so much anymore. I push away from him a little.

Frowning deeply, he wipes the tears off my cheeks before cupping my face. "Tell me what happened." I feel anger vibrating off him.

I take in a shuddering breath. "His name is Mr. Whitechapel. He—he tried to touch me..."

But those aren't the right words, are they? He *did* touch me. He wouldn't stop until he'd pinned me down, telling me the entire time that I wanted this. That I'd been driving him crazy the entire semester. That he'd noticed every one of my suggestive looks.

He'd unbuttoned the top of my pants, he'd pushed my shirt up...

That was as far as he got. Too far.

I still don't have full control of my gift, but fear brings it out. The siren told him to stop, told him to let me go.

And then I ran here.

And now I'm dying inside, falling back into who I was before the Bargainer saved me from my past.

I hate my face. I hate my body. I hate who I see in the mirror. I hate my ability to reel people in with a single look and command. I hate everything about me that makes me who I am. I hate that anyone can still make me feel weak.

I manage to get the story out, and then I begin to cry again. And again, the Bargainer pulls me into him. I lean my head against his chest, for once not thinking about him in a romantic sense. Just comfort.

"Cherub, I'm proud of you using your power like that," Des eventually says.

Why that makes me cry harder, I can't say.

"Want to know a secret?" he says, his hand smoothing down my hair. He doesn't wait for me to respond. "People like him were born to fear people like us," he says, his voice sinister.

I pause amid my sobs.

What? What does that even mean? And why is he telling me this? I've been a victim my whole life. People like Mr. Whitechapel *use* people like me. It's not the other way around.

"That's a shitty secret," I decide.

The Bargainer brings his lips close to my ear. "It's the truth," he whispers. "Eventually you'll understand. And eventually you'll embrace it."

Unlikely. But I nod anyway because I don't feel like debating with Des at the moment.

For about fifteen seconds, I'm good—I might even be over it—then the memory of my teacher's hands on my body drags me under all over again.

I don't know how long I cry, only that Des holds me the entire time. I'm not sure I'm even crying about what happened today at this point. I think I'm crying about all those days when I didn't get away in time.

Eventually Des moves us from the floor to the bed, humming some fae hymn beneath his breath. And eventually I stop weeping like a maniac and instead just hold him close like he's my own personal safety blanket.

I nod off like that, wrapped up in the Bargainer's arms.

The next morning when I wake, he's gone.

It's only later that I learn Mr. Whitechapel has disappeared. And that, when he resurfaces a week later and countries away, most of the bones in his body are broken, several teeth and toes are missing, and the Bargainer's calling card is on his person.

No one can get him to talk about what happened to him. But he is apparently quite eager to discuss his gross misconduct with his students.

Students. Plural. Apparently I'm not the first.

Des is no longer just my savior; he's also my vigilante. And I have to come to terms with the fact that the man who let me cry in his arms is also the Bargainer, a wanted criminal known not just for his deals but also his immense cruelty—the same cruelty the fae are infamous for.

And Lord save me, I am just fine with that.

Present

I'm still reeling when our surroundings reappear.

My breath catches as I look around.

Des and I stand among ruins, the white marble glittering in the moonlight. Flowering vines wind around the worn arches and the toppled statuary.

The Otherworld.

The sound of rushing water surrounds us on all sides, the mist from it dappling my skin. I turn in a circle, staggering back at the sight of the giant waterfall that crashes against the opposite end of the outcropping we stand on, plumes of mist rising up around it.

"What is this place?" I ask, wonder entering my voice.

"The Temple of the Undying Mother—one of the first gods my people worshipped." Once more, Des wraps his arms around me. "Hold on."

My arms slip around his waist as his wings unfurl. He tenses, his wings beginning to flap, the force of each stroke whipping my hair about.

Then the two of us rise, and I get a better look at the ruins. They sit on a small rocky island that protrudes out from the middle of a giant waterfall.

I tear my gaze away, only to find that the Bargainer has been watching me with those riveting eyes of his, his face soft.

The longer I hold his stare, the faster my pulse races and the more that old longing returns. I want to look away, but I can't.

A smile begins to spread along his lips, and it's so very different from his usual expressions.

"Where are we going?" I shout over the wind, just to break the moment.

His hold tightens. "My palace."

The place where Des reigns. Despite my reservations being here, I'm excited to see it. I can't even count how many times I wondered what it looked like.

We rise higher and higher into the night air, passing through one billowing cloud after the next.

A group of tiny glittering fairies—pixies?—fly past us, then circle around Des, chittering excitedly.

"Of course I'm back," he says by way of greeting. "No, I didn't bring any candy, and yes, she is pretty."

I feel a gentle tug on my hair and hear the sound of high-pitched laughter. When I glance over my shoulder, I see several of the little fairies diving through my hair, playing what appears to be hide-and-seek. One of them has latched onto a lock of it that billows in the breeze, squealing with excitement.

Um…all right.

"This is Callypso," Des continues. "Callypso, these are the pixies of the west wind."

"Hi," I say over my shoulder, trying not to freak out at the fact that little people are using my hair like a jungle gym.

"Fairies believe it's a blessing to be touched by pixies," Des says quietly.

"Oh." And now I smile.

One of them flutters over and pets my cheek, speaking softly.

"She says you have kind eyes."

I can hear the pixie's voice squeaking near my ear as the rest of them climb up my hair and perch on the crown of my head.

Whatever she says next wipes Des's expression clean.

"What is it?" I ask.

"Nothing of importance."

Angry chittering.

"End of discussion," he says to the tiny pixie, his tone no longer indulgent. "Go ahead and tell the palace we're coming."

With a huff, the pixies scatter into the sky, ruffling my hair as they go. I watch them fly off until the evening clouds swallow them up.

"They were sweet," I say.

"Mmm," he says, looking distracted.

"What's on your mind?" I ask.

"Nothing, cherub."

That's obviously a lie, but I don't push.

We rise above another layer of clouds, and then the sky clears. An ocean of stars fills the night sky, brighter than any I've seen on earth. They're so prominent, I feel I could almost reach out and touch them.

And then I catch sight of Desmond Flynn's palace, and all thoughts of stars vanish.

Rising above the clouds is a castle made of the palest white stone. In the moonlight, it shimmers brightly, drawing attention to the tall spires and the maze of bridges and ramparts that connect them. Descending down on all sides of it is a walled city, every building made of the same milky-white stone.

With the way the clouds spread out around the base of the city, it appears to float on the fluffy plumes. But as we get closer and the cloud cover dissipates, I can see the *bottom* of the slate-gray mountain the city is built on.

An island in the sky. Impossible, and yet here in the Otherworld, it exists.

Even the base of the floating island appears to have been cut, chiseled, and faceted to look like more buildings. I make out columns and balconies, spiraling staircases and light flickering in cut-glass windows.

"Wow," I breathe.

Out of my periphery, I can feel Des's gaze on me again, but for once, I'm too distracted to glance at him.

More pixies circle around us as we begin to descend. Soon I can make out the streets that run between buildings, and then I notice the fairies.

Most pause to watch our entrance. I feel every one of those foreign, predatory eyes on me, and I'm painfully aware that I'm a human in a world that enslaves my kind. Being a siren means very little to these beings. Not when they see my rounded ears and sense my mortality. What is a little power in light of all my human coarseness and fragility? The Bargainer holds me closer than necessary, and he's making a very public entrance, as though he's proud to show off the human in his arms.

Or he just doesn't give a fuck.

Knowing Des, I'm actually kind of betting on the latter.

He beats his wings faster as the white stone courtyard in front of his palace gets closer and closer. An elaborate bronze gate encircles the palace. Beyond it, men and women with pointed ears gather, their curious eyes trained on us. Several fae guards dressed in white and silver keep them back. They appear to be just as curious about us as I am about them.

Des and I land softly, his head bowed over mine. I step out of his hold, but I don't attempt to shrug off the arm he keeps looped around my waist.

The crowd gathered around us is silent. Then, one by one, they begin to cheer.

I stare out at them, my eyebrows hiked up. Next to me, Des's wings are splayed out, the span of them dwarfing us. If I'm being perfectly honest, I'd like to curl up in one of them and hide.

"Why are they cheering?" I whisper to him.

"There's much you don't know about the Kingdom of Night." With that enigmatic response, he nods to our audience and then leads me toward the castle.

There are dozens of people gathered in the entrance

hall—what I can only guess are his soldiers, officials, and aides—but none of them approach us, and Des doesn't stop to speak to them, though he does acknowledge them with the tilt of his head.

My eyes move everywhere, because everywhere there is some enthralling sight to take in, whether it's the massive bronze chandelier overhead whose flames spit and flicker like sparklers or the ceiling that's made to look like the heavens outside.

It's all so impossibly lovely.

Des bends toward me. "I've wanted to show you this place for a long, long time," he admits.

I tear my gaze away from my surroundings to look at him. "You have?" I don't know what to make of that.

"I wanted even more for you to like it," he adds.

My eyes move over his face before I catch sight of the simple circlet of hammered bronze that rings the fae king's head.

His crown.

I touch his simple headpiece. "When did you put this on?"

"When we landed."

He wasn't carrying it on him, which meant…magic.

"It looks good on you." It really does.

"I hate it," he confesses quietly as he leads me down one of his halls.

"Why?" I ask.

"I've never felt particularly kingly."

I realize then, as he leads me through his palace at the center of his kingdom, that a king is *exactly* what Des is. It isn't just some pretty title; it's all this. Whatever parts of him I got all those years ago when he visited me, those were something else.

Back then, I had only seen his wicked side, his dirty deeds. I'd never seen his righteousness.

This is a side of him I don't know. And I think it might be the best side of him.

His crown isn't the only item he wears. Three bronze bands circle his bicep.

He sees where I'm looking. "War cuffs," he explains. "For valor."

A warrior king. And my lady parts were having trouble enough around him as it was. I'm now officially a lost cause.

Des leads me through the palace, nodding to people we pass as he goes. Their eyes linger on me, and most dip their heads.

I crane my neck to follow the fae woman who stopped and actually curtsied to me. Not just the king but also me.

What in the world? Did he tell everyone that I'm here to fix their problems? Because I seriously doubt I'm going to get anything out of these humans that Des couldn't.

"Where are we going?" I ask distractedly.

"To the servants' quarters. You'll be interviewing an off-duty nursemaid today."

No sense wasting time, I guess. The thought of glamouring these humans makes my palms sweat.

"Have all the kingdoms stopped taking change-lings?" I ask.

Des shakes his head. "Just the Kingdom of Night. The Kingdom of Day has considered it, but neither the Kingdoms of Fauna or Flora will."

Which means that humans are still being plucked from earth.

"And yours are free? There aren't any slaves here?" I ask.

"None, cherub."

I nod to myself, wiping my sweaty palms off on my dress.

The servants' quarters are located in an auxiliary building on the side of the palace. We exit the back of the castle and pass through a moonlit garden before we enter the building.

Inside, the space is only slightly less adorned than the palace itself and the corridors a bit narrower. We stop at a dark wood door.

"Did you memorize the questions?" Des asks.

I give him a look. "I agreed to do this. I'm good for my word."

"I'm taking that as a yes," he says, searching my face.

It is a yes.

Des raps his knuckles on the door. A moment later, it swings open of its own accord. Inside, a single human woman sits at a desk, her quill poised over a letter.

By the looks of the living quarters—and the several pairs of boots in various sizes resting just inside the doorway—she must share the space with roommates. But at the moment, she's alone.

As soon as she notices Des, she rises to her feet, bowing deeply. "My king, it's an honor," she murmurs.

The Bargainer turns to me, giving me a heavy look. "Your repayment begins now," he says.

Immediately the magic takes hold, prickling my skin, urging the siren out.

"I hate it when you do that," I mutter.

"Don't make deals with bad men, cherub," he says, leaning against the wall, folding his arms.

The woman's eyes move to me. The first thing I notice about her are the bruises. They dot her neck and her chest, continuing on beneath the curved neckline of her dress. There are rings of them, some obviously newer than others.

When she sees me looking, she self-consciously covers the marks, but there's another bruise around her wrist. I can almost make out the small handprint from whoever must've squeezed her there.

"H-how can I help you?" she asks, her eyes moving to me and Des.

"Do you know why I'm here?" I ask, taking a few tentative steps toward her.

She shakes her head, her gaze lingering on my shimmering skin.

"I'm here to ask you a few questions concerning the disappearances of fairies across your kingdom," I explain.

She sucks in a breath, her face visibly paling. Now, now she has an idea.

She begins to shake her head, backing up and bumping into the chair behind her. "*Please.*" She places a hand over the bruises on her chest once more. "I–I can't."

Seeing her fear, I would expect her to play dumb. But perhaps both of us know it's no use.

Her eyes begin to dart about, looking for an escape. She edges away from me, clumsily banging into things.

"There's nowhere for you to go," I say. "We both know this."

Despite my warning, she tries to slip past me, feinting to the left before she runs, like I'm going to try to tackle her.

Unfortunately for this woman, I'm used to targets running from me.

"*Stop,*" I command, my voice unearthly.

Immediately her body halts, her shoulders trembling. When she looks over at me, a silent tear slips down her cheek. The sight of it breaks my heart.

"Please, you have no idea what he'll do if I talk," she pleads.

He?

"Let's sit down," I suggest, my voice soothing despite the glamour.

Robotically, she moves to the small couch, more tears following the first. When she looks at me, I can see the resistance in her eyes, but she can't do a damn thing about it.

"What's your name?" I ask, sitting next to her and taking her hand. It's already clammy with sweat.

She stares down at her hands in her lap. "Gaelia."

A human woman with a fae name.

"Were you born here?" I ask.

Drawing in a shaky breath, she nods.

"What do you do in the palace?" I ask, already knowing the answer.

She peers over at Des, who's still leaning in the room's entryway, before returning her attention back to her lap. "I work in the royal nursery."

My eyes move back to the bruise on her wrist. Again, the impression it's left on her skin makes it look as though a tiny hand squeezed it too hard. A child's hand...

I force my gaze back to her. "Why does your king believe you know something about the disappearances?" I ask.

Her expression crumbles, her eyes and mouth pinched as she cries. "Please," she begs again.

Gaelia looks at me with agony, and I can tell this is her last-ditch effort to stop the rest of the conversation from unfolding. She's pleading for my humanity with her eyes, but she doesn't know that I have no more control of the situation than she does.

I press my own lips together, my eyes stinging. I don't

want to do this to her. She's not a criminal, just the last in a line of humans who were once slaves in this world. She's a victim, one who's had the misfortune of working in the wrong place at the wrong time. And thanks to me, she's probably going to suffer for her forced confession.

My eyes flutter as I say, "*Answer me*," the siren heavy in my voice.

She draws in a deep, stuttering breath. "Some of the babies in the royal nursery are the children of the sleeping warriors."

"The women in the glass caskets?" I ask.

She nods. "They are unlike the other children under our care," she continues. "They are…*peculiar*."

Fae in general are peculiar; I can't imagine what an oddity among the fae looks like.

"Peculiar how?"

Gaelia begins to openly weep even as she answers, "They are listless, almost catatonic at times. They don't sleep. They just lie in their cradles, their eyes focused on the ceiling. The only time they do anything at all is when…is when…" She touches the bruises on her chest. "…they feed."

Her fingers curl around the neckline of her blouse, and she pulls down the edge of the material. I lean in to get a better look. Beneath the material, extensive bruising covers her chest. Among all the dark discoloration are strange, curving cuts.

Bite marks.

I rear back at the sight. Now that I'm looking, I see the little puncture marks where their teeth split Gaelia's flesh.

"And when they feed," she adds, "they prophesize."

Prophecy. Even earth has supernaturals that can prophesize…but children prophesying? This *is* peculiar.

Not to mention the fact that said children are *gnawing* on humans.

"How old are these children?" I ask.

Gaelia is beginning to rock in her seat, holding her arms close to her. "Some are as old as eight." Her lips tremble over each word. "The youngest is less than three months."

"And which ones prophesize?"

Her eyes focus on something on the floor. "All of them." All of them?

"Even the three-month-old?" I ask skeptically.

Gaelia nods. "She speaks and feeds like the rest of them. She told me you and the king would come. She said, 'Bare them no secret, tell them no truths, or pain and terror shall be your bedmates and death the least of your fears.'" She releases a shaky breath. "I didn't believe her. I hadn't even remembered her warning until you mentioned you wanted to ask me some questions." Her arms tighten around herself. "They all show me so many things, so many horrible things…"

"Is that normal?" I probe. "For a child that young to even be talking?"

More tears. "No, my lady. None of this is normal." Gaelia's shaking, which had died down somewhat, begins all over again.

"I don't understand. What is so terrible about telling me this?" I ask.

She hesitates.

"You're going to have to tell me, one way or another," I say. "It might as well be on your own terms."

She covers her mouth with her hand, her sobs beginning anew. I hear her whispering to herself, "Forgive me. Forgive me." Her rocking has increased.

"Gaelia."

Slowly her eyes move to mine, and she drops her hand from her mouth. "He doesn't want to be found," she whispers. "The children tell me he is making many plans. That he is wary of our king, the Emperor of the Evening Stars," she says, her eyes moving to Des. "But that he fears no others."

Des comes over now, placing a hand on my shoulder. Gaelia notices.

"He still needs more time," she continues, wrapping her arms around herself once more. "He's not unstoppable yet."

"Why would he tell you this?" Des says.

She doesn't respond, but her fingers squeeze into the flesh of her upper arms.

"Answer him," I say softly, my glamour forcing her to answer.

Still, she fights the words for another second or two, until they force themselves out anyway. "Children say whatever is on their minds. Even these ones. In this way, they're not so different from ordinary children."

"Why do you believe them?" I ask.

Her lips quiver. "Besides the prophesying? Because for years, the nurses on rotation have been complaining of a figure that leans over these children's cradles. And lately, I've started to see him as well."

The back of my neck prickles. The Otherworld is chalk full of boogeymen, and this sounds exactly like one of them.

"What does he look like?" I ask, going off script. Up until now, I'd managed to pepper Des's questions into the natural flow of the conversation, but now I abandon the rest of them altogether.

Gaelia shakes her head manically. "He's just a shadow... just a shadow."

"Where is he?" Des asks.

She shivers, not even bothering to fight our questions anymore. "Everywhere."

Her words raise my gooseflesh.

"Do you know his name?" I ask.

"Thief of Souls," she mutters. "Thief of Souls."

That name again.

"What does he want?" the Bargainer growls.

Her eyes meet ours. "*Everything.*"

CHAPTER 13

February, seven years ago

Tonight, Douglas Café is bustling, a dozen different conver-sations filling the air.

I stare into my coffee cup. "Des, why haven't you made me repay my debts?"

Des leans back in his seat, his legs kicked up on another chair he's dragged over. He sips an espresso from the world's smallest cup, his hand dwarfing the tiny glass.

He sets the cup down. "Are you eager to, cherub?"

Under the café's soft lighting, his eyes glint with anticipation.

"Just curious." I search his face. "Are *you*?"

"Am I what?" His attention moves casually over the rest of the room. I'm not fooled, just as I wasn't earlier, when he deliberately took a seat in the corner of the room, making sure his back was to the wall.

Ever since Mr. Whitechapel reappeared with a few less

toes and fingers and the Bargainer's calling card on his chest, the Politia has been on the hunt for Des.

"Eager for me to repay my debts," I say.

"If I was, then you would have already paid them."

But why *wouldn't* he be eager? Based on the deals I've witnessed, I know Des is religious about making his clients repay him in a timely fashion.

My bracelet is now nine rows deep and steadily growing. Not once has he made me repay him. Not for a single wish.

"All these beads make me nervous," I say, twisting my bracelet around.

His gaze drifts back to mine. "Then stop buying favors."

I stand, the chair scraping back. "You're crappy company tonight," I say.

Maybe it's not him. Maybe it's me.

Because at the moment, I feel so damn disappointed. Disappointed by this evening, by all the others just like it. By wanting something I just can't have. By being too weak to give up this stupid crush even though I know I should. By collecting lifetimes and lifetimes of debt and shackling myself to a bad man who wants nothing to do with me.

"Sit down," Des commands, and I feel the brush of his magic in the order.

My legs begin to fold, my body bending to take my seat. I fight the command, but it's not much use.

I glare at him. And now I understand a bit better why my own power is just so terrible. It's a peculiar kind of torture, to have your body answer to another person. Peculiar and vile.

"That's what your repayment will feel like," he says. "Only the compulsion will be worse. Much worse." He leans forward. "Don't be so eager to repay your debts. Neither of us will enjoy it."

163

"If you won't enjoy it, Des," I say, trying to stand up. His magic presses down on me, forcing me to stay seated. "Then why don't you stop making deals with me?"

Again, his eyes glint. "You play a dangerous game with me, siren. Making deals is its own sort of compulsion." His voice is so low that only I can hear it. "And you offer them to me so easily." He pauses, his eyes shining wickedly. "Don't think I'll ever stop taking them—because I won't."

Present

Des and I are quiet as we leave the servants' quarters.

Next to me, the Bargainer looks grim.

Bloodsucking children, phantom visitors, and a man who goes by the name of the Thief of Souls. It's enough to give me nightmares.

I rub my arms. "How long have these disappearances been going on?" I ask as we enter the garden.

"Almost a decade."

And in all that time, nothing has been solved…

I've done my job. I've glamoured an innocent woman at the Bargainer's behest. I can wipe my hands clean of this task and leave that woman to her fate, a fate that made her mad with terror. A fate she had been warned about by a baby who should be too young to talk.

I pause, stopping in the middle of the stone pathway.

The Bargainer turns to me, his brows drawn together.

"If I'm able to get more information for you from the children, will you take off more beads?" I ask.

He cocks his head. "Why do you wish to see them?" he probes.

As if it isn't obvious. "That woman back there is frightened

164

of these children and of what they've told her. *They* are the ones we should be interviewing."

Des sighs. "I am oath-bound against using my magic on fae children, and short of that… I have been to the nursery a thousand times, and a thousand times I've tried to talk with them. Not once has it worked."

"But you've never brought a siren with you," I say.

Every time I close my eyes, I see Gaelia's beseeching stare and her hopelessness. I can't seem to just leave it alone.

The corners of Des's eyes crinkle. "This is true. I've never brought a spitfire siren to do my dirty work." He stares at me for a bit longer. Finally, *reluctantly*, he nods. "I'll take you to the children. I doubt it will be very helpful with me there, but I'll take you all the same. However," he adds, "the moment I sense anything amiss, we're leaving, no questions asked."

The protectiveness in his voice sends shivers down my arms.

"I can work with that. Whose children does the royal nursery take care of?" I ask as we make our way through the palace once more, on our way to that very nursery. It seems strange to me that these *peculiar* kids, as Gaelia put it, are right inside the castle, in the very heart of the kingdom.

Des clasps his hands behind his back. "The nursery takes care of children orphaned by warrior parents—our way of honoring their final sacrifice—children of nobility working in the palace, and of course, any children of the royal family—including mine."

"Y-yours?" I echo.

Why had I never considered the possibility Des might have children?

A warrior king like him? He'd have no shortage of women… It's possible.

Des peers over at me. "Does that bother you?"

I shake my head, not meeting his gaze, even as my stomach twists.

I can feel his eyes on me.

"Truth," he says. "How would you feel if I told you I had children?"

The moment the question leaves his lips, his magic closes around my windpipe.

I clutch my throat, glaring at him. "Some warning would be nice," I rasp out.

My windpipe constricts. Not the response it wants.

I feel the magic drag the words out, much like my magic dragged answers out of Gaelia.

"I would be jealous," I say.

God, am I glad we're the only two people walking down this particular hallway. It's embarrassing enough to admit this to Des without having any additional audience.

"Why?" he asks.

The magic doesn't let up.

I grit my teeth together, but it doesn't stop the answer from slipping out. "Because I'm a horrible person."

The magic squeezes harder. Not truthful enough, apparently.

"B-because," I try again, "I don't want anyone else to share that experience with you."

"Why?" he presses.

You've *got* to be kidding me. The magic's a noose around my neck.

"Because that's an experience I'd like to share with you," I rush to say. Immediately, my cheeks flush.

The magic eases up, but just barely.

Des's eyes soften. "You'd want to have my child?"

"Not *anymore*," I wheeze.

But even now the magic senses I lie. It squeezes my windpipes, choking me.

"Yeeesss," I hiss out.

All at once, the magic releases me, and I know several beads have just disappeared without even looking.

I don't give a flying fuck.

I'm seeing red.

Des looks so pleased. Pleased and *aroused*.

"We will be returning to this conversation, cherub," he promises.

That's about the moment I pounce on him.

He grunts as I push against the wall and loop my arms around his neck.

Oh my sweet baby Jesus, am I angry.

He steps away from the wall, forcing me to lose my footing as he pries my arms off his neck. Before I can attack him again, he pulls me in close, our torsos flush with one another.

"You had no right to do that," I say, whisper soft.

Technically, he *did* have every right. That's what happens when you bargain with Des. He can take whatever he wants as repayment.

His eyes move to my heated cheeks. "You're embarrassed."

Of course I'm embarrassed. Who wants to tell the guy who ripped her heart out that *hey boy hey, I still want your babies*.

He runs a hand down my back. "You would not be so embarrassed if you knew my thoughts."

Now my breath catches.

"Rest assured, cherub," he continues. "I don't have any children." He pulls me closer, his lips brushing my ear. "Though I'm always willing to change that."

I feel my cheeks flush. His hand slides down the back of one of my thighs, and he loops my leg around his waist.

"Des, what are you doing?" I demand as he wraps my other leg around his hips and lifts me into his arms.

It's a useless question. The Bargainer is doing what he always does—throwing me and my emotions off-kilter.

Next time I fall for someone, it won't be a conniving, manipulative—

His hand moves lower, cupping my ass.

—*horny* fae king.

Next time, it will be a good boy.

"I don't even want kids," I mutter.

Des just smiles.

Fairies.

Then, naturally, someone chooses that moment to turn down the hall. The Bargainer doesn't make a move to put me down. Instead, he begins walking with me wrapped around him like a koala, nodding to the fae woman as we pass her.

So awkward.

It's not until we reach the double doors that lead to the nursery that Des finally puts me down.

In this section of the palace, it's unnaturally silent. I keep expecting to hear...*something*. The young are always noisy.

I reach for one of the knobs. Before I can grab it, the Bargainer catches my hand.

"Remember my words," he says. "Anything unusual happens, we're out of here."

I stare into those silver eyes, his chiseled features on edge.

"I remember," I say. Shaking off his hand, I open the door.

It's almost quieter inside the nursery than it is outside. Even the air here feels still, like everyone's holding their breaths.

A lone servant fluffs the pillows of one of several ornate couches that rest in the sitting room. Beyond her, a set of French doors opens up to a private courtyard.

She startles when she sees us, dipping into a hasty curtsy. "My king, my lady," she says, greeting each of us. "What an unexpected surprise."

"We're here to see the casket children," Des says brusquely.

Casket children—what a morbid name for them.

"Oh." Her eyes move between us. "O-of course."

Do I detect unease?

She dips her head. "Right this way."

As we follow her down one of the side halls that branch off the common area, I notice she discreetly cracks her fingers one by one.

"They're fairly quiet at the moment." *Catatonic* is what she means. "We've had to separate them from the other children. There were complaints..." She doesn't finish her thought. "Well, you know about that already, my king."

"Complaints about what?" I ask.

She takes a deep breath. "That the children were feeding off the other children. We decided to move them. They don't...prey on each other."

As we trail behind her, stepping over some glass toys and a lyre playing a cheerful tune, I give Des a *what the fuck* look. He raises an eyebrow and shakes his head, his expression dark.

She stops at a door and knocks as she enters. "Children, you have company."

The room we step into is cloaked in shadow, and none of the lit sconces seem to drive away the darkness. The far side of the room is made up of a wall of windows. Several children stand in front of them, staring out at the night beyond. Just like Gaelia said, none of them move a muscle. More lie on the row of beds pushed against the walls. I can't see inside the cribs, but I know there must be infants in at least some of them.

A wet nurse sits at a rocking chair to our left, pressing a tissue against the skin just above her breast, wincing as she does so. She drops her hand, hiding the tissue in her fist when she sees me and Des, hastily standing and bowing to us both.

The Bargainer nods to her, while my eyes linger on the beads of blood forming where she'd been pressing the tissue to her skin.

"You both can leave us," he tells the two servants.

The woman who led us here wastes no time leaving, but the wet nurse hesitates briefly, casting a fearful look about the room before she dips her head. "If you need me, I'll be right outside," she says, filing out. The door clicks shut behind her.

Now that the two of us are alone with all these strange children, I'm spooked, every instinct shouting at me to leave the room.

Almost as one, the children at the window begin to turn toward us.

I go cold all over at the sight.

Their eyes move to Des.

All at once, they begin to scream. Not moving, just screaming. Even the babies are wailing.

Des leans in close. "I forgot to tell you. They don't like me so much."

You don't say?

He steps in front of me, using his body to blockade mine, and I'm not going to lie, right about now, I'm ridiculously grateful for my shield.

You were the one who wanted to see them, Callie. Grow a backbone.

I force myself to step out from behind the Bargainer, scraping together the last of my courage.

What had Gaelia said? That strange though they may be, these were just kids.

Just kids.

I take a tentative step forward, and then another. They're still screaming, their gazes transfixed on Des.

I begin to hum, hoping that in between kids' love of music and my own abilities, they might stop shrieking long enough for me to actually interact with them.

All at once, the children's eyes move to me, some of their screams hiccuping a bit as I begin to glow, the tune I hum beginning to have a magical pull to it.

And then I begin to sing. "Twinkle, twinkle, little star…"

So sue me for not being inventive.

One by one, the children stop crying and begin to watch me, mesmerized. I walk toward them, really hoping this is a good idea.

When I finish the song, the children blink, like they're waking from a dream. I can't glamour fae—my powers only work on beings of my world—but music doesn't need to be controlling for it to captivate.

Their eyes move to Des, and they tense up again.

"Be calm," I say, my voice ethereal. "He means you no harm. *I* mean you no harm."

It's a tense few moments while I wait to see how they'll react. When they don't begin to scream again, I relax. At least I relax as much as I can, considering I'm surrounded by a gaggle of creepy kids. A couple of them have dried blood caked around their lips.

I try not to shudder.

"My name is Callypso, but you can call me Callie. I wanted to ask you all a few questions. Will any of you speak to me?"

Their eyes move to me, and they stare unblinkingly at me. I'm seriously concerned that they've gone catatonic again when, as one, they nod, circling around me.

"Where are your mothers?" I ask.

"Sleeping below," one little boy murmurs.

"Why are they sleeping?" I ask.

"Because he wants them to." This time, it's a girl with a lisp who responds. As she speaks, I catch sight of two sets of fangs.

I try not to recoil.

"Who is 'he'?" I ask.

"Our father," another girl says.

A single father to all these children?

I swear I feel a ghostly breath on the back of my neck. There is no earthly reason why they should know this—or anything else I've asked so far—yet they do. And I have a feeling in my gut that they have most of the answers Des is looking for. Whether they'll share them is another matter altogether.

"Who is your father?" I ask.

They look at one another, and again I get the impression that they make decisions as a collective unit.

"The Thief of Souls," a boy murmurs.

That name—Gaelia had mentioned it, I'd seen it scrawled on Des's notes, and I'd heard it all those years ago.

"He sees it all. Hears it all," another boy adds.

Ten points to Slytherin for the creepy answer.

"Where can I find him?" I ask.

"He's already here," says a boy with raven-black hair.

My hackles rise at that.

"Can I meet him?"

As soon as I ask the question, the room darkens. The Bargainer doesn't say anything, but it's clear he's not happy about my question.

"Yesssss…" This comes from one of the *cradles* on the far corner of the room. "But you cannot bring *him* along." The children's eyes dart to Des.

"Our father will like you," a redheaded girl says.

"He already does," another adds.

"He likes pretty things."

"Likes to break them."

Again, that chilling breath is breathing down my neck as the children speak, their unwavering gazes fixed on me.

Des's shadows circle my lower legs protectively. "*Callie.*"

The children tighten their circle around me, throwing glances over their shoulders at the Bargainer.

Earlier, I'd worried they wouldn't talk. Now I'm worried that they might be too fond of me.

"Do you know where I can find him?" I ask.

"He will find you."

"He always finds the ones he wants."

"He's already begun the hunt."

"The hunt?" I shouldn't ask. I feel like coming to the Otherworld has exposed me in exactly the way I feared it would.

"He'll make you his, just like our mothers."

All right, I'm done.

"I have to leave," I say.

Across the room, Des begins moving toward me, clearly on the same page.

"Not yet," the children beg, closing in on me, their hands grabbing my dress.

"Stay with us forever."

"I can't," I say, "but I can come back."

"*Stay*," one of the oldest boys growls.

"*She said no.*" Des's sharp voice cuts through the room.

The kids recoil from him, several beginning to scream again. One hisses at the fae king, her pointed teeth bared.

"Stay," several say to me again. This time, they grab my exposed forearms, and when they do...

The air in my lungs leaves me.

I'm falling into myself. Down and down, into the darkness, past cages and cages of women, some who batter the doors of their cells, some who are lying far too still. Floor after floor of them blur together as I plummet.

Then the world flips until I'm no longer falling down but falling *up*. And then I'm not falling but flying.

I land at the foot of a throne, the wings at my back spread wide. My surroundings vanish, replaced by a forest. I'm soaring through it, and the trees seem to howl. I fly out of the woods only to crash into my old kitchen, the room soaked in blood.

My stepfather pushes himself off the ground, his body coming to life.

Oh God, *no*.

He looms over me, his eyes angry. From his head sprout antlers. They grow and twist with each passing second. He stares me down, his face shifting until I'm no longer staring at my stepfather; I'm staring at a stranger, one with chestnut hair, tan skin, and wild brown eyes.

The man in front of me is covered in my father's blood, and as I watch, he licks a stream of it off his finger.

"My," he says, "aren't you a pretty, pretty bird."

He and the room fade, and the darkness swallows me whole.

CHAPTER 14

February, seven years ago

My alarm goes off next to me, just as it has been for the last thirteen minutes. I don't have the energy to untangle my arms from my sheets and turn the thing off.

Today is what I like to call a Hail Mary day, because nothing short of a miracle can make me get out of this bed.

Most days, I'm good. Most days, I can pretend I'm like everyone else. But then there are the days when I can't, days when my past catches up to me.

Days like today. I'm too depressed to get out of bed. I'm being dragged under by all those bad memories.

The doorknob turning. The smell of spirits thick on my stepfather's breath. All that blood when I finally killed him…

One of my floormates bangs on the door. "Callie, turn off your freaking alarm before you wake up the whole school," she yells, then walks away.

Somehow I manage to turn the alarm off before burying my face in my pillow.

Not five minutes later, I hear the lock to my room click. I begin to sit up when suddenly, the door blows open, and in steps the Bargainer. If anyone's out in the hallway, they don't notice his entrance.

"Get up," he growls.

I'm still a few steps behind him. My mind's having a hard time comprehending that the Bargainer is here in my room at this hour. Technically, it's still dark out, so it's still the time that he reigns.

But a morning visit? That's a first.

He strides the rest of the way to my side, and just from his expression alone, I can tell that he means business. He pulls my blankets off me, a comforting hand touching my back. "*Up.*"

How did he know that me sleeping in thirteen minutes more than usual wasn't just plain laziness, it was a relapse?

He deals in secrets.

I groan and bury my head back in my pillow. I'm too tired for this.

"You want me to keep showing up every night? You need to take care of yourself."

And then he had to go and say that.

"That's a low blow, Des," I mumble into my pillow. I crave his continued visits more than pretty much anything else in my life at the moment.

"Deal with it."

I turn my face to the side and grimace at him. "You're mean." He also looks hot enough to catch fire in a Metallica shirt that hugs his muscles and a pair of black jeans, his white-blond hair tied back from his face.

He folds his arms over his chest, cocking his head to the side. "You're just now figuring this out, cherub?"

No, I had him pegged from day one, but since meeting him, he's softened up to me.

"Now," he continues, "*up.*"

To emphasize his point, my bed begins to tilt, one side levitating. I start to slide off the mattress.

I curse, clutching the edges of it so that I don't roll right off. "All right, all right! I'm getting up!" I slide the rest of the way to the floor, glaring at him as I pad across the room.

Des folds his arms, glaring right back at me. The man is remorseless.

I open my drawers and begin removing clothing items. I move slowly, my eyelids still droopy, my body still tired and sore.

"This is never going to happen again, understand?" he says. "You're not going to stop living your life because some days are harder than others."

I look over my shoulder at him like he's crazy. "It's not like I want this!" For my mind to suck me back into the worst parts of my past. To feel dirty and tainted and unlovable.

Even my annoyance is a pitiful thing right now. I don't have the energy it takes to truly get worked up over this.

"You feel like this again, you get help, or you call me and *I'll* get you help, but from now on, you're going to do *something* about it, all right?" Des says. His eyes are hard; I'm not going to get any sympathy from him.

"You don't understand—"

"I don't?" He raises his eyebrows. "Tell me, cherub, what *do* I know?"

He's baiting me. It's so obvious. I don't dare go on,

because how much do I really know about the Bargainer? And how much does he really know about me?

So instead, I glare at him again.

"*Yes,*" he says, "that's what I want to see. Your anger, your fight." His tone softens. "I'm not asking you to never feel sad, Callie. I'm asking you to fight. Always fight. You can do that, can't you?"

I suck in a deep breath. "I don't know," I say honestly.

His entire demeanor gentles with that confession. "Can you try?"

I bite my lower lip, then reluctantly nod. If that's what it takes to keep him coming back, I can try.

He gives me a smile. "Good. Now get dressed. I'll get us breakfast before you have to go to class."

Des spends the rest of our odd morning together doing everything in his power to make me laugh. And it works.

I don't know how he does it, but the Bargainer beats back my mood. As far as Hail Mary days go, apparently Des is just the miracle I need.

Present

When I blink my eyes open, I stare up at an unfamiliar room. I look around at the deep blue walls, my brow creasing.

"You're awake."

I startle at the Bargainer's smooth voice. He sits in a chair next to the bed, his steepled hands pressed to his lips. On the bedside table next to him sits an empty tumbler.

"Where am I?" I ask.

"We're in my room—back on earth," Des says.

His room. The one he hadn't been willing to show me before now. My eyes sweep over my surroundings, over the framed photo of Douglas Café and another of Peel Castle. Across the room, a golden orrery sits on a circular table, the metal and marble planets in our solar system hanging suspended around the golden sun in the middle.

There's nothing about his bedroom that seems worth hiding from me.

And then, among my musings, my trip to the Otherworld all comes back to me.

Air hisses in between my teeth, and my gaze snaps back to the Bargainer. "Those *children*."

Des grabs his empty tumbler and heads to a wet bar on the opposite end of the room, pouring himself a drink. He throws it back quickly, hissing at the burn of alcohol. He looks at his glass. "I understand why you crave the stuff," he says. Carefully he sets the glass back down, leaning against the bar. "Gods." He runs a hand down his face. "I've never wanted to throttle children so badly as I did when I saw them grab ahold of you. Their fangs came out; they'd been ready to drink you."

I put a hand to my throat. They were going to drink from me? All I remember are strange, nightmarish images I saw when they touched me.

I swallow at the thought of those images. Were these the prophecies Gaelia had mentioned?

I slide out of his bed. "Des, they showed me things," I say. I rub the skin where they touched me, noticing the beginnings of several bruises. "I saw cages of women, a throne, a forest, and a man with antlers."

"A man with antlers," the Bargainer repeats, his face grim.

"Does that help?" I ask.

"Unfortunately, cherub," he says, "it does."

He will find you.

He always finds the ones he wants.

He's already begun the hunt.

He'll make you his, just like our mothers.

I sit inside Des's guestroom, my eyes absently staring out the window at the dark night.

What have I done? I thought I'd been helping Des—and Gaelia—by interviewing those kids. A part of me had been proud of the fact that they'd talked to me when the Bargainer had been so sure they wouldn't.

But now, like Gaelia, I feel deep in my bones that the children's words weren't empty. That, irrational though it might be, I'd just caught the attention of whatever *thing* Des has been hunting. Only now it's hunting me.

I draw in a deep, stuttering breath.

I need to leave this place—this *house*—with all its connections to the Otherworld. Hell, there's a portal a few doors down from my room. It doesn't matter if the creature lives in another realm; so long as it knows how to manipulate ley lines, it would only take an instant for it to come crawling to earth.

I begin changing into the now dry—if salt-encrusted— clothes I wore here and swipe up the few items that I came with.

I can feel the same paranoia that claimed the royal nursemaid now crawling up my spine.

I'm hooking in my earring when I hear the door to my room open and feel an ominous presence at my back.

"You're leaving."

A thrill races down my arms at that silky smooth voice.

I turn to the Bargainer. "I'm not staying here."

"Your ex will find you if you go back to your place." His arms are folded. He is obviously displeased.

"Who says I'm going back?" I totally am.

"Where else would you go?"

"I have friends." Okay, I have *a* friend. One. Temper. And she's probably furious with me at the moment for going AWOL on her.

"You're not going back to their places." It's not a command, just a statement of fact.

"So what if I go home?" I would much rather face off with Eli, who cares about me, who's hurt and angry, *who I can control if need be*, than stay here and chance meeting an enemy that not even Des understands.

The air stirs, and suddenly, the Bargainer is at my side, his lips pressed against my ear. "If you go home, I'll likely have to steal you back from your ex, and that will displease me *greatly*."

I turn to look at him. "At the moment, Des, your feelings aren't my biggest concern."

The Bargainer stares at me for a beat. "You're scared of staying here," he says, reading me. He tilts his head, his eyes narrowing. "You think I'd let anything happen to you in my house?" I swear the man grows bigger, his presence overwhelming.

Judging by the look in his eye, I've offended the King of the Night.

Whatever.

I tear my gaze away and head toward the door.

A second later, the Bargainer materializes in the doorway, blocking my exit. His hands grip the top of the doorframe. Unwillingly, my eyes move to those toned arms of his.

"What if I told you that you couldn't go?" he says, his voice hypnotic. "That I wanted you to stay and use up some more of my beads?"

"I wouldn't believe you," I say, calling his bluff. "Now please, move."

Des is staring at me strangely. He releases the doorframe and prowls forward. "Truth or dare?"

I back up, suddenly nervous at the look in his eyes. "Des…"

"*Dare*," he breathes.

In the next instant, he's on me, his hands roughly cupping my cheeks. His mouth crashes into mine, his lips demanding.

Des is kissing me, and *God*, is it savage.

I kiss him back without thinking, swept up into the taste of him and the feel of him holding me.

I'm supposed to be leaving, reclaiming my house and my life, but nope. It's not going to happen, not while Des is demonstrating all the ways my taste in men was spot-on when I was a teenager.

I'm backing up, and one of the Bargainer's hands has dropped to my thigh, exposed by the high slits of my dress. His fingers move up and down the skin, up and down.

My back bumps into the wall. Des cages me in, holding me hostage with his body. My lips part, and Des's tongue sweeps inside my mouth, claiming mine.

His hand moves to my breast, and I arch into him, my breath leaving me.

"*Gods*, Callie," he rasps. "The wait…nearly unendurable…"

Des's wings materialize, spreading out and closing over the wall around me. While I kiss him, I begin to run my fingertips over them.

He groans, leaning into my touch. "Feels too good."

He slips a hand beneath my shirt and palms a breast, making really hot noises into my mouth as he acquaints himself with it.

My knees go weak at his touch, and he slips a leg between them, holding me up.

My skin begins to glow. I want to cry, this feels so right.

"Truth or dare?" he whispers.

Do I even care at this point?

"Truth," I murmur against his lips, refusing to give in to my baser impulses.

He pulls away from the kiss long enough to glance down at my swollen lips, a hungry look in his eye. "What did you miss the most about me while I was gone?" he asks.

I have to breathe several times to collect myself. His question is like cold water dousing a flame. His magic encircles me, forcing the answer out. "Everything. I missed literally everything about you while you were gone."

Des stares at me, his chest rising and falling as he catches his breath. His hand slips out from beneath my shirt, and his knuckles stroke my cheek. "You don't know what your words do to me."

"I wish I did." All this giving on my end, all this taking on his. This isn't what healthy relationships are made of.

He runs his fingers down my arms. "Stay, and I will tell you."

What I would give for that. To know exactly how he feels about me. I almost fall for it, just as I have everything else about this man. I'm about to start nodding when I remember.

Des is a fairy, a trickster. He collects secrets for a living; he doesn't give them up. And he's never been open to me in the past. He's not going to start tonight.

I made a promise to myself back when Des first left my life, a promise to be independent. Not to allow men like him to destroy my world. And now the very man who forced me to make that promise wants to burrow his way under my skin and into my heart once more.

I'd be the worst sort of person if I broke that promise at the first sign of temptation.

I run my hands through my hair. What am I doing? Really, *what* am I doing? I search the ground, as though it holds the answers. Then, letting my hands fall to my sides, I push past him.

It's been a long fucking day. I want my comfy pj's, a bowl of cereal, and some trashy TV I can fall asleep to.

In front of me, the door to the guestroom slams shut.

Apparently what I want isn't going to be all that easy to get.

I turn, exasperated, only to yelp.

The Bargainer crowds me, looking like he's about to rain retribution down on my ass.

"Don't go," he says. Even though he looks mad, his words are soft.

That in and of itself makes me hesitate.

So close to giving in.

"Why, Des?" My eyes move over his face. I can still taste him on my lips. "Why do you want me to stay so badly?"

A muscle in his jaw feathers. There are a hundred plausible lies he can feed me, but he doesn't voice a single one.

I wait. And wait.

His answer never comes.

I sigh and turn around, heading to the door. The air thickens, the static electricity of it raising the hairs on my arm. That's my biggest cue that Des is displeased. I'm practically suffocating on his power.

When I glance back again, his wings are out. They keep flaring and retracting.

Not displeased, I correct. *Out of control.* He's about to lose his shit.

Half of me thinks he *won't* let me go. And a large, twisted part of me wouldn't entirely mind that.

Instead, the heaviness in the air dissipates, and his wings fold tight to his back.

"Fine, cherub. I'll take you home."

Once we touch down in my backyard, Des checks the perimeter of my house, then my rooms, a manic look in his eye.

I'm still too shocked by my surroundings to do much more than stare. I forgot I had a *grown werewolf* trapped on my property. My place is in tatters.

As the Bargainer moves through my house, his magic mends the worst of the damage. Shredded walls are fixed, and my smashed table snaps back into place, the splintered wood fitting itself back together like a jigsaw puzzle. Shattered glass lifts from the floor and returns to the windowpanes, the cracks smoothing over until the surface is whole once more.

Des comes into the living room, looking agitated, his towering frame full of pent-up energy. "Everything's clear," he reports, running a hand through his hair. "There were two Politia officers parked down the street, but I sent them off. You should be safe for another day."

A day is all I need to hunt down Eli's furry ass and then rip him a new one.

"Thank you," I say, motioning vaguely around me toward the damage he fixed, and for, you know, scaring off the supernatural police, who'd cart me off to jail the first chance they got. It's still surreal to think I'm currently on the wanted list.

The Bargainer hesitates, fighting to hold his tongue. I know he doesn't want me to be here.

"Stay safe, cherub," he finally says. "I'll be back tomorrow evening." He crosses the room, heading to the door out to my backyard, not sparing me another glance.

That shouldn't hurt. None of this should hurt. But it all does. I don't want him to go. My heart wants to give in to him even if my mind knows better.

Halfway to the door, he pauses. Swearing under his breath, he turns and stalks back to me. He wraps a hand around my waist and takes my lips savagely.

I gasp into his mouth as he grinds into me. The kiss is over as soon as it's begun.

He releases me roughly. "If you want to see me for any reason before tomorrow, you know how to get ahold of me." He backs up. "I'll be waiting."

And then he's gone.

CHAPTER 15

March, seven years ago

"Tell me about your mother," Des says across from me.

The two of us play poker and drink booze in my dorm room, while outside, a rainstorm batters against the windows.

The booze had been his idea. "A little corruption will do you good, cherub," he'd said when he'd appeared in my room with the bottle, winking at me.

I'd sputtered at the sight of the alcohol. "That's not allowed."

"Do I look like the kind of guy who follows the rules?" With his leather pants and inked arm on display, he most definitely didn't.

So reluctantly, I'd rinsed out my mug and my water glass and let the Bargainer pour us each a glass of "really fucking good" scotch.

It tastes about as good as a dirty rim job.

"My *mother*?" I now say as Des deals out a new hand.

I pick up my cards distractedly, until I see the hand he dealt me.

Three tens. For once, I have a chance at winning a round.

His eyes flick from me to the backs of my cards, then back to me. "Three of a kind," he says, guessing my hand.

I glance down at the tens in my hand. "You cheated."

He picks up his drink and takes a swallow, his muscular frame rippling in a very pleasing way as he does so. "If only. You're easy to read, cherub. Now," he says, setting down his glass. He looks coolly at his own cards. "Tell me about your mother."

I fold my hand, taking a sip of the scotch and wincing a little when it hits my tongue.

My mother's one of those subjects that I never talk about. What's the use? It's just one more sad story; my life has enough of them.

But the way Des is looking at me, I'm not going to casually be able to change the subject.

"I don't remember much about her," I say. "She died when I was eight."

Des is no longer paying attention to the game or the drink. Those two sentences are all it takes to divert his entire focus.

"How did she die?"

I shake my head. "She was murdered while she and my stepdad were on vacation. It was a mistake. They were aiming for my stepfather but ended up shooting her instead." My stepfather, who was a seer. He'd failed to foresee it—or maybe he had foreseen it but couldn't or wouldn't stop it.

Innocent or guilty, that night haunted him.

"Her death was why he drank." And his drinking was why...

I suppress my shudder.

"Where were you when this happened?" Des asks. He still has a calm, lazy look about him, but I swear it's just as much of an act as his poker face is.

"Home with a nanny. They liked to go on vacation without kids."

I know how my life sounds. Cold and brittle. And that was the truth of it. Technically, I had everything—looks and money to go along with them.

No one would suspect that there were long stretches of time when I was left alone in my stepfather's Hollywood mansion with only a nanny and my stepfather's driver to look after me. Business always came first.

No one would suspect that those long stretches of loneliness were so much better than when he returned from trips. He'd see me and fall right back into another bottle.

And then...

Well, those are more memories I try not to dwell on.

My skin still crawls anyway.

"Why was anyone trying to kill your stepfather?" Des asks, our game of poker utterly forgotten.

I shrug. "Hugh Anders liked money. And he didn't care who his clients were." Mafia bosses. Cartel lords. Terrorist groups. He brought enough of his work home for me to see it all. "It made him a very rich man, and it made him a lot of enemies."

Maybe that was why he had the Bargainer's calling card in his kitchen drawer. A man like my stepfather walked around with a target on his back.

"Did you ever do business with him—before you met me?" I ask.

I hadn't meant to voice that particular question, and now

I find myself holding my breath. I don't think he knew him. The Bargainer hadn't acted like he knew him when I first called on him, but Des was made of secrets. What if he had known my stepfather? What if he'd helped him, the guy who abused me? The man who either directly or indirectly caused my mother's death?

Just the possibility has my stomach turning.

Des shakes his head. "Never met the guy until he was swimming in a pool of his own blood."

The image of his dead body flashes before my eyes.

"How about your birth father?" Des asks. "What was he like?"

"A nobody," I say, peering into my glass. "My mother accidentally got pregnant when she was eighteen. I don't think she knew who the father was; he was never listed on my birth certificate."

"Hmm," Des murmurs as he absently swirls his drink, his gaze distant.

I don't know what he's thinking, only what I would be—that my parents sound like shitty people. My mother, who was interested in giving me a good life but didn't want much to do with it; my father, whose greatest contribution was his sperm; and my stepfather, who starred in all my most vivid nightmares.

"Why don't you tell me about your parents?" I say, eager to take the spotlight off myself.

Des leans back and squints at me, a slow smile curling his lips. I can't stop staring at him.

"We share similar tragedies, cherub," he says, still smiling, though now it seems a bit bitter.

My eyebrows raise at his words. A fae king sharing anything in common with his human charity case?

I find that doubtful.

He pushes himself to his feet. "I've got work to do. Keep the scotch—and for the love of the gods, practice drinking without wincing." He turns to the door.

I don't bother trying to convince him to stay, though I want to badly. I already know he won't. Especially not after our—*my*—little heart-to-heart. Sometimes I imagine the Bargainer's mind is a vault. Secrets go in and they don't come out.

He pauses, then gives me a look over his shoulder, and his expression says it all. I may not have told him about how my stepfather abused me, but he *knows*.

"For the record, cherub," he says, "if your stepfather were alive, he wouldn't be for long." There's steel in his eyes.

And then, like magic, he disappears into the night.

Present

I spend over an hour cleaning my place up. There's stuffing and wolf hair everywhere. Not to mention the claw marks. My coffee table and a side table have to be thrown out. At this point, they're nothing more than kindling.

Should've asked Des to magic the rest of this mess away.

But then, he'd been so broody; I hadn't wanted to push my luck.

Des. It's been less than two hours since he left, and I'm already restless to see him again. I miss his house, his macarons, his fluffy guest sheets.

I miss his smell and his touch. I miss *him*. It takes being back in my empty house to remember just how lonely I am. I'd forgotten that while I'd been with Des.

I do what I can to straighten my house up, trying really,

really hard not to think of the man who seemed like he didn't want to leave me earlier—not to mention the one who destroyed this place fighting for me.

I should just swear off men. Nothing but heartache comes of them.

Heartache and trouble. Now, on top of hiding from the supernatural authorities and an Otherworld monster, I have to buy new furniture because my ex broke one of the most important pact laws and visited me when he was on the shifter equivalent of his period.

Once I clean up the bulk of the mess, I turn my attention to my cracked cell phone, biting the inside of my cheek nervously. I've been putting this part off, but I can't any longer.

Plugging it in, I check my messages. Thirty-one texts and twenty-five missed calls. Some from Eli, a couple from various interested parties, but most from Temper.

I don't bother checking any of them before I tap on Temper's number and, taking a deep breath, call her back.

She answers on the first ring. "Where the *hell* are you, Callie?" she says, panicked.

"I'm back at home."

"Home? *Home?*" Her voice rises. "Your house was *ransacked*, there's a *bounty* out for your capture, and you're *home?*"

"It's fine. I'm fine."

"I thought you were *dead*." Her voice cracks and I hear her sniffle. "I couldn't find you." Temper's a pro at tracking people with her magic, but I never thought she'd use it to look for me.

"Are you...crying?" I ask.

"Of course not. I never cry," she says.

"I'm sorry I didn't call earlier. I really am okay," I say softly.

"What happened to you? You just fell off the map, and Eli's been blowing up my phone, but he won't tell me anything."

I press three fingers to my temple. "Um, it's a long story."

"*I've got time.*"

I sigh.

She huffs, her voice hiccuping a little. "Don't you *sigh*. I spent the last twenty-four hours thinking my best friend *died*."

"Temper, I'm sorry. I'm all right. I'm sorry and I'm alive." Obviously. But it feels important to reiterate the obvious.

"What happened?" she repeats. I can tell she's pacing by the subtle jangle of her jewelry. "I mean, the best possible scenario I could come up with was that you had some angry makeup sex with Eli and that...ohmygod he probably went beastie on you. That's so freaking gross." It all comes out in a rush. "And yeah. He shredded stuff up in the process."

I wince at that.

She lets out a breath. "Don't tell me he turned you. Please don't tell me that. I remember how much the thought frightened you. And if he has, so help me God, I will smite that hairy little shit and make a coat out of his fur. I swear I'll do it."

The line goes quiet, and it's just the sound of Temper's heavy breathing.

"Holy shit," I finally say. I clear my throat. "Um, no, we didn't have angry animal sex; no, Eli didn't turn me; and good lord, woman, please don't make my ex into a coat. He didn't hurt me."

"Then what *did* happen?"

It's only when she asks for a third time that I realize

I've picked up on some of the Bargainer's bad habits, like withholding secrets.

I glance down at my bracelet, which is missing over a row of beads. "Can you come over?" I ask.

"Is the sky blue?"

I give a shaky smile, even though she can't see it. "Good. I'll tell you when you get here."

Just like I promised myself, I fish out some comfort food and turn on a show that will rot my brain while I wait for Temper to get here.

None of it helps.

I'm disturbed by my trip to the Otherworld, I'm upset by what happened here in my house, but most of all, I'm annoyed that I keep replaying every single intimate thing Des has done since he came for me.

Ten minutes later, my front door opens, and I hear the *click-clack* of heels.

Temper stops in the entryway when she sees me, blinking rapidly. "*Callie.*"

We close the distance between us, hugging each other tightly. When we finally break apart, Temper sniffles, her gaze moving about my place. Her eyes linger on my restored table and the unbroken windows.

"I was here this morning," she says, brushing her braids away from her face. "Your kitchen table was broken."

"That's, uh, part of what I have to tell you about."

"I'm all ears." She sets down her stuff, then plops on my couch. A tuft of cotton flutters into the air as she does so.

Missed a spot.

Temper grabs my bowl of popcorn and begins eating

it. "Where's the booze?" she asks, looking around. Usually nights like this always have a beer or a glass of wine to accompany them.

Crap, she doesn't yet know.

"Um, I'm trying out this whole sober thing," I say, gingerly sitting down next to her.

She swivels to fully face me, popcorn forgotten. "Okay, *what* is going on?"

I scrub my face. "Way, way, waaaaaay too much."

Where to even start?

Dropping my hands, I glance down at my wrist. "You know this bracelet?" I begin, lifting my arm.

"Yessss." She has no idea where I'm going with this.

"Each one of these beads is an IOU." I run my thumb over them, not meeting her eyes. "I'm in a lot of debt."

She settles into the couch. "So pay it off," she says, and now she resumes eating my popcorn. "You have money." She snaps her fingers as an idea comes to her. "Or, better yet, glamour it away."

I clear my throat. "It's not that simple. I can't glamour this guy. And I am paying it off. That's why I've been gone."

Now she squints at me. "Who's the guy?"

I give a nervous laugh. "He's…um…he's the Bargainer."

It's quiet for several beats.

Temper raises her eyebrows. "Wait, *the* Bargainer? The same Bargainer who nearly killed that teacher a decade ago? The same guy who's been linked to over twenty disappearances? The same guy who's always at the top of the Politia's wanted list because that *same guy* is always breaking the law?"

"All that stuff is alleged," I say.

She snorts. "You and I both know that dude's not innocent."

"He's a decent guy." And he kisses like a rock star.

"You're defending him," she says, astounded.

"It's complicated."

"He's a *bad guy*, Callie. And this is *me* you're talking to. I *like* them bad. But even I think he's too naughty to tap."

I roll my lips together and stare down at my hands.

She takes one look at my face and blows out a breath. "Oh no, don't tell me you like him?"

I don't say anything.

"*You do*." She reaches over and grabs my hand. "Let me tell you a crappy truth—it always ends terribly with the bad ones."

Unfortunately for me, I already know that all too well.

———

It's deep night by the time I eventually go to sleep, my mind too consumed by my thoughts.

Earlier, I managed to fill Temper completely in, starting from eight years ago. She'd always known someone had broken my heart, but until tonight, she'd never known the details. I'd told her about my deal with the Bargainer and the mystery I'd gotten myself involved in, and lastly, I told her about Eli coming here during one of the Sacred Seven days and shifting on me.

Poor Eli. I'm no longer the only supernatural he's going to have a reckoning with. And personally, I'd be much more scared of Temper's wrath than mine.

Outside, the wind whistles against my windows, shaking the glass panes against their frames. It sounds like a dying creature. The waves crash angrily against the cliffs, the whole thing so loud that once I do fall asleep, it becomes the soundtrack to one anxious dream after another.

I hear those fae children in my head.

He's coming for you. Coming to get you.

Their hands hold me in place while something in the distance creeps closer. Closer.

The moaning wind is speaking to me. Humming.

"*Fee, fi, fo, fin, I caught the scent of a sweet siren. Fey, fi, fah, fing, I'll pluck her feathers and make my bird sing.*"

I try to pull against the children's hold, but I'm stuck. I stare out my window, and I swear I see a dark silhouette against the night.

I drift, lost in the sea of my mind.

The doors and windows rattle. "*Let me in, siren. I'll give you wings to fly.*" I swear I can hear the voice right in my ear. "*Just open your door and part your pretty thighs.*"

My exhale echoes in the still air.

"*Callypso, it won't be long…*"

And then the strange dream evaporates away.

———————

I rub my eyes as sunlight streams into my room. My nose itches as a soft feather flutters down it.

Scrubbing my face, I glance at the clock next to my bed. Two p.m.?

I hadn't planned on sleeping that long. Then again, for most of the night, I wasn't really sleeping so much as gliding through one unsettling dream after the next.

I throw the covers off me, causing dozens of feathers to flutter into the air.

I make a face. Not the bedspread too.

Eli must've shredded my comforter. I hadn't realized…

I push out of bed, more feathers scattering along the floor. Ugh.

I lift up a foot, peeling the little bastards off my skin,

when I really take notice of the feathers littering my floor. Hundreds and hundreds of them are arranged in lines that arc away from my bed.

I back up, tilting my head.

When I see it, my blood runs cold.

It's a wing. The feathers are laid out in the shape of a *wing*.

Someone was in here. In my house. In my bedroom. Someone stood near me while I slept and meticulously placed hundreds of feathers.

I round the bed, my skin beginning to crawl, only to see another identical wing arcing from the other side of it.

I put a hand to my mouth. My heart feels like it's going to pound out of my chest.

Where did all the feathers come from?

I lunge for my bedspread and yank it down. But it's not the comforter that's been torn open.

The fitted sheet and the mattress are in shreds. Right where I slept. And I know for a fact it wasn't like that when I went to bed last night.

I can't wrap my mind around the horror of it. The invasiveness. Someone had practically reached under me to rip open my mattress and extract all those feathers.

How could I not wake up?

My breaths come faster and faster; I can't take in enough air. I back up, nearly tripping on my own feet.

I open my mouth, the words coming out almost reflexively. "Bargainer, I want to—"

Des materializes before I finish my sentence.

At first, he has eyes only for me. And he looks so damn happy—happy that I called him.

But then he notices the feathers. The fucking feathers, which are *everywhere*.

"What happened." It's not even a question; it's a threat to whoever did this. The edge in his voice makes the back of my neck prickle.

I'm shaking my head. "I don't know."

He walks around the bed, studying the patterns. He almost manages to pull off looking calm, but I can see the dark outline of his wings.

He places a hand on the mattress, gathering a fistful of feathers. "They did this while you slept?"

"Yes," I croak out. My voice sounds embarrassingly weak. Scared.

I hug my arms across my chest. I feel violated in my own home, my sanctuary.

Des drops the feathers and stalks to the other side of the room, checking the doors. From what I can tell, they're still locked.

He drags a hand down his mouth. I feel his magic then, building and building. Strands of my hair begin to lift at the static electricity in the air.

"You're under my protection," he says. "You have been for a very long time. Whoever did this was capable of sensing that."

As he speaks, the floorboards shiver beneath his feet and the glass panes behind him begin to rattle as they did last night. I hear one of them fissure.

"No one—*no one*—touches the people under my protection." His wings flicker in and out of existence with his words.

I'm woman enough to admit that right about now, I'm a little scared of Des. I can feel his fury riding the magic in the room. This is one of those moments when I have to recognize that fairies are very different from humans. Their anger is bigger and more ferocious than anything a human can conjure. And they're so much quicker to snap.

Des's face contorts into something merciless, and I'm pretty sure he's close to completely losing it.

"Please don't kill anyone on my behalf," I say. It's nearly happened before.

He laughs, but it's angry. "All the beads in the world couldn't make me agree to that." The Bargainer comes back over to me, clasping my wrist between his hands. His face still looks furious, but the longer he stares at me, the more that fury melts away. "Now, cherub." His words roll off his lips like honey. "The first repayment of the day: you're coming home with me, and you're not leaving until your debts have *all* been paid."

CHAPTER 16

March, seven years ago

Des sits on my desk, one of his boots perched on the back of my computer chair. He leans back against my window, sketching. Students walking to and from the dorms right now should be able to clearly see him. I live on the second story of the girls' dormitory, and my room faces out onto campus. Anyone loitering outside tonight should be able to see Des's big, hulking back.

But they don't. And I know they don't because if they did, our dorm's house mother would be up my ass in about two seconds tops.

The visiting hours here ended long ago.

Which means the Bargainer is masking his presence here yet again.

"What's wrong?" Des asks, not looking at me. He continues drawing, using the sketchbook and charcoal I recently bought him.

The sight wouldn't be so strange if the charcoal and sketchbook were in his hands. But they aren't. Instead, they float in midair three feet from him, and Des's drawing is coming to life without him ever touching it. His arms are folded firmly over his chest.

"Nothing," I say.

"Liar."

I sigh out a breath, staring at his drawing from where I lie on my bed. "Are you embarrassed to be seen with me?" I ask.

"What?" The charcoal comes to a stop.

My cheeks are beginning to flush. This is humiliating. "Are you embarrassed to be seen with me?" I repeat.

The Bargainer turns to me, frowning. "Why would you ask something like that?"

I feel my stomach plummet. He isn't denying it. "Oh my God, you *are*."

He disappears from his perch only to appear right next to me. A moment later, his sketchbook and charcoal hit the floor behind him.

"Cherub," he says, taking my hand, "I have no idea where you got this mad, mad idea. Why the hell would I be embarrassed to be seen with you?"

And just like that, my worry dissipates. I think I hate myself a little that Des has so much control over my emotions.

"You always use your magic to hide yourself around me," I say.

He squeezes my hand, and I feel his touch all the way to my toes. "Callie, you have this absurd notion that I'm a good person, when I'm at the top of the Politia's wanted list. There are bounty hunters looking for me this very moment. They're not the only ones either; I have clients and enemies who would happily use you to get to me. Masking my presence is second nature, especially around you."

That makes sense.

He hasn't let go of my hand, nor has he left the side of my bed. It's like we are poised right at the edge of something, and the longer he stares at me, the further I begin to tip over the edge.

His silver eyes darken, and I suck in a breath at the look. I've seen that molten expression on a few men before.

But they were never Des.

My pulse begins to race.

I'm pinwheeling over the edge, falling into those eyes, that face.

If only what I liked about Des ended at that face. Then it might be easier to deny what I feel for him. But the thing is, the Bargainer saved my life months ago, and he's continued to save it every day since. I like that he's fucked up like me, that he's wicked and sinful and makes no excuses for it. I like that he doesn't care that I might be a little wicked and sinful too.

I like that he's taught me how to play poker and that I've made him watch the Harry Potter movies…and read the books. I like that I get to travel the world with him every time he decides to take me on one of his bargains, that my room has become a collection of knickknacks of us.

I like that he drinks espresso in tiny little cups and that I can share my secrets with him, even if he keeps most of his to himself. He's the highlight of my evenings.

Scratch that—he's the highlight of my life.

And I'm content to be his friend, but tonight while he looks at me like that, I want more.

"Stay the night," I whisper.

Des's mouth parts, and I swear—*I swear*—I see a *yes* forming on his lips.

He blinks a few times, and just like that, the moment's gone.

He clears his throat, releasing my hand. "Cherub, that's inappropriate."

The Bargainer begins to stand, his impressive stature unfolding before my eyes.

I scramble to my feet as well. "Please don't."

We're beginning to sound like a broken record. I push him too far, and he flees. The scariest thing of all? The more distance he puts between us, the more desperate I am to close it, and the more I try to close it, the further away I push him.

I'm losing my best friend, and we both know it.

Des drops his hands. "Callie, if I stay, I give in. If I leave, I don't."

Then just give in.

But he doesn't, and he won't. Because despite everything the Bargainer says about himself, he's an honorable man when it comes to me. And that really is the root of our problems. He might actually be the best man I know.

Present

Well, shit.

Out of the frying pan and into the fire. That's all I can think about on the flight over to Catalina Island.

We land in front of Des's embarrassingly impressive house, and I walk out of his arms without a word. I can feel him at my back, his gaze assessing me.

The devious fucker is surely trying to figure out how to best approach me.

He's going to have to keep puzzling over it. Even *I* am not sure how to best approach me right now, because I have no idea what exactly I'm feeling.

Annoyance, definitely. My leash just got a lot tighter. Anger—and incredulity—that the Bargainer actually forced me to move in with him for the foreseeable future. Depending on how slowly he makes me pay off my debt, I could potentially live under his roof for the rest of my life.

I ignore the spark of excitement that comes with that thought; my heart is obviously an idiot.

Beneath all these frustrated emotions, there's relief. Relief that I didn't have to cave to my ego and stay inside a house that felt unsafe or swallow my pride and beg this man to let me stay with him again so soon after I left.

"I have no regrets, you know," he says behind me, his even voice carrying across the yard.

Ignoring him, I head up his stone steps and into his palatial house.

"Breakfast and coffee," I say. "I can't be civil with you until I have some breakfast and coffee."

I feel a hand on my back as the Bargainer materializes next to me. "Then let's get the lady what she wants. I have just the thing for you…"

Douglas mother-freaking Café. That's what he was hinting at earlier.

"It's been…years," I say, looking around the familiar café. The place looks unchanged, from the polished wood tables to the framed photos of the harbor to the glass case filled with pastries.

When Des led me to his portal room, I was more than

a little reluctant to venture down one of his ley lines again. But when we stepped off the line and onto the Isle of Man, my opinion did a one-eighty.

Outside the café, the sky is dark. It might be afternoon in Southern California, but it's already evening here on the British Isles.

Des leans back in his seat, stirring his coffee idly. Something a lot like nostalgia tightens my throat. Des used to take me here whenever he got bored of sitting around my dorm room.

His gaze follows mine to each detail of the café. "Did you miss this place?" he asks.

"Not as much as the company," I admit.

He looks almost pained at that.

"Why did you leave, Des?" I whisper. We're going to have to go over all this at some point if we're living under the same roof.

His expression turns grim. "*That* is a conversation for another time."

I almost groan in frustration. "It's been so long, what does it matter?"

I'm such a goddamn liar. It still matters. Desmond Flynn is a wound that's never healed.

"It matters" is all he says, echoing my thoughts.

Beautiful, frustrating man. He's eyeing me like a cornered animal would. That's never a good position to put a super-natural in, especially a fae king.

I know all this, and yet I still can't let the subject go.

"Tell me," I insist.

He rubs his eyes, hissing out a breath. "It's not in my nature to tell you. *None of this* is in my fucking nature. I will explain it all when the time's right."

All my hopes plummet at that. "Des, it's been *seven years*. How long do I have to wait for the time to be right?"

The atmosphere at our little table darkens. "Do you even *know* the meaning of waiting?"

I reel back at the bite in his words.

He leans his forearms on the table, a lock of his white hair escaping the leather thong he tied it back in. "Seven years, Callie, and how many of them did you spend single?" He seems to swell with the emotion in his voice.

"*What?*" I reel back, eyeing him. "What does that have to do with anything?"

"*Everything.*"

Is Des...jealous?

"Tell me," he repeats, the shadows deepening in the room, "how many years of those were you single?"

I'm still staring at him, dumbfounded. Of all the millions of ways I could spend my day, I hadn't imagined this would be one of them.

Des grabs my wrist, taking hold of a bead. "Answer me."

The words are ripped from my throat. "None of them."

Ugh. Fuck magic. And fae debt collectors.

"None of them," the Bargainer repeats, angry but satisfied. He releases my wrist.

I glare. "And I expect you kept your hands to yourself as well?" I've heard enough stories about the King of the Night and his revolving door of women. "You *asshole*. You *left* me. You broke my heart and you left me. You don't get to be jealous of what came after that."

He leans forward, his face menacing. "I didn't *leave* you, Callie."

Now I'm pissed. "You fled my room that night after the dance. Tell me how that's not leaving."

"You don't know anything."

"*Then enlighten me.*"

We stare each other down. Shadows are collecting around us as Des's emotions get the better of him. The other patrons don't notice it, thanks to the dim lighting and the night sky outside, but I do.

Just seeing him this worked up should be satisfying, but under my anger, I'm baffled by it. He left all those years ago, and now he's insisting he didn't. And it's been so long that I'm wondering if I am remembering incorrectly.

But no, that particular night is burned into my brain.

I wait for him to explain himself, but as usual, it doesn't come. I push away my drink and the last of my croissant, losing my appetite.

His eyes linger on the action. "Cherub, what happened last night?"

"You're going to have to take a bead if you want any answers out of me," I snap, annoyed. If he's going to fight explaining himself, then I sure as hell will as well.

A little bit of the anger dies in his gray eyes, replaced by that curving smirk. This, he likes. My feistiness, my engagement.

He wraps his hand around my bracelet, and briefly my gaze flicks to his elaborate sleeve of tattoos.

"Tell me what happened last night," he repeats, and this time there's magic behind his words.

I shudder as it takes hold, and instantly I regret baiting him. "Nothing."

I begin to feel pressure against my windpipe.

"My magic seems to disagree," the Bargainer says.

I want to groan. "What else do you want me to tell you?

After you left, I cleaned up my house, hung out with my friend for a few hours, and went to bed early. When I woke up, I found my bedroom exactly how you saw it."

Des resumes stirring his coffee. "My magic isn't releasing you, so you might try thinking a little harder."

I narrow my eyes at him.

He raises an eyebrow. "Or you can slowly suffocate. Your choice."

"I don't know what you want me to say," I wheeze. "I watched TV, I went to sleep, I woke up on a shredded bed."

Still no relief. And now I feel like just another of the Bargainer's clients, squirming under his power.

He takes a sip of his coffee. "What happened in the time between you going to bed and you waking up?"

I give him a bewildered look. "I slept."

The magic presses down my chest.

"Soundly? Fitfully?" he probes. "Did you have nightmares?"

I remember the storm that shook the house and the moaning wind that invaded my sleep.

"I did dream," I say.

Is there a tad less pressure on my chest?

"About what?" Des presses.

I try to remember. It's just out of reach.

"Since when do you read into dreams?" I say.

"Since always. I am the King of the Night. I rule over everything that encompasses, including dreams."

That makes some sort of sense.

I grab my drink and stare down into it, shaking my head. "I don't know. Those children I met, they were there, holding me down. And there was a voice—a male voice."

What had he said?

Let me in, siren. I'll give you wings to fly. Just open your door and part your pretty thighs.

My cheeks heat.

Jesus.

"What did the voice say?" Des asks.

"I'm not repeating that in public."

The fae king looks intrigued.

Now that I recall the dream, the magic intensifies like it knows I'm willfully withholding the information.

When I still don't answer, his eyes move over me. "You're really going to hold out, babe?"

Not for long. The magic's squeezing the life out of me.

"Not in public." I'm nearly begging.

The Bargainer studies me for a moment longer. He snaps his fingers, and the noise around us lowers, becoming muffled. "That's as much privacy as you're going to get."

It's enough. Well, to be honest, it's *not* enough—I don't exactly want to admit the content of my dreams to Des—but I've already admitted I want his babies, so there's really nothing left of my pride to protect.

I stare down into my drink. "He said, 'Let me in, siren. I'll give you wings to fly. Just open your door and part your pretty thighs.'"

The pressure leaves my chest.

Finally.

Around us, the noise rises once more.

Across from me, Des's shadows are back. Moody man.

"You never saw who spoke?" he asks.

I shake my head and take a sip of my drink. I set the mug down gingerly. "Are you actually taking my dream seriously?" I ask.

Des runs a thumb over his lower lip. "Perhaps," he says

distractedly. "In the Otherworld, dreams are never just dreams. They're another sort of reality."

I let that sink in. "You...you think something from the Otherworld visited me last night?"

"I don't know."

I might have a fae stalker.

One that can infiltrate my dreams.

I feel so *dirty*. Dirty and vulnerable. My mind can be manipulated by some creature, and I can't do anything to stop it. I thought staying back at my home would offer me some extra measure of protection, but it didn't.

"You think this has anything to do with the disappearances?" I ask now.

I'm sitting on the Bargainer's couch, watching him as he paces back and forth across the room, his arms behind his back.

He cuts a glance my way and, frowning, gives me a jerky nod.

Well, shit.

How many times had Temper and I dealt with a similar situation? How many criminals had threatened us over the years?

Countless. And when that happened, the only surefire way to guarantee our safety was to nab the bad guy before they got to us.

I take a deep breath. "I want to help you solve this case. Not just interview servants but actually solve it." *Before my stalker makes good on his promises.*

Des stops pacing. "You wish to help me and my people?" He gives me a strange look.

I shift a little on his couch, made uneasy by the odd intensity in his eyes.

"That's not what I said."

He prowls closer to me, tilting his head like he can divine my secrets from my face. "But you mean to." He reaches the couch, looking down at me. "Helping me any more than you already have will place you in danger—danger that even my protection might not save you from. We can find other ways for you to repay your debts."

"This isn't about repayment," I say.

His eyes deepen. Almost reluctantly, he tears his gaze from mine, rubbing his chin. His shadows have lovingly wrapped themselves around my legs.

"I should say no," he muses aloud. "There are so many reasons why I should say no." His eyes slide to mine. "Even knowing the danger, you're still interested in helping me?" he asks.

I hesitate, then nod, squeezing my thighs. Am I frightened? Of course. But that's never stopped me in the past from taking on a case.

"All right, cherub, we'll figure this out. Together."

CHAPTER 17

March, seven years ago

My stepfather is alive.

I stare in horror at him as he picks his bloody body off the ground, his neck wound still gushing.

I knew it. I knew he'd come back. Hugh Anders was too big, too terrible, too powerful to be killed.

I stumble back as his eyes focus on me, and there's such murderous rage in them. He'd never looked at me like that when he was alive. There was a different sort of sickness to his gazes then.

But now that I killed him, things are a little different.

"No," I breathe. I'm covered in his blood and still edging away from him. My heel slides in a puddle of it, and I lose my footing.

My elbow hits the ground first, the impact making my teeth click.

The monster is *alive*. It's not over. It's never going to be over. He's been killing me slowly since I was twelve. He's simply here to finish the job.

He stalks toward me, blood still pouring from his neck wound.

I scramble backward as he keeps coming at me.

"You thought you could kill me?" he says, "*Me?*"

Oh God, oh God, *oh God.*

He's going to lay his hands on me. I'm not going to escape this house, not ever.

There are drumbeats in the background. Or maybe that's my pulse.

He reaches for me.

The noise swarms around me. Louder, louder, louder. It's all I hear.

And then it shatters.

"Callie, Callie, Callie," he says. "Callie, Callie, Callie—"

"*Callie, wake up!*"

I gasp, my eyes snapping open.

Gazing down at me, the Bargainer looks half-mad, his jaw clenched impossibly tight and his brows sitting heavily above his wild eyes. His pale hair hangs loose around his face.

I suck in a heaving breath, wiping away the moisture on my cheeks.

A nightmare. It was nothing more than a nightmare.

Des's hands grip my upper arms, and now I reach out and squeeze his hard forearms, just to make sure he's real.

I'm breathing heavily, and now we search each other's eyes. He's seeing everything in mine—all the dark little pieces of me that I lock away during the day. Deep in the night, they get stripped away.

I hate it, that he's seeing how scared I am of my past.

But I'm also seeing things I shouldn't be seeing in his expression. Like fear, concern. He's all raw edges right now.

"He's gone, Callie," the Bargainer says. "He's gone and he's not coming back."

I don't bother asking how he knows any of this. I simply nod. It's the thing he and I don't talk about.

Then awareness seeps in. Des is mostly on my bed, and our hands are all over each other. If he were anyone else, his presence would scare the living shit out of me.

But Des is…Des is my moonlight.

A chilly breeze raises my gooseflesh, and I look past him, toward the window above my desk. Only a few jagged pieces of glass are still lodged in the frame. The rest of the windowpane is scattered in shards on my floor.

I blink a few times, then turn back to the Bargainer.

He lifts a hand to the mess, and the shards of glass rise into the air. Piece by piece, they fit themselves back together until the pane of glass is whole once more. "I used the window."

"You *flew*?" I ask, skeptical and a little curious. I've still never seen what his wings look like.

He gives a slight nod.

"You wouldn't wake up," he says, and I hear a thread of concern in his voice.

I don't usually wake up. Not when I'm that far under the pull of my nightmares. I have to let them play out.

"How did you know?" I ask. "About the nightmare, I mean."

He's still searching my face, like he's trying to make certain I'm okay. "It doesn't matter." He releases my arms. "Scoot over." I do so, and he settles in next to me, his back resting against my headboard. "The guy was a real asshole, wasn't he?"

I know he means my stepfather.

I work my jaw, then nod.

I swear the shadows in the room deepen, and I remember all over again who's next to me, hogging all the room on the mattress. For several seconds, we're both quiet as the darkness lays claim to my dorm room.

My pulse is pounding, partly from the aftertaste of my dream and partly from Des showing up out of nowhere like some kind of dark savior. And now he's a hairsbreadth away from...something. Anger, madness, retribution—I still can barely read the man.

"Rest easy, cherub," he says. Then, softer, "I won't let anyone else hurt you." The violence that laces his voice... it's another reminder of how fierce he can be and how well earned his reputation is.

"You're...staying?" I say, brushing some sweaty strands of hair from my face.

He was pretty adamant about not sleeping over only a couple of weeks ago.

He's quiet for so long that I assume he's not going to answer me.

"Yeah," he eventually says, "I am."

Present

"So what's our next move?" I ask, my eyes drifting over the framed photos in the Bargainer's living room.

Des sits down next to me on the couch and pinches his lip. "Tomorrow, I'd like to show you the sleeping warriors."

Unwillingly, a shiver courses through me. Just because I agreed to this doesn't mean I'm thrilled to return to Des's kingdom. But sitting around and letting someone fuck with me while I sleep isn't a good option either, so…

"Do you think me seeing the women will help us figure out what's going on?" I ask.

He stares at my lips. "No," he says plainly, "but I'll show you them nonetheless."

I look around us, at his living room. "And after that?"

The corner of his mouth curves up. "I'll give you my case notes to read over, and we'll go from there. Other than that, you'll pay off your debt and make yourself at home."

Caught in the spider's web. Isn't that what I felt last time Des brought me here? That every single thing that happened forwarded some interest of his, and I was hopeless to know what it was.

I take in his strange fae beauty. He belongs to a race of beings that kills savagely, *brutally*. Forcing me to live under his roof and play his games day in and day out isn't particularly cruel or out of character.

"Do I literally have to sleep inside your home every single night?"

"Don't worry about that, cherub."

I laugh humorlessly. "That's not an answer, Des. What happens when I leave your house to stay the night with a friend? Am I going to spontaneously die?"

"A *friend*?" he asks derisively. "Is that what you call your men? Friends?"

Your men?

The only reason I haven't launched myself across the couch and throttled Des is because, like earlier today, I detect jealousy in his voice, and that throws me off.

I narrow my eyes at him. "You're presuming a fucking lot right now," I say. "I was talking about Temper, my *completely platonic* best friend, you ass." She and I had sleepovers from time to time. So sue us for not wanting to grow up.

A corner of his mouth curls up. "You won't spontaneously die. My magic understands nuances."

Judging by how weirdly upset he got just now, I bet those nuances don't count *my men*.

My heart begins to pound as the reality of my situation sets in.

Living with the Bargainer.

How is this going to work, practically speaking? What if paying off my debt does take years? What if I have to watch Des date other women? What if I date other men?

Living together is going to be b-a-d.

Bad. Bad. Bad.

I slip back into my bedroom, pulling out the phone I remembered to pack earlier when I left my place with Des. I scroll down to Temper's number.

Considering that I now temporarily live on an island, I have to get my affairs in order. Namely, I have to warn Temper that I'll be out of the office for a bit.

I don't think too closely on how long *a bit* might actually be.

You knew that one day, this was going to come, I admonish myself.

I'd been prepared for the possibility that I would have to leave West Coast Investigations while I paid off my debt to the Bargainer. It doesn't make me any less sad.

"Hey, chick," she answers. "What's up?"

We've been texting each other back and forth all day, so she knows I'm alive and well and free of the Politia's clutches. But she doesn't yet know I now live with Des, largely because I'm a coward, and I didn't know how to break the news to her.

"Hey, Temper." I rub my forehead, trying to keep my voice light.

"Callie, you missed a good day. That hundred-thou client that called in asking for you? Well, today he came in, and my God, the dude is a *looker*. No wedding ring either."

I bite my thumbnail. It's the perfect segue, and yet I don't interrupt her.

"You need to get yourself off that wanted list," she continues, "because the way this guy keeps asking about you, I'm starting to think he's interested in mixing a little business with pleasure—and you'd have to be dead to not want this one."

"You should take him," I say, and then I wince.

She snorts. "Listen, if he were open to it, the agreement would be signed, sealed, and delivered. He was adamant about working with you."

"About that..." I take a deep breath. "I'm going to have to take a leave of absence."

"And this is news how?" Temper says.

I pull the phone away and stare at it for a moment. That was not the response I'd imagined.

"Callie, you're on the wanted list," she continues. "I understand. I've taken on your cases until you can come back."

I sag against the nearby wall. The wanted list. Of course.

"Temper, I love you."

"Of course you do. I love you too. Now"—I can hear her shuffling in her office—"I still think you should get ahold of this client. Want me to give you his number?"

"No," I hurry to say. I didn't want to worry about clients on top of everything else.

"You're right." I can almost see her nodding to herself. "Too dangerous. He could narc on you."

I don't bother mentioning that this call can also be traced. These are all things that both Temper and I are well aware of. The thing is, when you have powers like ours, dealing with pesky things like phone records is child's play.

"Temper," I say, my voice going low and a little hoarse, "I might be gone for a long time."

"You won't. I'm already working on removing your name, and once Eli gets back, I'll make sure that whatever strings he's pulled, *he unpulls them.*"

I wince at the threat in her voice.

"Temper, it's not just the wanted list. I wish it was just that." I gather together my courage. Now for the hard part. "You might have to find a replacement."

The line goes quiet for several seconds.

Finally, "No."

Temper's tone raises goose bumps along my arms. I know that if I were in her office, the place would be vibrating with her magic. This is but a glimpse of her magnificent and malevolent power.

"All right, all right," I say, backing off on the subject. "You don't have to find anyone else, but the thing is…the Bargainer has recruited me to help him with a string of disappearances in the Otherworld, and while this is happening, I'll be staying with him."

Silence. But this time, when the line goes quiet, it doesn't feel ominous like it had moments ago. It feels…judgy.

"What?" I finally say.

"Nothing."

I roll my eyes. "Just say it."

"Nothing."

I wait.

She clears her throat. "Now you're sleeping over at the Bargainer's place?"

"Not by choice!"

"Mm-hmm."

"Oh my God, Temper—"

"Just tell me the truth: Are you bobbing for this guy's bananas? Is that what this is about?" she asks.

"No, no, it's *not* like that. This is strictly professional."

Liar.

She snorts, seeing right through me. "Does *he* know that?"

"Um…" I don't really know how the Bargainer feels.

"Okay, babe, let's regroup for a reality check: You're a hot siren. He's a bad guy. Like I've-had-nightmares-of-him bad. He wants your goods. Hell, I want your goods, and I'm straight as an arrow. So if you stay there, you know what's going to happen, I know what's going to happen, Jesus knows what's going to happen, and most importantly, the Bargainer knows what's going to happen: you and he are going to get some serious nookie."

"Temper," I groan.

"Don't even act like it isn't true. And as for your leave of absence, I'm *not* filling in your position. Do what you need to do to get out of there, *or I'll make it happen*."

———

That evening, I sit with Des in his dining room, Temper's earlier words echoing in my mind.

She just might be powerful enough to take on the Bargainer, and that frightens me.

Perhaps I should just give in to his dares. I'd get rid of beads quicker that way. And physically, I'd enjoy myself—oh,

222

would I enjoy myself. With Des, I'm not scared of getting intimate. I'm scared of the fall that's sure to follow.

Across the table littered with takeout food, the man himself leans back in his chair, his legs splayed open wide, his face all insolent beauty. This is his broody, regal look. All he needs is his crown.

My gaze moves around us. Des's formal dining room is almost fantastical. Carved onto the chairbacks are all sorts of scenes from what I can only guess are fairy tales. Above us, candles flicker from a hammered bronze chandelier, and the walls are painted with scenes from a moonlit garden.

Hard to imagine that this man—this *thug*—commissioned someone to design his dining room like this. It looks like ovaries exploded all over it. Sleek, sophisticated ovaries, but ovaries nonetheless.

Sitting with my heels kicked up on his table, I pick up a carton of lo mein. I dip my chopsticks in and expertly scoop out several noodles.

I pause, midbite, when I realize Des is just watching me, his expression fascinated.

"What?" I glance down at my chest, just to make sure I haven't spilled food on myself.

It was the Bargainer's idea to pick us up some Chinese, but he hasn't touched his food since we sat down.

"You've changed."

I have changed, haven't I? Somewhere along the way, I'd gotten a little more hardened. Maybe it was Des leaving, maybe it was my line of work, or maybe it was just growing up.

I eye him. "Should I be offended?"

"Not at all, cherub. I find all versions of you quite… intriguing."

Intriguing. That was one way of putting it.

I raise my eyebrows as I dip my chopsticks into the carton again. "You haven't changed much," I say.

"Should I be offended by that?" Des echoes my words, his voice huskier than usual.

I set down the white carton and push the last of the food away.

"No," I say.

He shouldn't be offended, but I should be worried. The same things that made me fall for him long ago are getting to me all over again.

"Hmm," he says, holding my stare for several seconds.

Then, with a wave of his hand, the cartons of takeout disappear from the dark wood table.

"You didn't want any?" I ask.

"I'm not hungry."

Then why is he here with me?

"You didn't have to sit with me," I say. "I'm no longer a needy teenager."

I cringe to think of that girl who carelessly collected beads from the Bargainer to get a few hours with him.

"Trust me, I know."

Silence falls thick over us. In the past, it had never been this way. Then, the silence was always comfortable. Hell, there were evenings I'd ask him to stay and we wouldn't talk at all.

But now the two of us have all this unresolved *baggage*.

"What are we doing here?" I finally ask.

Anything to lift this weight off my chest.

The Bargainer crosses his muscular arms over his chest. "You're repaying your debts."

"Stop it, Des," I say. "You and I both know that's not what I meant. Last night, you were going to tell me."

He leans forward, resting his forearms on the edge of the table. "But only if you stayed, Callie. You didn't stay."

"I could say the same for you." All those lost years. "Do you even like me?"

"I've kissed you, I've begged you to stay with me, and I've spent most of the last week with you. What do you think?" he says softly.

How can an answer manage to be everything I want to hear while also making me want to pull my hair out?

"What do I think?" I say, swinging my legs off the table so that I can lean forward. "It doesn't *matter* what I think. That's all I've been doing for the last seven years—thinking about what went wrong. I'm tired of trying to figure you out."

Des stands, towering over me even from across the table. He rests his hands against the surface. "There is something, Callie, that you've never asked me: how I felt about our seven years apart."

The audacity! "That's *exactly* what I've been asking you," I say.

"No, you've been trying to figure out why I left. Not how I felt."

Only a fairy would make this sort of distinction. And for my part, I always assumed that how he felt was tied up in why he left.

"Ask me, Callie," he says softly, his luminous eyes beseeching me.

Just looking at him...it's hard not to be sucked in by his ferocious beauty and his velvety voice. It's all so achingly familiar.

And now he's trying to deconstruct our past and make it something it wasn't. And I'm just enough of a sucker to allow it to happen.

I can't believe I'm about to say this. "How did you feel, leaving me?" I ask.

He holds my gaze. "Like my soul was ripped in two."

I still.

Is he serious?

I feel like my world's being overturned.

"And the seven years that followed?" I breathe.

He stares at me, unwavering. "A nightmare."

He's taking a hammer to the walls I've built around my heart, and he's systematically smashing them down. And I want him to. If what he's saying is true, then maybe I do want him to get past all my defenses.

By his own admission, his experience sounds worse than mine.

"If it was so bad, why didn't you just come back to me?" I ask, my voice pleading.

The Bargainer opens his mouth, and I think he's going to answer, when instead he says, "Truth or dare?"

You have *got* to be kidding me.

"Seriously, Des?"

Just when the two of us begin to disambiguate our relationship, he stops it dead in its tracks.

"Do this for me, and I'll give you something in return."

"Fine," I say, fixing him with a challenging look. "*Dare.*"

His lips curl up into a satisfied smile, relishing my answer.

"Do something to me that you've always wanted to do."

Well, shit.

That's what I get for daring the King of the Night.

I swallow.

There are so many inappropriate responses to that command. Because there have always been an unending list of things I wanted to do with Des.

Des waits for me, his arms hanging loosely at his sides.

Gingerly I walk around his dining room, his magic compelling me onward.

This is going to be embarrassing.

I stop in front of him. When I glance up, he wears a serious expression.

My gaze drops to his jaw. That strong, razor-sharp jaw of his. Carefully, I wrap an arm around his neck and pull his face closer to me. He bends to accommodate me.

Our eyes meet briefly, his glittering as he stares at me.

This feels too raw. Like we aren't bound by debts. Like I'm something other than his client right now.

He didn't want to leave me seven years ago.

Softly, I brush a kiss along that defined jaw of his.

I forgive you for breaking my heart, I think as I kiss him.

Angling his face to the side, I press another kiss to his jaw.

I still want you.

Another kiss.

I think I always will.

Des stays still, letting me trail kisses along the edge of his jaw.

Touching him, kissing him draws up goose bumps along my skin. It feels like there's a storm on the horizon, something big and unstoppable that's rolling in. Something that will sweep us away. And dear God, I want to be swept away.

The Bargainer's magic continues to press against my skin. I nip his ear, earning a low noise from Des. My mouth moves down the strong column of his throat, the siren awakening within me. Dragging the collar of his T-shirt down, I touch my tongue to the hollow at the base of his throat.

The magic dissipates.

I blink several times, as if waking from a dream. My

mouth still hovers right over his skin. With effort, I straighten, releasing his shirt.

"You've always wanted to do that to me?" Des asks gruffly.

Shaking off the last of my daze, I nod. His brows are pinched together, his mouth stern.

"Since I was sixteen."

Back then, I'd wanted to kiss him along his jaw and neck because it seemed romantic, erotic. To a teenage girl who wanted a relationship but was afraid of sex, kissing a man there seemed like a good compromise.

Des covers my hand with his, holding it against his neck, his nostrils flaring with some strong emotion.

"Do it again," he says.

My eyebrows rise. So it wasn't all just in my head? Des felt that spark between us too?

I slip my hand from his to tilt his jaw to me. Once more, my lips skim his skin.

He'd agonized over our time apart.

He called it a nightmare. And I believe him.

But where does that leave us? What does any of it mean?

My mouth moves down his neck once more.

Des holds himself so still, like the slightest movement will scare me off. And now I wonder for the first time if he's ever been insecure about my feelings for him. I assumed they were always obvious, but it's like the two of us have held ourselves back from making that move that will expose our true feelings. I'd once assumed it was because he felt none for me. I'm no longer sure that's true.

My thumb strokes the skin of his cheek as I kiss him.

And now we're afraid of each other. That's what the two of us are. Afraid of hoping when all hope's ever done is break us. Afraid of getting exactly what we want.

And I might be wrong. Des might actually be uninterested in me despite all the signs. But I'm going to stop denying the possibility. And I'm going to stop denying my own feelings.

So after I finish kissing his throat, my hands reach for the edge of his shirt.

The Bargainer's hands grip my upper arms, and I can feel his heated, curious gaze on me, but I ignore it.

Don't overthink this.

I lift his shirt up, breaking away only to help him take it off.

My gaze moves to his sculpted chest. I run my fingers over his shoulder, where his tattoos taper off. His muscles flex beneath my touch.

I smooth my hands over his pecs and down his hard abs. I was wrong earlier when I said that he hadn't changed. When I was a teenager, he would've never let me touch him like this.

I press my lips between his collarbones and begin trailing kisses down his sternum.

I risk a glance up at him.

Des is looking at me. He's looking at me like I personally put up all the stars in the sky. A second later, he shutters the look.

"Callie…"

Around us, the room's darkening. How much further can he be pushed before his wings come out?

Better question: how much further can I push this until the siren comes out? Already I can feel her demanding to join in. She'll either speed us the hell up, or she'll make good on her earlier threat to hold out on Des.

"Tell me what you're thinking," I breathe.

"I'm afraid that if I do anything, you'll stop." I see him swallow. "I don't want you to stop."

I pause to give him a shy smile, a genuine one. "I won't," I say, punctuating my words by pressing a kiss to his sternum.

He hisses out a breath. "You keep doing that and I'm going to cash in more favors."

My skin lights up. The wicked grin that spreads across my mouth is all siren. "Tell me," I say, glamour entering my voice, "have you been thinking about what I told you earlier?"

I play with the top button of Des's pants, running a hand over his groin.

"About all those dark desires I would've *gladly* fulfilled," I continue.

"I've thought about it," he admits. He caresses my face, some of the passion in his eyes changing into something... sweeter. "I'm sorry, siren. I had to leave you. I didn't want to."

I frown as I unbutton the top of his pants, the siren in me not entirely sure what to make of his words. The rest of me knows he's being genuine.

He really didn't want to leave me.

That changes everything.

He catches my hand just as I begin to tug his pants down. "Not like this," he says quietly.

"Still holding out on me?" I say.

"Still holding out *for* you," he corrects. His thumb brushes against my cheekbone.

His words are another blow to those walls of mine. He's mercilessly ripping them down.

"Now," he continues, "it's my turn, cherub, to do something with you that I've always wanted to."

My skin brightens at that.

He picks me up and, still shirtless, carries me through his house. I resume kissing the underside of his jaw, the siren in me eager. So, so eager.

He groans. "Never realized how good that feels. Please... have some mercy."

My breath fans out against his skin, and I ignore his plea, kissing him more, my blood thrilling at his reaction.

A moment later, his wings appear. They expand, only to curve around the two of us. I reach out and stroke one.

"Jesus..."

I never thought that Des would melt beneath my touch. This, I can get used to.

Moving into his bedroom, he forces his wings back so that he can lay me out on his bed. Stepping away, he closes his eyes.

I push myself up on my forearms, trying to figure out what he's up to.

A second later, Des's wings disappear. Only then does he join me on the bed, propping himself up against the headboard and pulling me against him. My head nestles on one of his sculpted pecs, and my breath hitches. Even the siren in me is caught up in the moment. She's used to running the show, but now she wants to be seduced—rather than do the seducing.

He stares down at me, a wily spark in his eye. "Comfortable, love?"

Love.

That one's new.

I smile like an idiot in spite of myself.

I'm not sure what his next move is going to be until a laptop floats through his doorway, landing neatly on his stomach.

My lips part when I realize what's going on, my pulse in my throat.

Our movie nights. Back at school, we used to do this all the time.

Opening the laptop up, Des clicks open *Harry Potter and the Deathly Hallows: Part 1*.

"We never got to finish the series together, so…I thought we might watch the last two movies."

This is what he always wanted to do with me?

My throat constricts. I hadn't realized he'd enjoyed our movie nights as much as I had.

"I'd really like that," I finally say, because he's waiting to hear something.

Giving me a small smile, he tucks a hand behind his head and starts the movie. And then we settle in, just like we used to. For once, our closeness, our silence does feel just as comfortable as it did years ago.

Two odd hours later, tears are silently streaking down my cheeks as the movie ends. They drip down my face and onto the Bargainer's chest.

I feel his eyes turn to me.

"Are you…*crying*?" he asks.

Cat's out of the bag.

I sniffle. "Dobby was *such* a good friend."

The Bargainer pauses. Then his stomach begins to shake. A second later, I realize he's *laughing*.

He tilts my head so that I'm gazing up at him. "Cherub, shit, you're too adorable." Carefully he wipes my tears away with his thumb.

Adorable. Another compliment I tuck away. Later, when I'm alone, I'll pull it back out and savor it.

Des's gaze falls to my mouth, and his look goes from

affectionate to hungry. He hesitates, and I think he's going to kiss me, but then his eyes move to the computer and he exits out of the movie.

"Are you still good for round two?" he asks.

To be honest, lying here on my human pillow, I *am* getting sleepy, despite the fact that said human pillow has kept my anatomy awake for quite some time.

"I'm still good," I lie.

As if I'm going to opt out of this. I'd like to see someone try to pry me away from this man's sculpted body.

I swear the Bargainer's eyes miss nothing as he stares at me. Giving his head a shake, he starts up *Harry Potter and the Deathly Hallows: Part 2*, and I resettle against his chest.

My mind drifts as I began to watch the eighth Harry Potter movie.

Aside from some intense kisses and some minor groping, the Bargainer hasn't pushed things any further with me. And now, much to my chagrin, I actually kind of want him to. Especially, if I'm being honest with myself, after what he told me tonight about how it felt leaving me.

Like my soul was ripped in two.

He admitted his feelings. Gave them freely to me. I'm still reeling from that. For any fairy, that's a big deal. Secrets are like currency. The more you have, the more powerful you are.

For a fae king to give up his secrets?

I can only imagine.

I snuggle deeper into his chest, some strange, light emotion taking hold of me.

I could get used to this.

CHAPTER 18

April, seven years ago

The Bargainer and I step out of a taxi.

"Is it weird for you—taking a car rather than flying?" I ask.

We're on another gig of his. Someone whose debts he needs to collect.

"Not as weird as bringing you along," he says, paying our driver.

Tonight, the two of us are still on the Isle of Man, though I've never been to this particular part of it. I think we're on the north end of the island. The houses in this particular area are built close together, many of them with peeling paint and mossy roof tiles.

"Are you ever going to show me your wings?" I ask, watching him as he walks away from the taxi, tucking his wallet into the back pocket of his pants. I force my eyes not to linger on him or on the way his clothes cling to his muscular body.

Oh, to be that faded shirt.

"Trust me, you don't want to see my wings," he says, walking past me up the paved road.

"Why wouldn't I?" I ask as I follow him, pulling out a pistachio-flavored macaron from the bag I carry. We made a pit stop at Douglas Café right before this.

"Something you should know about fae," he says over his shoulder. "The only time our wings come out is when we want to fight or fuck."

Considering how frequent and in-depth my textbooks' descriptions of fairy wings were, those bitches must be losing their shit all the time.

But not Des, apparently. I've never seen his wings. Not a once. The good news: so far he hasn't wanted to kill me. The bad news: he hasn't wanted to rock my world either.

Damn.

I catch up to him. "You're an unusually well-behaved fairy," I say, taking a bite of the macaron.

Sweet baby Jesus, these pastries are good.

He raises an eyebrow, his eyes drifting to my mouth as I polish off the cookie. "Not always. Get a few drinks in me, and I'm a nightmare."

"A few drinks, huh?" I say, dusting off the crumbs that have trickled down my chest.

Is that really all it takes? He and I have drunk together...

He must see my interest. "Cherub, catching me drunk is never going to happen."

Our conversation is cut short when we approach a modest-looking house, the paint on this one especially faded.

Des knocks on the door.

"See, so well-behaved for a fairy," I say next to him.

He gives me a long-suffering look but doesn't respond.

When no one answers the door, Des bangs again.

And again, no one responds.

"Fucking idiot," he mutters, backing up.

"I don't think anyone's in—"

Des raises a booted foot and kicks the door clean off its hinges, the force causing the metal to shriek.

My eyes are wide with shock as it crashes inward.

Des looks like Death come to collect a new soul when he straightens, dusting bits of wood off himself. "Stay here, cherub."

My heart is in my throat, but I do as he asks.

The Bargainer strides inside, the evening shadows clinging to him like wisps of smoke.

He disappears around the hallway.

Each second of silence is agonizing. I eat another macaron to distract myself, but it tastes like sawdust. Suddenly, I feel like a fool, holding my bag of macarons, waiting for this wicked fae king to do who knows what to the poor soul who lives here.

I shouldn't be here. Good girls don't do this. And bad girls...well, I'm not one of those, am I?

You've killed a man. You're worse than a bad girl.

A shriek sounds from somewhere inside the house, startling me enough to drop my bag of cookies.

"Please, don't hurt me!" the man inside the house pleads.

When Des comes back to what's left of the front door, he's dragging a man by the scruff of his neck. The shadows clinging to his body have deepened. I look pointedly at his back.

Still no wings.

"Just for being difficult, you're getting charged interest," the Bargainer says, dragging him down the front steps and onto the man's lawn.

"Please, please, I'll pay. Just give me a week."

"I don't want your repayment in a week. I want it now." He throws the man onto the grass. Over his shoulder, the Bargainer says to me, "Pick up your bag, cherub. It's rude to litter."

"Says the man who just destroyed a door," I mutter as I grab the bag, my gaze fixed on what's happening in front of me.

The Bargainer throws me a smile. "That's not littering, that's B and E." He pauses, and I hear a series of odd groans behind me. "And now it's just E."

Without looking, I know he's fixed the door.

"Show-off," I say, the beginnings of a smile forming on my lips.

For the second time this evening, the Bargainer's eyes drift to my mouth.

Beyond him, his client shakes on the ground, his gaze meeting mine. "Please, help me," he begs.

All humor drains from Des's face as he turns back around.

The Bargainer steps in front of me, and I swear the night darkens. "You shouldn't have done that." Thunder rumbles in the distance.

Des stalks over to the trembling man, who's now crab-crawling away from him. The Bargainer puts a boot on his chest.

"Give me the name," Des demands.

"I–I don't know what you're talking about."

Des sizes the man up for several seconds, then nods. "All right, Stan. Get up."

Don't get up, Stan, you fool.

But Stan the Fool does get up, a disbelieving spark of hope in his eyes. Like the Bargainer ever releases a man from his debts.

"C'mon." Des jerks his head toward a beat-up car parked in front of the house. "Get in."

Now Stan hesitates, confused.

The Bargainer is already walking toward it. "Keys," he demands.

When Stan doesn't hand them over, they float out of his pocket of their own accord. Des catches them in midair.

He raps on the hood of the vehicle. "In. *Now.*"

"What are you doing?" Stan demands. I can see the whites of his eyes.

"We're going to visit the Otherworld." Des unlocks the driver's side door. "And once we get there, I'm going to feed you to the scariest motherfuckers I know."

That's enough to break the mighty Stan. The man begins to whimper even as he gets into the back of the car, and his fear is the most pitiful sound in all the world. I grimace at him. It's as though he hadn't known this day would come when he bought a favor from the Bargainer.

When Des's eyes fall on me, they soften. "Apologies, cherub, for the wrench in our evening. I'll drop you back off at your dorm. Get in."

I head to the car and slide into the front passenger seat, the interior smelling like stale cigarette smoke.

More begging comes from the back. "Please, you don't understand," Stan says, leaning forward. "I have a family."

"You have an estranged girlfriend and two children whom you don't spend time or money on. Trust me, they're better off without you." The Bargainer pulls onto the dark road.

"I don't want to die." Stan begins to weep.

"Then tell me what I need to know," Des says.

"You don't understand," Stan whines. "He'll do worse things than kill me."

Once again, the darkness expands around Des. "You know who I am, Stan," the Bargainer says, his voice icy. "My reputation precedes me. So you've heard of what's happened to past clients who've tried to stiff me."

More sobbing.

"And they paid," Des says, his voice ominous. "Before they died, they paid."

Oh *shit*.

Stan weeps harder, and when I look over my shoulder at him, a snot bubble has formed in one of his nostrils.

That's just wrong.

"Please," he begs, softer. "Please. I have...I have a family. I have..."

Maybe it's the snot bubble, maybe it's the fact that a grown-ass man is being cowardly, and maybe it's that I have to sit in a smelly car and thus can't eat my macarons in peace, but this man is kind of ruining my entire night by being difficult.

I will the siren out, a soft glow rushing over my skin as I turn my body around to face Stan.

"Cherub—" Des warns.

Too late.

"Fulfill your oath to the Bargainer and tell him what he needs to hear," I command, glamouring the Bargainer's client. "*Now.*"

Stan spends a good several seconds fighting his mouth, but it betrays him. He begins to cry even as he says, "They call him the Thief of Souls. I don't know his real name or the names of the people who do his dirty work."

Next to me, the Bargainer's mouth is a thin, angry line.

"He has many bodies and none at all..." Stan's voice dies away into sobs. Somewhere in there I hear him mumble, "You bitch."

Des slams on the brakes and the car skids to a halt. A moment later, he's out of the car, hauling Stan out by his hair. He drags the man into the darkness, and I can tell he cloaked himself in shadows by the way the night deepens.

I hear Stan shriek and the meaty sound of flesh hitting flesh. Then that too grows distant. Finally, there's silence. Several minutes go by like that, and I'm halfway convinced that the Bargainer forgot about me.

But then, out of seemingly nowhere, Des *lands* a dozen feet away from the passenger side of the car, rubbing his knuckles.

"You flew!" I say, amazed. He also did God knows what to Stan, but I'm not going to linger on that.

The Bargainer wouldn't kill him. Right?

Des doesn't respond to my words, and it's only as he gets closer that I realize he's pissed.

He opens my door and pulls me out, holding me close. "Don't *ever* do that again, cherub." His chest is heaving. "Never again."

The glamour?

"But I helped you," I say.

He squeezes my arms, a muscle feathering in his cheek. "You put a target on your fucking back."

I still don't understand. "I did the same thing in Venice."

"Which was also problematic," he says, "but this is different. You made a man talk who was willing to die for his silence." He lets that hang in the air.

He was willing to die for his silence.

A sliver of fear blooms. I haven't been taking Des's bargains seriously. The proof runs up my wrist. To me, they always felt like games. Macabre, violent games, but games nonetheless.

And games aren't real.

But this is real, and because I interfered, I might've ruined someone's life—well, ruined it more than it already was.

Des clenches his jaw. "How many girls can glamour someone? Just think about that for a second."

I don't know.

He leans in close. "Precious few." His eyes narrow. "Do you know what happens if someone comes after that man? If that someone didn't want Stan to talk in the first place? They're going to torture him, and what allegiance does Stan have to you? He's going to squeal as soon as he can, and then whoever he was so afraid of is going to come after you."

Jesus.

"I can make him forget," I say, my voice rising. "Just bring him back to me." I peer over Des's shoulder and into the darkness.

"Making him forget won't change the situation," the Bargainer says. "If the wrong person was interested enough, they could sense your glamour even without the aid of Stan's memory. And then they could trace it back to you."

I feel my nausea rising. Not just on my own behalf but because my meddling might've screwed over Stan and Des as well.

The kicker of it all is that I thought the Bargainer would be impressed—proud even. I'd proven myself useful.

I let out a shaky breath. "I'm sorry," I say softly.

Des's eyes search mine, and little by little, his anger evaporates. He pulls me into him, wrapping his arms around me. "It's not your fault," he says, deflated. "I should never have brought you along. I was a fool to let you convince me in the first place."

I go rigid beneath him. As screwed up as it is, I like coming along with him.

"I want to keep coming along with you," I say.

"I know, cherub. But neither of us can live like this."

His words make my heart pound harder, though I'm not sure if I feel dread or excitement. I guess it all depends on his reasons.

"Like what?" I ask.

He just squeezes me harder. "Nothing. Forget I mentioned it at all."

———————

Present

I wake to near darkness. A large leg has been thrown over mine and an arm is wrapped around my midsection.

Des.

Sometime during the final *Harry Potter* movie, I fell asleep in his arms, my body spooned against his. And in the hours since, I've been reeled in tight against his chest, his body nearly encasing mine.

My clothes are still on, as are his, and yet something about this feels incredibly intimate.

I rub my eyes, dazedly taking in the dim room. Des's shadows lurk in every corner, the sight of them making me feel...*safe.*

I begin to move, only for Des's grip to tighten on me, pulling me even closer. I let out a little squeak. I'm an overgrown man's teddy bear at the moment.

The Bargainer stirs, nuzzling the back of my head. "You awake?" he asks, his voice sleep-roughened.

Instead of answering, I angle my head up and look into his eyes. Gone is the calculating edge to them. Gone is his wiliness. Gone are the shields he hides behind.

Right now, he's just a tired, happy man.

He reaches up and runs a thumb over my lower lip. "I lied to you earlier, cherub. Sleep does very much become you."

I feel my face heat.

I don't know how he sees my reaction in the darkness, but his eyes move to my cheeks. "As does blushing."

Tentatively, I reach out and run my hand through Des's white locks. "Tell me another secret," I say.

His mouth twitches. "You give a siren a secret…and she asks for another."

"You have so many of them," I say. "Don't be a grinch."

He lets out a long-suffering sigh, but the effect is ruined by the smile spreading across his lips.

He leans in close. "I wasn't going to tell you this, but if you want a secret…"

I wait.

"You drooled all over my chest during the second movie," he confesses. "To be honest, I thought you were crying again."

I push at him, laughing in spite of myself. "That's *not* what I meant when I asked for a secret!"

He rolls onto his back, hooking an arm around my waist and taking me with him. And now he's beginning to laugh as well. "I don't make the rules, cherub. I just bend them."

I straddle him, leaning in close. "I should be an exception." I don't even know what makes me say it, but it's too late to take it back.

I expect Des to raise an eyebrow and spin my words with that silver tongue of his.

Instead, his face sobers, his expression turning serious. "You are." His eyes drop to my mouth, his fingers pressing into my skin.

Most of the time, this man leaves me confused. But not right now. Right now, he and I are on the exact same page.

Slowly, I lower my head, and I press my mouth to his.

What's better than waking up with Des in the morning?

Kissing Des in the morning.

My lips skim over his, savoring the taste of him. He pulls me closer, making a guttural noise as he deepens the kiss, working his tongue into my mouth.

This feels like unfinished business. He and I are that storm on the horizon, but now, finally, that storm is rolling in.

I move against him, wanting more, impatient for it.

"Callie," he says, his voice strained, "can't do that, love."

There it is again.

Love.

"Say that again."

"Love?"

I nod, pressing myself tighter to him. "I like the endearment." I move against him again despite his warnings.

He makes a pained sound.

"So do I," he breathes.

Slipping a hand between us, I unbutton his pants and dip a hand in. "I *really* like it."

Des hisses out a breath. "Careful," he warns against my lips. His eyes say an entirely different thing. They're daring me to go further.

I break away from his mouth. "What if I don't want to be careful?" I say, grabbing hold of him. My breathing deepens at the feel of him. Never have I done this with him. It feels righter than our kiss. "What if I don't want *you* to be careful?" I punctuate my words by moving my hand up and down. Up and down.

He rocks against me.

I lean in close. "The tough Bargainer isn't so tough anymore."

"Callie—"

"Love," I correct, the siren beginning to seep into my words.

"*Love*," he says. "I was planning this...the other... way...around."

"Too bad," I say.

"Wicked woman," he says, his mouth curving into a smile.

I'm tempted to bring him to the edge, only to stop. That's what the siren wants. Enjoy his lust, and then make him suffer.

But a bigger part of me wants to see this through to the very end. This man who left me but agonized over it. This love who seemed jealous of my exes. This usually polished king who's going to come in his pants because I want him to fall apart under my touch.

I watch him with awe, my eyelids lazy. His high cheekbones are even sharper at this angle, his crafty eyes focused on my face as his hands squeeze my thighs.

"Too good, Callie—"

I move my hand faster.

He hisses out another breath, his hands moving over me like they're trying to find exactly what they want to touch but can't decide. Eventually, they settle on my hips.

I work him, feeling his body tense beneath me.

He groans. "Going to come..."

I lean in and kiss him as he jerks against me, again and again and again. His fingers tighten against my flesh, trying to pull me closer to him.

I smile against his mouth when I finally feel him relax.

He breathes heavily against me, leaning his forehead against mine. "You want to know a real secret?" he rasps.

I nod against him.

"I want to wake up to you every single morning."

This time when we head to the Otherworld, I know the drill.

We cross over, arriving at another set of fae ruins—this one a stone circle made up of statue after statue of solemn fae men and women—before Des flies us to his palace.

He holds me close, and I catch him more than once staring at me with an unguarded look in his eyes.

Like he wants more of me.

I never gave him the chance earlier. Right after he came, I slipped away from his bed.

Why did I run? Perhaps because I was scared of what I did to our relationship. And perhaps because I wanted to give him something to fixate on, the same way I've fixated on his confession last night.

Only now I'm beginning to fixate on this morning too. With every heated look he gives me and every silent promise in his eyes that he's going to finish what I've started.

The fae king is hungry, and he's used to getting what he wants.

I try to focus on the task at hand—visiting the sleeping warriors—but it's no use. I'm more aware of the Bargainer than ever.

We break through the cloud cover, and once again I catch sight of that magnificent city of his.

"What's it called?" I ask, nodding to the Bargainer's floating city.

"Somnia," he replies, his breath tickling the shell of

my ear. "The land of sleep and small death. The capital of my kingdom."

The land of sleep and small death. That sounds dark and magical…which is Des in a nutshell.

He banks sharply to the left, circling the city as we begin to descend. People creep out onto their terraces and into the streets to watch us land. More gather outside the gates in front of the castle.

"The next biggest city," the Bargainer continues, "is Barbos, then it's Lephys, then Phyllia and Memnos— sister cities connected by a bridge. Arestys is the smallest, poorest…" His expression darkens.

"Are they all floating cities?" I ask.

"They are."

"I want to see them."

What am I saying? Surely that didn't come from my mouth? The last thing I want to do is spend more time in the Otherworld.

Des looks down at me.

"Starting with Arestys," I add breathlessly.

Seriously, Callie, you crazy bitch, stop talking.

But I *can't*, not when he's looking at me like that.

"Then I'll take you to them all," he says, his silver eyes shining like he can't get enough of my words.

I might as well have hammered the last nail in my coffin myself.

Just had to open your mouth…

Des soars over the front of the castle, and unlike the grand entrance we made last time, the two of us land softly on one of the palace's back terraces.

He eases me to my feet before his wings disappear.

"No fancy entrance this time?" I ask.

"Tonight I didn't want to share you." His wings shimmer out of existence as he speaks.

Just as his wings disappear, his simple bronze circlet materializes. Under the black T-shirt he wears, I see the lowest of the three bronze war bands appear as well.

I smile at the sight of him, my crooked king, with his frayed shirt and simple crown. Right now he looks neither fae nor human. He looks like something better than either.

Casually, he takes my hand and leads me inside the palace. We head down a wide hallway and through a room full of swords and scepters on display.

The fae we pass don't spare a glance at Des's attire, though they themselves wear embroidered dresses and tunics and suits with fancy buttons and beadwork.

What his subjects do stare at is *me*. Me and my hand, clasped in the king's. When I catch them looking, they bow low, murmuring *Your Majesty* to us as we pass.

I'm antsy to remove my hand, if only to stop them from staring. Des, meanwhile, is unfazed by any of it.

He leads me outside the palace, down a suspended arched walkway that connects two of the castle's spires, and I have a moment to take in the sweeping architecture of this place. The palace sits at the highest point of Somnia, the rest of the buildings dropping away on all sides.

From here, the world looks to be made up of thousands and thousands of stars, each one brighter than the last. Beneath us, levels and levels of white stone houses dot the land, some even trailing down chasms cut *into* the city. It gives a whole new meaning to the fae term *under the mountain*.

Once again, I'm struck by how magical, how impossible,

this place is. The city of dreams and small deaths looks like something from a dream. Something I'm sure I'll wake from.

The two of us enter another tower, leaving the night sky once more. Des steers us down several more hallways until, eventually, we stop in front of a hammered bronze door, the top of it curved like a Moroccan archway, and he ushers me inside.

As soon as I step in, I realize where we are.

The king's quarters.

I should've known from the door alone we were heading here, but I mistakenly assumed the Bargainer was taking me straight to see the sleeping women.

A plush sitting room spreads out before me, and beyond it, a large balcony. Off to the left, I catch a glimpse of bedroom furniture. To the right is something like a dining area.

Bronze lamps are mounted along the walls, those same starbursts of light I saw last visit floating inside each glass case.

When I turn to look at Des, the shadows have curled closer around him.

The hunger in his eyes...

He catches one of my hands and kisses my knuckles.

"Truth or dare?" he whispers. He's had carnal thoughts on his mind ever since that *handy* little wakeup call I gave him this morning.

And so have I.

"Dare."

His nostrils flare.

One breath, he's across from me, and in the next, I'm wrapped up in his arms, his lips hot on mine. He carries me through his chambers to his bedroom, kissing me all the while.

Lamps dangle from the high ceiling, a small starburst of light glowing in each. On the far side of the room, a line of windows with those distinctive Moroccan arches surrounds a set of double doors that lead out to the balcony.

The Bargainer lays me on a huge bed with a hammered bronze headboard, his eyes gleaming in the light. He doesn't follow me onto the mattress, choosing instead to stand at the foot of the bed and gaze at me.

He drops to his knees, a hand caressing my leg, some of his white-blond hair sliding over his face.

No, I want to see his expression. I push myself up and reach forward, brushing his hair away from his face.

He leans into the touch.

Both hands wrap around my legs. "Once the repayment begins, the magic takes on a life of its own, Callie. Do you still want my dare?"

Judging by where we are, how Des is touching me, and the heat in his eyes, I know this is going to be something physical.

I should say no. I should protect myself from further emotional entanglements with this man. But after last night and this morning, I've decided to try a new tactic. One where I'm brave with my heart.

"Yes."

Triumph flares in his eyes. He pushes my chest back down. Already I can feel the magic coiling around us, waiting, *waiting.* Unlike most other times when I feel it bearing down on me, now the Bargainer's power feels warm, pleasant, like it's just there to add to the experience.

Hands returning to my calves, he pulls me to the edge of the bed, my legs hanging off the mattress, the chiffon dress I donned this morning now hiking up nearly around my waist. Up Des's hands slide, over my knees and along my inner thighs.

I gasp when his fingers brush against the lacy panties I'm wearing.

Des's breath hitches as he draws my dress up higher, getting a good look at my lingerie.

"How I have imagined," he murmurs, his eyes roving over me, "and it has never done you justice."

He imagined this?

Hooking his fingers around the lace edges, he drags my panties off, uncovering me inch by inch.

Under my mounting desire, I'm scared.

Fate's too cruel to ever give you more than a taste of what you want. I'm afraid this is my taste.

"Cherub," Des says, tossing my panties aside. He stares at my core, mesmerized. "I am going to make you feel good. So, so good."

Pushing my dress up even higher, his lips begin to kiss the skin just below my belly.

"Des…" My heart's going to hammer out of my chest.

I lick my lips, my throat dry.

Des runs a finger over my core. I gasp out in surprise, my skin beginning to brighten.

He does it again, and now my hips move. A low sound comes from Des.

A finger dips into me, and my mind goes utterly blank.

He slips in another finger, and I let out a low moan.

"That's it, Callie."

"Des." I need more. Far more.

He removes his fingers, and while I'm watching, he licks them one by one.

That is *so* filthy. And Lord help me, I'm aroused by it.

He lets out a groan. "Better than my imagination."

He hitches one of my legs over his shoulder, then the

other, opening me to him. It's all so very indecent. The Bargainer's gaze moves from my core to my eyes.

"Fair warning: I'm not stopping until you come." And then he leans in.

At the first touch of his mouth, I suck in air. It's going to be too much, I can already tell.

He licks around my inner lips, throwing in a nip here and there, *teasing* me. Soon I'm making sounds I'm not proud of. I don't know what to do with my hands, so I twist them in the sheets.

"My cherub. So sweet, so responsive," he says between kisses, his voice rough.

Jesus, this man wasn't lying when he said he was the overlord—or king, *whatever*—of sex. Has oral ever felt so good?

That's a rhetorical question. Answer's no. And he hasn't even made it to my clit yet.

He toys with me, and I don't fucking care, because the Bargainer is between my legs and he's not going to stop until I come.

But then he does stop toying with me, and suddenly, he means *business*. His tongue moves over my clit, again and again.

Oh God.

Too much. Far too much. My hips move of their own accord, my body glowing brighter than those sparklers hanging throughout the room. I can't take this.

I try to crawl backward, away from his mouth, panting.

"Ah, ah, cherub," he says, dragging me back. "You're not going anywhere. Not until I'm finished with you."

He won't release me. He won't release me, and I'm bucking against him.

I let out a strangled sob. "Des, *please*." There's way too

much sensation down there, and it's building. Building, building, *building*.

"Come for me." He's now just sucking on my clit.

Impossible to think through this.

"*Des.*" My body is just a bundle of nerves, all of them taut. I can't get away, and I can't stand much more of this. I'm right on the edge, and with each stroke of his tongue…

"Come."

I begin to fall.

"*Oh my god, Des.*" The siren's entered my voice.

I stare blankly at the beautiful ceiling, my vision going unfocused, as my orgasm lashes through me, lasting longer and burning brighter than any others I've ever had.

By the time I come down, the Bargainer is kissing my inner thighs, his touch still proprietary. My legs slip off his shoulders, and he catches them, closing them gently and pulling my dress down.

He gathers me in his arms and moves us to the head of his bed.

I stare at him with astonishment.

"That was…" Incredible. Mind-blowing. Unbelievable.

"A long time in coming," he finishes for me.

Des strokes my hair back, his eyes filled with such longing. My heart squeezes at the sight of it. Leaning in, he kisses me, and I taste myself on his lips. It's vulgar and arousing, and my dimming skin brightens all over again.

His fingers trail across my arm.

I stare up at him, trying like an idiot not to think about the fact that Des just went down on me. This beautiful man who'd always been so out of reach took a bead just so that he could give me an orgasm.

The world is utterly backward—and I never want it to right itself.

"What are you thinking about?" I ask.

"So much, cherub."

I finger the bronze war bands that circle his upper arm.

"I've imagined you in my bed a thousand times," he continues, his gaze on me.

This moment is surreal to me.

"A thousand times?" I don't know what to do with the woozy, light-headed sensation that rolls through me. It's somewhere between elation and flattery and hope so sharp it hurts. Once again, I'm scared—of him, of us. Of having everything I ever wanted within my grasp, only for it to slip through my fingers. Because it will slip through my fingers. That's just the nature of things.

He presses his lips close to my ear. "Do you want to know a truth of mine?"

"Always," I say, turning my head to better face him.

He takes my hand and presses it against his chest. Beneath my palm, I feel his heartbeat racing.

My eyes move from his chest to his face.

"It does that whenever I'm around you," he says.

———

I stand out on his balcony, looking out at the night sky. Once I regained the use of all my limbs, I explored Des's rooms, ending up out here.

I stare out at all those pale buildings and gardens that spread out from the castle.

The Bargainer reigns over all this.

Over all this and more.

Des steps out onto the balcony.

"Most of the time, I forget that you're a king," I say.

"I'm glad," he says, coming in behind me. He braces his arms on the railing, caging me in. "I don't want you to think of me as a king. I want you to think of me as a man."

I understand that. Labels can be dangerous, dangerous things, even when they're seemingly desirable.

"I want to know about this side of you," I say.

I want to know how he came into power, how many years he's been ruling. I want to know whether he makes decisions by himself or if he has a committee of trusted advisers. I want to know all the boring, inane things that go along with his position because I simply want to know more about him.

He presses a kiss to my shoulder. "One day, cherub, I'll tell you," he says.

I turn toward Des, staring down at the skin he just kissed. I catch sight of the intricate tattoos running along his left arm and begin to trace them.

Beneath my fingers, I feel him shiver.

"Where did you get these?" I ask.

"That is also a story for another time."

Des and his secrets. Always his secrets.

I sigh, returning my attention to his kingdom.

The two of us stand together like that for a long time, not talking.

"Want to know a secret?" the Bargainer asks.

This must be a consolation prize; I'm not to know about who Des the king is or about the ink that stains his arm, but he will give me a secret—forget that it might not have anything to do with anything.

"Yes," I breathe. I'm pathetic enough to take what I can get.

He wraps an arm around my midsection, pressing my back flush against his chest. "The Kingdom of Night is the strongest kingdom in the Otherworld. Tell that to fae of any other realm, and they'll argue with you. But it's true." He points over my shoulder to the sky above. "Tell me, what do you see out there?"

I follow his finger, looking up at the night sky. It glitters with thousands and thousands of stars, each one so much brighter than any I've ever seen on earth.

"Stars," I say.

"That is all you see?" he asks.

"Other than the night, yes."

"The *night*," he repeats, his thumb stroking the skin of my stomach through the fabric of my dress. "That is precisely why people take my kingdom for granted. No one *sees* the darkness, and yet it's everywhere. We are surrounded by an entire universe of it. It came before us, and it will live on long after us. Even the stars might form and then die, but the darkness will always be there.

"That also happens to be why the Night Kingdom is considered the most romantic of realms. Not only do lovers meet under the cloak of darkness, darkness is the most eternal of all things. To declare your love until the end of night is the most sacred and undying of vows." More quietly, he adds, "It's the oath I will take when I bind myself to my queen."

Knife wound to the gut.

I don't want to hear about Des's future queen, not on the wings of what we've done together. It's not like he's making the proposal to me, after all.

I'm embarrassed that I even care. I shouldn't, but it's like I can't help but open myself up to him.

"Lucky girl," I say, pushing away from the wall and him along with it.

I feel Des's eyes on me as I cross through his room.

"No," he corrects. "She won't be the lucky one. I'll be."

CHAPTER 19

April, seven years ago

This can't last.

I lie in the Bargainer's arms, my eyes drifting closed as he strokes my hair. I fight sleep, not wanting to lose a moment of this.

Ever since I woke from that nightmare, my window in pieces and Des inside my room, he's stayed with me each night until I've fallen asleep. Perhaps even longer.

His body feels like it was made for me, every dip and groove of it fitting against mine like puzzle pieces. But it's more than just the way I fit against him; it's the way he smells, a scent there is no name for, and the way his arm curls around my back.

Right in the base of my stomach, there's a sense of rightness being in his arms, like this is the only place I truly belong.

Does he feel it too? Or am I simply making fairy tales out of smoke and shadows?

These are question I come back to often.

My eyelids lower, and I fight to keep them open, my gaze moving to the Bargainer's ear. I reach out and trace the pointed edge of it.

Fae ears.

Beneath my touch, Des shudders.

"You hide these," I say. I swear that most of the time, they look blunted—*human*.

"Sometimes," he agrees. Gently, he removes my hand.

It's quiet, and the lights around the room have long since gone off. Even in the darkness, I can sense Des's shadows blanketing me, and they make me feel safe. Before him, I had so many reasons to fear the night.

Now, I anticipate it, because it brings me him.

"Thank you," I murmur.

"For what, cherub?" he says.

"Everything."

He stops stroking my hair for a moment. When he begins again, I swear I feel his thumb brush across my temple. The lightest of caresses.

I begin to drift off to sleep, so I'm not sure whether I imagined the final words he breathed into the night—

"For you, no less."

———

Present

After our conversation, the two of us get back to business. Namely, seeing the sleeping warriors. If the Bargainer notices that I'm being distant, he doesn't say anything.

What is there to say? That he's sorry? In this, he's not at fault. Love isn't something you can fake. And while Des has been affectionate with me, kind to me, and physical with me, he hasn't mentioned anything about love.

I'm the one who can't smother these feelings that have been festering inside me for years.

The Bargainer takes me down flight after flight of stairs, deep down into the bowels of his castle, until we arrive at a balcony that must be located on one of the lowest levels of the palace. Beyond it, the land drops away and the buildings are terraced one on top of the other, all the way down into the darkness.

We approach the edge of the railing, brisk night air whipping my hair.

I lean over it. "Where to now?"

Des's arms wrap roughly around my waist.

"What—" I barely have time to stare at the bands of muscle that grip me and his intricate sleeve of tattoos before he leaps into the air, his claw-tipped wings unfurling.

I yelp as my body jerks up with him.

I should've known as soon as I saw the balcony that we were flying somewhere.

Only Des has stopped flapping his wings. That's about the moment I realize that we're not flying up. We're *diving*.

Nothing can describe the sheer terror of falling into an abyss headfirst. The wind thrashes my hair about my face and steals away my breath as we plummet. A dizzying number of balconies and gardens blow by us, terraced along the inner rock walls of this strange island. The whole thing looks like a dollhouse. I see cross sections of homes and shops, temples and gardens. And as we dive, each level gets dimmer and dimmer.

We continue down until the buildings are cloaked in darkness. Down here, it feels less like the city of night and more like a void.

Our descent slows, and the Bargainer's great wings unfurl

above me as he angles us toward an unassuming balcony almost at the bottom of the chasm. The buildings around us are less adorned than the ones above, and the thorn-covered vines that snake around the railings and column-lined porticos appear almost sinister.

As soon as we land, my body sways in his arms from the rush of blood.

His grip on me tightens when I try to pull away. "Give yourself a moment, Callie," he says, his voice low.

I do, not entirely minding his embrace.

Once Des senses that I've stopped swaying, he releases me.

I glance around what must be one of the lowest levels of the city. It's cold here, colder than the open air above. "What is this place?"

"Welcome to the capital's industrial district, where Somnia's exports leave and its imports arrive."

So people don't live here per se. That's a relief. Compared to the rest of the city, this area is kind of a bummer. I mean, it's beautiful, in a creepy way, but it isn't a place I would want to linger.

I glance toward the simple wooden door that leads inside from our balcony. Unease stirs low in my belly. I can't detect magic the same way a fae might, yet even I don't want to walk through that door, though I'm sure that's precisely what we're going to do.

Not a moment later, my suspicions are proven correct when Des steers me toward the door.

"This used to be a storage facility," he explains, "just like the rest of the buildings in this area. It was converted to a temporary shelter for the sleeping when we ran out of space..."

Ahead of us, the door creaks open, and the two of us step into a cavernous, windowless warehouse.

The Bargainer nods to a guard on the far side of the room who appears to be keeping vigil.

Without a word, the guard exits a far door, giving us privacy.

I glance around. Like many of the rooms in the palace, someone's used magic to depict the night sky on the ceiling. Tiny starbursts of light shine softly from sconces set into the wall, but they do very little to ease away the darkness that gathers in this room.

That's all I notice of the warehouse itself because—

All those coffins.

There are *hundreds* of them—maybe thousands. Rows and rows of glass caskets. My eyes sweep over them.

"So many," I breathe.

Next to me, the Bargainer frowns. "Almost twice this number of women are still missing from my kingdom alone."

I suck in a breath of air. Practically a city's worth. Albeit a small city, but still.

Such staggering numbers.

Inside each casket, I catch glimpses of the women, their hands folded over their chests. So eerie.

"Each one had a child with her?" I ask.

The Bargainer nods, running a thumb over his lower lip. Those lips that were all over me not an hour ago.

He catches my eye, and whatever look I wear, it causes his nostrils to flare.

I have to rip my gaze away. I don't really want to have a moment with this man while we stand inside what's essentially a morgue.

"Where are all the children?" I ask. There were no more than two dozen in the royal nursery.

"They're living with their remaining family."

I raise my eyebrows. Hundreds of those odd children are now living in fae households?

"Have there been any complaints?" I ask.

Des nods. "But more than that, there's been a steep increase in infanticide in the last few years."

It takes me a second to actually connect the dots.

I suck in a breath. "They kill the kids?"

He sees my horrified expression. "Are you really so surprised, cherub? Even on earth, we have a reputation for being ruthless."

Of course I'm surprised. Children are children are children. No matter how disconcerting they are, you don't just…kill them.

"Before you judge my people, you should know that there have been cases of caregivers falling into the same…*sleep* as these women. And in plenty of these cases of infanticide, these children aren't the victims. They're the perpetrators."

The thought of it all makes me queasy. I don't envy Des his job as king. I can't imagine any of this.

"Have any of the servants working in the nursery fallen into this same sleep?" I ask, looking out across the room.

"A couple," he admits, casting a glance back over the coffins. "The fae ones. Humans seem to be somewhat immune, so now they're the only ones who have direct contact with the children inside the palace." Des jerks his chin toward the caskets. "Go ahead, cherub," he says, changing the subject. "Have a look at them."

I drag my gaze back over the room. Just the sight of all those women lying so still has the hair on my forearms rising.

Warily, I leave Des's side, my footsteps echoing inside the cavernous room. I walk toward the closest row of coffins, almost afraid to peer down into them.

The glass glints under the low lighting, making the caskets shimmer in the near darkness.

I step up next to one of the caskets and force myself to look down at the woman. She has raven-dark hair and a heart-shaped face. A *sweet* face, one that you wouldn't imagine would be on the body of a warrior. Her pointed ears peek between her locks of hair.

I swallow, staring down at her. Last time I saw a body this still, it was my stepfather's.

Blood on my hands, blood in my hair...never be free.

I force my gaze away from her face. She wears a black tunic and fitted breeches that are tucked into suede boots. Her hands are folded across her chest, resting on the pommel of a sword that lies against her torso.

She's so still, so serene, and yet a part of me expects her to open her eyes and use that sword to break free of the coffin.

The vision is so realistic that I force myself to move on to another before I chicken out and leave prematurely.

This one has hair that looks like spun silver, and it's bluntly cropped just past her chin. Despite her silver hair, she looks young, her smooth skin taut over her high cheekbones and square jaw. This woman is all soldier; even at rest, I can tell her personality is all hard edges. But not even that saved her. Clutched beneath her hands is a bow, and next to her feet is a quiver filled with arrows.

Another warrior. But not *just* a warrior. This one has a silver band on her upper arm. A *medaled* warrior.

I begin to wind my way through the coffins. All the women wear the same black attire, and each carries a weapon. Warriors who are now victims.

The whole thing is putting me on edge. Some of the

strongest women in Des's kingdom lie inside these coffins. How did this happen to so many who were so capable?

And if this monster could do this to these women, what could he do to an average person? What could he do to *me*?

I begin to hum to alleviate my growing anxiety.

I touch a casket here and there, noticing that the glass feels warm.

My skin prickles. This situation is...is *unnatural*—wrong at its most basic level.

Without thinking, my humming shifts to singing.

"Wake from your slumber.
Rise from your sleep.
Tell me your secrets.
They're mine to keep."

The siren in me likes to string together rhymes, much the same way a witch does spells. I'm sure it has something to do with how effective my glamour is, but to my ears, it's simply pleasing.

"Open your eyes.
Breathe in the fresh air.
Tell me your secrets.
They're ours to share."

I throw a glance over my shoulder at Des. Arms folded, feet planted apart, and wings out—he looks like he's channeling something between rock star and fallen angel. The leather pants and the sleeve of tats don't help. His eyes move over the coffins, almost as if he expects someone to move...

I follow his gaze, instantly tense, but nope, the women are as still as they were when I walked in.

Turning my body back toward the rows of women, I resume my song.

"Rouse from your rest.
Shake off this dark spell.
Open your mouth.
You have secrets to tell."

I knew before walking in here that my glamour couldn't rouse these women. They are all fairies. And yet I still hold out an inkling of hope that I can help them.

A minute goes by, then another. I wait for any sign of life, but no one moves. And now I feel silly. Singing to a room full of fae who haven't stirred since they were brought here.

I begin walking back to the Bargainer, my footsteps echoing.

A tinkling laugh rises from behind me.

I pause, glancing over my shoulder. There's no one there—at least no one walking or talking.

I begin to move again, my muscles now tense. I'm spooked and imagining things.

"Slave…"

I pause midstep, my eyes going wide as they meet Des's.

He puts a finger to his lips. A split second later, he evaporates into smoke.

Shit. Where'd he go?

A spectral breath tickles my cheek, laughing softly, and I realize right about now that I might have bigger problems.

I twist around, sure I will find someone standing next to me. But no one's there.

Another laugh rises from the depths of the room, followed by a hum. The voice comes from nowhere and everywhere. It's all around me, multiplying on itself.

"Sleep, fair one,
Or are you afraid?
This is a game in which
You are far outplayed."

I glance around for the singer, but I already know this is some sort of magic beyond my comprehension.

A phantom hand strokes my hair.

"You ask us to wake,
When we want you to sleep.
Secrets are meant
For one soul to keep.
So sing your songs,
And rhyme your rhymes.
He's coming for you.
These are dark times."

The singing dies away until the room is quiet once more.

"Holy fuck," I breathe.

Time to get the hell out of this place.

I eye the coffins as I pass row after row of them, expecting any second for these women to attack me.

Just had to stir up trouble, didn't you, Callie?

Ahead of me, the shadows swirl together, coalescing into a winged man.

Des.

The Bargainer's wings are spread threateningly, and his

face is unreadable, which means Des the killer has come out to play.

Someone's losing their shit.

"Oh, so nice of you to join me," I say, my voice high. I'm about to lose my shit too.

"I never left you," he says.

I'm not going to think about that comment. This situation is weird enough as it is.

He stares out at the coffins. "If I were any crueler, I would burn this room down, women and all."

Normally, a statement like that would shock me, but right now, when I can still feel those phantom fingers trailing down my skin, I'm thinking that leaving these women here, in the core of Des's capital, is a very bad idea.

CHAPTER 20

April, seven years ago

My dorm room has become a collage of me and Des. A string of prayer flags hangs across my ceiling, courtesy of a trip to Tibet. The lantern perched on my shelf is from Morocco. The painted gourd on my desk is from Peru. And the striped blanket at the foot of my bed is from Nairobi.

The man's taken me around the world, mostly on business trips, but sometimes just for the hell of it. I think he likes seeing my excitement. And out of all these trips, I've collected a room full of souvenirs.

Pinned to my walls, between my trinkets, are the Bargainer's sketches. A couple of them are of me, but once I noticed I was a recurring theme in his art, I asked him if he could draw me pictures of the Otherworld. Originally, my intent had been to minimize portraits of me, but once he began drawing images of his world, I was ensnared by them.

Now my walls are covered with sketches of cities built

on giant trees and dance halls nestled beneath mountains, monsters both terrifying and strange, and beings so beautiful they beckoned me closer.

"Callie," Des says, pulling me back to the present. He's sprawled across my bed, the edge of his shirt hitched up just enough to give me a glimpse of his abs.

"Hmm?" I say, twisting my computer chair back and forth.

He hesitates. "If I asked you something right this instant, would you answer me honestly?"

Up until now, our conversation had been lighthearted, humorous, so I think of nothing when I say, "Of course."

Des pauses, then says, "What really happened that night?"

I freeze, my chair coming to a stop.

He doesn't need to elaborate on just which night he's speaking of. We both know it's the night he met me.

The night I killed a man.

I'm shaking my head.

"You need to talk about it," he says, tucking his hands behind his head.

"Are you suddenly a shrink now?" There's a lot more venom in my voice than I intended. I can't go back to that night.

Des reaches for my hand and holds it tightly in his own. The same trick that I've used dozens of times on him he now turns on me: touch.

I stare down at our joined hands, and damn but his warm grip makes me feel safe.

"Cherub, I'm not going to judge you."

I drag my gaze up to his. I'm about to beg him not to push me any further. My demons batter against the walls of their cages. He's asking me to unleash them, and I don't know if I can.

But when I meet his eyes, which stare at me with so much patience and affection, I say something else entirely.

"He came at me like he always did when he drank too much." I swallow.

Shit, I'm really doing this.

And I'm not ready, but I am, and my mind makes no sense right now, but my heart is speaking through my mouth, and I'm not sure my mind has anything to do with it. I've carried this particular secret with me for years. I'm ready to unburden myself.

My eyes move back to our joined hands, and I take a strange sort of strength from his presence.

"That evening was a long time in coming. It began several years before then." Long before my siren ever had a chance to defend me.

To know the story, I have to go back to the beginning. Des had only asked me to explain a single night, but that's impossible without knowing all the hundreds of nights that preceded it.

"My stepfather...raped me...for years."

I drag myself back to that dark place, and I do one of the hardest things I've ever done: I tell him. All the gory details. Because there really is no such thing as dipping a toe into this discussion.

I talk about the way I used to stare at my closed door, that I came close to wetting my bed watching that knob turn. How I can still smell the bite of his cologne and the sour spirits on his breath.

That I used to cry and sometimes beg. That despite my best efforts, it never changed anything. That eventually, I became numb to it, and that's perhaps the detail that hurts the most.

Will the fear and disgust ever go away? Will the shame? Intellectually, I know what he did to me wasn't my fault. But emotionally, I've never been able to believe it. And God, have I tried.

My knuckles are white from how tightly I grip his hand. In this moment, he's my anchor, and I'm afraid when I let him go, he'll drift away from me.

I'm a dirty, tarnished thing, and if he couldn't see that before, now he will.

"That night, the night he died, I couldn't take it anymore." It was him or me in the end, and to be honest, I didn't really care which. "Killing him wasn't premeditated. He came at me in the kitchen, and he set that bottle on the counter. When I got the chance, I grabbed it and held it out like a weapon."

What are you going to do with that? Hit your father with it?

"I smashed it against the wall." My eyes go distant, remembering that encounter. "He laughed at that." A mean laugh, one that promised pain. Lots of it. "And then he lunged at me. I didn't think. I swung the broken bottle at him." It felt good to fight back. It felt like madness, and I gave myself over to it. "I must've nicked an artery."

My body's shaking, and the Bargainer squeezes my hand tighter.

"He bled out so fast," I whisper.

And the look in my stepfather's eyes when he realized he was going to die. Mostly shock but also a healthy dose of betrayal. Like after all he'd done to hurt me, he assumed I'd never hurt him back.

I swallow thickly, blinking back the memories. "The rest you know."

I expect a million terrible reactions but not the one the

Bargainer gives me. He releases my hand only to wrap his arms around me and pull me out of the computer chair and into his embrace. And I'm so, so thankful he's touching me, holding me, giving me this physical comfort right when I thought I was incapable of being cherished.

I crawl the rest of the way onto the tiny twin bed we now share, and as the moon sets, I cry in his arms. I let myself be weak because this may be the only time I'll ever get this.

A weight lifts from my chest. The pain is still there, but the dam's been broken, and all that pressure that existed within me now rushes out.

Finally I understand why the Bargainer is so alluring to me. He's seen Callie the victim, Callie the killer, Callie the broken girl who can barely keep her life together. He's seen all this, and yet he's still here, stroking my hair and murmuring softly to me. "It's all right, cherub. He's gone. You're safe."

I fall asleep like that, locked in the strong arms of Desmond Flynn, one of the scariest, most dangerous men in the supernatural world.

And he's right. In his arms, I feel absolutely safe.

———————

Present
Back in Des's Otherworld chambers, I pace, my skirt floating behind me.

He's coming for you.

The Thief of Souls.

Des warned me it would get worse. I just hadn't really understood.

"Have those sleeping women ever done that before?" I ask, glancing over at Des.

The fae king watches me from a side chair, his fingers steepled over his mouth.

"No."

He doesn't even try to dodge the question like he's usually so fond of doing.

"And you heard everything they said?"

"You mean their little rhymes?" he says. "Yes, I did."

He's been uncharacteristically somber since we left the chamber of sleeping warriors. His wings only disappeared a few minutes ago, but I know better than to assume he's unaffected by what we heard.

He's just better at hiding his meltdown than I am.

"First the children, and now this," he says, his seat groaning as he leans forward in it. "Apparently this enemy has taken a liking to you." A flash of anger in those silver eyes.

My panic rises all over again.

The Bargainer stands, his presence almost menacing as the darkness curls around him. His hammered crown and war cuffs only serve to make him look more intimidating. He comes up close to me, placing a finger under my chin.

"Tell me, cherub," he says, tilting my chin up, forcing me to meet those silver eyes of his, which look almost feral. "Do you know what I do to enemies who threaten what's mine?"

Is he referring to me? I can't tell, nor can I tell where he's going with this.

He leans in close to my ear. "I kill them." He pulls away to meet my gaze. "It's neither quick nor clean."

His words send shivers up my arms.

"Sometimes I feed my enemies to creatures I need favors from," he says. "Sometimes I let the royal assassins practice their skills on them. Sometimes I let my enemies think they've escaped my clutches, only to recapture them and make them suffer—and *how* they suffer. The darkness cloaks many, many deeds."

It scares me when Des gets like this. When his Otherworldly cruelty surfaces.

"Why are you telling me this?" I say softly.

His stares into my eyes. "I am the scariest thing out here. And if anything tries to touch you, they will reckon with me."

The next few days, Des spends in the Otherworld, doing his kingly duties, while I stay back at his Catalina home. He's invited me along, but, um, yeah, I'm good on this side of the ley line for now.

Meanwhile, I've read over some of Des's case notes, which largely restate what he's already told me. It mentions the human servants with their bruises and haunted eyes, the fairies who fall into that deep sleep after caring for those strange children, and the people who chose death over answering Des's questions. The whole mystery is one sad, disturbing trail of destruction.

When I'm not reading up on the case, I'm either exploring the island of Catalina or Des's house. Right now, I'm up to the latter.

I wander into the Bargainer's room, flicking on the lights. My eyes move from the art hanging on the walls to the metal model of the solar system to the wet bar.

I've been curious as to why Des didn't want me to see this room when he first gave me a tour of the house. There's nothing much in here.

I move over to his dresser, opening the drawers one after the other. Inside each are piles of folded shirts and pants.

The mighty King of the Night stores his clothes just like the rest of us.

I close the last drawer and move farther into the room, not seeing much else I can rummage through. Seriously, this is one of the most spartan rooms I've come across, and I do my fair share of snooping in my line of work.

My eyes land on one of his bedside tables. The only thing resting on it, besides a bedside lamp, is a leather-bound portfolio. I remember from our time together that Des loved to sketch; I even got him a sketchbook at one point.

I move over to the book, my hand curving over the soft cover. But then I hesitate. This is private—it's essentially Des's journal.

But he's never been unwilling to share his artwork before.

Making a decision, I open the portfolio.

I stop breathing the moment I see the first picture.

It's of...me.

The portrait is quite simple, just a basic sketch of my head, neck, and shoulders. I run my finger down the penciled slope of my cheek, noticing how bright my eyes look in the drawing, how hopeful I appear. I remember Des drawing this in my dorm room over seven years ago. I also remember seeing the image and completely not connecting with it. I'd been so lonely then, so full of my own demons, I couldn't imagine that anyone looked at me and saw this beautiful girl. But I'd been flattered nonetheless.

After all this time, he kept it.

I feel more of my defenses crumbling. The wall I built around my heart is in shambles, and apparently Des doesn't have to be here to destroy it.

The next sketch is of me sitting on the floor, my back against my dorm room bed, giving a petulant look to the artist drawing me. Scrawled beneath the picture is a note: *Callie wants me to stop drawing her. This is how she looks when I tell her no.*

I grin a little as I read that. Mighty words, but Des had at least partially caved in to my request; he drew me all sorts of landscapes and Otherworldly creatures in addition to the portraits of me he was so fond of.

The next drawing is one I've never seen, and unlike the other sketches, this one's more painstakingly executed. At first, all I can make sense of is the odd angle of the drawing, like the artist was on his back, looking down the length of his body. Then I make out the woman curled up against the chest we're looking down at. I recognize my dark hair, the top of my nose, and the contours of my face, which is somewhat buried against Des's chest.

This could've been one of many nights when I fell asleep curled against him, but something about the image... something about it makes me think it was one of the bad nights, the nights when Des stuck around to scare off my nightmares. I can feel an echo of that old pain even now.

Those evenings were what made me realize I loved the Bargainer. That it wasn't just infatuation but something I could feel on my skin and in my bones. Something that couldn't be extinguished.

I didn't fall for Des because he was handsome or because he knew my secrets but because he stuck around when I was least lovable. Because he was a man who didn't try to take anything from me even when I lay next to him but instead gave me peace and comfort. Because each one of those nights, he saved me all over again, even if it was from myself.

And if this picture is anything to go by, it was a moment Des wanted to remember as well.

I flip to the next image, this one in color. Most of the drawing is set in deep shades of blue and green. In it, I'm smiling, a ring of fireflies resting on the crown of my head. I remember this night too—

A knock on the front door jolts me from my thoughts.

What am I doing? I definitely shouldn't be looking through these. Even if I am clearly the Bargainer's muse.

Hastily I close the portfolio, arranging it how I found it. I throw several glances back at it as I cross the room. He kept those old drawings all this time. Again I'm reminded of his confession about how he felt leaving me.

Like my soul was ripped in two.

And once again, I feel hope so sharp it's almost painful.

That too is whisked away when someone pounds on the door again.

Who would visit Des here?

I get my answer a few seconds later, when I peer through the door's peephole.

"Shit," I mutter under my breath.

"I heard that, Callie," the familiar, gravelly voice says.

The Bargainer doesn't get visitors here.

I do.

CHAPTER 21

May, seven years ago

"Holy fuck," Des says, materializing in my dorm room. "It's a war zone out in your hallway."

In the hallway, I hear a muffled shout as some girl loses her shit because her nail polish smudged *and ohmygod there's no time to fix it.*

I close my laptop and swivel around in my chair. I glance down at my bracelet. I hadn't called the Bargainer tonight, nor had I the day before and many nights before that. Somewhere along the way, Des started inviting himself over.

Des crosses my room and peers out my window. Far below us, girls in gowns and boys in tuxedos cross the lawn. "What's going on tonight?"

"May Day Ball."

Des glances over at me, his eyebrows raised. "Why aren't you getting ready?"

"I'm not going," I say. I pull my legs up onto my chair.

"You're not going?" He sounds surprised.

Isn't it already obvious? I'm wearing boxer shorts and a worn T-shirt.

I suck in my lower lip and shake my head. "No one's asked me."

"Since when do you wait for permission?" he asks. "And also, how is that possible?"

"How is what possible?" I ask, staring down at my knees.

I'm grumpy. Officially grumpy. If I still went to my former high school, I wouldn't have to hear the excited squeals of girls as they got ready, and they wouldn't notice how my door was ominously shut.

"That no one's asked you."

I shrug. "I thought it was your job to understand people's motives."

When I look up, Des's arms are folded across his chest, and I have his full attention.

"What?" I say, suddenly self-conscious at all the attention.

"Do you want to go to the May Day Ball?" he asks.

Oh God, I'm not admitting this to him. I tuck a strand of hair behind my ear. "I don't see how that matters."

He cocks his head, and sweet baby angels, he's going to read me. He's *already* reading me.

"It does matter. Now, do you?"

I open my mouth, and I know that everything is in my eyes. That I don't fit in, and people don't entirely like me. That I'm an outsider and I want in, I always want in, but I don't get to walk inside that particular door. I'm forever banished to watch other people live their lives while I wait for mine to begin—or end. It really could go either way. My existence so far has mostly consisted of me holding my breath, waiting for the other shoe to drop.

Des is moving, closing the remaining space between us, and I'm just staring at him like a fool, my knees pressed close to my chest.

He kneels in front of me, the air shimmering beyond his shoulders. He takes my hand, his eyes serious.

My heart's in my throat, and I can't swallow it back down. I feel bare in the most exquisite way, and I'm not sure why that is.

He begins to smile. "Would you, Callypso Lillis, take me to the May Day Ball?"

————————

Present

Eli. The most wanted list. That's all I can think about as I step outside Des's home and face my ex.

Our last confrontation feels like a million years ago. Honestly, after everything that's happened in the Otherworld, this just seems so insignificant by comparison.

"Were you trying to get caught, or did you just not give two shits about it?" Eli asks.

"I didn't give two shits about it." I fold my arms over my chest and lean against the entryway wall. Now I feel the heat of my anger coming back. This bastard. "I can't believe you had the audacity to come into my home and threaten my life *and then*, as if that weren't enough, you put my name on the goddamn wanted list."

"Callie, I never would've hurt you," he says, his voice soft. He looks almost wounded. And I'm sure it is wounding on some level, considering he is the protector of his pack.

"You came into my house during the Sacred Seven," I say. "Of course you could have hurt me."

He shakes his head. "You're pack. Or at least you were."

I feel my hackles rising at his reaction.

"Do you put all pack members on the wanted list?" I ask.

Let's see just how big Eli's balls are.

Eli runs a hand down his face. "What I did, all of it, was a mistake," he says, his voice defeated. "I was angry, and my wolf was demanding justice..." He sighs. "It's no excuse, but I regret it, if it makes any difference."

I press my lips together. It's not like I handled things well either, but putting someone on the supernatural wanted list far outweighs any wrongdoing on my part.

"I'm not going to let you arrest me," I say.

He lets out a breath. "I'm not taking you in. I just... needed to talk to you."

"You could've just called."

"I'm sorry," he says, his voice genuine. Coming from an alpha like him, an apology is a rare thing.

I work my jaw. I'm still so peeved at the whole thing. Pushing down my frustration, I nod, looking away. I'm not sure whether I'm acknowledging Eli's apology or accepting it. All I know is that I want to bury the hatchet between us.

The shifter's eyes move to the Bargainer's house. "My offer still stands, Callie."

I glance at him.

"What I did was wrong, but what this guy's doing, that's worse. He's taking away your free will," he says. "The Bargainer is a wanted man. Just give me the word and I'll go in there and take care of the issue."

It takes several seconds to register what he's saying. When it does, horror washes over me. "No, I don't want that."

"*Callie.*" The alpha is in his voice.

"Don't," I warn. He no longer has the right to exert his pull over me. "There's so much you don't know."

"Then tell me," he says. "Or else I'm just going to keep assuming the worst."

Isn't that exactly what I've been demanding of Des? To stop keeping secrets? And here I am being a hypocrite.

But this secret...

"I never told you about my past." I rub my face.

Even now, I hesitate to tell Eli. It hurts to remember, and then there's the shame. Always the shame.

But perhaps if I tell him, he'll understand why I acted the way I have. And perhaps it will help him feel better, about me, about Des, and about the situation.

"When I was a minor," I begin, "my stepfather...my stepfather..."

Eli goes still.

"He sexually abused me." I force the words out.

I hear a low growl. This is what I've always loved about shifters—about Eli. Abusers earn swift deaths in packs. No one fucks with their young. No one. That's always made them feel safe to me.

I blow out a shaky breath. "It went on for years. And it only stopped..." I pause again, pinching my forehead.

I can do this.

"When I was almost sixteen, he came at me, and I fought him off with a broken bottle. Nicked an artery." *All that blood.* "He was dead in a matter of minutes."

Eli's growl is growing louder and louder.

I stare at my hands. "I *killed* a man. I wasn't even an adult. I thought my life was over before it had begun, all because I finally fought off the person abusing me." My voice drops. "He was such a powerful seer. Had I done things the legal way, I just...I don't know if it would've ended well for me."

I take a deep breath.

"So I called on a man infamous for his deals…"

That's all I manage to get in before Eli pulls me into a hug, holding me close. "I'm so sorry, Callie. So fucking sorry."

I shudder a little as the memory runs its course through me and I nod against him.

"You should've told me this. All of this," he admonishes me quietly.

"I'm bad at sharing," I admit.

He holds me for close to a minute, and I appreciate the comfort.

Eventually, I step out of his arms, wiping away a tear that's managed to sneak out from the corner of one of my eyes.

"What you have to understand," I say, "is that the Bargainer *saved* me. He cleaned up the mess, enrolled me in Peel Academy, hid my crime."

Telling Eli this is a gamble. The shifter is one of the good guys. He could drag me away, dig up that old case, and let the system do its work.

I'm sort of banking on the fact that Eli's sense of justice—*pack* justice—will align with my actions; people who do bad things to innocent shifters just sort of disappear.

"The Bargainer didn't charge me then," I continue. "I know you think he did, but he has his own code of ethics. Because I was a minor at the time, he wouldn't allow me to do business with him like that."

Now knowing what I do about fairies, true favors are kind of a big deal. The fae live to take advantage of a situation.

Eli seems to understand this too. The werewolf raises his eyebrows.

"It was only later that I called him again. And again. And again. I came up with all sorts of favors just so that he could stick around for a while." Because I was intrigued by him.

Because I was infatuated by him. Because I wanted a friend who wasn't scared off by my darkness—and Des wasn't.

"He should've never made those deals with you," Eli growls.

I play with my bracelet, rolling the beads round and round my wrist. "No, he probably shouldn't have," I agree. "But we've all given in to our baser natures a time or two, haven't we?" I say.

Eli grunts, looking out over the Bargainer's property. He rubs his face. "I wish you would've told me all these things long ago."

Could've, would've, should've. It does no use getting upset about it now.

"Did I ever have a chance?" Eli asks.

I glance over at the shifter. "I don't know. But I do know that you deserve someone who can give you far more than I can."

Stepping in close, Eli rests his palm against the side of my face. "That son of a bitch is a lucky man."

The words are barely out of his mouth when behind us, the front doors slam open.

I turn just in time to see Des striding out from his home, his wings visible. His stormy eyes flick to Eli, who's still standing close to me, and I see a flash of possessiveness in them.

Reflexively, I step away from the shifter.

It's broad daylight out here, which isn't exactly Des's favorite time of day. He was supposed to be in the Otherworld for several more hours. Clearly, something changed.

Did he think I was in distress? How would he even know that?

The ground shivers with Des's power, his gaze intent on Eli as he stalks toward him.

I step in front of the Bargainer, placing a hand on his chest to stop him from whatever he's thinking of doing.

He glances down at my hand, his nostrils flaring, before his eyes move back to Eli. "You have two seconds to get off my property before I make you," he says to the shifter, his voice smooth as liquor.

Eli stares at Des's wings for a long moment, looking stunned. Finally, he tears his gaze away. "I didn't know," he says.

I look between the two men. "Know what?"

The Bargainer watches Eli for several seconds. Then ever so slightly, he inclines his head. "Now you do."

"Callie told me what you did for her when she was a kid," Eli says. "Thank you for helping her," he continues. "No more bad blood between us, okay? I didn't realize the situation—any of it."

Again, Des inclines his head.

Eli backs away, casting a glance in my direction. "Take care of yourself, Callie," he says, raising a hand goodbye. And then he turns and walks off the property and out of my life.

My brow is still furrowed long after Eli leaves. Nothing about what just happened makes a terrible amount of sense.

I was expecting a confrontation of some sort between the two men, but instead, I get apologies and understanding. I should be relieved, but as Des leads me back inside, my eyes drift to his wings.

That's what Eli was staring at with such shock. The fae king's wings. The same wings Des studiously hid from me in the past.

There's something I'm missing, and I'm going to figure out what it is.

———

Before Des and I can talk about any of what just happened, I mumble some excuse about needing to go to the bathroom and slip away to my room.

Locking the door behind me—not that it would stop the Bargainer—I grab my phone and dial Temper, pacing back and forth across the room.

"Hey babe, what's up?" she answers.

"Temper, you know a fair bit about fairies, don't you?" I say, jumping right in.

Before we became private investigators, when Temperance Darling was just another misfit at Peel Academy, she had a minor obsession with fairies. When I originally met her, she'd wanted to be a diplomat stationed in the Otherworld.

"Mmm, *fair bit* might be taking it too far, but I know a few things. Why? What do you need to know?"

"Eli confronted me and—"

"He *found* you?" Temper interrupts, her voice incredulous. "Already? Wow, you suck at hiding."

"And how do you think he found me? Could it be because he tapped your phone?" I say.

There's a pause over the other end of the line.

"Well, shit," she says. "That is just messed up."

"It's fine. We talked through our issues, and now we're good."

Another pause. Temper has a habit of those around me. "Are you telling me you managed to talk your way off the most wanted list?"

When she says it like that...

"Oh my God, you *did*." She barks out a laugh. "Callie, you must have a vagina of gold."

I chew on a thumbnail. Outside my room, I can hear

the Bargainer moving around, impatient. I'm going to have to go out there and talk with him soon. He and I both have questions that need answering.

"Listen, Temper, I need to talk to you about something important."

Immediately, her tone changes. "What is it?"

"What do you know about fairy wings?"

"Um…they're sparkly—at least some of them. They come out most commonly when a fairy loses control of their emotions—you know, anger, lust, if a fairy drinks too much… Um, I know there's more. Let me think. It's been a while since I read up on this stuff…"

I remember the look in my ex's eyes today when he saw those wings: *game over*.

"Today, when Eli saw the Bargainer's wings, he backed off. It was really weird, and I just wanted to know…"

What do I want to know?

"Those two met? Again?" And then the rest of what I said catches up to her. "Wait. What do you mean Eli saw the Bargainer's wings?"

"It's not like this is anything new," I say. "Eli saw them before, when he came to my house around the full moon."

"Yeah, but they would come out when the Bargainer was under attack if he needed to use them to fly," Temper says. "What happened today?"

I fiddle with my bracelet. "There was another confrontation between the Bargainer and Eli, and this time when Eli saw the Bargainer's wings, the whole dynamic changed. It was weird. I mean, Eli *apologized*."

Perhaps it was because of everything I told him. Perhaps I was barking up the wrong tree.

More silence.

Finally, "Has the Bargainer shown you his wings?" Temper sounds...odd. "Outside of situations when they're needed or when he was being attacked? Has he just, you know, walked around with his wings out? And flashed them like they're his favorite accessory?"

"Yes," I say slowly, my stomach tightening. "Why?"

She exhales. "*Callie.*"

"*What?*"

"There is one instance when fairies are particularly fond of keeping their wings out and flashing them whenever they feel like it. Especially the males."

She just stops speaking.

"Oh my God, your silence is killing me," I say. "Temper, whatever it is, just say it."

"Fairies only do this with their betrotheds."

CHAPTER 22

May, seven years ago

This can't be real life.

An hour ago, I didn't have a date, a dress, or a ticket to the May Day Ball.

Now I have all three, thanks to the man next to me.

I glance over at Des as we wait to enter Peel Academy's ballroom, and my knees go a little weak.

There is a God and he loves me, I think as I drink Des in. I've never been particularly fond of men in tuxedoes, but then, I'd never seen Des in one.

His face looks a touch softer, younger, and I don't know whether to blame magic for it or simply his clean-cut attire. His white-blond hair is free of the leather band he usually wears, and it skims his shoulders.

Des runs a hand through that hair now, looking untouchable. And yet I swear he's uncomfortable.

Perhaps it's because tonight people can see him.

Ever since the two of us walked out of my dorm room, people have come to a grinding halt. Callypso Lillis, the pretty but weird outsider, is going to the May Day Ball, and the guy taking her is a *babe*. At least that's what I assume they're thinking based on their wide eyes and lingering looks.

It could also be the fact that Des simply looks like trouble, with his staggering frame and rakish features. His tattoos are hidden, but there's no masking the edgy vibe he's giving off.

We make it up to the entrance and hand our tickets over, and then we're inside.

I can feel dozens of eyes on us, and I realize I'm beginning to tremble from the attention. This is high school, where students excel at making undesirables feel invisible. I'd been invisible for so long, and that was fine with me. So fine.

But tonight I can already tell no one's going to ignore me. Not with my beautiful and dangerous date at my side. And not while I wear this dress, with its choker of diamonds that holds the fitted silver silk taut against my body. The backless expanse of it dips to just past the small of my back. More strings of diamonds trail down my spine, holding the edges of the silk in place. The hem of the gown drags against the ground. It's a dress a celebrity should wear, or a queen—or a fairy. Not me.

But I really didn't have a choice in the end. It's not like my closet came stocked with prom dresses. And this was the one Des procured for me.

We're only inside the school's ancient ballroom for a minute before Trisha, one of the girls on my floor, approaches me.

"Callypsie!" she squeals, and ugh, shoot me now, that nickname needs to die.

"Callypsie?" the Bargainer says under his breath.

"*Don't*," I warn. "If you care for your balls at all, *don't*."

At the beginning of the year, one of the girls on my floor started calling me that, because for whatever reason, Callie wasn't a good enough nickname, and it just never fucking went away.

The Bargainer snickers. "Whatever you say…Callypsie."

I don't have time to make good on my threat before Trish is on me.

"I didn't realize you were coming!" she says, pulling me in for a hug.

This is awkward. Trish is one of those girls who I must've pissed off at one point in time, because her hobbies include studiously ignoring me.

Except for right now.

I pat her back, willing her to release me so I can understand what sort of hex has been put on her to make her address me. And as *Callypsie*, of all things. I thought she'd missed that nickname during all that time she pretended I didn't exist.

And then she turns to the Bargainer, and *holy shit*, she is giving him one hell of a predatory look.

I move a little closer to him. I find I don't really like sharing Des. It's a pretty illusion to believe that he's mine and mine alone, but among this crowd, he might as well be. No one here knows him. No one here has seen him orchestrate a deal or collect repayment. No one has played poker with him or sipped tea and chatted over pastries with him. No one has had movie marathons or heart-to-hearts with him. No one here knows that he's kind and cruel and wicked and funny and everything in between.

But the way Trisha's staring at him, like if she had five minutes alone with him, she could win him over, is making me question my decision to come to the dance. Because maybe five minutes is all it would take. I really don't know, and I'm afraid to find out.

"Um," I say, "this is my date—"

"Dean," the Bargainer fills in for me, extending his hand.

Trish looks moonstruck as she takes his hand. I seriously hope I don't wear that expression around Des.

I probably do.

"How do you and Callypso know each other?" she asks as Des releases her hand. She smiles shyly, like she's some coquettish little flower. I can't decide if I want to smirk or grimace at that.

I turn to Des, and I'm so scared he's going to tell the truth.

Oh, Callie and I met right after she murdered her stepfather. She's quite vicious if you really get to know her...

Des drapes his arm around my waist and looks at me fondly. "I saved her life. At least that's how she puts it, isn't it, cherub?" He gives me a little squeeze as he does so.

His eyes twinkle as I gaze up at him. The man is definitely playing us up and having entirely too much fun doing so.

I can't find the words to respond, so I nod.

"Oh," Trish says, furrowing her brows. "That's...odd. Wow, so are you two a thing?"

Her eyes move briefly to me before returning to the Bargainer. The girl is undressing him slowly in her mind's eye, and damn it, I had a corner on that particular market up until today.

The Bargainer's gaze moves past Trish's shoulder. "Your date's waiting for you, Trish Claremont. Don't leave him hanging."

"How do you know...?" Her words trail off at whatever she sees on Des's face. She glances over her shoulder, backing away. "Uh, yeah, well, it was nice meeting you, Dean." She doesn't bother saying goodbye to me before she hastily retreats.

He watches her walk away, his eyes narrowed.

"That was weird," I say.

Weird is just a euphemism for an emotion I can't actually put a name on. Obviously a part of me is territorial, which is embarrassing because Des isn't even mine, but it's more than that. It's being both pleased and disappointed to be recognized for the first time in your life by someone you don't like. And it's shame that a part of you even feels pleased at something as basic as human recognition. But then again, Trisha *hadn't* really seen me tonight. Not as a friend, not as a threat. My existence began and ended with the introduction I gave her.

Bringing Des here might've been a very bad idea.

The Bargainer's lips brush against my ear. "Let's find a table. Maybe I'll even let you straddle me and pretend that we're a thing for the next girl who asks."

That's all it takes to wipe away my somber mood.

My skin begins to brighten just from the thought of getting to straddle Des. In other words, this siren totally popped a lady boner.

Des doesn't have time to remark on it before more acquaintances come over.

And so we do that same little song and dance all over again. And again.

Right in the middle of introductions to Clarice, a girl from my myths and legends class, the Bargainer takes my hand and leads me away. I barely have time to throw her an apologetic glance over my shoulder before I'm swept off.

"Where are we going?" I ask.

Students part as soon as they see Des. "Dance floor," he says over his shoulder.

I slow a little. Dancing is not really my thing.

He gives a little tug, and what pathetic resistance I have falls away.

I catch up to his side. "That was insanity back there," I say, because I can't think of anything better.

"That was hellacious," he says, "and I'm used to events like this. Thank fuck I never went to high school." That gets him a look or two from people who've overheard us.

"You never went to high school?" I ask as we weave between couples. I don't know why I'm surprised; nothing about Des seems particularly normal.

But still.

"My upbringing was a little more unconventional."

Because Des is a king of the Otherworld. A *king*.

I brought a fae king to my supernatural prom.

Jesus. All I need is the "Monster Mash" playing in the background to round this out.

We step onto the dance floor just as one song ends and a slow one begins.

I suck in a breath, about to be like, "Oh, ew, a slow song, let's sit this one out," despite wanting to latch on to the Bargainer like a koala. But before I can get a word in, he pulls me in close, one of his hands going to the small of my back, where my skin is exposed.

There's something oddly intimate about his hand touching the bare skin at the base of my spine, something that has my cheeks flushing.

I have no idea what to do with my hands. No freaking clue.

The Bargainer leans in. "Put your arms around my neck," he says.

Tentatively, I do so.

I've fallen asleep draped along this man, and yet this feels oddly more exposed, what with him looking down at me, his silver eyes shining strangely.

I give him a nervous smile, one I'm sure he sees right through.

His head dips down to my ear. "Relax, cherub."

His thumb strokes the exposed skin of my lower back, and my mouth goes dry. My eyes drop. I can feel the pull to give in to the siren. I don't have a good handle on her yet. But as the song goes on, I get more comfortable. I decide to peek up at Des.

I'm not prepared to see the tormented expression on his face.

"What's wrong?"

"Everything, cherub," he says. "Everything."

———————

Present

I stare at my phone long after I hang up with Temper.

Fairies only do this with their betrotheds.

Technically, Des and I are lovers, but we aren't in any sort of relationship. And we definitely aren't *betrothed*, to use Temper's outdated word.

But Des *has* been flashing his wings—to me and now to Eli—without bothering to mention that it meant he was staking some sort of claim on me.

My blood is beginning to boil.

How dare he.

I storm out of my room only to find the Bargainer pacing, looking agitated as hell.

"Is it true?" I demand.

He pauses. "Is what true?"

I'm almost surprised he's not aware of what I talked about with Temper. So much for being Master of Secrets, or whatever the fuck his title is.

"About your *wings*," I say. "Is it true that you've been flashing them to let everyone know that I belong to you? That I'm your betrothed?"

He goes utterly still, but his eyes...his eyes are bright. Around us, shadows begin to gather in the room.

Alarm bells are going off in my head.

"It *is*," I say as the truth dawns on me.

Carefully, he approaches me.

"You *bastard*," I say. "Were you ever going to tell me?"

He stops in front of me, looking a little menacing.

And I don't give two shits.

I poke him in the chest. "Were. You?"

He looks down at my finger, like I personally offended him. And then I see the corner of his mouth curl.

He steps deeper into my space, his chest brushing mine. "Are you sure you want to know my secrets, cherub?" he says. "They will cost you much more than a wrist full of beads."

"Des, I just want answers from you."

I'm surprised to see his eyes deepen with excitement. He picks up a lock of my hair and rubs it between his fingers. "What can I say? Fairies can be incredibly jealous, selfish lovers."

"You should've told me."

"Perhaps I was proud to have my wings out," he admits, setting my lock of hair back down. "Perhaps I enjoyed the way you looked at them and the way others looked at them. Perhaps I felt things that I haven't felt before."

As he speaks, his wings slowly unfurl. And with each

297

word he says, my irritation dissipates. In its place is something more uncomfortable. Something that makes my heart ache.

"Perhaps I didn't want to tell you only to find out that you didn't feel the same. I know how to be lethal, Callie. I know how to be just. I don't know how to deal with you. With us. With this."

"With what?"

He's still being cryptic, even now after he promised to tell me his secrets.

He runs a finger along my collarbone. "I haven't been wholly honest with you."

This isn't exactly a shocking revelation.

"There was a question that you asked me," he continues. "*Why now?* I've been gone seven years, Callie. So why do I come back now?"

I furrow my brows. "You needed my help," I say. The mystery, the missing women. He'd been very clear about that.

He laughs, and the sound has an edge to it. "A lie that became the truth."

Now I give him a strange look. If not for that reason, then why?

He touches my cheek gently.

"*Callie.*" It's not so much that he says my name as it is the way he says it. His wings spread fully out, the span of them stretching across his living room. The things are huge. "A fairy doesn't show his wings to his betrothed." He slides his hand behind my neck, his thumb stroking my skin. "A fairy shows them to his soul mate."

CHAPTER 23

May, seven years ago

After the dance, Des walks me back to my dorm, disappear-ing only long enough to slip past the girl manning the main desk in our lobby.

Now he hesitates at the threshold of my room, looking conflicted as hell.

Rather than question the look, I grab his hand and tug him in, closing the door behind him. I drop the hem of my dress, which I've been carrying since we left the dance, afraid to dirty it any more than I already had. It's the prettiest piece of clothing I've ever worn.

I run my hands nervously down the bodice. "Thank you," I say quietly, staring down at my feet.

Des doesn't respond, but I feel his eyes on me. Those wicked, calculating eyes.

"Tonight was…" Something from a dream. I can still feel the way he held me when we danced. "…wonderful."

The Bargainer sits down heavily on my bed, running his hands through his hair.

I wait for some reaction, but it doesn't come.

The silence inside this tiny little room stretches on, and for once, it isn't comfortable.

"Is something wrong?" I ask. I can feel worry churning inside me; I can practically taste the bitter bite of it at the back of my throat.

This can't just be the best night of my life. I don't get to have anything that sweet.

Poor Callie. Always on the outside, always looking in.

He drops his hands from where they cradle his head. "I can't do this anymore."

He looks up at me, and I nearly stagger back. For once, Des is the one with his emotions laid bare, and he's staring at me like he's been waiting for me his entire life.

Maybe I do get to have this night with all its sweetness.

Maybe I'll get more than just this night.

"Des? What are you talking about?"

I see his throat work as he stares at me, his gaze challenging. He pushes off my bed, standing once more. The way his jaw squares is making my heart race. He looks sinister. Dangerous.

He begins stalking toward me, his eyes raking over my body, his gaze hungry.

I despaired that this man felt nothing toward me. Now a good dose of fear floods my veins because a small voice is whispering, *Oh, but he does, and that is the much worse fate.*

"Give me one good reason why I shouldn't take you away from here tonight. Right now."

"Take me away?" I flash him an odd look. "Do you have another bargain tonight?" He hasn't been taking me on as many lately, not since I glamoured one of his clients.

He begins to circle me. "I would take you away and never release you. My sweet little siren." He runs a hand along the bare skin of my back, and I shiver. "You don't belong here, and both my patience and my humanity grow thin."

Something's not right.

"I could make you do so many things—so many, many things," he whispers. "You would enjoy them all, that I promise you. You would enjoy them, and so would I."

I swallow, my gaze darting down to my bracelet. I can feel his magic coaxing me toward something elusive.

"We could start tonight. I don't think I can bear another year," he says, eyeing me again. "And I don't think you can either." Just the way he says this is full of so much hunger.

As he moves around me, I catch his hand, trying to stop him and these weird, cryptic confessions of his.

"Des, what are you talking about?"

He threads his fingers through mine, holding our hands up between us. "How would you like to begin repayment tonight?"

Now there is nothing but sex and desire in his eyes.

For the past year, the only things that struck me as particularly fae-like about Des were his trickery and his brutality. But right now, Des is all fairy. It's in his words and his frightening expression. This version of him is dark and foreign.

Dark, foreign, and compelling.

And as he looks down at our intertwined fingers, his lips spread into the brightest, cruelest smile yet. I almost draw my hand away; something like self-preservation keeps me from running. I have a feeling this man is dipping his toes into treacherous waters right now, and any wrong move I make will send him tumbling headfirst into them.

I draw in a shaky breath. "Desmond Flynn, whatever's going on, I need you to snap out of it."

I sound a lot calmer than I feel. My pulse pounds like a drum between my ears.

He brings our joined hands close to his lips and closes his eyes. He stays like that, unmoving, for at least a minute. Long enough for me to worry. But eventually he does blink his eyes open, his nostrils flaring. And I know with just that one look that the Des I've come to know and rely on is back.

His expression holds a world of remorse. "I'm sorry, cherub," he whispers, his voice husky. "You weren't meant to see that." He continues, "I am...not human, for all I appear to be."

There's something singing in my blood, and I'm pretty sure a good portion of that is still fear, but mostly it's hope.

I'm not particularly brave, but I decide to be so now. "Do you...like me?" I ask. There's no mistaking my meaning.

The Bargainer releases my hand. "*Callie.*" He's pulling away, physically, emotionally.

"Do you?" I push.

Because I got those vibes when he was promising to take me away and make me repay him.

One of his thumbs brushes against my cheekbone. Still frowning, he dips his head.

He does.

My skin illuminates, its glow blindingly bright, and I'm happy, I'm so goddamn happy because he *likes* me, and I like him, and he took me to a dance, and maybe, just maybe—

This can work.

Even though he's more than a little scary, and even though my siren would love nothing more than to take advantage of him, he's the moon in my dark sky.

My dark king. My best friend.

I rise to my tiptoes.

"Callie—"

I cut him off with a kiss. It's a bit of an indulgence to call it a *kiss*. My lips graze his, and there they linger.

The Bargainer's hands move to my upper arms and he squeezes them. I swear he wants to pull me closer, but he doesn't.

His lips stay rigid beneath mine, and I'm going to lose courage fast.

But then he lets out a pained sound and his mouth does begin to move. Suddenly, it goes from being a "kiss" to being a *kiss*.

He gathers me into his arms, his lips sweeping over mine and his mouth moving desperately, like he can't get enough. Like this is the first, the last, the only kiss he'll ever get.

The whole thing takes my breath away. I slide my arms around his waist, feeling like I'm holding on for dear life. Every part of me fits perfectly against every part of him.

Hell couldn't give me a more wicked man; heaven couldn't give me a more perfect moment. A year I've waited, a year I've agonized, a year I've despaired that this would never happen.

And now it is.

One of Des's hands threads into my hair, roughly gripping it. He can't hold me any tighter, and yet I sense that he's trying. That he's trying to fill himself with my very essence.

And here I thought I'd worry about how crappy my kissing technique would be. I hadn't imagined this—that he'd crave me like a dying man craves life.

My lips part as I gasp in a breath of air, and it's like the action breaks a spell. One moment, Des's mouth is on mine; the next, it's gone.

He releases me, staggering back, his breathing heavy. Shadows gather around him, thicker and denser than I've ever seen them. They wrap around me too, looking like billowing black storm clouds.

But I only have time to wonder at his shadows before my eyes are drawn up—up, *up*.

Behind Des, two wicked, silvery wings flicker into existence, the sharp talon-tipped ridges of them rising above the Bargainer's head.

"Your wings..." I say, awed.

The only time our wings come out is when we want to fight or fuck, he'd said.

And I don't think he wants to fight me.

Des doesn't bother looking over his shoulder. He's still staring at me. "I'm sorry," he says. "It was never supposed to happen like this. I should've waited. I'd intended to wait."

"Des, what's wrong?" I say, taking a step forward. My stomach is plummeting. I can already sense his regret.

He drags a shaky hand through his hair. "I have to go."

"No," I say, my skin dimming.

"I'm sorry," he repeats. "I meant to give you more time. I never should have done this—any of it."

Any of it?

He can't be saying what I think he's saying. Especially not when his wings are still out. They've been twitching, like they want to spread themselves.

"But you *like* me," I say, not understanding what he's rambling about but hearing regret threaded throughout his voice.

"I'm a king, Callie. And you're..."

Broken.

"Innocent."

"I'm not innocent." God, I'm not.

He stalks forward and cups my cheek. "You are. You are so painfully innocent in so many ways, and I'm a very, very bad man. You should stay away from me, because I can't seem to."

Wait. "Stay away? But why?"

"I can't just be your friend, Callie."

I can't just be yours either.

"Then don't," I say, my voice hoarse.

"You don't know what you're asking," he says, searching my face.

"I don't care." And I really don't.

"But I do," he says quietly. There's a finality to his words.

I feel a tear drip out, because I know what this is.

It's a goodbye. And I don't understand any of it.

His voice drops. "*Don't cry.*"

"You don't have to go," I say. "Everything can go back to the way it was. We can just…*pretend* tonight never happened." I practically choke the words out. I don't want to pretend any of this away.

Des frowns. Still holding my chin, he pulls my face forward, kissing each of my tears.

When he pulls away, I see something in his eyes, something that makes me think the Bargainer's feelings run deeper than I assumed. That only confuses me more.

"Just…give me some time." Almost reluctantly, he releases me, backing up.

"How long are you going to be gone?" I ask. In the last year, I'd never gone more than a few days without seeing him.

His lips press together. "Long enough to figure out what I want and what you deserve."

The way he says that causes panic to unfurl inside me.

This is the end of something. I thought it was the beginning...but it's not. It was foolish of me to be so optimistic.

"What about my debts?" All 322 of them. They're a lifeline suddenly.

"They don't matter."

They don't *matter*? This is the Bargainer, the man who has made an empire off his deals. He wouldn't just squander hundreds of them.

Now it's more than just panic I feel. I'm terrified. He's leaving, not just for the night but for many. Perhaps for the rest of the nights of my life.

His hand falls to my doorknob. And I know this is it: the moment he walks out of my life.

All because of one single kiss. One kiss that revealed his wings.

Never before had I seen them. The one single time the unshakable Des slipped up was with me.

That has to be worth something, right? Something worth fighting for.

"One final wish." My voice is harder than I imagined. More resolute.

He bows his head. "Don't, Callie," he says, almost begging me.

His one weakness—a bargain. He can't seem to help himself when it comes to granting me favors.

I don't know what comes over me, what strange compulsion pushes me to say words that I have no right saying to the Bargainer. I only know that my very world has come to a standstill, and if I do nothing, it will fall off its axis.

I close my eyes, and words from an old book flow from my lips. "From flame to ashes, dawn to dusk, for the rest of our lives, be mine always, Desmond Flynn."

All I hear is his ragged breathing.

I don't even have the presence of mind to be embarrassed. The old binding verse spoken between lovers felt right leaving my lips.

I open my eyes, and the two of us stare at each other. I've never seen horror and wonder share space on someone's face, but he manages to wear both. And then he vanishes in a wisp of smoke.

I didn't know then that he wasn't coming back.

Present

A fairy doesn't show his wings to his betrothed. A fairy shows them to his soul mate.

I stop breathing.

The entire world goes quiet, until all I can hear is the pounding of my heart, my stupid, hopeful heart.

"You lie," I whisper.

He gives me a small smile, his eyes shining so brightly. "No, cherub, I'm not."

I feel like I'm on the verge of breaking. "So you're saying…?"

"That I'm in love with you? That I have been since you were that obstinate teen with way too much courage? That you're my soul mate and I'm yours? Gods save me, yes, I am."

My knees nearly buckle.

Soul mates.

Yes, my heart whispers, *soul mates.*

Seven years ago, I buried my past and recreated myself. Seven years ago, I fell in love.

I fell in love, and I never fell out of it. Which was problematic, because seven years ago, my first love broke my heart.

"But you left," I say softly.

He stays rigidly in place. "I did," he says, his eyes sad. "But I never meant to stay away."

"Then why did you?"

He runs a hand through his hair, looks away, then takes a deep breath, his gaze returning to me. "You were so damn young," he says quietly, his eyes searching my face. "And you'd been abused. And my heart chose you. I felt it that first night, but I didn't believe it, not until the feeling grew until it couldn't be ignored. I couldn't stay away. I could barely resist you at all, but I didn't want to push you into something. Not when you'd just escaped a man who took and took. I didn't want you to think that was all men were good for."

I can't breathe. A silent tear tracks down my cheek. Then another.

Des wipes my tears away, his expression so gentle. "So I let you play your game, buying favor after favor from me, until the day I couldn't take it. No mate of mine should *owe* me. But my magic, it has a mind of its own... Like your siren, I can't always control it. It thought that the more you owed me, the longer I could guarantee that you were in my life. Of course, that strategy came to an abrupt end the moment you cast your final wish."

Tears are still dropping down my face as I rack my brain for the wish he's referring to.

"That final wish of yours," he continues, "it was bigger than either of us. You wanted me, I was falling for you, and it wasn't right, Callie. I knew it wasn't right. Not when you were still recovering from what your stepfather had done. But I could be patient. For my little siren, my mate, I could."

He flashes me a soft smile, his eyes brimming with some deep emotion.

And I feel light as air. This is everything I wanted to hear all those years ago. And now it's making me cry harder. I thought my scarred heart had fallen for the one man who couldn't love me back.

His eyes go distant. "But that wish...I was a prisoner to it."

"What *wish*?" He keeps mentioning this ominous wish, and I have no idea what he's talking about.

Des's focus sharpens. "Your last one. On the night of the dance—'From flame to ashes, dawn to dusk, for the rest of our lives, be mine always, Desmond Flynn,'" he says, quoting the binding verse I spoke long ago.

My face heats. "You never granted that one."

"Are you sure about that?"

My skin goes cold as his words sink in. "You...you granted it?"

"I did," the Bargainer says, his eyes moving to my lips.

He'd agreed to be mine. My brain is exploding at that.

I glance at my bracelet. "But the beads never showed up..."

"They wouldn't, since you were already paying them off. We both were."

My breath catches, and a lump forms in my throat. "What do you mean?" I barely get the words out.

"A favor as large as the one you requested requires steep payment," the Bargainer continues. "Do you think my magic would allow you to buy yourself a mate so easily? That kind of favor requires a good dose of heartbreak and years of waiting—seven years, to be precise."

Seven years.

Oh God.

The Bargainer's magic is subtle; if you aren't looking for it, you'll never notice it.

That entire time I'd tried and failed to move on, all

that time I'd resented the Bargainer, it had all been part of my wish.

"Every day after your last wish, I worked myself raw trying to get close to you," Des says. "And every day, I was stopped by my very own magic, which had turned on me."

I'm shaking my head because I can't speak. The binding verse I'd spoken out of sheer desperation. As that final evening seven years ago replays itself in my head, I watch it from a new perspective—Des's. I inhale sharply when I realize how the events unfolded according to him.

He'd been bound to my wish just as much as I'd been. I'd never realized he couldn't just stop his own bargains.

"Then one day," Des continues, "the magic's hold on me loosened. I tried to approach you like I had a thousand times before, and this time, the magic didn't stop me." His silver eyes shine as he looks down at me. "Finally, after the longest seven years of my life, I was able to come back to my love, my mate. The sweet siren who loved my darkness and my bargains and my company when I was no one and nothing more than Desmond Flynn. The woman who took fate into her own hands when she spoke those ancient vows and declared herself mine."

A sly grin lifts first one side of his mouth, then the other. "Callie, I love you. I've loved you from the beginning. And I will love you long after the last star dies. I will love you until the end of darkness itself."

"You love me," I say, letting that sink in.

"I love you, Callypso Lillis," he repeats.

And then...I smile. My heart feels like it's going to burst.

"Do you...want to be with me?" I ask, suddenly shy. Part of me is still in disbelief.

Des pulls me in close. "Callie, this may be oversharing, but I'm getting the sense that you want that at the moment."

My smile widens. "I do."

His eyes move over my face. "I want to wake up every morning to you, cherub, and one day, in the future, when I've made myself worthy of it, I want to marry the shit out of you, and then I want to have lots and lots of babies with you. If, that is, you will have me."

I stare at Des, with his white-blond hair and striking silver eyes. It's all laid bare, his love, his excitement, his *yearning*. Des, who saved my life, who is looking at me like I'm his moon and his stars.

For once, the King of the Night is not in control of the situation. He doesn't hold any of the cards, but he has shown me his hand. And his hand is everything I ever wanted. He wants a future with me, one that includes marriage and children—and love, so much love.

And now he's asking me to make the decision of whether I still want him in my life.

I wanted him seven years ago, and all that time between then and now, I continued to want him, even when I knew it was impossible. Even when I hated him, I wanted him. I wanted him yesterday, I want him today, and I'll want him tomorrow and the day after. I want him for the rest of my life.

I always have.

"I'll be yours, if you'll be mine," I say.

Des smiles so bright that it reaches every corner of his face. I'm almost bowled over by it. "I'll always be yours, cherub."

And it's pure reaction, but I begin to grin back at him, even as a happy tear slips out.

My heart is breaking, and it's reforming, and my whole body is lit up from the inside out.

Des clasps my cheeks. "And mountains may rise and fall, and the sun might wither away, and the sea claim the land

and swallow the sky. But you will always be mine." He runs his knuckles over my cheekbone. "And the stars might fall from the heavens, and night might cloak the earth, but until darkness dies, I will always be yours."

CHAPTER 24

I blink several times once Des finishes speaking. "That was—"

"My land's version of a vow." He still hasn't dropped his hands from where they cradle my face. "I've wanted to say those words to you for *years*." He leans his forehead against mine. "Humans aren't the only ones with archaic lovers' vows."

And then Des kisses me.

A kiss to end all kisses. Love is another sort of subtle magic. It can bring people together and tear lives apart. It can wash away sorrow. It can forgive.

It can redeem.

Des's wings wrap around us until we're in our own little world. "Truth or dare?" he whispers.

"Truth," I say.

"Do you love me?" he asks. I swear once he asks, he holds his breath. But maybe I'm imagining things.

"I've never stopped."

For a moment, he closes his eyes, taking in my admission.

When he opens them again, they're full of so many emotions, and I know what happens next.

His hand drifts up from my chest and cradles my neck. He gazes at me like I'm some archaic deity he worships.

"Desmond."

His eyes move to my lips, and ever so slowly, he lowers his head. I meet him halfway, our mouths colliding. Both his hands move to either side of my face, tangling in my hair.

I don't try to stop the siren from taking the lead as soon as I give in. My skin glows brighter, and I wrap my arms around him, pulling him in close.

He breaks away, trailing kisses along the underside of my jaw, my neck, the juncture between my collarbones.

I make a small noise at the back of my throat, and I feel his smile along my skin. His hair tickles my flesh where it touches me, and the Bargainer's lips...they're moving lower, toward the valley between my breasts.

We're not stopping with just kisses. Not tonight.

His breath fans out along my skin, and I arch into him. He pulls away long enough to remove my shirt, then my bra. Tossing the garments aside, he spends several seconds gazing at my exposed torso. The look in his eyes is hungry.

I've never stood naked before him—and I've never seen him naked before, for that matter. The realization is shocking, considering all we've done.

Reaching behind his back, Des shrugs his own shirt off, and I marvel at his sculpted pecs, his toned arms, his rock-hard stomach. I skim my fingers over each of his abs, for the first time ever feeling like I have a right to touch him. He looks carved from marble, his skin taut over thick ropes of muscle. Not bulky like Eli is, but every bit as chiseled.

Soul mates.

He is mine, and I am his.

I'm almost dizzy with joy. Have I ever been this happy in my entire life?

The Bargainer scoops me up and carries me down the hall and into his bedroom, kicking the door shut behind us.

He lays me out on his bed, then lowers himself over me, his narrow hips nestled between my thighs. Even just that contact has me moving against him, impatient for more.

But unlike me, Des seems to have limitless patience, his gaze moving to my bare chest. His hand cups my breast, his thumb moving in circles around my nipple until it hardens. He bends down to it, his lips replacing his fingers. His tongue moves over it, and I arch into him.

Jesus, he's going to make me come before we're even fully undressed.

My hands move over the muscles of his back, my fingers clutching him close.

His mouth trails down my stomach, his hands sliding down either side of me. The Bargainer glances at me through his lashes when he hits the waistband of my jeans.

"Take them off," I breathe.

He doesn't do anything for a second, and I get the impression he's savoring this moment. Then he moves back up and kisses me. While he does this, I feel the brush of his magic. A moment later, my pants unzip themselves and slide off.

I can't help it. I break off the kiss to laugh.

The man himself grins down at me, but the humor in his expression fades into something far more wicked.

His face is inches from mine, his hair hanging down around his face.

"My mate," I say wondrously.

"Your mate," he repeats.

Even this is almost too much. My heart and my body can't take so many good sensations all at once. I feel like I'm going to come apart, and when I finally put myself back together again, I won't be the same Callie I once was.

I feel the breath of his magic again, and this time it's his pants that slide off. I only have a couple seconds to appreciate his black boxer briefs before they drag themselves off as well.

I've imagined this so many times, yet my mind has never done him justice. Every curve of muscle that wraps around his thighs, the defined V that points to his very large cock, the way his waist tapers in and fluidly transitions to his narrow hips and sculpted ass—it's better than anything my mind could conjure.

He lets me drink him in for a moment, and then he drapes himself back over me, his erection pressed firmly against my leg.

I'm glowing as brightly as I ever do. Normally, I have to withhold some of my powers when I make love; otherwise, my glamour can turn innocent words into commands that control my partner.

But with the Bargainer, I don't have to worry about that; he can't fall under my spell the way other men can. The sensation of being myself fully and completely—something I've never felt with anyone else—is liberating.

His hand touches my lacy panties. "These have to go." The second the words are spoken, I feel an invisible hand tugging them off.

There's no longer anything funny about the magic. Not when the Bargainer—Des—is staring at me with a promise in his eyes.

He kisses my lips, softly, gently, then positions himself. I can feel him at my entrance.

He pulls away from my lips, his eyes moving over my face. Again, I get the impression he's memorizing the moment. As he watches, he pushes into me.

My pelvis rises to meet his, and inch by inch, he slides inside me. My lips part in silent surprise, our eyes locked together. All those years of waiting, of hoping, of despairing, it all led to this moment.

Perfection.

A shiver racks his body when he's fully seated in me. "Want to stay here...forever."

My throat works as my hands move over his shoulders, then slip around his back. I want him to stay right here too, the two of us wrapped up in each other.

He slides almost all the way out before thrusting into me hard. I moan at the sensation, the sound unearthly.

The smile he flashes me is pure sin. "I like making my sweet siren moan."

He moves in and out of me, his strokes powerful.

God, he's staggering to look at. His brows are stitched together, his lips parted, and with each thrust, his abs flex. The sight of him doing this to me is itself nearly enough to get me off.

He lowers himself, his slick chest meeting mine, and his hands comb the hair away from my face.

He pulls me even closer, his cheeks brushing mine, his pace slow and tender.

Making love. That's what this is. He's being gentle, romancing me even after he's received my love and found himself between my legs.

This is how it might always be.

Nights like this that stretch on and on into the future. My heart hurts at the possibility. True love—it always seemed just beyond my reach. I only ever believed in it because I had acutely felt its absence all those years we spent apart.

For so long, I thought something was wrong with me emotionally. That I couldn't love fully, that I couldn't be myself, that I was weak. Here in this man's arms, I realize for the first time in a long time that I'm not broken. Not even close.

I'm his mate.

He's mine.

My hands slide up his corded back, then run along his arms, drinking in each one of his sculpted muscles.

The Bargainer bends down and nips at my breast, and suddenly I'm right there on the edge of an orgasm that's been building long before Des even entered me.

As if he can sense how close I am, Des deepens each thrust, his eyes riveted to me. He dips down and kisses me roughly.

"I like this look on you, cherub," he says. "And knowing I'm responsible for it."

My arms tighten around him, pulling him closer as my eyes close and my mouth parts.

"Don't you dare close your eyes," he says. "I want to see everything I do to you."

A burst of magic courses through me, forcing my eyes open.

"*Desmond,*" is all I have time to say before my orgasm rips through me.

I cry out, the sound its own sort of melody. My skin shimmers, its glow reflected in Des's eyes.

The Bargainer's thrusts become faster until his body stills.

And then, with a groan, an orgasm racks his body, forcing him into me harder and deeper than before.

As soon as he finishes, he rolls next to me and gathers me into his arms. He holds me tightly to him, like he can't bear even an inch of our skin apart. His skin is still slick with sweat, and mine is slowly dimming as the last remnants of my orgasm are replaced by a satiated exhaustion. He smells like me, and I smell like him.

He looks at me, wearing a wondrous expression. His eyes are happy, so unbearably happy.

"My siren," he says. "My mate. The years I've waited for you."

I can't stop the grin that spreads along my face lying in the Bargainer's arms. For the first time in my life, my world has felt unequivocally *right*.

One of Des's fingers traces my lips, his gaze transfixed on me.

"Why didn't you say anything that first day you came back to me?" I ask curiously. That could've saved us so much angst.

He huffs out a laugh. "If only, cherub. I wanted to, but you hadn't seen me in seven years, were currently in a relationship, and pretty much wanted to flay my ass alive. My options were limited."

I smile a little at that.

He pulls me closer. "Ah, I would give my kingdom for that smile alone."

I could bathe in Des's words. Words that normally taunt and tease and coax. Words that have seduced me over and over again. Tonight they're the sweetest serenade.

I run my fingers over his sleeve of tattoos. "What do all these mean?" There's a rose melting into tears. There are angels and smoke and scales that morph into an eye. All of it twists and turns down his shoulder and arm. It's beautiful and macabre.

Des strokes my hair, his eyes still full of uncharacteristic softness. It's a strange look on the normally terrifying Bargainer. It's a look I never want to leave his face.

He hesitates before answering. "I got them when I was a part of the Angels of Small Death," he finally says. "A brotherhood of sorts."

That has me craning my neck to peer at him. "You were in a *gang*?" I ask, putting together what he isn't saying.

He smiles wryly. "Semantics. We policed the streets when the Kingdom of Night was…under different leadership." He glances down at his sleeve, a frown forming. "It was a long time ago."

He really was a thug before he was ever a king. I don't know what exactly to make of it, except it seems somewhat fitting.

Fitting and petrifying.

"I thought you were a king," I say.

"I am a king."

"I thought you were *always* a king," I clarify.

"Disappointed?" he asks. His body stiffens, on edge.

I never realized just how much my words affect him.

I trace the lines of the weeping rose. "Not at all." I like the idea that this man didn't grow up in a castle. "I don't think I could've dealt with an entitled Desmond Flynn."

A blatant lie. I would've taken Des just about any way he came. I *had* taken Des without fully understanding his past.

But to know that he ruled the streets in the Otherworld like he ruled the streets here…it makes me appreciate who he is all the more. There's undoubtedly a sad story behind his past. Just like mine.

I hug him closer. "Tell me another secret," I say.

I can hear the smile in his voice when he speaks. "The night I first met you, I couldn't get you out of my head..."

I fall off to sleep to a soundtrack of the Bargainer's most intimate secrets.

In the early hours of morning, Des wakes me up. Rolling over me, he begins kissing me, his lips demanding.

I feel him hard against me, ready to go.

I moan a little, the siren in me already waking up. "Again?" I say, opening my arms to him even as I speak. "Aren't you even a little tired?"

I already throb from the two previous times tonight that he's woken me up. But in spite of myself, I smile like a cat that's licked up all the cream, utterly pleased.

Des lets out a husky laugh. "Cherub, there are benefits to being the Night King's mate."

My skin begins to glow all over again. Normally, my siren is left wanting. Always wanting. But the King of the Night knows exactly how to satisfy her.

How to satisfy me.

I move against him as his lips skim over my skin.

"Can't get close enough to you, love," he murmurs. "You leave me wanting, even when I'm buried inside you."

I know the feeling. Already there's this urgency that buzzes along my skin, to touch him, to taste him, to breathe him into me and never let him go.

And under all that is pure unadulterated awe.

Des *loves* me. Des spent seven years trying to get back to me.

Des has no idea what it means to be *my* mate.

I push him onto his back. His arms lock around my waist, and I end up straddled on top of him, my hair cascading down my back.

He reaches out and takes a handful of it, staring at it like he's never seen hair before.

I lean forward, my hands running over his chest and down his arms. "Sweet little fairy," I purr, my voice melodic.

Des raises a cocky eyebrow at that. He doesn't even need to say anything for us both to know that *sweet* and *little* are the last things he is.

"I'm going to give you *all* your wickedest desires," I whisper, the siren thick in my voice. I begin trailing kisses down his chest, moving lower, lower. "One…at…a…time."

He sucks in a breath when he realizes what I intend.

Lowering myself between his legs, my mouth closes around him.

His entire body tenses.

"*Gods*," he curses.

His hands delve into my hair, tangling it.

I move up and down, up and down, working him with my lips and tongue, my hands moving over every pleasure point until I have him bucking against me.

His breathing hitches, becoming ragged and uneven.

He's not going to last long. The thought makes me smile wickedly against him.

All at once, he pushes me away. When my eyes meet his, I see rampant hunger in his own.

"You do play dirty, siren," he says, rolling me onto my stomach.

Lifting my hips up, he rubs the head of his cock over my entrance. Up and down, up and down.

Gathering my hair into a fist, he leans forward, tilting

my ear toward him. "You didn't think the King of the Night would just be gentle, did you?" he says, his voice husky.

His hand moves between my legs.

He pinches my clit, and I let out a moan.

Des nips the shell of my ear. "Mmm, I like that sound."

"Des…" I lean my forehead against my pillow, panting.

Suddenly, he's pushing himself into me. I can feel my inner walls giving way, making room for him.

And now I let out another moan as he fills me.

Once he's deep inside me, he doesn't move.

"Cherub, never could I have imagined it would feel so good…"

It's been like this, every single time. Like the electric, restless chemistry between the two of us is finally, finally sated.

Then he does move, thrusting in and out of me with gathering force. He holds me against him, my hair still caught up in his fist. I'm trapped in his arms, arching back into him.

Our bodies begin to make wet, slick noises as we sweat. Darkness gathers around us, and my glowing skin is the only illumination in the room.

Des releases my hair all at once, only to tweak my nipples a moment later.

That's all it takes.

My orgasm shatters through me, going on and on and on. Somewhere in the middle of it, I hear Des shout, and then he's coming too, his cock driving in and out of me.

The two of us collapse together in a boneless heap.

From heartache to this. Life could not possibly get better.

The next morning, when I begin to wake, I stretch, my body sore in all the right places. Des's arm tightens around my midsection.

I'm smiling before I even open my eyes. When I do, I first catch sight of the Bargainer's white-blond hair. I skim a hand through it, enjoying touching him, exploring him, even when he's not awake.

His wickedly curving lips are slightly parted. Like this, he looks like an angel. He'd absolutely loathe the compliment, but it's true. Everything about him is perfect.

When he doesn't wake and I begin to feel like a creeper for staring at him, I slide out of his bed.

I swing by my bedroom to throw on some clothes, and then I pad over to the kitchen. The stupidest things make me smile, like the way the sunlight shines in through the windows or the sight of yesterday's bag of macarons.

I brew a cup of coffee and make my way to the back of the Bargainer's house. A grand set of French doors opens to a palatial backyard. A garden full of flowering vines and exotic shrubs lines it. A gurgling fountain sits right in the middle of the garden, aquatic plants growing from it.

Where the garden ends, land gives way to cliffs. Beyond the cliffs, a blue expanse of ocean spreads out for miles and miles. Today is a clear enough day that I can see the California coast.

I think back to all those days I'd sat on the edge of my property and stared out at Catalina Island. I'd never imagined that across that water, Des was right here, possibly staring back…

Forced to stay away from me because I made a foolish bargain seven years ago. And yet he was always just within sight.

It's all over now.

He's my soul mate.

I don't understand how it's possible. Here on earth, supernaturals know whether they have soul mates, much the same way I know I'm a siren. When we're teenagers, our powers awaken, including mating bonds.

And nothing of the sort was awakened in me.

But perhaps...perhaps it works differently in the Otherworld. Perhaps soul mates aren't predestined there as they are here. Or perhaps the bond manifests differently.

All questions I need to ask Des when he wakes.

I sit down at a patio table near the edge of the property and sip my coffee.

I glance down at my bracelet. It appears unchanged from yesterday, but as I count the beads, three whole rows are missing. I don't think Des even knowingly removed them.

His magic did.

I notice, however, that last night didn't remove the entire bracelet. Clearly, the Bargainer's magic doesn't believe that one night of revelations and proclamations of love (and a shit ton of sex) is enough to seal the deal.

It seems Des's magic is as capricious as my siren is naughty.

I close my eyes and breathe in the briny air, listening to the crash and the sea.

"Callypso Lillis, I've been looking for you."

I freeze at the sound of my full name and the strange, masculine voice at my back.

I turn in my chair and squint, staring at the sun. It dims, and in its place is a man of staggering beauty. His hair looks like spun gold and his eyes are the cerulean blue of the sky.

Some sort of supernatural. Nothing but magic makes a human look like that.

A moment later, my brain catches up with me.

Why is a stranger on Des's property—in his backyard no less? And how does he know my name?

Everything about the situation feels *wrong, wrong, wrong*, but I'm too shocked at the moment to react.

My siren, however, isn't.

Luminescent light ripples across my skin as she surfaces.

I stand abruptly. "How did you get back here?" I demand, my voice ethereal.

That's all I can say. Not *Get the fuck off this property*. Not *I'm going to call the cops*. Not *DES!*

He steps closer. "I told you, I've been looking for you."

He answers my question, but I don't think the siren compelled him to do so. He doesn't look like a glamoured man. He's not clamoring to get closer to me, waiting for my next command.

Which means…

Fairy.

Shit. The only other Otherworld creature I know is looking for me is the Thief of Souls.

Is this…him?

He saunters forward. "You are surprisingly difficult to get alone," he says.

I back up, bumping into the table behind me.

He's going to grab me.

I act on instinct, grabbing my cup of coffee from the table and throwing it at him. He lifts his hand in the air, and the mug and the liquid arcing out of it freeze in midair.

He extends his hand palm out, and ever so gently, the cup floats onto it, the coffee funneling back into the mug.

I open my mouth. "*DE—!*"

His eyes narrow on my lips, and my voice cuts off, my shout now silent.

I clutch my throat. "What have you…?" I might as well be mouthing the words, because my vocal cords are no longer producing any sound.

"Your colleague, Ms. Darling, said you were busy, but it doesn't look like you're busy."

The client who's been pestering me.

I continue backing up, my eyes darting to the house.

He smiles, and it's like he invented the act of smiling, it's so blindingly bright. "He's not going to save you."

The man disappears. A moment later, his arms lock around me as he grabs me from behind.

I go hellcat on him, kicking out, my hands scratching at anything I can reach. I scream and scream, uncaring that my voice has been muted.

"*Enough*," he breathes.

Magic slams into me, and the world goes dark.

CHAPTER 25

My eyes flutter open, and I rub my head, my mind groggy.
Above me is a rough-hewn rock ceiling. Sitting up, I glance
down my body. I'm no longer wearing my outfit from
this morning. Instead, I'm sheathed in a wispy copper-
colored dress, the edges of it embroidered in intricate,
shimmery patterns.

Don't remember changing...

I shiver. I'm cold. Really, really cold.

I look around. Three rock walls surround me. And
the fourth...

The fourth is a wall of iron bars.

Imprisoned. But where? Why?

I roll off the pallet I woke on. In the corner of the room,
there's what I would indulgently call a toilet. More like a
bowl set into the ground.

Scratched onto the wall nearest me are tally marks.
Dozens and dozens of them. None are slashed through, and
I can't decide if that's because the last prisoner intentionally

tallied the days this way or if several separate prisoners began tallying and never made it past four.

I notice the bastard who took me is nowhere to be seen. Was he the Thief of Souls or someone else entirely? He never even attempted to explain himself or his motives.

I make my way to the front of my cell, ignoring the sour taste at the back of my throat—the taste of residual magic. My eyes are fixated on the sight across from me.

A cavern of prison cells are cut into the shale. Row after row, level after level. They extend as far as I can see in all directions—up, down, left, right.

Inside each is a woman dressed similarly to me.

Goose bumps break out along my skin.

It looks just like my vision.

Are these the missing women?

If so, then I'm totally fucked. Des hasn't figured the mystery out, and it's been ongoing for nearly a decade. I'm not holding my breath that'll change simply because I'm here.

Where *is* Des? What must he think?

"Hello?" I call out.

No one answers.

In the distance, I hear quiet murmuring and the soft click of shoes along the walkways outside the cells, which must belong to prison guards. I grimace. If that's the case, then there are at least a handful of people who know what happened to the warrior women who disappeared from the Otherworld. And they're facilitating it.

Other than those few sounds, the cell blocks are eerily silent.

This is the place where hope comes to die.

And then, a thought strikes me, one that gives me courage.

"Bargainer," I rush to say, "I'd like to make a deal."

I wait for the air to shimmer and Des's large body to take up space in my cell.

A second passes. Then another. And another.

The cell remains exactly how I found it.

"Bargainer, I'd like to make a deal," I repeat.

He's always come in the past. *Always*. And after last night, I know that he will come for me now that our seven years are up.

Again I wait.

Nothing happens. My room remains empty. Horribly empty.

And now I have to accept that Des *can't* get to me, either because he's been incapacitated—an idea I reject with every fiber of my being—or something is preventing him.

Something like magic.

Something so powerful, a fae king cannot get immediately around it. That's what I now have to contend with. And if I want to make it out of here alive, I'll need to figure out a way to get past it.

Captivity is boring.

Frightening, but boring. It consists largely of me sitting in my cell, wondering what exactly is going to happen to me and how I managed to land myself in an Otherworld prison. One that is secretly capturing fae females for some nefarious purpose.

My thoughts are only interrupted every hour or so, when a set of guards makes their circuit past my cell. The first time I saw them, I'd startled at the sight. Each one looks like a blend of animal and man. Some have snouts instead of noses, others haunches instead of legs, and some whiskers, claws, and fangs.

To a human like me, the sight is…off-putting. But then again, the guards are also currently my enemies, so I'm a bit biased.

The only time the guards stray from their hourly patrol is when, like now, two of them cart a fae woman by the armpits back to her cell.

I press my face to the bars, taking in her slumped shoulders, her bowed head, and her lank hair, which hangs loosely in front of her face. Her bare feet drag along the ground behind her. I watch until they move past my line of sight, their footsteps echoing in the cavernous room.

My eyes drift to the other prisoners. Most either sit or lie unmoving inside their cells. I don't think they're dead, but they don't look all that lively either.

Not dead but not alive.

And is that going to happen to me too?

I'm no fae warrior. I'm what fairies derogatively call a *slave.* A human. To be fair, I'm a supernatural one, but at the end of the day, I'm still human. I have no value here as a prisoner.

So why was I taken?

The answer is right there in front of me.

Because you mean something to the King of the Night.

Somehow his enemies learned this, and they captured me to get to him.

I stare down at my wisp of a dress. Not even going to think about the fact that I didn't put this on. My situation has enough horror in it as is.

An evening of bliss, followed by this. I got to enjoy the perks of being the Night King's mate for a whopping day.

Here it is, the fall after the high. And in my world, there's always a fall. I knew it was too good to think that I would just get a man like Des after all this time. He was always meant to be someone just out of my reach.

Two sets of footsteps head in my direction, interrupting my thoughts. Another rotation for the prison guard.

Only, this time, they halt in front of my prison.

The iron shackles clang between my ankles and my wrists as the guards on either side of me lead me away from my prison cell. My nose itches as the blindfold one of the guards tied around my head now tickles my nose.

Overkill much?

I don't even get to be flattered by it either. It's probably standard procedure for the incarcerated warriors.

It could be worse. If I were a fae, the iron cuffs wouldn't simply be rubbing away skin; they would be sizzling my flesh and draining me of my energy.

Gradually, the quiet murmurs die away and the air begins to smell fresher, though it's still musty, heavy with the scent of…animals.

It takes another five minutes before I'm deposited in a room. The air here feels heavy, ominous.

Bad things happen here.

Bad things are going to happen to me.

I try not to panic. I spent years making sure I'd never again be a victim, and it was all for naught. My glamour doesn't work on any of these beings, and without it, I'm simply a human woman up against powerful fairies.

The guards release me, their footsteps retreating behind me. A moment later, the door opens, then closes softly, and I'm alone again, shackled and blindfolded in this room that feels evil.

My awareness stretches out. I can hear someone breathing.

Fuck, not alone after all. My panic spikes.

"Desmond Flynn's one weakness." The deep, vibrating voice fills the room, and I can feel the creature's power in his words. "And I have her."

My heart's pounding, and as my fear rises, so does my siren.

I hear the sound of heavy footfalls crossing the room toward me. It takes most of my willpower not to stumble backward.

"I would not have imagined the great King of Chaos to choose a slave for himself." The man stops right in front of me.

I jolt when I feel his touch along my cheekbone, which must be glowing by this point.

"Not even one such as you." He runs a thumb along my lower lip. "The people here call you an enchantress. But tell me, human, could you enchant me?"

Instead of answering, I swat away his hand with my shackled ones. The action earns me a chuckle, and then his hands are back on my face, stroking my skin.

"Stop touching me," I growl.

"Oh, my lady, have you not heard?" I feel his hot breath against my ear. "That's what I'm best at," he whispers.

The siren is restless inside me.

He wants an enchantress, let's give him an enchantress, she whispers. *Let him think we are willing right up to the last second. Then we'll stand over his body and laugh as he takes his own life. Foolish to cross us.*

My siren either doesn't realize or care that this man cannot be glamoured. Not if he's fae.

He pulls the blindfold off my face, and I blink against the light. The first things I notice are the man's antlers. Sharp, towering antlers that add another two feet to the already large stature. Silky chestnut hair frames his tan face.

It's the man from my dreams.

The slitted pupils of his golden eyes expand as he takes me in.

"You *are* quite beautiful," he says. "I can see why the Lord of Secrets has taken you for his mate."

He knows Des and I are mates?

"But you are painfully weak," he continues. "What a vulnerability. He should know better."

"Who are you?" I ask, my voice ethereal.

His eyes dance at the hypnotic pull of my words. "My manners!" He bows. "I'm Karnon, King of Fauna, Master of Animals, Lord of the Wild Heart, and King of Claws and Talons."

The King of Fauna? The mad king?

Fuckity fuck, that's not good.

He straightens, splaying his arms out to display the room around him. "Welcome to my kingdom."

I glance around at the room—*bed*room, I amend. The place is covered in furs. Thick wood and ivory furniture is scattered throughout the room, each piece intricately carved, though none are so impressive as the staggering headboard on his bed. A hunting scene is carved into the wood, embellished with bits of ivory, mother-of-pearl, semiprecious stones, and flecks of gold.

A bed for a king.

Out of all the rooms to meet him in, this is the one he chooses. Also not good.

I tear my eyes away from the massive bed to look at Karnon, who's studying me with a small smile.

He leans in close, his antlers nearly touching me. "I already have a casket picked out for you. A special coffin for a special lady. We'll deliver you right to your mate's feet."

Karnon's finger hooks over the low neck of my dress. "I wonder if it will break him to see his love like that—still as death and holding another man's baby. Will he kill it? Keep it? Oh, the possibilities..." He runs the backs of his fingers over my chest.

I notice that blood's dried into the creases of his hand. I swallow at the sight. So far, he's only been a bit eccentric, but I have no doubt that at any moment he could snap.

"I've never been with a human woman," he continues. He lowers his voice. "In the Kingdom of Fauna, it's taboo to sleep with a slave. You earthly beasts are so dirty. But you are pleasing enough to look at." His eyes run over me. "Yes, quite pleasing. I'm eager to see the rest of you."

Jesus.

No one will ever hurt us like before, my siren promises. *He will pay.*

The King of Fauna tilts his head. "Perhaps we should begin now?"

Before I have time to react, he grabs my jaw. Looking me in the eye, he leans in and presses his lips to mine.

It's not a kiss. Not in the truest sense. Instead, he forces my mouth open, then exhales.

A rush of magic is forced down my throat, tasting like rot. I struggle against him even as my knees begin to buckle.

His arm comes around my waist, holding me up as he continues to breathe into me.

I try to bring my knee up to his crotch, but my leg only comes up inches before the shackles around my ankles jerk tight.

Karnon doesn't even notice.

My chained arms are trapped between us.

Completely immobilized.

As a last-ditch effort, I jerk my head away, then headbutt the King of Fauna. He staggers back, placing a hand to his forehead.

Without his grip holding me up, my legs now do buckle.

Karnon's lips curl back into what might be a smile. All I see are several sets of fangs. "The slave has a little fight in her."

I force myself to stand, swaying on my feet. I'm choking on whatever corrupted magic he force-fed me. "What did you do to me?" I croak, my voice hoarse.

He tilts his head, surveying me with those strange eyes of his. "I look forward to seeing more of that pretty skin," he says. "Guards!" he calls, not glancing away from me.

Two fae soldiers rush in, one who has feathers for hair, the other who has claws.

"We're finished here," Karnon says.

Again, I sway on my feet, feeling dizzy and disoriented. Each moment I stand here, I weaken. Something's very wrong with me. Everything's moving slower—my limbs, my mind.

Roughly, the soldiers blindfold me again. Gripping my upper arms, the two drag me back to my cell, dumping me carelessly on the pallet in the corner.

I'm barely aware of it. Whatever was forced down my throat is slipping through me, turning my veins to ice.

They don't bother removing the cloth around my eyes, and I don't have the energy to do it myself.

Drifting, drifting...

My mind darkens until all that surrounds me is endless, hopeless blackness.

CHAPTER 26

Choking. Choking on magic. It's pounding behind my forehead, tensing up my muscles, squeezing my insides.

I wake with a scream, the sound echoing down the cell block. Somewhere in the distance, a guard growls out a warning.

I sit up, panting, placing a sweaty hand to the column of my throat.

Just a dream. The stifling darkness, the corrupted magic, Karnon...

Only it isn't, I realize as I finally catch my breath. I can still feel his viselike grip on me, his lips on my mouth, the insidious darkness that seeped into my veins.

My face is coated in sweat, and my stomach is roiling—

I barely make it to the toilet in time to vomit. I spend the next several hours like this—either shivering on my pallet or purging my stomach of every last ounce of its contents.

At some point, the guards slide a meal through a hatch at the base of the barred wall. The food sits untouched at the edge of my cell.

Eventually, the sickness dissipates. Not completely, but enough to function. Stomach growling, I drag myself out of bed toward the tin bowl. One glance at the gruel and I decide going hungry is better than spending several more hours with my head in a prison toilet.

I lean my sweaty forehead against the bars and stare out of my cell just as a guard approaches.

I eye him as he passes, noticing the lion tail that swishes behind him.

Do all Fauna's fairies share aspects with beasts?

The guard slows, flashing me a cold look. "Don't stare at me, slave."

I'm so fucking sick of this world already.

"Nice tail, asshole," I mutter.

That stops him in his tracks, and I'm just enough of an idiot to smirk at the fact that I got under his skin.

He slams his gloved palms against the bars. "Consider yourself lucky that the king wants to put his dick anywhere near you," he growls.

My smile grows, turning mean. Then I chuck my bowl at the bars, the gruel splashing against his face. "Fuck you, pig."

I never would've guessed beforehand, but I don't make a very good prisoner.

For one second, the guard does nothing, his face shocked. And then he lets out a lion's roar, rushing at the bars.

I spin to my feet, ignoring a wave of dizziness that rushes through me, just as he makes a grab for me. His hand closes on nothing but air.

"You filthy, vile slave!" he bellows. "I could kill you right now! Right where you stand!"

Light ripples across my skin as my siren surfaces.

"Could you kill me?" I say, my musical voice taunting. "Why don't you come in and find out?"

He roars again. Because obviously he can't lay a finger on me. Not the one bargaining chip Karnon believes he has over Des.

"Or are you scared?" I lean against one of the stone walls. "The lion who's scared of a little woman."

He snarls, banging against the bars until another soldier—one with horse ears—pulls him away, flashing me a glare that's supposed to scare me. But nothing is more frightening than the fate that already awaits me.

I watch them walk away, glad for once that my siren fears nothing and no one. Animals can scent that kind of thing, and that's what these guards are—part animal. Not so different from Eli when it comes down to it.

I slide down the wall, leaning my head back against it. I'm exhausted, and it's only been what? A day?

This place breaks us fast.

"Psst, human," a female voice calls from the cell next to mine once the guards' voices have disappeared. "Are you all right?"

"Yeah," I call back weakly. My skin's stopped shining, and all the strength that comes with the siren has fled, leaving me exhausted.

"That was brave, what you did there. Rash—stupid even—but also brave."

I manage a laugh. I don't know much about fae, but rolling an insult into a compliment seems like something they would do.

I lean my head back against the wall. "What's your name?" I ask her.

"Aetherial," she says. "Yours?"

"Callypso."

"You're new here, huh?" she asks.

"Yeah," I sigh out, my eyes moving to those tally marks.

"How many times have you met the Fauna King?" she asks after a beat of silence.

Apparently I wasn't the only one who got special visits with him. I'd figured as much.

"Just once."

"Oh, fun's only beginning for you," she says.

That makes me crack a smile. My fellow inmates are fae *warriors*. These women are the toughest of the tough. Somewhere along the way, I'd forgotten that. I'd only associated them with the sleeping women trapped inside those glass coffins. I hadn't thought that they might've fought their fate every bit as much as I was planning to. But right now, hearing Aetherial make light of our terrible situation, I remember.

"How many times have you met him?" I ask.

"Four," she says. "I've lost movement in my arms and legs. He takes out those first. Doesn't want his women to be difficult."

"That's what that kiss was?" I say, surprised. That, after all, was the only time Karnon forced his magic on me. "A way to immobilize us?" I wiggle my fingers and toes as I speak. I haven't lost any use of my limbs.

"Among other things," she says darkly.

A shiver races down my spine. "What does that mean?" I ask.

She pauses. "Tell me you don't feel it—that sickness making itself at home in your bones."

I did when I woke, but after puking my guts up, the sensation went away. Now I just feel weak. Incredibly weak.

"And then of course, there's the whole matter of us getting pregnant," she adds. "You know about that?"

"I do. Sorry to ruin the surprise," I say. "I'm still holding out hope that immaculate conception is involved in that whole process," I add, not really joking.

"Immaculate conception?" Aetherial repeats, amused. "Now that would be something. All of us prisoners just magically getting knocked up." She chuckles to herself. "I like you, human," she says.

"I'm a siren." I'm not sure why I make the clarification. Perhaps so that I don't seem quite so helpless among all these strong warriors.

"A siren?" She whistles. "And here I was hoping Karnon wouldn't touch you—you being human and all that. No offense," she adds. "I've dallied with plenty of human women in my time, but it's a thing for some fae."

I remember Karnon's earlier words. "So I've heard."

We lapse into silence for a bit, both of us likely musing on our fates.

"What kingdom are you from?" I finally ask.

"Day." She exhales. "Royal guard turned prisoner. That's irony for you."

It all stings. Hearing her story, knowing her fate, knowing mine.

"So tell me," she continues, "how does a human come to be trapped in this hellhole with the rest of us?"

"I have unusually bad luck," I quip, even as I grimace down at my hands.

I hear her gruff laughter. "Apparently that kind of thing is contagious around here."

Another small smile stretches across my face. Who would've thought I'd become fast friends with a fae warrior while imprisoned?

Absently, I watch the guards patrol the rows of cells

across from me. Most have some obvious animalistic feature, like whiskers, tails, or hooves. But then there are some who walk these halls that don't have these obvious characteristics.

Could they be fae from another kingdom? *Humans?*

My heart pounds at that last possibility.

"Hey, Aetherial, can you do me a favor?" I ask, my eyes studying a uniformed cook delivering tray after tray of prisoner meals. He looks fully human from here, but I'm so far away it's hard to tell.

"What would you like, siren?"

I watch the uniformed man as he moves down a cell. "Can you tell a human from a fae on sight?" I ask.

"Almost always," she says. "Why?"

I can't help the spike of excitement I feel. "Have you seen any humans here since you were taken?"

"Hmm, not that I remember. I wasn't looking for them though."

I continue to stare at the cook as he moves down the cell block. For the life of me, I can't tell what he is.

"If you see any," I say distractedly, "will you let me know?"

If I can get a human to bend to my will...the possibilities are endless.

I'm tempted to try out my powers right now, but a healthy dose of fear keeps me quiet. I'm afraid that if I glamour one of these guys prematurely and it doesn't work, the guards will stop me from getting another opportunity.

"My view is pretty limited at the moment, but yeah, I'll let you know." It's silent for a beat. "Is it true then, what they say about a siren's voice?"

My mouth forms a grim line. "It's true."

"Your idea will probably get you killed."

I guffaw. "You prefer the alternative?"

I hear Aetherial's husky laughter. "I was right about you. Stupid and courageous."

Neither of us speak again until a series of guards approaches a cell across the way, one of them carrying two large poles over his shoulder. At the back of the cell, a fae woman with flame-red hair lies limp on her pallet.

The bars to her cell slide back, the metal scraping along its tracks.

The guards file inside the cell, and the guard carrying the poles snaps them open. That's when I realize I'm not staring at *poles*, per se, but a crude gurney. A stained wisp of cloth is stretched between the two shafts.

They set the gurney on the ground, then grab the woman, situating her body on the flimsy material.

Then, as one, the two prison guards lift the gurney and cart her out. I watch them until they're out of range.

"They remove the lifeless ones," Aetherial says from the cell over, clearly watching alongside me.

They're paralyzing the women.

"Stay here long enough," Aetherial continues, "and it'll happen to you too."

I frown, even though she can't see it.

All those sleeping women in Des's kingdom, all the paralyzed ones here…it can't be a coincidence.

Which means—

I know who the Thief of Souls is.

Karnon.

———

This time when I'm deposited in what I can only presume to be Karnon's room, I know what to expect. The ominous press of air, the silent retreat of the guards, Karnon's approach.

I'm once again shackled and blinded, completely at the whim of the monstrous fae king. However, the moment he speaks, something about our dynamic feels different.

"My precious bird, they *blinded* you," he says, aghast. A moment later, his claws slash through the material, leaving the cloth hanging in ribbons around my neck. "Beautiful creature," he murmurs, taking me in. His nostrils flare as his gaze rakes over me. "Human…but *not*. Creature of the heavens and the sea." His gaze halts at my hands. "Shackles too? This is preposterous. You are my guest."

He rips the iron cuffs binding my wrists clear apart, hissing as he does so. I startle at the show of strength. I assumed he was powerful, but seeing a live demonstration is sobering.

"Cursed metal!" he spits out as the cuffs hits the ground. He clenches his fists, and I can hear his skin sizzling.

Iron burns.

In spite of the pain, he reaches between my ankles and rips apart the cuffs there as well, howling once again at the pain.

This is what the warriors endured when they wore these?

A guard pokes his head in. "Your Majest—"

"*Out!*" Karnon cries.

The door slams shut not even a moment later.

To me, he mumbles, "They're getting too daring, those guards, coming and going without knocking. Must make an example of one of them—and soon." He's completely unaware that as he talks, his palms are smoking.

Karnon rises back up, those antlers of his towering over us. His eyes are bright and unfocused, his pupils dilated.

He cups my face, and immediately I tense, his burning palms heating my skin.

"Frightened little bird, you have nothing to fear from me." He begins to stroke my skin. "All I want is to calm you. Pet you."

Ugh. Mad king indeed.

His hands run down my arms. Halfway down, he stops and turns them over. "What is this bare flesh?" he says. "Where are your markings?"

Um, what?

His hands move to my neck, and he probes the skin there. "And your gills!" he says, horrified. "Where are they?"

I give him a cautious look. Today, Karnon seems kinder but definitely crazier than the last time we met.

He spins me around and sucks in a breath. "Your wings! Who clipped you?"

He turns me around, and once again, I get a close-up of those wild eyes and the fangs that his lips can never quite hide. His claw tips dig into my flesh.

I realize after a moment that he expects me to answer.

I blink a few times, dazed by all the manhandling. "No one clipped my wings. I never had any to begin with." *You crazy bastard.*

"None to begin with?" He moves behind me, making me tense up again, and he presses his hands flat against my back. "No, no." He shakes his head vehemently. "*Dormant.*" He strokes my skin, and I'm beginning to get the willies. "Oh, but they *must* bud."

I don't follow any of this. I don't speak psycho.

"Beautiful bird. Tragic bird. *My* bird. You are not like the others. They smell of trees and sunbaked earth. Some feel cold like the winter freeze. No beasts among them— save for my sacrifices. Must be made, must be made."

If I tried to run right now, how far would I get?

His hands move down my back to my waist, and I decide that I don't really care what my odds are of escape.

I turn around, letting the siren out.

His eyes glitter as he takes in my shimmering skin. "Breathtaking creature. Caged, flightless thing. You are a rare—"

I slam my knee into his crotch.

He makes a small, choked sound, his body folding in as he clutches himself.

His mistake to see me as harmless.

I bolt for the door.

I hear a snarl behind me. A moment later, he materializes in front of me, blocking the door. His eyes flash, and a menacing growl rumbles in his throat. "If you run, I will chase you, and I will break you, pretty bird."

"Stay away from me," I say, my voice becoming ethereal.

The Fauna King's eyes flicker, and I sense I'm no longer staring at Karnon.

Those eyes...I'm looking down an abyss at the monster that lies at the bottom of it.

They are the same eyes I stared into yesterday.

He runs his hands through his hair, taming his wild mane. This man's not bestial, not like Karnon. He's cultivated. His eyes are focused, shrewd.

Interest sparks in his gaze. "Beautiful slave. We meet again."

This is not the same person I was speaking to a moment ago. I'm used to having two aspects of myself, so I know the signs fairly well.

The way Karnon is now studying me, his expression piqued—and hungry—makes me worried. The Karnon I met earlier was crazy, unpredictable, feral, but he didn't seem evil. Not like he does now.

I begin to back up. In response, the fae king prowls forward. This man is brutal, violent, unforgiving. He's the kind of man who takes and takes and takes.

He closes the distance between us, wrapping his hand around my wrist. Karnon's palm moves over my bracelet. "What is this?" He fingers the beads. "You are not to wear anything but what I give you." As he speaks, his fingers curl around the bracelet. He yanks hard on it, and I let out a small sound as the beads dig into me. But it doesn't break.

Frowning, he tries again. Again, my charmed jewelry holds fast. I'd enjoy his frustration if my arm wasn't getting flayed in the process.

"What is this magic?" he growls, peering closer at the beads. All at once, he jerks his head back. "The Bastard of Arestys," he snarls, releasing my hand. "*Guards!*"

They enter the room.

"Why was I not informed that she wears Desmond's magic?"

They look at each other, obviously confused. As if they would know. These guards are obviously just muscle.

"Your M-Majesty," one of them stutters, "we weren't aware—"

Karnon takes a menacing step forward. "Not aware?" he says. "Are you blind?"

He waits for a response.

The guards shake their heads.

As the three speak, I begin to edge toward the door. My heart pounds faster and faster. This might be my one opportunity to escape.

"You brought foreign magic in here," Karnon says. "It can be traced."

Traced?

"Your Majesty, we had no involvement—"

But the Fauna King is done listening.

Karnon roars, slashing a clawed hand through the air. Several feet away, the guards scream as each of their stomachs rip open in four long, jagged lines. *Claw marks.* Karnon did that with his magic.

Almost immediately, blood and innards spill out from their guts.

Not wasting another second, I bolt for the door.

I never make it out.

Karnon grabs me from behind, his claws slicing into my skin as he spins me around. "We're not done," he whispers into my ear. He grasps my jaw, squeezing it to the point of pain. And then he breathes into me once more.

CHAPTER 27

I'm dying, my body rotting from the inside out.

I think a day or two has gone by since my last visit with Karnon, but I can't be sure. All I know is that my life consists of shivering, sickening, and sleeping.

The guard I've dubbed Lion Tail walks by my cell every so often, banging on the iron bars with his gloved hands, taunting me. I weakly manage to flip him off, but I have no idea whether flashing someone the bird is even offensive in the Otherworld. All I know is that Lion Tail didn't freak out at the sight like I hoped he might.

"Hey, Callypso," Aetherial calls out.

My head rolls weakly toward her voice.

"Siren!"

"Yeah?" I croak weakly.

"Drag your bed over here," she says.

"I don't know if I can," I mumble.

"You can, *I* know it." She doesn't even sound sorry, her voice commanding. Weak, but commanding.

Ugh, fae warriors are way too tough.

It takes an embarrassingly long time to move my pallet, but eventually I do just that.

"How are you holding up, siren? Still have enough movement in your limbs?"

"You had me drag my bed over here and now you ask me that?"

She gives a wheezy laugh. "I'm making polite talk. Don't question it."

My lips curve up slightly.

The two of us fall silent again, and my mind drifts.

"The shackles…" I finally say. "I didn't realize how painful they must be."

"I've endured worse."

Geez.

After a moment, she adds, "We wrap cloth around the cuffs. The barrier stops most of the pain."

But not all of it.

As I listen to her, I realize her voice is slurred, her speech much slower, like she picks her words carefully.

Losing the ability to move her mouth.

"Are you all right, Aetherial?"

She doesn't speak for a long time.

Finally, she says, "Everything's going. Even my mind feels foggy."

From the little I know of her, I can tell Aetherial is too proud a creature to say that she's not all right.

She sighs. "You know, the worst thing about this is that my wife's going to have to see me like this."

I don't bother to comment. What would Des do when— *if*—I came back to him in a coffin?

"She's going to take in that creepy little monster

I'll inevitably birth. I know she will, that sweet, foolish woman."

"You've also seen them?" I ask.

"I was *bitten* by one of those creatures."

I cringe, remembering that Des had told me those children had been close to biting me as well.

Des. Just the thought of him guts me. I don't know if I'll ever get to see him again, hold him again, talk to him again.

"You're married?" I ask, changing the subject and forcing my mind from the one thing that will make me go soft. Because there is no softness in this place. And if I want to hold out for as long as possible, I have to be the hard-ass I've learned to become in Des's absence.

I hear Aetherial exhale wearily. "Yeah," she says. After a moment, she adds, "We got married in the Night Kingdom. Technically, our marriage isn't recognized in the Day Kingdom—relations with humans aren't the only thing taboo here. But technically, I don't really give a shit."

I smile at that.

"By the way, Callypso—" she says.

"Callie," I correct.

"Callie," she repeats. "Just an update: I haven't seen a human in the prison—other than you, of course."

My heart plummets. I've been here days, and I'm getting weaker with each one. I'm losing my window of opportunity.

I stare down at my bracelet, twisting it around my wrist. Not all hope is lost. If I understood Karnon correctly, Des might be able to track my magic.

But if he could, wouldn't he have shown up already?

"Callie?" Aetherial interrupts my thoughts.

"Yeah?"

"No one gets magically impregnated here."

Her meaning doesn't register at first, but when it does…

My eyes close at that. At what she's not saying. Strong Aetherial immobilized, powerless to stop what happened to her.

"It was Karnon?"

"The devil himself," she affirms.

I don't have words. It's happened to me before, it might very well happen to me again, and somewhere between it all, you'd think I'd have something to say, but I don't. Not for brave Aetherial.

She clears her throat the best she can. "Just thought you should know."

I swallow. "Thank you for warning me," I whisper, my voice hoarse.

But I'm not sure I'm better off knowing what happened to her, what awaits me.

Sometimes knowing is just another kind of hell.

———————

It's not working.

Whatever venom Karnon's trying to feed me isn't taking.

I huddle in the corner of my cage, my body covered with a sheen of sweat. My entire body shakes violently. From my best guess, it's been nearly a week since I arrived. I've gone through two more of the Fauna King's ministrations, and each time my body rejects his poisoned magic, he gets more and more frustrated.

He hasn't touched me yet. Perhaps the monster doesn't like victims who fight back. Though I doubt at this point I'd present much of a challenge to Karnon; I'm too weak to do much on my own. Despite my sorry state, I'm not being dragged under by his magic, not like the other women here.

A horrible sort of malaise is settling into my bones. It feels like the magic will either do Karnon's bidding or I will cease to exist. And so far, it's not doing Karnon's bidding.

I'd assumed that all fae magic worked on humans. After all, the Bargainer could use his magic on me. But perhaps my assumptions were wrong. Perhaps there are some limits to fae magic. Perhaps being a human right about now is a good thing.

Although, it's hard to call the state I'm in a good thing. I lie listlessly on the pallet, my dress hanging loosely on me. Now the guards simply carry me to Karnon's chambers without a fight. There's no more small talk.

If I'm greeted with the evil version of Karnon, he gets right to work. If I'm met with the kinder, crazier version of Karnon, he rocks me against him, murmuring nonsense about wings and gills, claws and scales.

"Aetherial?" I call out.

Silence. It's been like that for the last several days.

I begin talking to her anyway, just in case she can still hear me, telling her anything that crosses my mind. But not once do I mention the one thing that weighs most heavily on my mind—

I'm going to die here.

CHAPTER 28

Day who-the-fuck-knows and visit number six with Karnon, the guy who's beginning to star in all my nightmares.

When we arrive, the guards drop me unceremoniously on the ground before retreating.

Groaning a little, I push myself onto my forearms, reaching for my blindfold. Lately the guards have stopped binding my wrists and ankles. What's the point? I'm too weak to escape.

I pull off the cloth around my eyes, blinking against the brightness of the room. I freeze when I take in my surroundings.

The first thing I notice is that I'm not in Karnon's bedroom. Here, dead leaves are scattered across the floor, and spindly, dead vines cover most of the walls and much of the ceiling. They're even wrapped around the great antler chandelier ending far above me. This derelict room looks like it's been left to the elements.

A wild room for a wild, mad king.

My gaze falls to a raised dais at the far side of the room. The massive chair perched in the center of it is made entirely of bones. And sitting on it is Karnon.

He assesses me from his throne. "Precious bird," he says, "you are dying."

He stands, and that simple action alone sends a shiver down my spine.

Today won't be like the other visits.

His footsteps echo as he descends down the stairs in front of him, leaves crunching beneath his boots.

I get a good look at his eyes, and it's my stepfather all over again. The half-mad lust that looks more animal than man. The trigger-short temper that can veer to anger at the slightest provocation.

He stops less than a foot away from me. It's just the two of us in this room; whatever guards or aides or officials are normally stationed here are now gone.

Karnon kneels next to me. I try to scramble away, but my limbs are heavy and sluggish. I want to shriek in frustration. I'd vowed long ago to never again be a victim. And here I am, powerless beneath the will of a mad king.

He begins petting my hair. "What a pretty, pretty bird. A shame you cannot fly, trapped as you are in this cage of a body." He cups my face. "You are dying because the animal in you is being smothered."

Right, that's why.

"I'm dying because you're poisoning me," I say.

He stares back at me, his gaze distant, and I can already tell my words didn't register with him. He begins petting my hair again. "How can a creature survive when she doesn't have gills to breathe or wings to fly?"

When I don't answer, he gives me a look like my silence

is making his point for him. His touch moves from my hair down my back.

I try to bat away his hands, my limbs sluggish. It does no good.

"Sweet creature," he says, stroking my back, "fret not." He leans in close to my ear. "Today I will set you free."

I turn to look at him, my gaze locking with those slitted pupils of his. We stare at each other for several seconds, his hands lying heavily on my back. His body begins to tremble, and then, all at once, he releases all his magic right into me.

His magic is like a sledgehammer to my back, driving down into my skin, into my bones with the force of a freight train. The shock wave from it ripples out around us, shaking the very walls of his throne room.

Then comes the pain, pain more vast and acute than anything I've ever felt. My siren rises in response.

I open my mouth, my eyes rolling back, and I scream and scream as agony unlike anything I've ever felt rips through me. My body feels like it's unmaking itself, my bones breaking, my muscles ripping, my skin flaying itself.

It's unending and unfathomable, the force of it pinning me to the ground. I'm helpless beneath Karnon's grip on my back, a grip that I can't possibly shake at this point.

The Fauna King laughs himself hoarse as a sound like thunder rumbles in the distance. "My beautiful bird sings best when she hurts." He presses down hard against my skin. "Siren," he shouts, "come forth!"

Another wave of power slams into me.

My screams hit a new decibel, the sound harmonizing with itself.

My spine and ribs feel like they're cracking, shattering.

I'm no longer made of muscle and bone. It's all been pulverized under Karnon's magic.

"Yes!" the madman cries. "*More!*"

My body seems to buckle as another wave of energy floods through me. My skin is burning, burning. And my back!

My back is on fire! It must be; that's where the worst of the pain is.

Karnon releases me, but the agonizing power he's shoving into me doesn't ebb. If anything, it's getting worse. Because it's changing course; rather than burrowing into me, it's now trying to force itself *out*.

I hunch over, breathing heavy, my hair plastered to my face.

"*More!*" Karnon shouts.

I'm tearing apart from the inside out. My skin no longer fits my body. It's much too small. I heave over and over, barely able to endure the pain I'm in.

"*More!*"

My screams become increasingly more agonized as his power batters against the inside of my flesh.

"*MORE!*"

All at once, my screams cut off and the magic erupts.

My skin splits down either side of my spine, and I hear the sound of wet popping and snapping.

And then…I feel it. Two sticky, wet protrusions push out from my ripped flesh, unfolding down my back.

Then finally, finally, the magic abates.

I collapse in on myself, shivering, shaking.

Blood, everywhere.

"Yes! My beautiful bird, you are set free!" Karnon says gleefully.

I can't move. No energy left. As I lie there, I catch sight

of my hands. Where once were nails, now I have sharp, black claws. And my forearms...delicate, semitransparent scales cover them, glittering gold where blood spatter doesn't cover them.

I can barely make sense of the sight.

But then I glimpse something over my shoulder. Something dark, something bloody... And there's a weird weight against my back...

The siren within me is whispering, the worlds curling themselves around me,

I am powerful.

I am vengeance.

I am unleashed.

Karnon's steps approach me.

He grabs those dark, bloody things behind me, stretching them up and out. I feel my muscles stretch as I extend my arms.

But my arms are right in front of me...

I catch another glimpse of those dark things. And then I understand.

Wings.

I grew *wings*.

CHAPTER 29

At the sight of them, I heave again. This must be a bad dream.

Claws and scales and wings. I'm now more beast than woman.

"How do you like them?" Karnon asks, his words taunting.

I roll my forehead against the bloody marble floor.

Can't bear the sight.

Far behind me, someone pounds on the doors that lead in, the wood shuddering against the force of the strikes. If I had any more energy, I would've jumped at the noise.

Instead, I just lie here.

The doors continue to bang. And bang.

Karnon drops my wings, and with a wet smack, they flop to my sides. His footfalls retreat.

BOOM!

The metal doors blow open, wood splintering every which way. The massive double doors hit the throne room's floor, their impact shaking the walls of the room.

I sense him before I hear his agonized bellow.

Des.

He found me. A weak thread of happiness pushes through my exhaustion.

Shadows curl around me like smoke. I stare tiredly at them.

"So your mate found you after all," Karnon says. "Took him long enough."

The air shifts, and a moment later, Des is crouched at my side.

I feel his hand glide over the sensitive flesh of *my wings*. His eyes...his eyes look at my disfigured body in agony. Des pulls his hand away and stares down at the blood coating it. I sway at the sight of it, feeling weak and dizzy. Des makes a noise that's so unlike him. He sounds nauseated—distressed.

"Gods," he breathes, looking helplessly over me. "Is anything...broken?"

Now a keening noise makes its way out of me.

Everything. Everything is broken.

I pinch my eyes shut, even as Des's shadows thicken and coil around us. The Bargainer pulls me close.

"I'm so sorry, cherub," he whispers, his voice breaking. "For everything. He will pay."

I begin to shake.

Somewhere behind us, I hear Karnon's approaching footfalls. My weakened body still manages to tense at those terrible footsteps, and one of my—my—*wings* shifts behind me. I want to retch at the sensation. Des's grip tightens around me.

"Tell me, how do you like your mate now?" Karnon says mockingly. "She's improved, no?"

I catch another glimpse of myself—my golden dusting of scales, my sharpened fingernails...my wings.

Suddenly, I can't look at Des.

I'm monstrous. Not a woman, not anymore.

Des brushes a kiss against my temple, then his hands leave me. He stands, and the atmosphere of the room feels suddenly ominous. I turn my head just in time to see the Bargainer approaching Karnon. He's swathed in shadows, the darkness gathering around him.

"You know it's breaking the most sacred law of hospitality to attack a king within his own castle," Karnon says, backing up.

The Bargainer doesn't bother responding. He is the embodiment of wrath. I can see it building beneath his skin, burning in his eyes. A bottomless abyss of it.

It reminds me of Karnon's cold gaze...

But my mate is so calm. All that fury is contained within him as he moves, and it only serves to make him appear all the more menacing.

"I never imagined you'd go for a slave. But weak attracts weak," Karnon taunts, trying to get a rise out of Des even as he begins to back away.

The reaction never comes. The Bargainer continues stalking after Karnon with the same steady, coiled rage as before, his face set in uncompromising lines.

"Though I did enjoy her moans."

And still, Des doesn't react.

Karnon growls, clearly growing impatient. Suddenly and without warning, he swipes his hand through the air. I feel the magic brush by me, and too late, I let out a thin cry, remembering those guards Karnon disemboweled days ago.

Des doesn't even try to block the attack. I see cloth and skin split in four jagged claw marks across his stomach, and his blood begins to spill.

"No," I croak out weakly, beginning to drag myself across

the floor. The edges of my vision darken and my arms shake from the effort.

The Bargainer's face is still a mask of anger. And as I watch, I see his wounds begin to stitch themselves up.

But even as he heals, Karnon swipes his hand through the air again. And again, Des's flesh is rent open. A cry slips from my lips.

Need to help him.

I struggle to get my feet under me as Karnon strikes out with his magic again and again and again, carving up my mate. Jagged, awful lines blossom along Des's arms, his legs, his torso, his face. The Bargainer does nothing, says nothing—he doesn't even so much as cry out as his flesh is ripped open. Just heals himself as he continues stalking toward Karnon.

The mad Fauna King, for his part, continues evading Des, moving around his throne room, the rotted leaves crunching beneath his feet.

"Your woman tasted good too—have I told you that?" Karnon says. "Mortal flesh is so sweet when ripe. But humans, they break so easily. Look at yours"—he gestures to me—"nearly dead from a simple metamorphosis."

As he speaks, my legs give out, folding before I can fully stand. A pained cry slips from me as my elbow slams into the floor.

The Bargainer's emotionless façade slips. He glances my way, and for an instant, I see a world's worth of emotion in those light eyes—love, pain, and the ferocious protectiveness he feels toward me.

The Bargainer's attention returns to Karnon, his face smoothing out and becoming emotionless once more. I sense Des's magic building and building; it thickens the air as it fills the room.

The Night King is all darkness. It gathers around him, dimming the room. Bit by bit, the shadows snuff out the lights. His face is as sinister as I've ever seen it. Even Karnon looks a little unsure at this point, taking a stumbling step backward even as his magic continues to strike out at Des.

The Fauna King glances at me, and something dark and devious alights in his expression. He moves toward me, and shit, it's obvious he means to grab me.

I want to rage at the fact that I'm too weak to run or fight back. Still, I try to drag myself away. Before I've made it more than a couple of feet, I feel those horrifying, deplorable hands on me, pulling me up.

Karnon presses my back to his front, and I cry out as my new appendages are crushed between us. The mad Fauna King wraps a hand around my neck, his claws pricking my flesh.

"I will hurt her," Karnon threatens, staring out at the Bargainer.

Des has stopped in his tracks, the shadows billowing about him as his power continues to gather. My gaze meets his, and I expect to see fear or panic in his expression.

Instead, I see something dark and resolute, something that warns me that though he lost me once, he will not again. His shadows begin to slither over the floor, moving like snakes, dragging the darkness along with them. The Bargainer's gaze flicks to the man holding me hostage as the shadows sweep over the room, blanketing me and everything else until the room is black as pitch.

"You think I cannot see in the dark?" the Fauna King says.

It's quiet.

Then—

"*I am the dark.*"

Des's power detonates, blasting through the room, whipping my hair back.

Had I thought that Karnon's power was staggering? It's nothing—*nothing*—next to the fury and sheer strength of the magic that moves through me. Warm liquid sprays against me, splattering against my hair, my face. I taste the coppery tang of it on my lips.

Blood.

Whose?

With a deafening shriek, the walls and ceiling explode outward, bits of marble and plaster scattering to the four winds, the building essentially vaporized.

And then it's over.

The darkness recedes, and when it does, the first thing I see under the dim twilight sky is…meat. Meat—and bits of bone smeared across the room.

That's all that's left of Karnon.

Kneeling behind him is Des, who doesn't have a fleck of Karnon's blood on his clothes, nor a strand of white-blond hair out of place.

I glance around us. This must've once been a grand castle, but now all I can see of it is its foundation and bits of furniture that weren't completely obliterated in the explosion.

Beyond the castle walls, the dark evergreen trees that surround it are utterly untouched.

Des did all this. I shiver at the sight of all of it.

The Bargainer raises his head, his eyes locking with mine. "The King of Fauna is no more."

Des comes up to me, his hands sliding under my body as he lifts me up.

I let out a small, pained noise. Everything aches: my scalp, my teeth, my bones, my toes—my heart.

Especially that last one.

"It's all right, cherub. It's all right."

I make a choked sound and turn my head toward his chest.

It's not all right at all. I can feel the tips of my wings dragging along the ground. A faint dusting of scales covers my arms, and I have claws.

Monstrous. Just as monstrous as my captors. And now I'll always carry the reminder.

The only thing that tempers my revulsion is my will. I'm struggling to stay conscious.

Des keeps casting worried glances down at me. "Stay with me, love."

I force my eyes to remain open.

"Good girl," he says, stroking my hair back. "We're going home." His expression is filled with such agony.

It's painful for him to even look at me.

Perhaps it was better when he was simply out of my life. Then it was a single blow I managed to live with. Seeing him look at me this way over and over again—each moment is a dagger to the gut. In response to my anxiety, my wings tense, ready to lift.

"Be calm, love," Des says.

Slowly, I force myself to relax my back, my wings going limp again.

He bends his knees, tensing. A moment later, we shoot into the sky.

I stare at the stars, the beautiful, desolate stars, my body at the end of its rope. My eyelids close.

"Callie…"

But not even Des's voice brings me back from the darkness.

CHAPTER 30

I wake to the sensation of a hand petting my back.

I wearily blink my eyes open. I don't immediately recognize my surroundings. Not until I notice the bronze wall sconces and a Moroccan archway.

Des's room. I lie splayed out on my stomach in the middle of his bed, nestled among all his sheets.

Why am I on my stomach? I never sleep on my stomach.

"Cherub, you're awake." The Bargainer's smooth voice raises goose bumps across my skin.

I begin to smile, still confused, when I remember.

The prison, Karnon, my metamorphosis.

My metamorphosis.

I reach behind my back. When my fingers brush against feathers, I let out a choked cry.

It wasn't a dream.

"They're…beautiful," Des says. His hand moves over them. Under his touch, they *move*, my feathers making a whisper-soft noise as they rub against each other.

I squeeze my eyes shut. "*Don't,*" I say, my voice hoarse.

I don't want to hear about how pretty they are. They were forced on me by a madman. By a psychopath who would've laughed had the transformation killed me. The same monster who raped thousands of women.

I was ready to die. I was even ready to live in a state of suspended animation.

I wasn't ready for this.

And I know it's not the worst fate, but it feels that way. Because now I look like all those fauna fae. My captors. My tormentors. It was one thing to endure the punishments. Another to look at myself and see them.

"Don't what?" Des says. "Don't touch you? Compliment you?"

"All of it," I say, opening my eyes. I'm horrifying to look at.

My arms shake as I begin to push myself up into a sitting position. I catch sight of those dusky gold scales that run up my forearms like plated armor.

I have an itch to pluck them from my skin, one by one.

As soon as I begin to sit up, I feel pressure at my back. My unwieldy wings are too long, the bones too delicate.

I can't sit up in bed.

I feel a frustrated tear leak out as I flop back on my stomach.

So weak.

A moment later, Des scoops me up. My wings tangle behind me, the tips dragging along the ground. The feathers are pitch-black, but under the light, they have an iridescent sheen.

They *are* pretty, and I hate them all the more for it.

As he carries me, my fae king looks at me like he's the one drowning.

He catches me staring. "We will get through this," he

swears, "just like we did the last time. We've done this once before. We can do it again."

"I don't know if I can." My voice breaks.

Des sets me on my feet in front of a full-length mirror in his chambers. "Tell me what you see," he says.

I frown, first at him, then—reluctantly—at my reflection. I don't even want to look. I don't want to see if I'm more monster than human. But when I do look, I see my face, and it is utterly unchanged. Forgetting Des is standing by me, I touch my cheek. I thought that maybe...that maybe I wouldn't recognize myself in the mirror. That I'd truly be a beast. But I'm not.

My eyes move to my hand. For a long moment, I stare at the sharp claws, and then my gaze moves to my fingers. Those are still human. In fact, if I filed my claws down, other than my nails' black color, they would look like regular hands.

My forearms have a delicate sheen of scales, which glitter under the light. They begin at my wrist and end before my elbow, and a few rows of them ring my upper arm before fading back into my normal flesh. They don't continue up my neck or chest or face. I lift the skirt of my dress to look at my legs. Those too are free of scales. They look how they've always looked. And my feet are still human feet—no claws adorn my toes.

And when my gaze moves back to my reflection, I still have the same proportions. I'm the same woman I've always been, just with a few additions. And while those few additions—claws, scales, and wings—are painful to look at, I'm not the monster I thought I might be.

In fact, if anything, I look a little fae.

"What do you see?" Des asks again.

I swallow. "I see Callie."

"As do I." He dips his mouth close to my ear. "Cherub, people like us are not victims. We're someone's nightmare."

I'm not a victim.

I'm not a victim.

How had I forgotten this? Because somewhere along the way, I *had* forgotten. And it nearly broke me.

I'm not a victim.

Here in the Otherworld, I lost my most powerful weapon—my glamour. But I gained claws and wings.

My eyes move to Des. "Teach me again how to be someone's nightmare."

I need to feel dangerous, powerful, traits I lost somewhere along the way.

A hint of his wicked smile appears, and cloaked in his shadows, it's menacing. "With pleasure, mate."

I stand inside one of the Kingdom of Night's reappropriated warehouses, staring at the multitude of sleeping female warriors. Thousands of them.

Killing Karnon should've released all these women from whatever dark magic held them under.

But it hasn't.

And now there are so many more sleeping women, uncovered from the subterranean rooms far below Karnon's castle.

The partially empty warehouse is suddenly teeming with coffins. And the women in all the new ones are pregnant. No one knows when—or if—they'll give birth.

The other kingdoms have also received their share of sleeping warriors recovered from the bowels of Karnon's prison, warriors belonging to the Kingdoms of Day, Flora, and—strangest of all—Fauna. Karnon had been abusing his kingdom's female soldiers.

I can barely wrap my mind around it.

There's still the matter of the male warriors, the men who are still missing. And then there are the female captives, like Aetherial, who are recovering from their ordeal. Captives who have all complained of a darkness that still lingers within them.

Nothing's solved.

I touch my hand to one of the coffin lids, my claw tips clicking against the glass. "*Wake up*," I whisper, glamour slipping into my voice.

If the sleeping women hear, they don't obey.

I even wait for the sound of wraithlike voices to rise around me, just as they had before.

But all is silent. All is still.

Smoke and shadows wrap around my arms. A moment later, they coalesce into hands.

"Cherub," Des whispers into my ear, squeezing my arms gently.

At his voice, my wings stir, brushing themselves against his chest.

I shouldn't be surprised that he found me. He's the Bargainer, Lord of Secrets, Master of Shadows, and King of the Night.

He touches my jaw, turning my face.

I close my eyes and swallow. It feels good to have the Bargainer touch me like this, despite the fact that Karnon did the same thing, day after day. Because with Des, it's different. It always has been. It always will be.

"I woke and you were gone," he says.

I understand what he doesn't say. That he feared he lost me all over again.

"I had to see them." The words are barely audible.

I had to see the women who were less fortunate than me. The ones who were unable, even after Karnon's death, to escape his clutches.

My eyes scan the room, my chest tight at the sight. Had I not been human, I could've been among them, my body laid out like all the others, my lungs not breathing, my heart not beating, my body not alive.

But not dead either.

Suspended somewhere between the two. Waiting.

He's coming for you.

Goose bumps break out across my skin.

"It's not over," I whisper. I can feel it in my bones. We'd simply fired the first shot.

"Let our enemies come," Des says, his silky voice lethal. "They have a reckoning waiting at the end of my blade— and my siren's vengeance to deal with."

I turn to face Des, his white-blond hair swept back beneath his crown. His tattoos and war cuffs are hidden under his fitted fae attire, but even without them showing, he is so obviously a dangerous thing, with his glittering eyes and hulking wings, which have been out almost constantly since the night he killed Karnon.

He cups the side of my face. "Let our enemies come, and I will kill them all. So long as you're at my side, cherub, I have something to fight for."

This is perhaps the most amazing mystery of all in the aftermath of Karnon's death. My physical changes haven't dimmed what Des feels for me. He actually seems quite... *fond* of the changes. And every time he looks at my wings, my claws, my scales with adoration, I tolerate them a little more. And I fall for my mate over and over again.

This man who's saved me so many times, who's pulled me from my own tormented darkness into his. This man who waited seven years for me. This man who, against all reason and odds, is my mate.

I lean in and brush a kiss along his lips. "I'll be at your side," I promise, "till darkness dies."

EPILOGUE

That night, when I fall asleep, I dream.

My surroundings are indistinct; there's simply the impression of darkness and the sense that other things are hidden within it.

I hear children's laughter, the sound echoing through the inky night, and my body tenses. It gets louder, closer, even though I don't see any children. I don't see anything at all.

Abruptly, the laughter dies away, and the only sound left is my own hitched breathing.

My eyes move over the darkness.

Just as I'm about to take a step forward and explore what I can, someone exhales against the nape of my neck. I have to swallow my scream.

I spin around, looking for the person sharing space in the darkness with me, but there's no one there, only the impression of something terrible waiting just beyond my sight.

Panic tightens around my windpipe. I take a few deep breaths, trying to calm my racing heart, when a phantom hand brushes the hair away from my ear, and lips press against the shell of it.

"*Fee, fi, fo, fum,*" the Thief whispers. "I'm not done, siren. Oh no, I've just begun."

Dear readers,

Thank you so much for reading Rhapsodic*! Reviews and word-of-mouth recommendations are really helpful to authors, so if you loved Des and Callie, please consider leaving a review on your favorite book website or telling your friends and family about it.*

Hugs and happy reading!

Laura

**Keep a lookout for the next book in
Laura Thalassa's The Bargainer series:**

A Strange Hymn

CHAPTER 1

Wing.

I have wings.

The black iridescent feathers glint under the dim lights of Des's royal chambers, now black, now green, now blue.

Wings.

I stand in front of one of Des's gilded mirrors, both horrified and transfixed by the sight. Even folded up, the tops of my wings loom well above my head and the tips brush the back of my bare calves.

Of course, wings aren't the only thing different about me. After a particularly nasty skirmish with Karnon, the mad King of Fauna, I now have scaly forearms and claw-tipped fingers too.

And those are just the changes you can see. There's nothing—except maybe the wounded look in my eyes—that I have to show for all those parts of me that were altered in different, more fundamental ways.

I'd spent the better part of a decade fighting the idea that I was a victim. I'd done a damn fine job of it too—if I do say so myself—before I came to the Otherworld. And then came Karnon. A small shiver courses through me even now as I remember.

All those cleverly crafted layers of armor I wore were shucked away by a week of imprisonment, and I'm not quite sure how to deal with it.

To be honest, I really don't *want* to deal with it.

But, as bad as I have it, the Master of Animals got it worse. Des vaporized the dude so completely that all that's left of him is a bloodstain on the remains of his throne room.

Apparently, one does not fuck with the Night King's mate.

Mate.

That's another thing I've acquired recently—a *soulmate.* I'm bound to Desmond Flynn, the Bargainer, one of the most wanted criminals on earth, and one of the most powerful fae here in the Otherworld.

But even that—matehood—is more complicated than it appears.

I still have so many questions about our bond, like the fact that I never knew I was a soulmate until a few weeks ago. Other supernaturals find this kind of thing out back when they're teenagers and their magic Awakens.

So why didn't I?

There's also the fact that most soulmates can feel the bond that connects them to their mate like it's a physical thing.

I place a hand over my heart.

I've felt no such thing.

All I have is Des's word that we are soulmates—that and the sweet ache in my bones that calls for him and only him.

I drop my hand from my chest.

Behind my reflection, stars glitter just beyond the arched

windows of Des's Otherworld suite. The hanging lanterns dangle unlit, and the sparkling light captured along the wall sconces have long since dimmed.

I'm stuck here in the Kingdom of Night.

I doubt there are all that many supernaturals that would complain about my situation—mated to a king, forced to live in a palace—but the simple, sobering truth is that a girl like me cannot waltz back onto earth with giant wings protruding from her back.

That sort of thing wouldn't go over well.

So I'm stuck here, far from my friends—okay, *friend* (but, in all fairness, Temper's got the power and attitude of at *least* two people)—in a place where my ability to glamour, a.k.a. seduce, others with my voice is essentially useless. Fairies, as I've learned, cannot be glamoured; my magic is too incompatible with theirs.

To be clear, that's not a two-way street. They can still use their powers on me; the bracelet on my wrist is proof enough of that.

My eyes return to my wings, my strange, unearthly wings.

"You know, staring at them isn't going to make them go away."

I jolt at the sound of Des's silky voice.

He leans against the wall in a shadowy corner of his dark bedroom, his expression irreverent, as usual. His white blond hair frames his face, and even now, even when I'm bashful and exposed and oddly ashamed of my own skin, my fingers ache to thread themselves through that soft hair of his and pull him close.

He wears nothing but low-slung pants, his muscular torso and sleeve of tattoos on display. My heart quickens at the sight. The two of us stare at each other for a beat. He doesn't make a move to come any closer, though I swear he wants to. I can all but see it in his silver eyes.

"I didn't mean to wake you," I say quietly.

"I don't mind being woken," he says, his eyes glittering. He doesn't move from his spot.

"How long have you been there?" I ask.

He crosses his arms over his bare torso, cutting off my view of his pecs. "Better question: How long have *you* been *there*?"

So typical for Des to answer a question with a question. I turn back to the mirror. "I can't sleep."

I really can't. It's not the bed, and it's definitely not the man who warms it. Every time I try to flip onto my stomach or my back, I inevitably roll over a wing and wake myself up.

There's also the little matter of the sun never rising in this place. The Kingdom of Night is perpetually cast in darkness as it draws the night across the sky. There will never be a time when the sun glances into this room, so I can never know when exactly to wake up.

Des disappears from his spot against the wall. A split-second later he appears at my back.

His lips brush the shell of my ear. "There are better ways to spend long, sleepless evenings," Des says softly, one of his hands trailing down my arm.

My siren stirs at his words, my skin taking on the faintest glow.

His lips brush the side of my neck, and even that lightest of touches has my breath hitching.

But then I catch sight of my reflection, and I see the wings. The glow leaves my skin in an instant.

Des notices the moment my interest wanes, moving away from me like he was never there. And I *hate* that. I can feel the distance between us. I don't want him to give me space, I want him to pull me closer, kiss me deeper, make me extinguish this new insecurity I have.

"These wings…" I begin to explain, but then I stop.

Des comes around to the front of me. "What about them?" he asks, blocking my view of the mirror.

I lift my chin. "They'd get in the way."

He raises an eyebrow. "In the way of what?"

As if he's unaware of exactly what we're dancing around.

"Of playing chess," I say sarcastically. "*Of…intimacy.*"

Des stares at me for several seconds, then his mouth slowly curls into a smile. It's a smile full of tricks and mischievous things.

He steps in close, only a hair's breadth between our faces. "Cherub, I *assure* you, your wings will not be an issue." His gaze dips to my lips. "But perhaps your mind would be better put to ease with a demonstration?"

At his suggestion, light flares beneath my skin, my siren immediately ready to go. Whatever my insecurities are, she doesn't share them.

I look over my shoulder, at my wings, and my worries come roaring back. "Aren't they a major turnoff?"

The moment the words leave my lips, I wish I could catch them and shove them back down my throat.

The only thing I hate worse than feeling like a victim is airing my insecurities. Normally all that emotional armor I don hides them—sometimes so deep I forget they're there— but after my ordeal with Karnon, that armor is lying in scattered pieces somewhere around my feet, and I haven't yet had the time or the will to refashion a new set for myself. I'm horribly raw and painfully vulnerable.

Des raises an eyebrow. At his back, his own wings, which

I haven't noticed until now, expand. The silver, leathery skin of them pulls taut as they extend to either side of him, blocking out most of the room.

"You do realize almost all fae have wings?"

I know they do. But *I* never have.

I hold up a forearm. In the dim light, the golden scales that plate my arm from wrist to elbow shimmer like jewelry. On the tips of each of my fingers, my nails glint black. They're not sharpened at the moment (thanks to meticulously filing them down), but the second my siren gets a little angry, they'll grow back into curving points.

"How about this?" I ask. "Do most fae have this?"

He clasps my hand in his own. "It doesn't matter one way or another. You are mine." Des kisses the palm of my hand, and somehow he manages to make my insecurities feel small and petty.

He doesn't release my hand, and I stare at the scales.

"Will they ever go away?" I ask.

His grip tightens. "Do you want them to?"

I should know that voice by now. I should hear the warning notes in it, the dangerous lilt to it. But I don't, too consumed with my own self-pity.

I meet his eyes. "*Yes.*"

I get that I'm being a poor sport. Rather than making lemonade out of lemons, I'm pretty much cutting open those lemons and squeezing them into my eyes.

My heart begins to speed up as he fingers one of the hundreds of beads that still circle my wrist, each one an IOU for a favor I cashed in long ago.

His eyes flick to mine. "Truth or dare?"

Des's gaze twinkles as he plays with the bead on my wrist, waiting for my answer.

Truth or dare?

This is the little game he loves to make out of my repayment plan. To me, it feels less like the game ten-year-old girls play at slumber parties and a whole lot more like Russian roulette with a fully loaded weapon.

I stare the Bargainer down, his silver eyes both so foreign and so familiar.

I don't answer fast enough.

He gives my wrist the lightest of squeezes. "*Dare*," he says for me.

The part of me that enjoys sex and violence quakes with excitement, wanting whatever Des offers. The rest of me is starting to think I should be scared shitless. This is the same man who's known around these parts as the King of Chaos. Just because we're mates doesn't mean he's going to go easy on me. He's still the same wicked man I met eight years ago.

Des smiles, the sight almost sinister. A moment later, a pile of leathers fall to the floor next to me. I stare down at them dumbly, not understanding what it is he dared me to.

For all I know, I just got royally fucked over.

Actually, I'm almost positive I got fucked over.

"Suit up," Des says, releasing my wrist. "It's time to start your training."

Glossary

Arestys: a barren, rocky landmass belonging to the Kingdom of Night; known for its caves; smallest and poorest of the six floating islands located within the Kingdom of Night.

Barbos: also known as the City of Thieves; the largest of the floating islands located within the Kingdom of Night; has garnered a reputation for its gambling halls, gangs, smuggler coves, and taverns.

changeling: a child swapped at birth; can alternatively refer to a fae child raised on earth or a human child raised in the Otherworld.

dark fairy: a fairy that has forsaken the law.

Desmond Flynn: ruler of the Kingdom of Night; also known as the King of the Night, Emperor of the Evening Stars, Lord of Secrets, Master of Shadows, and King of Chaos.

fae: a term denoting all creatures native to the Otherworld.

fairy: the most common type of fae in the Otherworld; can be identified by their pointed ears and, in most instances, wings; known for their trickery, secretive nature, and turbulent tempers.

glamour: magical hypnosis; renders the victim susceptible to verbal influence; considered to be a form of mind control; wielded by sirens; effective on all earthly beings; ineffective on creatures of other worlds; outlawed by the House of Keys because of its ability to strip an individual of their consent.

Green Man: king consort of Mara Verdana, Queen of Flora.

House of Keys: the global governing body of the supernatural world; headquarters located in Castletown, Isle of Man.

Isle of Man: an island in the British Isles located between Ireland to the west and Wales, England, and Scotland to the east; the epicenter of the supernatural world.

Janus Soleil: ruler of the Kingdom of Day; also known as the King of the Day, Lord of Passages, King of Order, Truth Teller, and Bringer of Light.

Karnon Kaliphus: ruler of the Kingdom of Fauna; also known as the King of Fauna, Master of Animals, Lord of the Wild Heart, and King of Claws and Talons.

Kingdom of Day: Otherworld kingdom that presides over all things pertaining to day; transitory kingdom; travels around the Otherworld, dragging the day with it; located opposite the Kingdom of Night; the eleven floating islands within it are the only landmasses that can claim permanent residence within the Kingdom of Day.

Kingdom of Death and Deep Earth: Otherworld kingdom that presides over all things that have died; stationary kingdom located underground.

Kingdom of Fauna: Otherworld kingdom that presides over all animals; stationary kingdom.

Kingdom of Flora: Otherworld kingdom that presides over all plant life; stationary kingdom.

Kingdom of Mar: Otherworld kingdom that presides over all things that reside within bodies of water; stationary kingdom.

Kingdom of Night: Otherworld kingdom that presides over all things pertaining to night; transitory kingdom; travels around the Otherworld, dragging the night with it; located opposite the Kingdom of Day; the six floating islands within it are the only landmasses that can claim permanent residence within the Kingdom of Night.

Lephys: also known as the City of Lovers; one of the six floating islands within the Kingdom of Night; believed to be one of the most romantic cities in the Otherworld.

ley line: magical roads within and between worlds that can be manipulated by certain supernatural creatures.

Mara Verdana: ruler of the Kingdom of Flora; also known as the Queen of Flora, Lady of Life, Mistress of the Harvest, and Queen of All that Grows.

Otherworld: land of the fae; accessible from earth via ley lines; known for its vicious creatures and turbulent kingdoms.

Peel Academy: supernatural boarding school located on the Isle of Man.

Phyllia and Memnos: sister islands connected by bridge; located within the Kingdom of Night; also known as the Land of Dreams and Nightmares.

pixie: winged fae that are roughly the size of a human hand; like most fae, pixies are known for being nosy, secretive, and mischievous.

Politia: the supernatural police force; global jurisdiction.

portal: doorways or access points to ley lines; can overlap multiple worlds.

Sacred Seven: also known as the forbidden days; the seven days surrounding the full moon when shifters remove themselves from society; custom established due to shifters' inability to control their transformation from human to animal during the days closest to the full moon.

seer: a supernatural who can foresee the future.

shifter: a general term for all creatures that can change form.

siren: supernatural creature of extraordinary beauty; exclusively female; can glamour all earthly beings to do her bidding; prone to bad decision-making.

Somnia: capital of the Kingdom of Night; also known as the Land of Sleep and Small Death.

supernatural community: a group that consists of every magical creature living on earth.

Thief of Souls: the individual responsible for the disappearances of fae warriors.

werewolf: also known as a lycanthrope or shifter; a human that transforms into a wolf; ruled by the phases of the moon.

Acknowledgments

This book was a labor of love that spanned several years, and no matter how many times I flip through it, I still feel the same magic I did when the idea for this story first came to me.

There are so many people who I need to thank for making this book happen. First, a huge shout-out to some of my earliest readers, who saw excerpts of this book back in 2014 and hounded me for more—I can honestly say it was your interest that convinced me to complete this story.

Thank you to my critique partners and friends, Sunniva Dee, DeAnne Negley, and Angela Mcpherson. You all helped shape this manuscript, and I still hold our late night chats close to my heart.

To my amazing agent, Kimberly Brower, I honestly cannot sing your praises enough. Thank you for always, always advocating for me and not taking any issue with my slightly feral writer tendencies. It's been such a joy getting to work with you.

Christa Désir, how did I get so lucky to land myself such an incredible editor? Thank you for catching all the things, answering all the questions, and giving all the encouragement. You have been such a compassionate, guiding force for me throughout this process.

To Jada Johnson, Sabrina Baskey, and the rest of the Bloom team—thank you for cleaning up this book, updating it in the best way possible, and giving it the polish it needed. It's been an absolute dream working with you all.

Readers, thank you for letting me share my characters and my world with you. I cannot tell you just how humbling it is to get to play some small role in your own journey.

Thank you to my children, who remind me why I do any of this. And lastly—and most emphatically—thank you to my husband. This book saw the light of day because you insisted it was amazing when I was steeped in my own self-doubt. You have encouraged me, celebrated with me, and cheered me on through every stage of this process, and you have been my safe place to fall through all the proverbial blood, sweat, and tears. Until darkness dies, love.

About the Author

Found in the forest when she was young, Laura Thalassa was raised by fairies, kidnapped by werewolves, and given over to vampires as repayment for a hundred-year debt. She's been brought back to life twice, and with a single kiss, she woke her true love from eternal sleep. She now lives happily ever after with her undead prince in a castle in the woods.

…or something like that anyway.

When not writing, Laura can be found scarfing down guacamole, hoarding chocolate for the apocalypse, or curled up on the couch with a good book.

You can find more news and updates on Laura Thalassa's books at http://laurathalassa.com.